SPELLS

OF

BLOOD

AND

KIN

SPELLS

OF

BLOOD

AND

KIN

· A DARK FANTASY ·

Claire Humphrey

THOMAS DUNNE BOOKS
ST. MARTIN'S PRESS ⚞ NEW YORK

THOMAS DUNNE BOOKS.
An imprint of St. Martin's Press.

SPELLS OF BLOOD AND KIN. Copyright © 2016 by Claire Humphrey. All rights reserved. Printed in the United States of America. For information, address St. Martin's Press, 175 Fifth Avenue, New York, N.Y. 10010.

www.thomasdunnebooks.com
www.stmartins.com

The Library of Congress Cataloging-in-Publication
Data is available upon request.

ISBN 978-1-250-07634-2 (hardcover)
ISBN 978-1-4668-8772-5 (e-book)

Our books may be purchased in bulk for promotional, educational, or business use. Please contact your local bookseller or the Macmillan Corporate and Premium Sales Department at 1-800-221-7945, extension 5442, or by e-mail at Macmillan SpecialMarkets@macmillan.com.

First Edition: June 2016

10 9 8 7 6 5 4 3 2 1

To my grandmother, who is also a writer.
Thanks for handing down some of your particular magic.

Acknowledgments

I started this book alone, or so I thought. By the time I finished it, I realized how wrong I was. I'm lucky to have many kinds of support and many wonderful people in my life, and many who are not mentioned here are still very much in my thoughts.

The first chapter of this book was workshopped at Viable Paradise XII. Instructors Jim Macdonald, Debra Doyle, John Scalzi, Steven Gould, Laura Mixon, Elizabeth Bear, Patrick Nielsen Hayden, and Teresa Nielsen Hayden all helped me hone my craft, but more important, introduced me to the writing community that still helps me thrive. Classmates I met there have gone from occasional conference meetups to valued colleagues and dear friends. Marko Kloos, Julie Day, Curtis Chen, Katrina Archer, Chang Terhune, and all the rest of you: Dirty Dozen for the win.

The Nachos and Narratives writing group, Nicole Winters, Stephen Geigen-Miller, and Melanie Fishbane, and past members Heather Jackson, Sean Davidson, and Greg Beettam: you are all quality writers and quality people, and I'm honored to share my work with you and share yours in return.

I've been part of a number of other writing groups, retreats, and informal clusters in the time it took to finish this book, and

I'm also grateful for the input and support of Bill Hopkins, Mike Rooks, Pam Chackeris, Michael J. DeLuca, Scott Andrews, Erica Hildebrand, Al Bogdan, Gemma Files, and Leah Bobet. Jennifer Brinn deserves a special mention for giving me a perfectly timed piece of advice on the ending.

Connor Goldsmith, my agent, is always a delight to work with.

My wonderful editor, Quressa Robinson, was unfailingly insightful and positive. I'm also thankful to copy editor Sara Ensey, interior designer Michelle McMillian, jacket designer Lisa Pompilio, and the rest of the St. Martin's Press/Thomas Dunne team.

I was immensely grateful to have help with some language: Nora Anderson with the Spanish and Alex Gershon, Leonid Gershon, Sophia Gershon, and Michael Gershon with the Russian. Any mistakes that remain are my own.

My parents kindled my love of Russian folklore by giving me a pair of storybooks illustrated by Ivan Bilibin. I'll be forever glad that they saw nothing wrong with their small daughter's interest in flying witches and fiery-eyed skulls. And finally, my most constant supporters: Olinka Nell, the one person in the world who has read everything I've written. Bevin Reith, who takes me and my work utterly seriously but is equally serious about making time for workouts, sunsets, and new microbreweries. My mother, Anya Humphrey, who combines high expectations with unconditional love, and is always willing to listen, even when I only want to talk about hockey.

SPELLS

OF

BLOOD

AND

KIN

O_{ne}

Baba had been dead for four days by the time Lissa got to speak with her.

The first day went by in a shocky stutter. 9-1-1. Waiting with Baba's body on the kitchen floor, even though by then she knew. One of the paramedics squeezing Lissa's hand before loading the stretcher into the ambulance.

The other paramedic was doing some kind of methodical re-suscitation drill, and Baba's body twitched dully with the move-ment and lay still again, and Lissa kept looking and then looking away. The ambulance siren blared, the paramedics passed each other implements, the radio buzzed with terse talk, and at the center of all this urgency, Baba was already past help.

Lissa could see a slice of Queen Street through the rear window: cars and bike couriers that had veered from their paths, a street-car immobile on its track. Within the ambulance, columns of neat drawers and coiled cables, between which the two paramedics moved with the ease of total familiarity, never quite brushing anything. Lissa sat still where they put her.

"You can hold her hand," one of the paramedics said.

Lissa did. It wasn't the right temperature, and the skin felt like candle wax. She let go as soon as the paramedic's gaze moved on.

"Are you her executor? Is there a religious official your grandmother would want present? What are her beliefs around organ donation?"

Yes, and no, and totally opposed, though Lissa could not go into the explanation with anyone. She had to answer the same questions three more times: beside the stretcher in the ER after the doctor had pronounced Baba dead, and then again with a different doctor while Baba's body was carried away somewhere Lissa was not invited to follow.

Even after the body was gone, Lissa's mind still kept jarring her with the image of Baba's face, open-mouthed, eyelids stuck halfway. And the froth at her mouth, which had spilled out and crusted on the kitchen floor. And how was Lissa supposed to get to the sink without coming near that spot?

"Is there someone you'd like to call?" said the last doctor, a young-looking Korean man, pushing a desk phone toward Lissa's hand.

Lissa flinched and tried to make it look like she'd meant to brush her hair back. "Um. No?" she said.

The doctor made a compassionate face. "Are you sure? You can take as long as you want."

There was the lawyer, and Father Manoilov, who would arrange the funeral, but Lissa knew that wasn't what the doctor had meant. He'd meant someone who would look after Lissa. And there wasn't anyone like that now.

Lissa took a taxi home, though it felt utterly wrong to leave Baba's body at the hospital. Before she had left, the doctor had handed her a manila envelope containing Baba's rings and the gold chain she'd worn about her neck. Lissa put the envelope in her pocket, took it out and put it in her purse, took it out again and held it with both hands, just to be certain.

And then there were those calls to make, and all the while, the image of Baba's face kept coming back to her, along with the feel of room-temperature skin, making her want to wash her hands over and over.

She did that as soon as she reached the house. She sterilized the phone too, which made no sense at all.

As soon as Father Manoilov had confirmed the booking for the church, Lissa found her shaking hands dialing her father's number.

Dad had never liked Baba, his mother-in-law; thought her superstitious, didn't like her influence on Lissa. But surely, he'd want to know; surely, he'd want to come—

It was late in London, and he didn't pick up. Lissa left a voice mail. She sat by the phone in case he called back. She woke up still in the chair, in the early hours, in the silent house. The phone never rang.

APRIL 25

🌒 WAXING GIBBOUS

Nick didn't actually remember being kicked in the ribs, but he was sore there and gagging for breath. When he leaned forward to pick up the smoldering joint he'd dropped, blood dripped down his shaggy hair and onto his hand.

"Well, that was . . . shit," he said, and he sat back on his heels, feeling a hot trickle down the side of his face. He groped around for his phone. Gone, of course. So were the credit cards. They'd left him some change, a pack of gum, and his student ID.

Jonathan was hanging over the edge of the Dumpster, heaving. "What the fuck?" he said between gasps.

"You okay?"

Jonathan shrugged limply. "Think so." He leaned in to puke again.

Nick got to his feet. Vicious spins rocked him, enough to make him grab on to Jonathan's shoulder. Sweat ran on him under his T-shirt.

He spent some time just leaning there beside Jonathan, smoking the rest of the joint to steady himself—long enough that the cockroaches started coming out from under the Dumpster again. Nick couldn't tell if his head was injured or if he just should have passed on that last round of shots. Figured the pot could only help, but it didn't seem to be kicking in.

Jonathan hauled himself upright and smoothed his rucked T-shirt over his bony chest. "'m okay," he said. "I think they took all my stuff, though. You?"

"Um," Nick said.

"Oh, hang on," Jonathan said, and he went back to vomiting.

"You are bleeding," said someone else. His voice had an accent— Russian or Polish or something.

"Jesus!" Nick said, surprised to find his eyes shut, dragging them open. "Didn't hear you coming."

"Show me."

Nick turned his face toward the light over the bar's back door. In its halo, all he could see was a brimmed cap and the glint of eyes and teeth in a man's face; muscular shoulders in a wifebeater, one bicep marked with a tattoo or maybe a scar. An army guy or something. The kind of guy you could maybe allow to take charge in an emergency.

Nick stood still while a fingertip prodded at his temple and forehead. "Do you, like, know first aid?"

"You will bear a scar," the guy said. "You should be careful in this neighborhood."

Nick gagged on laughter. He stubbed out the joint on the rusted flank of the Dumpster and carefully stowed the roach in his pocket.

"And your friend? Is he well?"

"Hammered," Nick said.

The guy was still standing really close. So close that Nick could see his lower lip was split, smeared with blood a little around the tear. It wasn't reassuring. Nick edged back against the Dumpster.

The guy leaned in as if to get a closer look at Nick's head. Instead, he laughed: a soft, bitter chuckle.

Nick laughed too, uncertainly.

The guy grabbed Nick's shoulder hard and kissed him on the temple, right over the jagged cut. Open-mouthed. His tongue probed the torn skin and lapped at the blood. Then with a choked sound, he wrenched away.

Nick belatedly got his hands up. "What the hell—"

The guy stumbled back a few steps. He wiped his mouth on the back of his hand and licked that too.

Nick got his only good look at the guy then, under the bar's security light: a tanned face, seamed with sun and wind. Dark eyes under the shadow of the weathered army-green cap.

Nick saw him take a breath as if to speak, but instead, the guy turned and ran away west down the alley.

"Jesus," Nick said.

"What?" said Jonathan, reeling up from his slouch and wiping at his mouth with the hem of his T-shirt. "Who the hell was that?"

"I don't know. Totally random," Nick said, staring down the alley at the runner receding into darkness. He raised his hand to touch the cut. Wet. He jerked his hand back.

"Shit. Your head," Jonathan said. "Should we call the cops?"

"No. No phone. And I just got baked—no way do I want to deal with the cops." He looked at his fingertips, smeared with saliva and blood. Was it only his own blood? What if the other guy had hepatitis or something? Nick shuddered. God, he was going to hurl if he kept thinking about it. He tried to shake it off. "It's fine. Come on, we should get out of here."

"Get a cab?"

"No money," Nick reminded him.

"Streetcar, then. Hope they didn't get our tokens," Jonathan said. "I'm not fucking walking all the way home."

"Streetcar," Nick agreed, shivering harder.

With the change Nick had left, they had just enough for two fares. The driver looked dubiously at Nick's bloodied face and the smears on Jonathan's shirt, but she let them board. A girl in the forward seats rolled her eyes. Nick and Jonathan stumbled to the rear. Jonathan took the window, and Nick sidled in close to him, chilled.

The doors flapped shut. The streetcar's great weight rumbled forward along Queen Street. The girl at the front talked on her cell phone; a couple in the middle leaned their heads in to whisper to each other.

Nick looked over at Jonathan to see his friend scrutinizing him, brown eyes puffy and red-veined. "What the fuck was that?" Jonathan said.

"What?" Nick said. "You're asking me? Come on. Like this was my fault."

"Whatever," Jonathan said. "I told you I didn't want to smoke that joint."

"You wanted to celebrate the end of finals, dude. Which, well deserved, by the way. And I'm pretty sure it was your idea to start with bourbon."

"It's just . . . you never know when to stop."

"Stop when I'm dead. Jerk."

"That was funny when we were first-years. Which was five years ago, in case you lost count." Jonathan closed his eyes and let his head drop against the streetcar window.

"It's still funny," Nick said. "Come on. I'm hilarious." There was drying blood on his fingertips. He tried to wipe them on his shorts, but the stickiness wouldn't come off, and Jonathan wasn't laughing, wasn't even looking at him.

APRIL 26

◯ FULL MOON

On the second day, the funeral was held in the church with all ceremony, though Baba had not been allowed to set foot in the sanctuary in life.

Lissa was still forbidden to enter the sanctuary, though Father Manoilov allowed her into the less holy parts of the building. Father Manoilov had always been polite to Baba, even deferent, as one practitioner of faith to another, both integral to their community, and he told Lissa he was thankful for the chance to welcome Baba's soul back to the fold.

Father Manoilov ushered Lissa in the side door and let her stand at the foot of the basement stairs. She could hear most of the service.

It was in Russian, which Lissa did not really speak.

She leaned against the wall, creasing her black dress, feeling sweat pool between her breasts. Even standing up, she nearly went to sleep, catching herself upright again with a jerk of knee tendons.

Her eyes stung and burned. She had wept, of course, yesterday, but she felt more weeping under the surface, and she wanted it to stay there, safely invisible, until she could be alone for as long as she wished. As she walked about the basement, Lissa pinched the web of her thumb and bit the inside of her cheek.

She found the church kitchen, where the trays of sweets were laid out, sweating under Saran Wrap.

She found the percolator humming to itself, smelling burned already; who would want hot coffee on a day like this?

She found the refrigerator, and she opened the door wide and leaned into the cold air. The refrigerator contained a bowl of individual creamers, several cartons of milk, one of soy milk; another bowl, this one of butter pats; five pounds of grapes; and, tucked in the door, a baby's bottle neatly labeled with today's date and wrapped in a Ziploc bag against leakage.

Lissa picked it up and tilted it back and forth. No sediment: not formula. Why bring milk to the church when there was already—oh!

She opened the bag and then the bottle and sniffed. Definitely fresh, sweet-smelling. Mother's milk.

After she resealed the bottle, she wrapped the bag around it again and slipped it into her purse.

And just in time: there was a recessional booming out from the organ upstairs and the great creaking shuffle of the congregation rising.

By the time the first of them came down, she was back at the foot of the stairs, composed and ready to receive condolences.

She did not want to stay in the prickling heat with the contraband bottle slowly warming inside her handbag, but she was a one-girl receiving line. Father Manoilov did not stand with her, though he patted her on the shoulder once. The entire congregation filed past and murmured the same things over and over and shook Lissa's hand. Several of the ladies even called her *koldun'ia*, crossing themselves: it was the ancient word for a village witch, but here in Canada the village had become a cluster of Russian immigrants centered on the church, and *koldun'ia* had become something more like an honorific.

Lissa was Baba's successor, so it was right and natural that they should transfer the title to her, but it sounded achingly strange to her ears, strange and undeserved.

Only one lady asked Lissa about her recipe. Lissa had Baba's list of orders posted on the side of the refrigerator, but somehow she had not yet thought to review it.

The full moon was that very night, and the spells would work for two more nights after, which would give her plenty of time, at least. Lissa assured the lady she would have it ready and hoped she was not lying.

When she got home from the funeral, instead of beginning on the recipe she checked her voice mail again. One message, and she could tell right away it wasn't from Dad, because the voice was a girl's, light and sweet and . . . British?

"Lissa? I thought I should call ahead in case . . . look, Dad told me what happened, and I—oh, it's Stella, I should've said. I'm coming. To Canada. I'm so sorry for your loss. I know she meant a lot to you, and I—look, they're calling my flight; I have to go. See you soon!"

Stella. Lissa hadn't seen her since the wedding of her dad to Stella's mother, twelve years ago. She remembered a thin, laughing child in a ribboned frock who had begged Lissa to spin her around.

Stella. Not Dad.

Lissa supposed she ought to be grateful she had any family at all. Some people didn't.

She didn't have the family she needed, though. Like a step-sister she'd barely met could possibly do anything for her in the face of losing Baba.

Maybe it was best Dad wasn't coming: he would have got all involved in the businessy parts, trying to make Lissa sell the house and invest in a new condo or something like that. He wouldn't be able to help her with the church ladies. He would want her to drop everything Baba had taught her and enroll in an accounting course. At least with Stella, she'd probably just get platitudes.

Lissa dropped the phone on the floor and lay down on the sofa, exhausted beyond anything, and after dark, she woke up briefly to shuck off her dress, and then it was the third day.

APRIL 26

◯ FULL MOON

Maksim slowed when the sun began to rise behind him, casting the shadow of his running form onto the dew-wet road. He veered off across unkempt grass and ducked through a stand of poplars. The buds smelled like vanilla caramel, intoxicating in the cool dawn air.

He was wringing wet with sweat, his hair and his shirt slicked to his skin. He peeled off his clothes, tossed them over a poplar branch, and strode naked right into the wavelets of Lake Ontario. The water was heavy with weed and cold enough to make him bare his teeth. He forged ahead and dove.

He burst up through the surface, blinked wet eyelashes. Lake water ran down his face, into his mouth; along with the rank freshness of aquatic life, he could taste faint lacings of city soot and jet fuel. The sunrise struck brightness off the glass towers of downtown. Maksim shook droplets from his hair and walked up through the water onto the beach.

He paced over the sand and up onto damp grass. The breeze lifted all the tiny hairs on his skin. Delicious.

With the cold and the light and the long run he'd had, Maksim came to a bit of clarity and recalled there was something not correct about walking naked out of doors beside the water.

Maksim ran his hands through his wet, matted hair and tried to think. He wasn't supposed to be doing any of this. Was he?

He circled back along the sand to where his clothes hung from the tree; the breeze carried the reek of his own dried sweat lingering on the fabric. And something else too, on the shirt, as he pulled it from the branch and over his head, something both enticing and horrifying. He settled his cap in place and looked down at himself.

Blood. That was blood on his clothing. Only a few droplets and smears, dry and brown, but he could smell it fully now, electric. The scent shot straight to his other nature, his worst and wildest self.

Maksim rubbed the stained cloth over his face. The blood smell, his own and another's. Whatever he'd been thinking was already lost in the intense and thoughtless pleasure his nature brought on him. His human will was nothing in the face of such intoxication.

He held still for a second with the shirt pressed to his mouth and nose. Something was not right.

Tossing his head didn't shake off the confusion. He barely remembered to shove his feet into his battered shoes. He strode quickly west along the water's edge and picked up speed, hitting the sand harder. Nothing in his mind but his body's command.

APRIL 26

○ FULL MOON

Nick woke to Hannah's voice. He wrapped his arm over his ears but couldn't quite block it out.

"You know better than that, even if he doesn't. Christ! You're like little kids. I don't know which of you is worse."

"Hannah," Jonathan said. "Are you seriously mad at me for getting mugged?"

"I'm mad at you for not taking your best friend to the hospital!" she said. "What if he has a concussion?"

"Me?" Nick said, squinting. "Come on, seriously? I don't have a concussion; I have a hangover." He sat up too quickly and saw flashes of color: pale-blue walls, burgundy Ikea love seat, salt-and-pepper shag rug, parquet floor. He pressed a hand to his head. "Why are we at your place, J?"

"You couldn't find your key," Jonathan said. He didn't look so great himself: black hair shower-wet, straggling over his pale forehead, his whole posture slouched and pained.

"I don't remember that," Nick said before he could censor himself.

"See?" said Hannah. "Short-term memory loss. That's not a great sign, in case you weren't paying attention." She was bent toward him, big brown eyes too intent and close. Nick thought her eyes were pretty, but not when she was pointing them at him like this.

"That's a sign that I was plastered," Nick said as firmly as he could manage. "And high. Also high."

Hannah shone a flashlight in his face.

"What the hell?"

"Your pupils are normal," she said, standing upright again and crossing her arms. "Any dizziness?"

"Jonathan, J, God, make your girlfriend leave me alone," Nick said, scrambling off the love seat and making for the bathroom. "You might've signed up for this, but I sure as shit did not."

"Head pain?" Hannah called after him.

"Yes!" he snapped. "You. You are a pain in my head. Also a pain in my ass. Hangover, remember? I'm helping myself to your Tylenol."

"Take the aspirin instead. Better for your liver," Hannah said.

Nick slammed the bathroom door and leaned over the toilet. The heaves tugged a bright net of pain over his left side. He tucked his elbow down reflexively, but it didn't help. His head throbbed in a hot, tight, feverish way.

He didn't look at himself in the mirror until he'd rinsed his mouth and swallowed a couple of pills. Then, with Jonathan's washcloth, he dabbed at the crusty dried-blood trail that led down from his temple. The cut itself was beaded with fresh red and clear ooze by the time he'd finished, and it looked gross but clean. Jonathan didn't seem to own Band-Aids large enough to cover the whole thing, but Nick put three little ones across the widest part, stretching them tight in the hopes it would pull the skin together.

His eyes looked okay to him: gray green with a dark ring around the iris, like his father's, usually vivid against his Greek coloring, when he wasn't busy looking like shit. Right now, his skin was weirdly sallow, and he could actually see why Hannah was freaked out, not that it was any of her business. He splashed cold water on his face until the sweaty dizziness began to recede, and then he had to redo one of the Band-Aids.

By the time he came out, Hannah had given up yelling at Jonathan and was curled up against his side on the cramped love seat, reading *Harper's,* her dark bangs covering the frown in her brows.

"Seriously, though," she said to Nick. "Can you assure me, as a grown-up, that you don't need medical attention?"

"Don't you count as medical attention? You're going to be, like, a brain surgeon by next week or something. You aced everything this year, right?" As if he didn't know; as if Hannah's transcript wasn't stuck to the refrigerator right here in Jonathan's apartment. Nick didn't know who was more proud: Hannah of her high marks or Jonathan of the genius he'd managed to convince to date him. It was kind of gross.

"No joking," Hannah said. "I need to know you're taking this seriously."

"Fine," said Nick. "I'm totally, completely fine. Swear to God."

"And you've learned your lesson."

"Yes, Mom."

"And you're not going to take Jonathan drinking in bad neighborhoods anymore?"

"Not even to celebrate the end of finals? There are only so many more finals in our lives, you know," said Nick. He shuffled over to the love seat and slouched down on the arm of it, ignoring the way it creaked. "And as soon as they're all over, you're going to make Jonathan marry you, and then neither of us is ever going to have fun ever again."

"There's fun, and then there's *fun*," Hannah said with one of her sudden little grins; she glanced up at Jonathan through her eyelashes, and he sighed happily and kissed the side of her head.

"Gross," Nick said aloud. "J, that was supposed to make you uncomfortable. The marriage thing, I mean. And you're just sitting there and taking it."

"It's not like we haven't thought about it," Jonathan said, yawning. "I mean, we've been together two years already. I'm only one more semester away from my MA, and then I do my doctorate and Hannah does her residency, and assuming the stress doesn't make us kill each other . . ."

"So romantic," Hannah said, rolling her eyes a little. "I just know he's going to propose while I'm in the middle of a thirty-hour shift, up to my elbows in placenta or something."

Nick groaned and wrapped his arms around his head. "You're going to make me puke," he said, and it didn't come out as jokey as he was hoping, given the upsurge of actual nausea in his throat. "I'm unfriending you and moving to Japan to teach English or something."

"Nope. No way. You'll be our best man," Hannah said, reaching up to pat Nick's cheek. "If you live that long."

Nick gingerly slid down to the floor away from her hand and propped himself against the love seat's leg. "If you have any sisters, I'll try to make it until the wedding."

"As if I'd ever let my sisters within a mile of you," Hannah said.

"Pick out my tux while you're at it," Jonathan said, stretching. "But let's do it over eggs."

"Eggs!" Nick agreed with an enthusiasm he definitely didn't feel.

He managed to keep it together through a diner breakfast, forcing down enough bacon and pancake to keep Hannah off his back. Jonathan kept going back over the mugging, making up details that Nick swore to. He didn't mention the other guy—maybe didn't even remember him—and Nick wasn't going to be the one to start that.

At least he'd found his house key in the bottom of the wrong pocket of his blood-smeared cargo shorts.

By the time he made it home, he was bagged—cold and exhausted and nauseated, and his ribs burned, and maybe he was being an idiot about not going to the doctor, but he just wanted his own bed.

He went to sleep right away. Sometimes he shivered himself back awake. Sometimes he sweated.

Everything hurt, bone-deep. Everything thrummed with a feverish energy.

Sometimes he heard a voice that might have been his own, whining quietly like a puppy—sometimes, outside, the rush and roar of the city as it rolled over from day toward night.

APRIL 27

◑ WANING GIBBOUS

The third day consisted of organizing the cremation, the transfer of the deed to the house, the bank account.

Also, it was time to wash the kitchen floor.

Lissa was just filling a bucket when the doorbell rang. The church ladies had been coming by since the funeral, but silently. Women brought rugelach and blood sausages and huge Tupperware bowls of borscht and left them on her doorstep. Gifts, as well as food: a little leather purse of subway tokens, a basket of herbal teas, and several envelopes of cash. But they did not interrupt Lissa in her time of grief.

Through the front window, Lissa saw a taxi departing. She dried her hands and opened the door.

A young woman stood before her, tall and smooth-haired, with a silk scarf around her throat and a characteristic way of tilting her chin down. "Stella?" Lissa said.

"Did I make it in time?" Stella said. "I flew out as soon as Dad called me, but I wasn't sure. He's in Belgium right now, closing a deal, and Mum couldn't leave the surgery, but I thought someone should come to you."

"You missed the funeral," Lissa said.

"Oh," Stella said. "I'm sorry." She stood there, hair and scarf stirring in the warm breeze.

Lissa stood, too, in the doorway of the house, which was her house now—every dim and dusty corner of it, every old book. She felt it hunched behind her like an injured animal, waiting to be put out of its misery.

Stella stepped forward and embraced her carefully. She smelled faintly of expensive scent. After a moment, she let go and patted Lissa's shoulder, fished in her purse, found a travel pack of Kleenex, and handed one to Lissa.

Lissa took it automatically and kept standing there, and then Stella's arms came around her again.

"You've been doing this all alone, haven't you?" Stella said. "It's okay. I'll help with everything. I can stay as long as you need." She took the tissue and wiped the tears from Lissa's face until Lissa pulled away, edging back inside the house.

Stella followed her in. "I'll just bring my gear in, shall I?" she said, and she started lugging things into the front room: two suitcases, one of which was tagged as overweight; a rolling laptop case; and a handsome leather tote with a scarf tied around the strap.

Lissa backed against the hallway radiator. "You . . . you don't have a hotel room, do you?"

"That's all right, isn't it?" Stella said over her shoulder. "Dad said the house was big. And the flight pretty much used up my budget." She came up with the tote and the laptop case and stacked them on Lissa's sofa. "Dad wanted me to tell you he's sorry for your loss," she said, a little stiffly.

"Um. Thanks." Lissa took the tote and the laptop case from the sofa and placed them fussily beside the lamp in the corner. Stella, seeming not to notice, put one of the suitcases on the sofa instead.

"He didn't even write a card, the arse," Stella burst out. "I shouldn't've said that! I'm sorry. I know he feels for you, of course he does, he's just—"

"He's just Dad," Lissa said, moving the suitcase into the corner with the other things. Dad called Lissa once or twice a year, on or near her birthday. On Christmas sometimes too, forgetting that Baba and Lissa followed the Russian tradition of celebrating the new year instead. "It's fine. I'm used to it."

"It's not fine. Family needs to stick together. That's why I came," Stella said.

"How long are you here for?" Lissa asked, taking the final suitcase out of Stella's hands and wheeling it into the corner.

"As long as you'll have me." Stella smiled tentatively. "I mean, I figured you might need some help cleaning the house."

"I don't have a guest room," Lissa said. The house had three bedrooms: Baba's, Lissa's, and the storage room. She wondered if she sounded like a jerk but didn't apologize.

"You have a chesterfield," Stella said, biting her lip. "You won't even notice me. And I can help—really, I can."

Stella didn't look particularly useful: all posh prettiness and sleek blown-out hair, even after however many hours on a plane. She looked like the receptionist at a high-end law office: someone who probably made a great cup of tea and knew people's official titles. Not what Lissa needed at all. And if Lissa was right, the quickest way to get rid of her was probably to take her up on her offer.

"The kitchen floor needs mopping," Lissa said. "That's where Baba died."

She led Stella into the room, where the bucket still stood, half-filled. She stopped short of pointing out the spot on the floor, not out of kindness but because the words backed up in her throat.

Stella was too tall to look up at Lissa, but with her head ducked down like that she gave a good imitation of it. After a stiff moment, Stella unclenched her hands, took the mop—wordlessly—and the bottle of Mr. Clean, laid her pair of gold rings on the counter, and went to work.

Lissa left her to it, shut herself in the upstairs bathroom, and had a very long shower. When she was as clean as she could get, she still didn't know what to do next.

She dressed and braided her hair. In the mirror, she saw a person who would never be mistaken for anything other than Stella's *step*sister: six inches shorter, heavier chested, lacking Stella's lean grace. Fair-haired but not quite blond. Peasant stock. When Lissa got old, she'd look just like Baba, lumpy and square.

That was half of why Dad had left Mum, she thought; bearing Lissa had used up whatever beauty had attracted Dad. Or maybe as he earned more money he'd felt himself entitled to someone more cultured, with less old-country baggage. He'd met Julie while he was on a business trip.

He hadn't married Julie until well after Mum died. Lissa didn't know why he'd waited.

She wondered if he'd ever talked with Stella about any of it.

Downstairs, Stella was just putting away the mop in the closet under the stairs. She rolled her head on her neck and said, "It's just drying. I was wondering—I'm starved—do you have a favorite takeaway? On me, I mean."

Lissa, feeling like even more of a jerk, picked her way over the damp spots on the kitchen floor to show Stella the refrigerator stuffed with the casseroles and soups from the church ladies.

"My God," said Stella. "How many people do they think are living here?"

They ended up eating cold borscht and piroshki, sitting on the porch steps. By the time she'd finished her portion, Stella was yawning every minute. "It's much later at home," she explained. "I found some sheets in the closet and set up the chesterfield. I was wondering if you have a spare pillow?"

As easy as that, Lissa seemed to have missed her chance to be firm and send Stella to a hotel. For tonight, anyway.

She gave up thinking of it after a minute and helped Stella get settled, locating towels and pillows and toothpaste. Stella went to hug Lissa again when she said good night, and Lissa let her, standing still within the circling arms.

Lissa shut the door and wandered back into the kitchen, where the floor was now clean and she could walk on every part without seeing Baba's face and the dribble of bloody sputum.

She saw it, anyway. She should have expected it, she said to herself, trembling beside the cabinet, unwilling to cross to the sink.

There were recipes to make for the ladies. Tonight was a day off the full moon, and her unexpected houseguest was sleeping. There would not be a better time.

She still could not face the kitchen. She turned away and went to bed.

And then it was the fourth day, and the lawyer called her to come by for Baba's lockbox, which turned out to contain the letter and the doll.

APRIL 27

◑ WANING GIBBOUS

Augusta lived in a squalid apartment at the top of a fire escape: iron stairs switchbacking up the side of a pitted cinder-block wall. The motion-sensor light at the top was long dead, but the ambient light of the city was strong enough to show Maksim the way. Some of the stairs were weak with rust. Maksim jogged up them carelessly, feeling the whole assemblage tremble under his weight, daring it to collapse.

"Augusta!" he called as he ascended. He thumped on the door with his fist. "Augusta!"

He couldn't hear anything from within. The narrow pane of safety glass in the door was dark. Midnight was long past, but from elsewhere in the building, Maksim heard percussive music and shouting. Maybe Augusta was there, partying.

He thought he could scent her near, though: warm and unwashed and boozy. Maybe she was sleeping. She should not sleep when he had need of her.

Maksim settled his weight and punched through the safety glass. It didn't break on his first try, so he kept at it. First the glass webbed into pale cracks, and then after a few more hits it fell inward, taking a few splinters of the frame with it. Maksim reached through and unbolted the door and let himself in.

Augusta sprawled facedown on her slumped sofa, head pillowed on one arm, the other flung outward. She was snoring very lightly. An army-surplus T-shirt was rucked up above her waist, exposing the worn waistband of her jeans and a few inches of skin.

Maksim kicked the leg of the sofa. "Augusta," he said, not quite a shout.

She stirred then, finally, with a sleepy murmur. "Maks?"

"Get up," he said.

"Mmm, nope." She buried her face in the crook of her arm.

Maksim took hold of the nearest object and threw it at her.

It turned out to be a glass, and it bounced off Augusta's shoulder and shattered on the floor.

"Asshole!" Augusta growled, sitting up. Her pale hair was crushed flat on one side and matted into a wild tangle on the other. "Stop breaking my shit."

"I must speak with you."

"What did I do this time? I don't remember doing anything." Her voice was rough with sleep and drink; Maksim wondered if she would even remember this conversation later.

"You did nothing. That I know of," he said.

"Then it can wait until morning." But Augusta was already sitting up, scrubbing a hand through her hair, tugging her khaki T-shirt roughly into place, groping around for something. She located it tucked within the threadbare cushions of the sofa: a mostly empty bottle of rum. She upended the bottle over her mouth. Most of the rum made it in.

Maksim sat down beside her, shoulder to shoulder, feeling the sleepy heat of her. "I wish you were sober just now," he said. "I need your help."

"You're being weird. And you're bloody," Augusta said, blinking sandy eyes in the dimness. She ran a fingertip over the split knuckles of Maksim's right hand.

"I broke your door."

"Haven't seen you lose your temper in so long, I didn't know if you were capable of it anymore," Augusta said. "It's kind of a relief. You're not so much better than me, after all." She raised Maksim's hand to her mouth and licked gently over the raw, broken skin, soothing it with her tongue.

"I have never been better than you," Maksim murmured. "I have been so, so much worse. You should turn from me. Maybe you will yet."

Augusta reared away from him. "What the fuck?" she snapped. "What the fuck is that supposed to mean?" She emphasized it with a sharp smack from the flat of her hand across Maksim's chest.

Maksim felt his mouth snarl. "I need help," he said again. "Something is wrong. I feel like . . . something is wrong."

"You smell different," Augusta said. She leaned in again and sniffed at his neck. "Better."

He could smell himself: sweat and blood and rust from the fire escape, and none of that was what Augusta meant.

"What did you do?" she said. "You gave up the curse, didn't you? About fucking time!"

His hand wrapped around her throat, silencing her, before he had even thought. "It is a balm, not a curse, and I did not give it up," he said. "I cannot. I would not."

Augusta shoved his hand away. "Then what?"

Maksim was on his feet, turning. "I wish I knew. All I know is that I feel wrong." Wrong, or all too right. The last couple of days had been too delicious, too much like the old days. The miles he had felt the need to run, the sweet ache in his calves only spurring him on faster. The hot sweat sliding down the hollow of his spine. The way he had not been able to resist that young man. All the pleasures Iadviga's invocation had blunted.

More than any of those, the craving for harm.

He should have thought of it right away, of course; only he had been drunk with it as he had not been in years. He should have known his pleasure for the ill omen it was.

"I must go to the witch," he said.

Augusta scowled. "No."

"You may not command me," Maksim said, fisting both hands in the denim of his jeans to stop himself lashing out.

"I know I can't. But you never fight me anymore," Augusta said and grinned through a yawn.

Maksim tipped her chin up to see her face in the angle of brightness from the streetlight outside. Her eyes looked puffy, lined, older than the rest of her.

"You are too foxed to fight," he said. "Go back to sleep."

"You were the one who woke me up, breaking shit," Augusta said. She tugged free of his hand. "Come on. Let's put some coffee on, and then you can punch my lights out. Just tell me you'll stay away from that unnatural piece of work."

Maksim hesitated for a second. Didn't he usually want to be kind? But Augusta's tone was too much to swallow when his body thrummed with this urge to move. He slapped her open-handed across the ear.

Augusta laughed and surged to her feet, butting her forehead right into Maksim's chin, knocking his cap off. "Yeah! Let's go. Come on."

He came back with a messy uppercut, catching her in the ribs and making her grunt. At the gym Maksim owned, he taught students of all levels, but none of them were *kin,* and Maksim was always pulling his punches. Here, and only here, he could let fly with close to his full strength.

"See?" Augusta gasped, ducking to let Maksim's fist overshoot her head and smack into the door frame. "That's it!" And he took her full in the cheek with his other fist, splitting the skin.

But she had been passed out drunk earlier while he was furious and on edge, and he shortly sent Augusta reeling backward into the scatter of broken safety glass.

She hit the wall hard with one shoulder and bit off a curse word.

"I take no pleasure in damaging you," Maksim said.

"Liar," Augusta said, without heat, twisting to tug down her torn shirt collar and inspect her shoulder.

Maksim picked up the rum bottle and held it up to the wash of light from the window—a finger left, at most.

"Give me that," said Augusta, stumbling over to drop to the sofa. "It wasn't my best fight. I'll do better tomorrow."

"That is what we all say," Maksim said, gulping the rum and tossing the empty bottle in the direction of the kitchenette.

Augusta cursed him, so he turned his back on her before he succumbed to the want in his fists again. He left her dim, stuffy room, jogged down the iron stairs, and vaulted over the last half story.

Then he went to see the witch.

APRIL 28

◖ WANING GIBBOUS

Lissa closed her bedroom door. The air hung still and stuffy. She'd told Stella she wanted a nap. She sat on her bed, back against the headboard, and opened the lockbox.

The doll, unclothed muslin body scalloped with faint brown stains, had eyes that opened and closed. Its porcelain head was capped with carefully sewn curls of auburn hair. Human hair. Baba's hair, it would be, cut when she was young enough that it held no gray. Lissa thought Baba must have made the doll originally for her daughter, Lissa's mother. Lissa tilted it back and forth, watching the clear, glassy gaze, and laid it on her lap.

The letter was on lined paper torn from a Mead notebook and folded small. Baba had written it in pencil, dark, spiky, and sprawling.

The letter reminded her again of the old story for which Lissa had been named: Vasilissa the Beautiful, or Vasilissa the Wise, depending on the version.

Vasilissa, like so many girls in old stories, grew up with a stepmother who hated her. The stepmother sent Vasilissa into the forest one night to ask the witch Baba Yaga for a light. Baba Yaga lived in a house that strutted about on hen's legs, and she rode through the sky in a mortar. Her house stood in a yard ringed with a fence of skulls mounted on spears, and the skulls' eyes burned with fire.

When Vasilissa explained her predicament, Baba Yaga said she might stay and work, and then she assigned her three tasks: cooking enough dinner for ten people, sorting and grinding a sack of millet, and squeezing all the oil from a sack of poppy seeds.

Vasilissa's sole memento of her departed mother was a doll, which she brought with her everywhere, even into the forest to visit the witch. At the full moon, Vasilissa could ask this doll three questions, because as usual in stories, everything came in threes. Vasilissa asked the doll to help her through the three tests Baba Yaga set for her, and the doll gave her such good advice that Vasilissa was able to do everything the witch had asked. Baba Yaga was so impressed that she agreed to give Vasilissa a light to take back to her stepmother: not just any light, but one of the fiery-eyed skulls.

When Vasilissa returned from the forest, bearing the skull aloft on its spear, her stepmother was at first grateful, for there had been no light in the home since Vasilissa left. But the skull's flaming eyes began to scorch the stepmother, and when she tried to hide, the skull followed her and burned her to a cinder.

Vasilissa then took up the skull again, went back into the forest, and asked Baba Yaga to teach her all her magic. With the help of her doll, Vasilissa was able to perform all the tasks Baba Yaga demanded in exchange. Eventually, Vasilissa became a powerful witch in her own right, so powerful that she drew the attention of the czar, who made her his wife; and the story said she carried her mother's doll in her pocket for all her days.

There were other stories about Vasilissa, or maybe there was more than one Vasilissa, but this one was important for the kernel of truth in it, or so Baba said: a witch could make such a doll and hand it down to her daughter or to her granddaughter. Once a month, around the full moon, such a doll could be of help.

Baba's letter ended with instructions and a charm, which Lissa read through a few times before sneaking down to the kitchen to pick up the supplies she would need.

Back upstairs, she set the doll on the bedside table, crumbled a slice of bread before it, and sprinkled salt from the shaker.

She felt almost embarrassed, even though she was alone: this was a new thing, this ritual, and she had only a folktale to suggest it would work. It wasn't like Baba could have tested it in advance. Maybe Lissa was getting her hopes up over nothing . . . and maybe, even if it didn't work, it would only be because Lissa herself didn't know how to do it correctly.

Before she could talk herself into a spiral of doubt, Lissa took a sharp breath and whispered the charm: *By the white rider of dawn, by the red rider of day, by the black rider of night, I call to you: Iadviga Rozhnata, your scion desires your counsel.*

"How long has it been?" said Baba from somewhere in the bottom of Lissa's brain. Her voice was a cold wind.

"This is the fourth day," said Lissa. "There was the funeral, and then Stella came, and the lawyer—"

"And on what business do you desire my counsel?"

"I don't know," said Lissa. She found she was crying again.

She wiped her cheek with the back of her hand and wiped that upon her skirt. "I don't know."

"*Vnuchka,* I am not to be called idly. Ask counsel."

Baba sounded a bit lecturing, Lissa thought, like always. And very far away.

"Where are you? What's it like?" Lissa said. "Can you counsel me about that?"

"I may not speak of it."

"I always thought that story was just a story. I didn't know you'd be waiting. . . ."

Baba was silent.

"I'm going to make up some spells for a few of the ladies," Lissa said. "Will they all still come to me . . . will they trust me to do it right?"

"You have learned some of my trade," Baba said. "They will have no cause to complain, so long as you remember your lessons."

Not quite the wholehearted endorsement she'd been hoping for.

Three questions. Lissa bit down on the tip of her tongue to stop herself from saying anything careless.

Finally, she settled on, "Was there anything you left unfinished?"

Baba did not answer quickly. Her silence felt alive and dark and chilly. Lissa began to wonder if this was another forbidden question or if she had somehow made Baba angry.

"Maksim Volkov," Baba said. "In life, I was sworn to help him. In death, I may do so no longer. If he comes to you, know that he is *kin.*"

"Kin? You mean we're related to him somehow?"

But silence was her only answer. Baba was gone. When Lissa said the charm again, nothing happened. She shook the doll. The eyelids fluttered open and shut; one of them stuck higher than the other, giving the thing an expression of drunkenness.

Lissa carefully jiggled it back into place and set the doll in her lap. She folded the letter up small and zipped it into a pocket of her purse.

"If you can hear me," she said, "I'll talk to you again as soon as I'm allowed, next month. I love you. If you're there."

When she came downstairs, Stella looked at her face and went to hug her again.

"I'm fine," Lissa said, backing into the banister and rubbing at her eyes.

"Another delivery came," Stella said. "I didn't want to wake you."

"What was it?"

Stella didn't answer but led her into the dining room, where a box sat on the table.

"It's the urn," she said. "A gentleman from the mortuary brought it over."

"I never asked her what she wanted done with her ashes," Lissa said.

"You didn't know she'd go suddenly," Stella said. "She was in good health, wasn't she? Dad said she was strong as a horse. You can't blame yourself."

"I should have asked," Lissa said. Three questions, and she had not managed to make this one of them.

She took the urn upstairs to put it on Baba's dresser, for now.

Stella followed her into the big, dim room. "How many rooms does this place have?" she said. "I'll bet this house hasn't been sorted in a dog's age."

"She had better things to do," Lissa flared, thinking of the third bedroom, a warren of boxes dating from when her mother was still alive. "I should've. It was my job to keep things clean."

"Even her knickers?" Stella said, wincing at the overflowing laundry basket.

"Don't," Lissa said. "Don't." She couldn't get anything else out of her mouth. She crowded Stella backward out the door and into the hallway. "Don't. Don't."

Stella stumbled, caught herself on the banister. "I want to help," she said. "That's all."

"I don't need your help," Lissa said. "Where were you before?" Which didn't even make sense, and damn it, when had she started crying again?

Stella had her hands tight together, and she was looking at Lissa with that face, and Lissa pushed past her into the bathroom and locked the door.

"Lissa? I'm sorry. I'm sorry." A breath. Feet shuffling.

Lissa shoved her fists against her temples and wiped messy tears all over. She unrolled a crumple of toilet paper and blew her nose.

"Lissa . . . I don't quite know what to do," Stella said through the door. "I'm getting it all wrong. I think I should go out for a bit, okay? So you can have some space."

"Yes. Please," Lissa managed to say, thick and wet.

Silence. Lissa blew her nose again.

Eventually, she heard Stella's footsteps moving away, pausing at the top of the stairs, and then descending.

A minute later, the front door opened and closed.

Stupid, this was all stupid and wrong, and she needed to do something different. Well, there was something she'd been avoiding, and today was the last day she'd be able to do it until next month.

She went to the house mains and shut off the breaker. The subterranean hum of the house cut off, leaving blank silence. Lissa wondered how the *kolduny* had discovered that electricity was unfriendly to magic: had they gathered somewhere in the old country to discuss it? Had they written each other letters? Baba had rarely spoken of such things, but when she did, Lissa could not always tell whether she was learning rules or merely Baba's habits. The most important *Law* she knew because of the way Baba looked whenever she mentioned it: flinty and staring, holding Lissa's eyes until she was sure Lissa understood.

Magic was to be done only on the full moon and the next two days after. Never on or near the new moon. That was *Law*.

"Like, the kind of law where if you break it other witches will arrest you?" Lissa had asked when she was a young girl. Baba had not laughed but had answered, "No, *vnuchka*. *Law* like the law of gravity. Nature imposes it, and if we break it the consequence is inevitable and severe."

So the kitchen corkboard always had a calendar with the phases of the moon highlighted, right underneath the cookbooks where Lissa could easily see it.

The grimoire of the *koldun* Anatoliy Ievlev stood on a shelf up higher, inside a cupboard, above the cookbooks and the calendar. It was a heavy tome with ragged-edged pages and a gold-stamped spine, printed in Moscow toward the end of the nineteenth century, probably as a curiosity more than a text; Baba had learned from a different grimoire, she said, but that one had been lost when she fled Russia, and so this one had been ordered at great expense from an antiquarian in Yekaterinburg on the occasion of Lissa's twelfth birthday. For Lissa's benefit, Baba had interleaved her own penciled translations, written on envelopes or notebook sheets, tucked in between the musty-smelling pages of Cyrillic. Lissa still had to stand on a step stool to reach that cupboard; she'd done it so many times now that her fingertips found the right book unerringly.

Lissa moved about the room in the dimness, setting out a row of tea lights. She couldn't see the floor in this light, the stain where Baba had lain, which wasn't even there anymore. She groped in a drawer for matches, felt a knife blade slide silken over the ball of her thumb.

The first match crumbled. The second fizzled. The third caught. She touched it to the wicks of the tea lights, and the unsteady light made the dark look darker. She licked at the cut on her thumb.

Next came the loosing of bonds. All the *kolduny* agreed that magic could not be done if the *koldun* wore anything knotted or clasped. Lissa unfastened her bra and wriggled it out through the armholes of her tank top and opened the clip that held her hair, letting the mass of it down over her shoulders.

She laid out her gear on the kitchen table: Baba's wooden spoon, the last thing her hand had touched in life; a Pyrex mixing bowl and a tiny spice-toasting pan; mortar and pestle; an assortment of flasks and test tubes, mostly purchased when Brunswick Collegiate closed its doors and sold off the contents of its classrooms.

From the cupboard over the refrigerator, the shoe box full of old baby food jars, some labeled in Lissa's hand, some in Baba's. From the fridge itself, a fresh dozen eggs.

The most recent orders from the church ladies were written on a magnetic shopping notepad. *For children,* Baba had written, in deference to Lissa's poor Russian. *For bones. For sleep.*

Lissa tugged strands of hair from her mouth and bent over the grimoire. Fertility was hard; she hadn't done it before. She would have to learn.

For the base, Anatoliy Ievlev suggested wine, but Stella seemed to have finished off the bottle of pinot grigio from the refrigerator; Baba had often substituted plain white vinegar, and Lissa did so again, splashing a cup into the Pyrex bowl.

Rabbit fur. Anatoliy Ievlev explained, "For they of all the animal kingdom are the best known for their increase." In one of the baby food jars was a rabbit's-foot key chain, some of the fur already scraped away for an earlier ritual. Lissa razored off another tuft and placed it in her tiny cast-iron spice-toasting pan upon the stove.

Baba's old gas stove was of the avocado-colored variety and had no automatic lighter; Lissa had to slide a lit match up to the burner to catch the gas.

Soon the rabbit fur twisted and charred. Another moment and it sprang into flame, and Lissa wrinkled her nose against the stink.

The ashes went into her mortar to be ground fine, and from there into the Pyrex, where they floated atop the vinegar. Lissa had asked once why so many ingredients had to be burned and put into the mortar before going into the recipe: was it something to do with the mortar the witch in the story used to ride around in? Baba had chuckled at that and said it was only that otherwise the texture would end up uneven.

Next, Anatoliy Ievlev directed her to add the more pedestrian clover and raspberry leaves, without explaining in what way they related to fertility. Both herbs toasted crisp and ground to powder, she passed on to the final item on the list: mother's milk.

From the refrigerator, she withdrew the baby's bottle she'd stolen during the funeral. You didn't pass up a chance like that. Anatoliy Ievlev had the right sense of it. The fluids of the body were always, always potent in spells.

She trickled the milk into the vinegar mixture and used Baba's spoon to stir it all together. She tilted in a few drops of red food coloring until the mixture achieved a dull pink color.

Lastly, the hokey part. When she was younger, she would blush at the sheer weirdness of it, especially the way Baba did it, intoning the words in a voice of drama and mystery.

She knew by now that the manner didn't matter so much. You didn't have to shout, either. The spirits would hear you, even if you spoke English, even if you stammered, even if you spoke in a whisper because your father slept upstairs. So long as the moon was full, or near full; so long as the speaker asked politely; so long as the speaker was a witch.

She took up the first egg in her left hand and dipped her right in the vinegar mixture.

"As the seed grows to flower; as the egg grows to chick; as the moon grows to full; so, I ask you, grant healthy increase. Riders of dawn and day and dusk, I ask you. I, Vasilissa, granddaughter of Iadviga, ask you this."

She finger-painted the egg with the curdled pink mixture and, with it, felt the spell sink into place.

APRIL 29

◑ WANING GIBBOUS

The doorbell rang sometime after midnight.

Right: Lissa had not given Stella a key. After a couple of hours of cooking and chanting and being alone in the house, she felt her earlier emotional reaction seemed out of scale, ridiculous. She set aside a just-completed egg in the carton, washed her hands quickly, and went to let her stepsister in.

It was a man, though, a stranger. Tanned arms, muscled like a martial artist. He wore old jeans and a brimmed cap shadowing his face under the porch light.

"You are the granddaughter," he said.

"And you are?" asked Lissa, blocking the entrance with her body.

"Maksim Volkov." His voice had a hoarse, strained edge to it.

"Oh. Yes. You knew my grandmother."

"For many years," he said. "Is she not at home?"

"She's dead," Lissa blurted.

Maksim Volkov tilted his head and stared at her. She thought he had a funny way of standing, absolutely still but somehow ready to burst into motion.

"I guess you hadn't heard," she said. "A few days ago. It was a heart attack."

"She left nothing for me?" said Maksim.

Lissa shook her head and spread her hands.

"You cannot help me?" He loomed toward her. She backed up a step into the hallway. Maksim crowded closer and caught her by the arm, gripping tight.

"Let me go," Lissa said, fighting to keep her voice steady.

"I must know if you are also a witch." His voice was rougher with each word, a dark rasp as of a file on granite.

So he knew and wanted something, and Baba had said he was kin. She nodded, and he abruptly let go of her arm. Mingled with the budding lilacs, she could smell him: a heavy reek of sweat.

"Tell me she taught you," said Maksim.

"I can do some things. She wanted me to help you. But you can't just, just push in here."

"Can you give me calm? Or sleep? I would not ask you," said Maksim, "except that I have a great need."

"I can see that," Lissa said, rubbing her arm. Sleep wasn't so hard. And Baba had given her his name. She fought down her unease. "Okay."

He sighed in relief and shuffled along behind Lissa as she led him down the hallway to the kitchen.

"Is it insomnia, then?" she said. "Because you sound like—"

Then she saw him in the light of the kitchen candles. Maksim was filthy: grit spattered his jeans halfway up the calf, and his tank top was far from white. Something dark spotted the fabric down one side of his chest; his lower lip looked bruised. His hair under the brim of his cap was stiff with salt.

He eased himself onto one of the high stools and hunched there, rubbing one palm against his thigh. A muscle in his jaw knotted and released, knotted and released.

"I was thinking tea, but maybe you'd like something stronger," Lissa said. "There's some rye. I could do you up a rye and Coke."

He nodded sharply.

Lissa found the rye and mixed him a fairly stiff drink. "How are you related to my grandmother?" she asked.

Maksim gave Lissa a flat look. "If she kept silence, it is not mine to break. But if you are wondering whether you should send me from the room, there is no need. I have seen your grandmother at her work."

"All of it?"

"I have seen her mix potions, and I have seen her say runes as she painted eggs. If that is not all of it, it is all I know to ask of you."

If Lissa hadn't heard it straight from Baba herself, she wouldn't have believed it: Someone who knew what they did yet wasn't part of the community around the church? Someone who had actually been in the room when Baba was working? Someone whom Lissa had never met in all the years she'd lived here?

But the cold voice in the back of her head had been perfectly clear. Lissa had asked Baba about unfinished business, and this man was the answer.

"Here," she said. "I'll leave the rye and the Coke beside you; help yourself. I don't want you walking around, spoiling my concentration."

To be honest, Maksim's presence would shake Lissa's concentration no matter what he did. Strangeness hung about him. But admitting this would not inspire confidence, and while she didn't really want him watching her, she wanted even less to let him sit unattended in some other part of her house.

She went back to the fertility eggs before the mixture could dry out, fetching another couple of cartons from the refrigerator.

Then she found another page in the grimoire and began on the sleep eggs.

The words were different, and this recipe called for the hair of cats and for valerian and lavender; but this spell was one Lissa had done before, and she moved through the ritual with a bit more confidence. She and Baba had been trading these off for years now, long enough that Baba had stopped bothering to test Lissa's eggs before handing them out to the ladies.

Across the room, Maksim waited in silence, flames reflecting from his eyes beneath the brim of his cap. Now and then, she heard liquid on glass.

Lissa finished the sleep eggs after another hour. She flipped the main back on, and the refrigerator hummed back to life.

Maksim was squinting at the rye bottle. "Very little is left," he said. "I apologize."

Lissa blinked. "Whatever. It's been in that cupboard for ages. I'm just surprised you got through it all." She settled on the other stool beside Maksim. "These are ready for you now. You'll want to take them at home, where you can—"

He took one of the fresh eggs and cracked it into his glass, where it slopped unattractively into the dregs of his rye and Coke. He downed the whole mess in a swallow, grimacing.

Lissa choked. "I was going to tell you to take it in a milk shake."

Maksim shrugged.

After a moment, during which Lissa watched him closely, Maksim let out a breath and slouched a little where he sat. "I think it is good."

He let his head sink onto his folded arms.

Lissa cleaned the kitchen around him, moving softly. Her newest patient shifted only once to turn his face against his forearm and settle more easily. He breathed slow and deep.

A success, then. She only hoped he could wake up enough to make himself scarce before Stella got back. She refrigerated the newly bespelled eggs, washed out the mixing bowls and spoon, and put away the grimoire.

By that time, Maksim was stirring. He lifted one eyelid and turned to pillow his cheek on his fist. "You are accomplished, *koldun'ia,*" he murmured.

"That's the first time you've used my title."

"I was not sure you merited it." He pushed himself up to lean against the wall and dumped the rest of the rye into his glass. He was too brown-complected to go truly pale, but he was very sallow, so the stubble stood out dark on his chin.

"I hope you didn't drive here," Lissa said.

Maksim blinked heavily. "I ran. If I do not keep myself fatigued, there is no telling what I will do." He quirked the corner of his mouth and swallowed some of the rye, straight. "I have done something that is not permitted already."

"Oh?"

But he shook his head, letting his eyes droop closed. He lay against the wall, boneless.

"I think I infected someone." Maksim's voice startled her just as she thought he'd fallen asleep. He sounded drunk, as well he should. "I was not trying. You must understand, I was not the one who hurt him. He was only there, bleeding, and I came upon him. The smell, the sight—it was . . . irresistible."

"What did you do?"

"You are right!" he snapped as if she'd accused him. "It is my duty to resist. But it is very hard, and this time I failed."

"Just tell me what you did."

"Licked him," Maksim said, sudden mad laughter in his voice. "Then I ran away."

"You found some poor guy bleeding—and you licked him and ran away."

Maksim slouched farther down, one hand over his face. "Part of me is not human, *koldun'ia*. And the other part is not good."

"I don't know what you're talking about," Lissa said. "You need to tell me from the beginning."

But Maksim slid down from the stool, supporting himself on the counter, and gave her a distracted half smile. "I must go," he said. "I will take these eggs with me, yes?"

"Yes," Lissa said. "But I'd really like to know—"

Maksim waved a dismissive hand. "I will tell you another time, when I have more words. These eggs are fine, *koldun'ia*."

"That's . . . good." Though he had only slept for a few minutes. Lissa had expected these eggs to be knockouts. "That's good," she said again to cover her worry.

He was already walking away from her, down the hallway, trailing his hand along the wall for balance.

"Are you sure you're okay to get home on your own?"

He chuckled, low and chilly. "No concern for me is warranted, *koldun'ia*." He slanted a glance at her from beneath his cap, nodded once, and let the door close.

Two

◑ WANING GIBBOUS

Maksim walked because he did not trust his balance quite enough
for running. The rye on its own would only have been enough to
loosen him up, but the witch's spelled eggs were something else:
a heavy drag on his limbs, a haze on his thoughts. He kept the
egg carton cradled in one hand and let the other hand reach out
to touch things: fences, lilacs, brick walls, walls covered in shin-
gle. Once, his head blurred enough that he found himself leaning
upon one of these walls, and he stayed there a moment, breathing thickly.

He walked past the mouth of the alley without seeing it and
found himself on King Street already, about to walk into a crowd
of black-clothed teenagers at a streetcar stop; he turned himself
around again and went back north, murmuring a curse.

Was this where he had found the young man? Was this where
he had begun to go wrong—this sodium-lit aisle of broken pavement? It held a shopping cart and a jumble of gas cans; he could
smell the gas, cloying, confusing the other scents. He held his

breath and went farther in. A Dumpster. That could be right. Stale beer, rancid grease, cat piss, mice. When he went to crouch beside the Dumpster, he fell to one knee, dizzy again.

He could smell blood, though, a bit, faint and tantalizing below the other smells. He got right down and snuffled at the ground.

Here: a fat drop, smeared by a shoe. Dry now, but there'd been no rain, and the scent of it was still true.

Under the blanket of the witch's magic, his other nature roused sleepily, sullenly. He drew the scent in. That made it better.

The young man had been just what his nature loved most: graceful body slowed by pain and shock, bruises just starting beneath the silky skin. Blood like liquor, and Maksim suddenly as thirsty as a sailor on leave. He'd let himself get closer, closer, never thinking his will would fail him so completely. Never thinking his nature would slip the collar of Iadviga Rozhnata's spell.

After what he'd done, Maksim had run off west. The young man would not have followed; he had been frightened, confused. He would be more frightened now, more confused, with Maksim's nature taking root in him. He would be all *kin* soon, and he would not know what it meant, and if Maksim did not find him in time . . .

Maksim dragged his mind from hazy, dire forebodings and back to what had happened, what evidence might be left to him.

The young man had been drunk. His sweat had tasted of it—his breath, his blood. Maksim wondered if this had made him even more appealing, because it reminded him of Augusta: drink and blood and the sweat of a healthy, athletic body.

The second young man had been drunk too, even worse off. They would have had to help each other or ask for help from some other person. East was downtown, heavier traffic, more taxis.

East was the way he'd entered the alley, and Maksim had not smelled the young man's scent on the way in. But he backtracked, anyway, slow and thickheaded, tracing and retracing, and sure enough, there was a hint of it, a trace of blood on a wall where he might have rested his hand.

So Maksim had managed to track the two young men a whole fifty feet. What next? He sat down on the hood of a parked car to think about it. Queen Street? Where there were streetcars and taxis and—wait, yes. He had already thought about this part. Surely Queen Street would be correct. He would just stroll down that way and keep scenting.

In a moment.

He started violently awake to a brush of warmth over his hand. He reached, snatched, caught nothing. Peered about, breathing hard.

On the roof of the car, behind him: a yearling cat, thin and hunched, peering back. When he stood up, it skittered away, paused, jumped down, and vanished into the alley.

Maksim braced against the drowsy slackening of his limbs. He did not sit back down on the car. He pushed off toward Queen Street.

A few steps down the sidewalk, he realized his hands were empty. That was wrong.

He turned around and saw his eggs, abandoned on the hood of the car. The little cat had come back and was sniffing at the carton.

He lunged at it, but he was just slow enough that his fingers only closed on a tuft of fine black fur. The cat darted under a nearby fence. Its wide-pupiled eyes gazed at him quite calmly as he took up the eggs again.

It should fear him more. His nature would have had him snap its neck before he could think. The eggs would wear off eventually, and he would be a danger to whatever, whoever, was near him.

He sighed. His eyes stung. He did not want to be a danger to small cats. He would sit down for a moment before resuming his search. Just a moment to rest his eyes before going on.

SHULGIN, RUSSIA: 1707

Smoke billowed up from the burning tents. The *ataman* was laughing, one side of his moustache singed to curling char.

The *ataman's* chest was bare, running with sweat, and his long *cherkesska* flapped open, buttons slashed off and one lapel scored with a ragged tear. He shook his saber in the air, and blood flew from the blade.

"A fine night!" he said. "A fine night, Maksim!"

Maksim heard the words as if through a waterfall, did not see the man's face at all, only the weapon and the blood scattering. He ran at the *ataman* and tried to slash his throat.

The *ataman* blocked him, still laughing. "You are very slow, and your saber is dull," he said. "You have been fighting-mad for many hours. Our foes are dead or have fled, and it is time for you to put your saber down."

Maksim tried to raise his saber again, but one of the nicks in the edge caught against the *ataman's* blade, and he could not seem to free it.

"Maksim," the *ataman* was saying. "Be calm now. The fighting is over for this day."

Maksim still had fight in his arms, but the *ataman* repeated himself until at last Maksim dropped his saber.

"It was a very good madness," said the *ataman*. "Come back from it now."

Maksim, at the touch of the *ataman*'s hand on his shoulder, startled and began to tremble.

The *ataman* soothed him like a beast, petting his arm. "Your brothers are over at the fire. Have you any hurts that need tending?"

But Maksim did not have his voice yet. He recognized the *ataman* now—a man he'd been following since last summer, through a long and messy campaign—and he was able to follow him dumbly toward the cooking fires, but when Maksim drew near the others, some of whom were wounded, the smell of blood and gunpowder made his lips draw back from his teeth. He covered his eyes with his hands so the *ataman* would not see the madness returning in them.

The *ataman* looked at Maksim's face and shook his head. "I will have someone come to you. But perhaps I should make sure you cannot forget that the fighting is over for now." The *ataman* took off his sash and used it to bind Maksim's hands together.

Maksim pulled mindlessly at his bonds until he hurt himself, and then he was still, mostly.

After some time, a woman came to help him strip off his scorched and slashed *cherkesska* and douse his injuries with vodka. He was still too much in his madness to answer questions, but he was able to make himself submit to her touch. After she stitched the worst of his injuries, he went to sleep there on the ground, still bound, wrapped in his battle-filthy coat.

When he awoke and freed himself, he found he was one of the heroes of last night's action. He drank with his brothers; he rutted with the woman who had cleaned him up. His injuries healed very quickly.

But the madness did not quite leave him. He fell into it again each time they fought, and each time took longer to return to himself. And when they were not fighting, he was quicker to anger, flush with energy that had to be wrestled out. He thought he had not always been this way.

He began to notice people flinching from him a little. He heard rumors about himself: that he was a shape-changer who became a beast at the full moon, that he was possessed by an evil spirit. None of the rumors he heard were true, but he began to understand there was something at the heart of them.

Finally, he sought out a *koldun*. The *koldun* was frail, stooped, blind in one eye; Maksim was a Cossack in the prime of his youth, and yet he feared the *koldun* so much that he trembled with it as he stood in the hut to ask his question.

The *koldun* demanded the price of a deer, which Maksim chased down on foot.

When Maksim returned with the animal slung over his shoulders, still steaming, the *koldun* said, "You have only to look to that hunt for the secrets of your nature."

"What do you mean?" Maksim said, growling a little, for the heated blood of the deer still stained his hands.

"You follow blood. You shed blood. You are kin to the others who share your blood. Blood is the only end," the *koldun* said as if that was all Maksim needed to know.

The *koldun* waited, smiling, his sighted eye bright in a web of wrinkles, while Maksim clenched his hands on the fine-boned limbs of the deer and fought down both the desire to run at him and the desire to run away.

"I can take it from you," the *koldun* said finally. "You will grow worse with age. I can make you as other men."

Maksim shuddered all down his spine. He thought it sounded like a threat, and he did not doubt the *koldun* would see it through.

He was losing his voice again, as he sometimes did when his madness rode him. But he made himself shake his head, and he laid the deer down at the *koldun*'s feet and backed away.

The *koldun* said nothing; he only turned away into the dimness of his hut and left Maksim standing there with deer's blood on his hands.

Maksim went away still believing the madness was a gift. Among the Cossacks, a violent man was a useful man. Battle was his natural inclination. His fellows learned to launch him in the right direction and then stay out of his way; his *ataman* learned how to command him, at least some of the time. When there was no fighting to quell his thirst, he could wrestle his brothers, he could fuck with abandon, or, failing all else, ride or run or drink until he dropped in exhaustion.

Maksim began to understand that he would live a very long life. He'd thought for quite a while that he would live all of it as a Cossack.

History happened, though. He did not change, or not quickly, but things around him did, and as his madness grew in him— and grew less welcome—he thought again of the *koldun*.

When he reached the place where the *koldun* had lived, he found that the man had died and left no successor. Maksim did not mind so much; he had already had another good idea. He left the Cossacks to their newfound gentleness and went looking for a war.

He did not have to look far. Not that year, and not for many years after.

APRIL 30

◑ WANING GIBBOUS

Lissa dropped off the fertility spell early the following day. She dressed carefully for it in a black shirtdress with long sleeves: ugly and unsuitable for the weather, but correct.

Stella had come back sometime in the late hours; Lissa could see her tousled hair hanging over the arm of the sofa. She tiptoed past and did not slam the door.

She couldn't help a thread of worry under her manufactured calm. The sleep eggs hadn't been as effective as she'd thought they should have been—what if she was off her game? What if the fertility eggs proved ineffective too?

Izabela Dmitreeva was staying with her mother-in-law and a gaggle of other relatives. When Lissa arrived, sweating in her heavy dress, two old men were watching television in the den; one made the sign against evil, and the other merely looked at her, his rheumy eyes level and cold. The mother-in-law had a familiar face; Lissa could not recall her name but thought she'd taken eggs for kidney stones the year before. Izabela Dmitreeva ushered Lissa into the kitchen and thanked her very graciously for taking the time in the midst of her own troubles.

The apartment smelled of boiled vegetables; when Lissa had finished explaining how to take the eggs, Izabela Dmitreeva pressed upon her a Tupperware container of cabbage rolls, calling her *koldun'ia* again.

Izabela Dmitreeva did not seem to have any doubt that the eggs would work. She had already begun knitting a baby blanket, Lissa saw; it lay in a basket on the windowsill, a jumble of knitting needles and pale-yellow yarn.

The old men weren't so sanguine. On her way out, she saw the sign again, and one of the men cleared his throat and hawked horribly into a Kleenex.

Lissa took the subway home and found Stella in the kitchen, making coffee. Making coffee for her, apparently.

"I didn't even hear you go out," Stella said, eyeing the ugly dress. "There's fruit salad. And muffins."

"I didn't know we had muffins."

"I made them," Stella said. "To say sorry."

"Hold that thought," Lissa said and jogged upstairs to change into a lightweight T-shirt and a denim skirt. Bare-legged, she came back down to find Stella setting out plates and cups in the kitchen.

The muffins turned out to be lemon cranberry and delicious. Stella picked at hers, and every time Lissa glanced at her, she glanced away.

"Look," Lissa said. "It was nice of you to bake for me."

"I want to stay," Stella said.

"With me? But—"

"There's so much I could do to help. This house . . . it isn't really yours yet, you know? And you shouldn't have to do it all by yourself. I was thinking you might be able to use some rent money. And—"

"But that's all about me," Lissa said. "I don't need all that."

"Oh," Stella said. "Okay." And her great dark eyes began to well.

"Hey . . . look, I'm sorry. It was nice of you to come, and . . ." And what else did you say to a stepsister you didn't know, anyway? Lissa filled her mouth with coffee.

Stella jumped into the gap. "That's just it; I don't think it's right that your only family is all on the other side of the ocean and never visits. And I can't change Dad, and Mum doesn't really count as your family, I guess, but there's me, and I want to know you better. You're . . . you're so quiet, and maybe you could use some fun sometimes. Or cry on my shoulder, if that would help. Or, you know—"

"I don't want to cry on anyone's shoulder."

"I do!" Stella said, dissolving.

Lissa, after a frozen moment of awkwardness, handed her a napkin.

"I can't go back," Stella sobbed. "I can't deal with it there. You know how many messages Erick's left on my phone in the last three days? Twenty-seven. Twenty-seven! He's scaring me."

"Erick?"

"Boyfriend. *Ex*-boyfriend. He just won't leave me alone."

"So you ran all the way to Canada?"

"I'll find a flat if you don't want me," Stella said. "I have everything I need. I have a job already."

"A . . . what?"

"Last night," Stella said, wiping smeared mascara from beneath her eye. "Everyone needs servers, right? And I don't have to worry about paperwork, because Dad got my Canadian citizenship set up ages ago. So I made the rounds of your neighborhood. And I found the Duke of Lancashire. You know, up near Bloor."

Lissa shook her head.

"The girls wear little kilts," Stella said. "They hired me on the spot."

"I wasn't expecting this," Lissa managed.

Stella tucked her head down. "Please let me stay until I find my own place. Please say I can."

"That's . . . wow," Lissa said. "Um. I have to think about that."

She thought she was being pretty awesome, not saying no right off the bat, but Stella's face went all crushed.

Lissa had no idea what to do with that. If Stella stuck around, she was either going to cave to emotional blackmail or kick her sister right out the door.

It was an hour too early to leave for work, but she did anyway. Behind her, the house felt smaller than usual, with Stella still sitting in it, drying her eyes at the kitchen table. Not hers. Not right.

At the print shop, Lissa's boss, Mustafa, welcomed her back, patted her on the shoulder, and told her he'd stocked the fridge with her favorite iced green tea. He didn't tell her the corporate orders were behind schedule, but she found that out quickly enough.

She'd have to put in some extra time to get everything caught up, but that was okay. She had to pay off the funeral somehow, and Baba had left her, in addition to the house, the property tax bill; the heating system, which still ran on oil; the new sofa, charged to the Sears card.

And if she worked late, she would not have to face Stella again just yet or the strangeness of the house or the people wanting eggs; she would not have to speak to anyone at all, only move quietly back and forth amid the scent of warm paper and the white noise of ink upon it.

APRIL 30

◐ WANING GIBBOUS

Maksim forgot where he was going on his way to Augusta's apartment. The hazy sunshine lulled him even as he walked. He stopped to watch two boys sparring in a backyard, and he leaned upon the fence and stared unabashed until a woman came out of the house and brandished a phone at him.

He shrugged at her. "No English," he said and wandered away. He took a nap on a bench for a half hour. He woke sweating and off-kilter, half-glad his egg was wearing off and half-desperate for another already. While he thought it all through, he knotted one hand in the other until his bones creaked and came to the remembrance that he'd meant to see Augusta. He rose from the bench and trudged off toward her street.

Her street was a shabby one, seen in daylight: rows of old Victorian rooming houses with sheets hung at the windows, and newer buildings with cheap brick frontages and cinder-block sides, all close-built right up to the edges of the lots so that the alleys were shoulder width and dark. People squatted in them sometimes in the summers. Many of Augusta's neighbors didn't seem to know how to wash. Some of them smelled ill. Maksim usually made Augusta come to visit him.

On this day, she must have seen or scented him coming; she stormed up the sidewalk, glowering, her boots heavy on the pavement. She had been choosing the same kind for decades now, plain black army boots with steel toes, and she would wear them until the leather wore down and the steel shone through. "You went to the witch," Augusta said. "And you didn't come back."

"I am here now."

"She couldn't help you properly. Could she? You need me, after all."

"She is dead," Maksim said, and he watched Augusta's eyes flinch. "Her granddaughter, fortunately for me, is also a witch."

"That explains the stink."

"What stink?"

Augusta flicked his scalp with her blunt fingertip. "You don't smell right, and you're all slow."

Maksim shrugged. "I have taken to the bottle also, and I have a piece of news to tell you, and I think you would prefer to hear it over a drink."

The look she gave him was wide-eyed and unhappy, but she led him to a dusty pub a few streets away. It was the kind of place where no one washed the windows or the floors, and the table-tops were sticky. The TV showed a soccer game; the announcer spoke in excited Portuguese, of which Maksim recognized a few words from his time in the Peninsula. Augusta ordered them each a glass of stout.

"I'm a bit short in the pocket this week," she said, flushing faintly over her nose and cheekbones.

Maksim groped in his pocket and found a crumple of bills. He dropped them on the floor, gathered them up, set them on the table; a breeze from the open door nearly scattered them again, and Augusta cursed and slammed the saltshaker down upon the bills.

"I don't like you like this. I hope you'll make this short so that I can go back to making some blunt."

"I can compensate you for your time," Maksim said. "Or not, if that gives offense. Really, Augusta—"

She bared her teeth at him. "Gus. Asshole. I've only been reminding you for a hundred years."

"Gus. Fine. The thing is . . . I may have made you a brother."

The pint glass shattered in her hand.

By the time the sighing bartender had brought damp towels and a fresh glass, Gus had recovered herself enough to laugh, if a bit breathlessly. "All these years . . . it's been just the two of us."

"The devil in it is, I do not know where to find him," Maksim admitted, covering his face with his hands. He emerged a moment later to add, "And I am out of practice. At managing myself. I do not feel it coming in time to rein myself in, as you do. If I go about unleashed, I am afraid of what else I might do."

"Come on. I do stupid shit all the time, at least when I'm sober. And I'm half your age, anyway; it hasn't hit me as much yet. But leaving that aside . . ." Gus said. "I want to know why you finally broke your streak. Why now. Why him, this fellow, and why can't you find him?"

"*Koldun'ia* Iadviga died, and her enchantment was undone," Maksim said. "Ill fate came upon me immediately. I think it has been waiting for me, ever since—"

"Ever since the thing you never talk about," Gus said, crossing her arms over her chest and squeezing her elbows.

"Yes." And for a moment, the memory roared over Maksim as it had not done in years: the red of it, the heat, the taste of gunmetal. He nearly gagged.

Gus laid her hands carefully on the tabletop, where Maksim could see them. He wondered if he'd made a motion or a sound.

"Take a sip," she said. "Good. Another. Don't worry, I won't press you. We've gone this long without talking about it, haven't we?"

Maksim shook his head, pressed his lips against the glass.

"Whatever it was," Gus said, "it drove you to take the spell. Didn't it? By the time I caught up with you that year, you were different. You were all bottled up. And now you're not, and that should be good, only you don't think so. Am I warm?"

Maksim nodded.

"Take another drink," Gus said. "This would be so much easier if it were last century, wouldn't it? We'd just get on a boat and go somewhere else for a while."

"No boats," Maksim said, hand tightening on his pint.

"Easy. Easy. I already used up our glass quota here. No boats."

Maksim gulped back the contents of the glass and set it down hard. Gus slid it out of reach across the table. "This is weird for me," she said. "You're always the one who knows what to do."

Maksim shrugged one shoulder, hand twisting at the collar of his T-shirt.

Gus blew out a breath and shrugged in turn. "One thing at a time, okay? Tell me about my brother."

Maksim drew a breath, felt it catch in his tight throat. He began, "I was running . . ."

But that wasn't right. That wasn't the beginning. He had been running when he came across the young man, but he'd been running for a while by then, ceaseless and demanding. When had he left the house?

He picked his way further through the slow backwash of his thoughts and said, "I was at my gym. Slavo—one of my students . . . we were working on his footwork. I thought he hit me. In the face. Lights flickered behind my eyes." Maksim paused. Even as he said the words, he thought they were not right. Not lights but a burst of brilliant darkness. It had been similar to getting hit, but he had been hit many times in his long life, and he should have known the difference. He shook his head and went on, "I was angry with Slavo. My own fault, but I wanted to punish him. I sent him away instead. Made him leave without his shower. I went some rounds on the bag, but . . . I needed air. You remember how I used to run?"

Gus nodded. She had seen him head out into the early mornings of three different continents and come back hours later, sweat-soaked and limping, all his temper bled right out of him. She had helped him bind his blistered feet now and then or ice his burning calves.

Since coming to Toronto, Maksim had not needed it the same way, but he had kept it up nevertheless, if not as desperate or driven as before. He usually ran as if he were training for a marathon, varying his distances and elevation, cycling through a series of favorite routes. But that was not the kind of running he wanted, the day he was trying to describe.

"I think I did not even lock up the gym," he said. "I went out and went far, and I went for hours. And instead of running it off, it got worse—the urge. I had not felt it so hard in years, and I was too drowned in it to think about why."

"You can't," Gus said. "I mean, I can't. Not when it's like that."

"It was late at night when I came on them," Maksim went on.

"Two young men in an alley behind a bar. Very drunk. They had been set upon, and one of them was bleeding."

Gus laughed without humor.

"You know what I did next," Maksim said. He was looking down at his hands on the tabletop, and he saw how tightly they were knotted together.

Gus followed his gaze and said, "I'll get us another round."

She brought back whiskey this time, in tough little shot glasses. Maksim drank his in a single long swallow; it eased the constriction in his voice somehow.

He said, "I ran away again right after. I did not think to stay. I went swimming."

"In a pool?" Gus said, shuddering. "But the chlorine—and even though it's so strong, it never quite covers up the smells of all the other people—"

"In the lake," Maksim said, remembering the deep chill of it, the myriad scents of waterweeds and shore weeds, the birds welcoming the dawn.

"So when you came to me and broke my door, that was the next day?"

"I was not sure you would remember," Maksim admitted.

"You left me a souvenir or two," Gus said, gesturing wryly at her face. "I wondered what was up with you."

"So did I," Maksim said. "And then I went to see the witch, and it came clear."

"So we have to find this guy, and we have to do it now."

Maksim shrugged. Nodded.

"And you don't have anyone else but me," Gus said. Not a question. She looked a bit horrified for a moment, but then she took a breath, patted Maksim's clenched hands, and said, "Go and relax or something. We'll find him."

She walked out without saying anything more, but she was whistling "Spanish Ladies," so Maksim didn't think she was angry.

Relax, she'd directed, and though he was not in the habit of taking advice from Augusta, Maksim took this as license to go back to his apartment and swallow down four eggs in quick succession. What came over him was not exactly sleep, but it was dark and blind, and it broke the tension in him like a blow from a sledgehammer. He slid down onto the floor before his refrigerator and let himself lie.

CADIZ, SPAIN: 1813

"Spanish Ladies": Gus had always liked it. Maksim had heard it sung by sailors a hundred times, no matter whether they were leaving Spain or headed toward it.

The day he boarded the *Honoria*, for instance, bound for Cadiz. The sailors were shouting it back and forth to each other, tuneless and rough, as they rowed Maksim from the pier out to the ship. Maksim was riding the rough edge of two days without sleep, running from a Mayfair flat to a hidey-hole in Southwark to the port and the first berth he could command. He'd committed a murder: the kind of murder he always ended up committing, a moment's unbridling of his nature and no turning back. He did not regret the murder—a young man losing at piquet and furious with it, who'd followed Maksim out of the card room to argue and ended in a sad huddle of limbs under a tree in Hyde Park—but he regretted being seen playing with the fellow and then leaving with him, and he regretted the new mare he'd had to leave behind in his rush to disappear.

The regret kept him on edge, despite the fatigue of his quick exit. He was unforgivably impolite to the captain, without realizing they would have to dine together; he wanted to drink heavily, but the drink was a Madeira, which he detested. He found the ship's motion made him almost ill, which was a thing his kind rarely suffered.

By the end of the five-day voyage to Cadiz, his neckcloths were all crumpled from constant tugging, he had opened his knuckles on the paneling of his tiny cabin, and between the missed dinners and the never-ending pacing, he'd lost enough weight to make his breeches begin to droop at the waist. He surged ashore, barely remembering his belongings.

He ran, first, away from the people and the bustling port, over the tumbled rocks along what was left of the ancient city wall and up a sun-scoured hillside. His legs itched with the time spent confined. He dumped his things under a patch of scrub, his coat and his neckcloth and even his boots, and he ran until his feet bled slick.

He limped back down toward the town in the evening to find that an animal had mauled his belongings about, and his coat lay spread in the dust. It smelled of herbs and dried shit. He put it to rights as best he could and went to find meat, drink, and the latest news of the war.

What he found instead was a dying woman.

She lay in a narrow cul-de-sac where a house butted up near to a high section of the fortification. Maksim had heard the city had been shelled in many places during last year's siege, but here the wall was as sturdy as ever. The woman was a faint, pale splash in the twilight of its shadow: white underskirts tumbled up over a torn spring-green gown. She whined very quietly.

She was bleeding. The smell came to Maksim like liquor, threading through the scents of frying fish and horse dung and ocean breeze. He was across the street in an instant, forgetting the more mundane needs that had driven him down from the hills. His mouth sprang with saliva.

Here was blood, and once blood had been spilled, more would always follow, and Maksim would be in the thick of it, one way or another. He did not stop to think that the war had moved on from here, that if this woman had been injured by a soldier it had been one of the allied soldiers stationed here or passing through, that any violence he would be drawn into on her behalf would only see him exile himself from yet another city. He did not think at all, just knelt on the dusty cobbles outside the spreading pool and reached to touch her throat. Her skin and hair were fair and fine. Her heart beat like a jeweler's hammer.

"*Ven aquí, cobarde,*" she murmured.

"I speak no Spanish," Maksim said in Russian. He looked at her eyes: one blue, one nearly all black where the pupil was blown. He looked at the injury to her head, but it was obscured by clots of blood dried messily into the curls of her hair.

He brought his face close to hers and sniffed along her brow, where the red ran freely, and he touched the tip of his tongue there, just for a moment.

"*Muere conmigo,*" the woman said, and she stabbed Maksim in the stomach.

Maksim swore. He rocked back on his heels.

The knife slipped free and blunted its tip on the cobbles. Maksim poked a fingertip into his injury and found it deep enough to bleed, but not at all vital.

"Would you care to try again?" he said to the woman, in English this time. He felt like laughing, the pain a bright bubble just below his rib cage: surprise was already becoming so rare a thing in his life.

"Yes," the woman snarled, almost soundless.

"Even though I have not hurt you?"

"You would," she said, and with that, Maksim could not disagree.

Moved by something he hardly recognized, he placed the knife in her hand and folded her trembling fingers about it. One of her palms was opened to the bone.

She could not raise herself enough to strike at his body again. Gasping, she lashed the blade across his forearm and then dropped it again.

"I have not the strength," she whispered. Maksim could barely hear her over the pleasant buzz of evening in Cadiz, gulls crying over the rooftops, hooves and wheels on the cobbles, the distant chime of bells from the ships shifting on the harbor waves.

"And if you had the strength, that is what you would do? Spend it on stabbing me?"

Her chin dipped in a nod. There were other people passing the mouth of the cul-de-sac, children playing with a hoop, bright saffron and poppy frocks catching the sunset light, and this woman had no thought of calling for help. She only clenched her blood-slick fingers closer around the hilt of her knife.

Maksim said, "You have a fine spirit for a woman."

The woman's eyes looked strange and flat; he wondered if she was still awake, really, and if she was afraid. Her heart was not beating so fast now. It skipped and started, the way a sparrow closes its wings in flight and then flutters them hard again.

The blood scent was too much; Maksim had kept himself on a leash all week at sea. He stopped considering and bent down to taste the freshest rivulet at her temple.

She twisted like a snake and bit him.

"I think you are meant to live," Maksim said. "Here." And he laid his opened arm to her lips and let her taste what it meant to be *kin*.

She spat and fought him for a moment, but he bore down, free hand tight on her jaw. Then she bit him again, right on the fresh cut, making him jerk and laugh and lap at her face. She was shivering now, heartbeat picking up again, stronger under the grip of Maksim's thumb.

"Easy," he crooned to her. "Easy." And her shivering abated until he could barely feel it, only a hint of it traveling through his frame as he lay with his head pressed close to her sternum and licked the dried blood from over her throat.

After a while, the woman's breath slowed to long, shallow sighs, and her eyes fell nearly shut, and her hand cupped lax over Maksim's elbow, almost cradling his arm to her slack open lips. Maksim sat up and spat on a handkerchief and wiped his face clean. He made bandages for the woman's gored hand and breast, as well as he knew how; the loss of blood would maybe have killed her if Maksim had not happened by, but more likely, it would have been a long death by fever, infection, her humors unbalancing themselves while she lay abed. That would not happen now. He felt almost as if he had done a good deed.

Maksim pillowed her head on his folded coat and went back out into the street. He felt lovely now, blood-drunk and exhausted and surging with life, all the tension of the last week spent. His head nearly spun with it, as with the best liquor, and he had to school his face to sobriety before he met someone.

Two women, Spaniards, came his way, carrying bolts of cloth. He called out to them in English, "There's been a crime. A lady is hurt." He pointed back toward the wall.

His own disarray, his unsteadiness, the blood on his clothing must have spoken for him. The women led him to sit against a salmon-colored wall at the edge of the cul-de-sac, and one of them gave him a drink from a wineskin while the other sought whatever passed for the law here. The siege might have left the city battered, but in the half year since it seemed to have re-bounded thoroughly—the street and the nearby plaza buzzed with people, sailors and soldiers of all the allied armies, fisherfolk and blacksmiths, priests and clerks, and, once they were aware of the incident, every one of them seemed to have a reason to come over and look at Maksim and the lady he'd found.

In no very long time, Maksim was following quite a procession uphill farther into the town: a litter carrying the injured woman, a pair of young men in official-looking uniforms, and a rabble of attendants, including the two women Maksim had approached and several young children, all of them chattering in Spanish.

They seemed to know where the injured woman lived; they brought her right to a townhouse door and made a hubbub there. Maksim followed everyone inside.

An elderly man ran into the parlor, wheezing with dismay. "Augusta! I did not even know she had left the house. Where is her servant? Has someone fetched the surgeon?" He collected himself and seemed to be repeating the same things in Spanish. A number of people ran out again; someone gave the old man a drink; others carried Augusta into another room.

Maksim went to follow.

The old man fixed upon him then. "Sir? You are?"

Maksim had not thought at all about who he might be, in this city, in this house.

He fell back upon a favorite subterfuge: stumbled forward, leaned upon the back of a chair, and pulled it down with him as he let himself drop.

As he lay boneless on the old gentleman's parlor matting, he thought how much he liked Cadiz already, with its sunny plazas and steep streets and its ships endlessly coming and going; and unless he very much missed his mark, he'd have a place here for a few days, at least.

Someone came to lift him to a settee, and he feigned awakening and weakly accepted a glass of what turned out to be canario. A sympathetic maiden held it to his lips for him, even.

When the surgeon had finished with Augusta, he came to Maksim, sleeves tied up and arms bloody to the elbow.

He carried a curved needle and a fine length of gut. He cut away Maksim's slashed shirt and sponged gore from the surrounding skin.

Maksim swallowed down some excellent whiskey and lay back with his eyes half-lidded as the surgeon placed his stitches, tiny piercing pains that spread into the duller flare of his injury, and though it was pain, it was also pleasure.

He slept in a narrow bed spread with a starched coverlet, and in the morning, he awoke to the sympathetic maid, who brought him black coffee and bread and told him that Miss Hillyard had survived the night, and she thanked him tearfully for saving the woman's life.

The maid had a romantic notion; Maksim could see it. She thought him a hero and a gentleman and probably had him as good as married to Augusta and herself elevated to a grander position. The maid would be disabused of it all soon enough: when Miss Hillyard began to feel the effects of Maksim's blood, she would cause a scandal one way or another. Maksim found himself eager to see where the madness would take her: he had never made a woman *kin* before, and he wondered if she would feel it as men did. She had not been raised to the sword as Maksim had—or any of the other *kin* he had encountered. She had probably been trained to sweetness all her short life, though Maksim thought, from her rage in the alley, that it had not quite taken.

For the time being, Maksim accepted the coffee, smiled bravely, and allowed that he was well enough to sit up and speak with Mr. Hillyard this morning. Two weeks, he gave it, and then

Mr. Hillyard could hang, while Maksim took his daughter to the devil.

Two weeks turned out to be too generous: barely a single one had passed before Augusta was well enough for trouble.

Maksim had formed a habit of looking in on her in the mornings, after breakfasting with her father. The first few days, she'd scarcely been well enough to greet him before sleeping again, but her new nature sprang strong in her, and before long, she was sitting up in bed, eyes bright below the new scars at her hairline and prevailing upon the sympathetic maid to very improperly wait outside the door while Maksim visited.

"I do not know precisely what you did to me, Mr. Volkov," she said, "but I fancy it was something un-Christian."

Maksim blinked. He had not been expecting such directness, though now that he thought of it, he should have: was this not the woman who'd tried to stab him even as her own life ebbed away?

"Un-Christian," he said. "That is true. What do you remember?"

Augusta flushed pink across the bridge of her nose. "Not much after the men left," she said and shut her lips tight.

"Tell me of these men, then. Were they strangers to you?"

Augusta nodded. "Soldiers," she said. "Spanish."

"Did they . . ." Maksim paused for a moment, but Augusta was already continuing.

"They wanted to despoil me," she said, looking at Maksim very straight as if shaming him for his delicacy in avoiding the question. "One of them tried, but he was dead drunk, and I scolded him, and he wilted like a cut lily, and it made him angry. Then they both beat me until I fell, and then they spat upon me and left me there to die. And I thought at first you were like them, but . . . you were not."

"I did not force my attention on you?"

"If you did, I do not recall it," Augusta said, eyes going distant and dreamy. "You gentled me and gave me something to drink and I felt . . . I felt . . ."

"I shared my nature with you," Maksim said. "It brings healing; you must have felt it straightaway. You will want to be careful to avoid questions."

"I am already monstrous tired of playing invalid," Augusta admitted.

"You must keep at it," Maksim said, "but if you are good, I will squire you out after the house is abed."

"I will be ready for a bacchanal at this rate," Augusta said moodily, fidgeting with her coverlet.

"It takes us all so," Maksim said. "But I had not expected it to come over you this early. Hold tight, and have your maid send for me if you have need."

Augusta made it through the day without issue, or so Maksim inferred from the absence of any message, but that very evening, as soon as her father's lamp was snuffed, she was scratching at Maksim's bedchamber door, already dressed and bearing a flask of her father's finest.

She knew Cadiz scarcely better than Maksim did; she and her father had come from London only after the siege had ended, pursuing some business. Augusta waved her hand impatiently at Maksim's questions and said, "Does it matter? You promised me a bacchanal, not a polite conversation. I expect you to deliver."

As it turned out, Augusta made a splendid maenad: fire-eyed, flushed with whiskey and exercise. Maksim watched her from the corner of the public house he'd chosen.

She led another girl down the floor, a dusky girl with wild curls tumbled from her scarf. Both of them were laughing, their skirts kilted up to display immodest ankles.

Around them, a circle of men applauded, clapped, and stamped.

Maksim scanned the faces: enthusiastic, lascivious, drunk, keen. Rough men, the kind of men he assumed Augusta had not had cause to meet before now.

Her father seemed to have kept her on the shelf, dressed in white, pouring tea for his associates. Maksim thought it a great waste.

The fiddler in the corner struck a triumphant finish. Augusta and her partner spun apart to curtsy to the room and back together to salute each other. Augusta kissed the girl's hand, laughing up at her with mocking eyes, and they parted—the girl to pour wine and wipe the bar, Augusta to stand beside Maksim, chest heaving, hand pressed to the spot where the knife had nearly gored her heart.

She fixed a pale curl behind her ear and looked expectantly to Maksim. "Well? Are you going to stand here like a great looby all night?"

"I do not dance."

"That much is apparent."

"I do not mind watching you dance, however."

"No one does," Augusta said. "I had an excellent dancing master. It seems a bit passive for you, though. I do not believe you to be possessed of a passive character."

"No, I am not." He covered a smile and poured her a tot of whiskey.

"My, this stuff is delicious," she said, knocking it back. "I often help myself to my father's, you know. It's fine, but I like it rougher."

Maksim bit his lip on the crude thing he could have said.

"I think it is time you told me what you're about," Augusta said. "I know you are healed, as am I, and you needn't linger. Yet here you are."

Maksim found himself bending close, the better to hear her;

Augusta's voice was low and cultured, and the room loud with the voices of fishermen and soldiers.

"I would follow you," she said. "I know you will not stay in Cadiz forever, and I would follow you when you go."

"Of course," he said. "The world has much to show us."

"You've already seen a great deal of it, I know. I hope you will not mind a protégée."

"On the contrary."

"I fear I have already made myself the subject of a bit of talk here. It would be best for my father if I did not stay to make more."

"He will miss you sadly," Maksim said.

"He cannot miss me, for he does not know me."

"I would know you, Augusta."

She smiled, wide and bright. The fiddler had struck up again, and Augusta unconsciously rocked her foot in time and looked away. She was blushing, or maybe it was only the whiskey; she smelled heated and honeyed, and in her smell was a thread of Maksim's own, her blood tuned to his now and forever-more.

She filled him with wonder, this thing he had saved. He touched a fingertip to her cheek.

She leaned into the touch a little, but her gaze was elsewhere, on the girl with whom she had been dancing.

"Look at her," Augusta said, just above a whisper. "Have you ever seen anything so fine? Look at the way her skin blooms in the light."

"Oh," said Maksim, understanding.

He took Augusta by the elbow with one hand, the whiskey bottle in the other, and shouldered his way to the door.

"I want to stay," Augusta said.

"Not now."

She tugged at his hand and then wrenched at it. "But Mónica said she would dance again."

"I am sorry," said Maksim. And he was. "I am sorry, but she is not for you."

"What do you mean? I thought you understood. I thought you were like me." Her eyes were black in the moonlight, all pupil, as she stumbled with him down toward the harbor.

"I am. Or you are like me now."

"Mr. Volkov," she said, throwing her weight back to slow him down. "Perhaps you do not take my meaning. I hope I have not led you to think I would accept a kind of companionship from you which I . . . which would be . . . indelicate."

Maksim stopped in the street and loosened his grasp, gentling her, smoothing her sleeve where his hand had creased it. "I do understand," he said.

His hopes, he did not mention. They had not been strong hopes, in any case. He had known for many years what it was to be alone, and now he had a friend.

He would endure. He knew what life held for him.

What he had done to her was another matter.

"I am sorry," he said again, very softly. "Come down to the water with me, and we will sit where we cannot be overheard. I have many more things to tell you."

APRIL 30

◗ WANING GIBBOUS

Hannah wrapped her hand around Nick's wrist, fingertips hooked over the tendon to count his pulse.

"Gold," she said, shifting back on the love seat and patting Nick on the cheek.

"So you'll get off my fucking case now?"

She sighed. "You're so healthy it's freaking me out. I'd kill to have your blood pressure. Your cut's healing beautifully. I'm still mad you didn't tell me about your ribs, but I'm almost over it. You got up early to run 10K, and you left Jonathan in the dust. Your resting heart rate is half what mine is. *Half.* That's practically pro-level fitness, Nick. And what do you want to do with it? Get hammered with my boyfriend."

"What? We're just going to the Cammie. I said we wouldn't go back to that other place again."

"Admirable restraint." She flicked Nick on the forehead. "Just, seriously, Nick, you're not going to have this forever. I hate to see you piss it away."

"You sound like my mom. Wait, is that it? Are you, like, practicing?" said Nick, arrested. He looked around the room: it was Jonathan's name on the lease, but there was plenty of evidence of Hannah's taste, given the couple of nights a week she spent there. An Audubon print over the nook table. Cushions on the armchair, printed with stenciled birds. Did people put birds on things when they were nesting? Was that a thing?

"Sure, I guess," Hannah said, completely comfortably. Did that mean it wasn't a thing or that she didn't care if it was a thing? "Don't you want to be a dad someday?"

"Jesus," Nick said, taking refuge in humor. "This is sudden, but I guess we'll just have to tell Jonathan—"

Hannah fished an ice cube from her water glass and threw it at him. "Seriously, you'll be a fine dad, Nick. If you ever stop being a kid."

"Jonathan!" Nick called. "Your girlfriend's being all grown up again. Make her stop."

Jonathan didn't answer. Nick, suddenly unable to sit still,

jumped up from the couch and hammered on the bathroom door. "Want to jog over there?" he called.

From inside, Jonathan groaned. "We already jogged. My legs are still sore. And I just got out of the shower, asshole."

"Walk, then? It's too hot for the streetcar."

"Doesn't that mean it's too hot to walk?" Jonathan said, coming out in a fresh shirt, combing his damp hair with his fingertips.

"I don't feel like sitting still," Nick said, pacing. He felt like running another 10K and then jerking off again, but a walk sounded okay too, if it was followed by about ten drinks. He jittered back and forth by the door until Jonathan had located his wallet and keys.

"Bye, Hannah," Nick said, waving his fingers.

"Bring him back in one piece," Hannah said.

She was muttering something to herself as she got up and stuck her head in the refrigerator, but Nick didn't want to hear it.

Jonathan had to stop and kiss her, though, and then he kissed her again.

"*Bye*, Hannah." Nick pulled Jonathan away by his shirt collar.

"Bye," Jonathan said softly. "Hang out here as long as you want. I won't be late."

"Yes, he will," Nick called, already dragging Jonathan down the hall.

CAPE TOWN, SOUTH AFRICA: 1814

Augusta left him for the first time as soon as they docked in Cape Town. She sat quietly enough in the cutter, though Maksim could feel her heel tapping the carpetbag beneath his seat. Once they had said their farewells to the captain, though, she began walking, fast and jerky, hands jammed in the pockets of her waistcoat.

"You have been warning me of this forever, and I am bound to say you were right," she said furiously, not looking at him, kicking at the cobbles.

"Handsome of you," Maksim said, laughing rather, though he too was affected with restlessness and appetite after the tedium of a sea voyage.

"It is not," Augusta said. "It is very grudging, and having said it, I feel even more as if I would like to throttle you and leave your body right here in the middle of the street."

"You may try," Maksim said.

She whirled on him. "Do not joke!"

"I do not. You will not win over me, not yet, but you'll find few other opponents to give you satisfaction."

"But I don't want to hurt you. You're my friend," Augusta said, wrenching at her own hair.

"That is why we may trust each other with this," Maksim said as gently as he could.

"You don't understand! I need to *wreck* someone—with my *hands*—"

"Run it out," Maksim said. "Tire yourself until you collapse. And if you must hurt someone, make it someone who heals—or someone who will not be noticed."

"How do you do this? How do you do this?" Augusta said, fingers tearing at her cuffs.

Maksim sighed and groped in his pocket and handed her the money he found there. "Go figure it out. I will take a room at the Two Sisters for some weeks," he said. "Find me there when you are ready."

She closed her fist over the money and ran from him.

Maksim found, at the Two Sisters, a clean bed, a stock of half-decent wine, and a young man whose skin bruised deliciously. He kept himself busy for a few days in this way until the young man began to complain of his roughness, and Maksim sent him off. Without company, the Two Sisters did not hold his interest; the mountain overlooking the town, however, proved a worthwhile excursion to occupy Maksim for a couple of days.

When he came down from the mountain, footsore and filthy and as satisfied as one of the *kin* could be, he still found no Augusta awaiting him, and he discovered his temper was not as quelled as he had wished.

The young man, bruised afresh, brought him bread and cheese and hot water to wash in, and he kept his eyes down. Maksim thanked him guiltily and promised not to break anything else, a promise he broke the next day.

Two full weeks, and finally Augusta returned. She had messily shorn what remained of her hair, and the inch-long crop looked bleached with sun and salt, shockingly pale against her newly browned face.

She would have looked savagely healthy, in fact, were her eyes open and her limbs properly arranged, but some boys brought her laid out on an old door and told Maksim she was not ill but only dead drunk and that she had promised them a British guinea if they would deliver her to Maksim Volkov at the Two Sisters.

Augusta did not so much as murmur when Maksim shook her. He paid the boys and carried Augusta up to his room, where she cast up her accounts all over his pillow.

She did not wake until after midday, and even then, she was stupid and sick for some hours; but she told Maksim she had done with her fit of temper and would like to explore the country with him now if he would be so good as to lay in a supply of victuals and drink.

"And the money I gave you?"

"Gone," she said. "Was I meant to husband it? I am sorry."

She looked sorry, all sallow and sore-eyed and thinner than she had been, tucked up in Maksim's dressing gown, sitting next to his window with the sun across her lap.

Maksim struck her, anyway, because he had not yet done so, and she was come into her own strength now and must learn the way of things.

"I apologized," Augusta said, blocking his fist with her raised forearms, cowering back. "I apologized."

"I am not punishing you," Maksim said, slapping Augusta's arms aside and grabbing at her throat.

"Yes, you are," she gasped, clutching his wrist. "Stop it; I said I was sorry."

"I have no one else," Maksim said, and he punched her in the side of the head. "Hit me back. Hit me back."

She shook her head, tears flying from her eye on the side where she'd taken the blow, but it wasn't a denial. She gave up trying to pry Maksim's hand off her and instead hammered him in the floating rib in an untutored but sturdy attempt.

Maksim chuckled low and tossed her bodily onto the floor. "Again. You can do it. Get up and hit me again."

And she did, and she did, and she did, and Maksim thought there was a smile starting on her swelling lip.

MAY 5

◖ WANING CRESCENT

Stella seemed to be trying. She wasn't around in the evenings—working, Lissa assumed. Her suitcase was neatly stowed behind the sofa, her clothes folded on top of it.

Lissa could only tell she was eating in the house at all by the occasional misplacement of a clean salad plate or cereal bowl; the reappearance of a fat, thorny brown pottery mug that Baba hadn't used in years; and the lowering level of milk in the carton. Stella replaced what she used too; the new milk was a different brand, but still 1 percent.

Stella left a little envelope of her tip money beside the grocery list. She cleaned the bathroom, right down to the grout. She didn't touch Baba's room or any of Baba's things; she might have dusted the shelves in the kitchen and living room, but she did it without changing the arrangement of the objects on them, so that Lissa was not even sure it had happened.

Lissa heard her in the shower late at night and smelled her shower gel and her expensive scent. Found a couple of her long hairs on her towel or in the sink. Saw her spare shoes neatly side by side on the mat.

Barely saw the girl herself, though. If Stella was just washing up her tea mug when Lissa came in to make coffee, she ducked her head and hurried out. One night when she wasn't working and Lissa had been out, Stella was still awake when Lissa came in: curled on the sofa under a light blanket, with her face scrubbed clean and her hair tied up for sleep. She had a magazine and a pencil, and Lissa thought maybe she was doing crosswords. She saw Lissa in the hallway and smiled shyly and waved good night.

Lissa couldn't remember whether she'd waved back.

The problem wasn't in anything Stella was doing or not doing. She seemed sweet. Well raised. More than Lissa would've expected, considering it was Dad doing half of the raising.

The problem wasn't in the idea of having a roommate, either. Lord knew she could use a bit of help with the household and the bills. Having to keep her rituals secret would be a pain, but she could invent something—a church meeting to pretend to host, something like that.

The problem was that Stella was family. Stepfamily, sure. Still too close for Lissa to pretend she was just some friendly but distant connection sharing a financial arrangement and alternating turns with the washing machine.

Family went one of two ways. They ruled you, or you ruled them. You couldn't be equal; you couldn't be neutral. If you didn't want to play, you had to go. Dad went: first overseas, then into a whole new marriage. Mama went too; exhausted and irritable at the end, she didn't seem sorry to be going. One of the last things Lissa remembered hearing from her mouth was a vindictive comment to Baba, that now she'd have Lissa all to herself, just like she wanted.

And Baba had wanted. As soon as Mama died, she began training Lissa in earnest. She put away all the photos of Mama and Dad with Lissa and had one taken of just the two of them at the portrait studio at Sears: Baba in her best gray dress, with her hair coiled around her head, and Lissa in a purple skirt and a blouse with purple kittens on it, hair in two long braids. She was nearly ten, and the other girls in her class were starting to pay attention to fashion and steer away from things that looked too childish, but Baba did not hold with fashion and thought children should be children.

That photo was still on Baba's dresser.

After a few days of tiptoeing, Lissa left Stella a note on the refrigerator.

They met at an organic-food café on Queen Street, which Lissa had picked because it was affordable but sounded trendy enough for Stella to appreciate. Stella was a few minutes late, which gave Lissa time to find a seat on the patio with a wall at her back. The air was humid and smoggy, but with the sun down behind the buildings, the heat was starting to lift; the smell of toner still lingered in Lissa's hair, and she unbraided it and shook it out, inhaling, instead, the fragrance of the blooms in a nearby garden and the café's aroma of toasting cumin.

She ordered a juice made from beet, ginger, carrot, apple, cayenne, and lemon, which arrived, capped with brilliant pink foam, just as Stella slid into the opposite seat.

"One of those," Stella said to the waitress, round-eyed. "Hey, Lissa." She made a motion that might have been an impulse to hug Lissa hello, but she checked it, instead slinging her purse over the back of her chair.

"Hey," Lissa said, and her mouth went dry and thick, and she blinked across the table at this stranger who was her stepsister, and the things she'd thought to say were gone.

Stella's juice came. They both sipped and raised their eyebrows and licked pink foam from their lips.

"Stay for now," Lissa said. "I don't want to make promises."

"Are you sure?" Stella said. "You don't seem very sure."

"I don't know what to tell you," Lissa said. "I haven't done any of this before. I'm not going to lie to you; I don't think I'm going to be easy to live with."

Stella paused and thought. "If you think it's not working, can you give me two weeks' notice? Because I don't think I can take it if I come home to find my stuff on the lawn and have to get a hotel like a cheating hubby." She grinned as she said it, but it wasn't a happy grin.

"Two weeks' notice," Lissa said. "Got it." She held out her hand across the table, and Stella took it.

Lissa had been expecting a handshake, but Stella put her other hand over top and squeezed.

"Thanks," Stella said, and she bit her lip, and damned if that didn't make Lissa tear up a bit too. With her free hand, she took a gulp of her juice so that she could blame the watering eyes on the cayenne.

MAY 5

 WANING CRESCENT

Maksim, snarling, slammed his fist into brick.

"Ouch," said Gus.

"There is nothing," Maksim said. They stood at the corner of Queen and Bathurst. A streetcar rumbled heavily past, followed by a string of cars and a rickshaw. The wall Maksim had punched was painted purple, and now flecks of that paint decorated the bloody scrapes on Maksim's knuckles. He brought his fist to his mouth and licked the injury clean.

"Maybe if we make a wider circle," Gus said.

"We already have. I cannot find it. Too many scents."

Understatement. Even Gus, used to Parkdale, had said she found this stretch of Queen Street difficult in the warmth of May—rotten fruit, pigeon droppings, Indian food, hot metal, motor oil, sweat, spunk, ammonia, liquor, coffee. People and all their mess.

"Maybe if we go back to Palmerston again," she continued. "Maybe if you weren't fucking yourself up with the witch's business—"

Maksim caught her gesturing hand in his own, roughly. He did not speak, but he let her lead him up to the alley, the capillary north of Queen. The people they passed did not look, absorbed in private business: urinating, making out, sharing joints or bottle tokes. Maksim kept his head lifted, searching for that elusive scent.

Gus stepped in too close beside him once, and he whirled on her, baring his teeth.

"You're stalking," she whispered. "You'll find no prey here."

Maksim watched his hand wrap itself around Gus's forearm and squeeze, bruising the pale skin.

She scowled and raised her other hand. "Does that mean it's time to hit you?"

"You promised," Maksim said. "You promised you would not let me hurt someone."

"Someone *else*," Gus said.

Maksim lunged at her, knocking her against a garage door, but not in an attack. He slid down until he was crouched against her legs and let go of her to wrap his arms tight about himself.

"I know," Maksim said. "I know, I know. I cannot remain among people like this."

Gus shook her head. "Okay. My place. We can fight some more, tire ourselves out."

"Give me something now," Maksim said. "I will go mad otherwise."

Gus hauled him up by his ear and punched him in the mouth. "I'm sober," she hissed. "And you're not."

Maksim licked blood off his teeth. "Keep going," he said.

Gus kicked him in the kneecap, and he fell, twisting.

"It's no fun if you aren't fighting back," she said. "Get up!"

Farther down the alley, a trio of heads turned, and a conversation ceased.

"I have already marked your face for you," Maksim said. "Mark mine."

A hammering blow across his cheek. "Well done," he said; it did not feel split, but the instant heat of a bruise rose below the skin.

The next one caught him almost by surprise a half second later, rocking his head into the garage door. He had sprung up and tapped Gus in the chin before he recollected his purpose.

Gus danced back. "That's it," she said. "Keep it up." And she darted in under his half-formed guard with a straight to his ribs and a second, random blow that caught him under the arm.

Maksim coughed. He dropped his hands and lifted his face, wide open to Gus's next punch, and it took him in the forehead and made him see gold-shot black.

When his eyes refocused, he saw that she was standing back, frowning fiercely and waiting for him to recover.

"I needed to know you would do it," he explained, although she had not asked. "I am ready to go home and sleep now," he said. When he tried to move away from the support of the garage door, he wavered.

Gus seized his arm and held him upright. "My turn to bully you," she said. "You're coming to my place, where I can keep an eye on you, and if you do decide to break something, it won't be something you love."

"What about," Maksim said and spat blood. "What about the things you love?"

"None left but you," Gus said.

Three

◗ WANING CRESCENT

Lissa came up her walk to find Maksim lying asleep on the porch steps. She could smell him as she got closer: stale sweat and rye, mixed uneasily with the heated lilacs. He slept heavily, with his face pressed into the crook of his arm.

"Evening," she said in his ear.

He bolted up and grabbed at her, catching her braid in his fist and pulling her head down.

"Hey—ouch!"

He sucked in a deep breath. *"Koldun'ia,"* he said, and his grip relaxed fractionally. Lissa yanked her hair back and pulled away, while Maksim blinked and stared and finally unlocked his posture and sank back against the stairs.

"It is not good to surprise me," he said.

Lissa backed off. "You hurt my neck."

"I am sorry. Only do not wake me up with a touch. It is best not to step close to me if I am unaware."

"You plan on crashing on my front steps a lot, then, do you?"

This seemed lost on him; he was rubbing his face with both hands and did not answer.

"Hey," Lissa said. "I haven't forgotten what you said last week. I'd like to help you. My grandmother said you needed help. But that means I need to hear the whole story."

"Your grandmother spoke of this?"

"Some." Close to the chest: she'd learned very early that being a witch meant mystery, and mystery was best preserved by keeping your ignorance to yourself. Maksim did not need to know that Lissa had no idea how they might be kin to each other or why Baba hadn't mentioned him earlier. Or that Baba was still able to communicate with Lissa, even if only under constraints.

Maksim asked her for a drink. She led him into the kitchen, where she could see that he was dirty again (still?) and had not shaved, and his face looked puffy and bruised.

She filled a bowl with borscht and made him up a plate of Izabela Dmitreeva's cabbage rolls and a stack of toast to go alongside, and she opened him a bottle of Stella's lager.

"You do not need to do this for me," he said.

"I didn't. Some other people did it for me. You're just getting the benefits."

This seemed to be the right thing to say. Once reassured, Maksim proceeded to eat everything in front of him, plus two more beers and a second helping of borscht.

"We all eat like this when we can. I thought you knew," he said when Lissa raised her eyebrows.

She hadn't spent enough time with her extended family to have any idea at all that they were big eaters, but she didn't care to admit as much to Maksim. "Anyway, don't stop on my account."

"The eggs are wearing off. I think you should give me more," he said.

"Already?" Lissa blurted. She'd definitely got the recipe too weak, then, somehow.

"You are not afraid of me," Maksim said, looking up at her from his slouch over the plate. "Why is that?"

"My grandmother was not afraid of you," Lissa said, hoping it was true.

"Ah—I see." He scraped his bowl clean and sprawled back in his chair. Quite different from the sleepy sprawl on the steps somehow; he looked tighter wound now and ready.

"So," she said. "Are you going to tell me?"

"I have figured out part for myself now. Why I have gone mad again. I have been many years without the madness, since your grandmother made a spell upon me. I believe the blessing has passed with her, and now I must make shift with my own weak will."

"My grandmother gave you a cure for . . . madness?"

"Not a cure—or so I see now. I thought it was one until I felt it slip with this full moon. Before I knew what I was about, I came upon the boy. You know the rest."

"Pretend I don't and tell me."

He knotted his hands together so that the knuckles stood out heavy and white. "He had the marks of violence on him, quite fresh. I think I could have run my madness out if not for that." He was silent again. Lissa could see his jaw clenching, the way it had the other night.

"So you . . . licked him," she prompted.

"I told you it was madness." He looked up from under sullen brows. "When I am sane, it is a madness I would never wish on another. When I am not sane . . . I do not rule myself as I ought. And it is a madness that spreads."

"You think you infected him? With your madness?"

"If I did, it will be some weeks before he is fully consumed. We have a space of time to find him."

"We?"

"Augusta and I. She is my . . . she is my family. And you—you said you would help also." Maksim hunched over and trapped his hands between his knees. "No. That is very forward of me. You have already helped me with your eggs, and if you will let me take more of them with me—"

"Of course. But I thought they were to make it easier for you to sleep."

"They are to stop me hurting anyone," he said. "So that I can go among people, to do my work and to find this young man, without my madness overtaking me."

"It would be better if I could figure out what my grandmother did for you and do it again," Lissa said.

"Yes." He sat up again restlessly and worked his hand upon the fabric of his jeans, over and over, kneading the muscle of his thigh.

"Will eggs be enough to tide you over?"

He shook his head and scrubbed a hand through his sweaty hair. "I do not know." He chuckled, mirthless and low. "I can feel it now," he said, rising and pacing to the window. "Perhaps I should have another one before I go."

She gave him two dozen; he cracked one in his hand and slurped it straight from the shell like an oyster. He grimaced, but the line of his shoulders slackened, and some of the tension in his face eased. At least they were doing something for him.

Lissa wrote her number on a blank card from Baba's recipe keeper. "Keep me posted. If you can't find him."

She locked the door behind him and went upstairs to the shelf in the sewing room where Baba kept her grimoires.

MAY 10

 NEW MOON

Nick met Jonathan at the coffee shop on Spadina, near the Graduate Students' Union building. The University of Toronto's downtown campus had seemed impenetrably huge and forbidding to Nick as a first-year, with its fifty-odd buildings sprawling over multiple city blocks linked by networks of footpaths traversing several different grassy commons. But five years in, the campus had shrunk, or Nick had grown, to the point where it felt like a pinching shoe, blistering him with its closeness.

"We can't stay here," he said, glowering, grabbing at Jonathan's book bag and pulling him back when he tried to choose a table. "It's only been, like, two weeks. I'm still having PTSD about fucking Boyczuk's seminar of doom."

"It's just convenient," Jonathan said. "But we can go to the Starbucks on College if you'd rather."

"It's too hot for coffee. I don't know why I agreed to this," Nick said, but he pulled Jonathan with him, anyway, hustling him through the door.

"There's such a thing as iced coffee," Jonathan said.

"Fuck coffee. I want a fucking beer."

Jonathan looked like he was going to protest for a moment, but then he shrugged. "I could use a break, anyway. Maybe you were right to go with the lighter course load."

"Summer vacation!" Nick exulted. "You wish you had one!"

"Maybe I would if I had a trust fund," Jonathan said.

"It's not a trust fund, and anyway, it's going to run out in, like . . ." Nick paused to calculate.

"Is it going to run out before 6:00 P.M.?" Jonathan said. "Because it's happy hour at the Palmerston tonight, and I think they have Great Lakes guest taps."

Nick chortled in victory, tugged Jonathan's bag out of his hand and slung it over his own shoulder, and led the way toward the Palmerston in a quick, jerky stride.

"Slow down," Jonathan said. "Let me just text Hannah—she gets out in half an hour."

"No," Nick blurted and then mentally kicked himself. "I mean, didn't she say she was having a girls' night tonight? You know, with Sue Park?"

"Did she?" Jonathan said. "Oh, Sue the violinist. Maybe? I don't remember." But he put his phone back in his pocket and followed Nick down the sidewalk. "You still into Sue Park?" Jonathan went on, half-teasing, half-serious. "I remember you calling her on my phone like five times after that music department social."

"That was years ago," Nick protested. "And I only called her on your phone because mine was out of minutes."

"Not because she started blocking your number, stalker?" Jonathan said, shoving him.

Nick laughed easily because it hadn't been like that at all, at all. He slung his arm around Jonathan's neck and tugged him in close for a second. "I forgot about Sue Park until today," he said and added, leering, "But I'll bet she hasn't forgotten me."

"Ugh, dude," Jonathan said. "Let go of my head and stop being gross about Hannah's friends."

"You were the one who said Sue Park had the most amazing rack you'd ever seen on an Asian chick," Nick said.

Jonathan dragged himself out of Nick's headlock and shaded his eyes with one hand instead. "This is the problem with knowing someone for, like, ever," he said. "You're always there to remind me of the stupid shit I've said and done."

"And get you to do more of it," Nick said.

"And that," Jonathan agreed, but he didn't really look like he minded, so Nick bought the first round.

The Palmerston was only moderately full, happy hour on a Tuesday; they got a table in the corner. Nick stretched out his legs, crooked his arms behind his head, kicked at the legs of Jonathan's chair. Drained his first pint in a few easy swallows.

He had lapped Jonathan by the end of his second, Jonathan sipping slowly and yawning a little and surreptitiously checking his phone. Nick laid his palm over the screen and said, "Buddy. Jonathan. J. I'm right here, and Hannah's out, and there's literally no one else in your life, so put the fucking phone down and—"

"I do have a family," Jonathan said mildly.

"Me too, but I don't take selfies at the bar for them," Nick said. "Turn it off and get the next round."

Jonathan put the phone away and obeyed, out of long habit. Nick watched from his chair as Jonathan ordered: more polite than he would have been a couple of years ago, eyes not straying below the bartender's chin even though she was wearing a Maple Leafs T-shirt with the neckline cut out to show a hint of royal-blue lace.

Jonathan was working as a teaching assistant now in addition to his own studies, and he seemed to think it required him to be a bit more formal, khakis and oxfords and a short-sleeved button-down, even though Nick knew for a fact he'd seen TAs in shorts and T-shirts before. It made Jonathan look older, or maybe he just *was* older; Nick didn't always look at him very closely, seeing instead the familiar blur of a dozen years of friendship, and now he wasn't sure when Jonathan had tidied up his haircut or when he'd switched his electric-blue steel hoop earring for a quieter silver stud.

Nick kicked out of his chair and joined Jonathan at the bar, scrubbing his fist into Jonathan's hair.

Jonathan twisted away, annoyed. "Give it a rest; I'm trying to buy you a drink."

"Arm wrestle," Nick said, grabbing at Jonathan's hand. "If you win, I'll help you mark that fuckton of papers you have in your bag. If I win, you're doing shots with me."

"I don't know what's with your new arm wrestling thing, but I am not going there. No way."

Nick ignored him, braced his elbow on the bar, centered his weight.

Jonathan only yawned and paid for their pints. "Nick, you're being such a freak. All this goddamned energy. Don't you ever just, like, relax anymore?"

"Not when there's arm wrestling to be had," Nick said. He pointed to a beefy guy at the bar and crooked his finger.

"That dude is a foreman," Jonathan said. "Meaning he's in charge of a bunch of construction workers. Know how he got to be in charge of them? Because he's the biggest motherfucker, Nick. They're like animals, you know: there's a hierarchy, and they fight their way up it. He's the king gorilla, Nick. Listen to me: didn't you practically break your head like two weeks ago? Do you really need a broken arm too?"

Nick stood up and crossed the bar. Jonathan followed a moment later, carrying both of their pints.

The foreman looked at Nick with pity and humor. "Okay," he said. "You've got something to prove. I get it."

"Go easy on him," Jonathan mouthed, beside Nick.

"I saw that, asshole," Nick said to him. "Just shut up and hold my drink."

He placed his elbow on the bar, clasped hands with the foreman.

"Count," he said to Jonathan.

"I thought I was supposed to shut up and hold your drink. Never mind. Fine. One . . . two . . . *three*."

The foreman's powerful wrist cocked forward, veins standing out along the tendon. Nick's much slimmer arm, in the same posture, held ground. Both men clenched their teeth and sweated for a half minute or so.

"Jesus," said the foreman. "Not bad for a little guy."

"Not bad yourself. Everyone else I've been up against lately has gone down by now."

"I pump a lot of iron," said the foreman. "Sorry, guy." He stepped up the pressure, forcing Nick's arm back, five degrees, ten degrees.

"No, *I'm* sorry." Nick paused. What kind of a confession could he make? *I think I'm turning into a superhero. I think I'm possessed.*

"I know kung fu," he said. He shrugged his other shoulder and cranked down until the back of the foreman's hand touched the bar.

"You know kung fu?" Jonathan said, baffled. "Since when?"

"It was a joke," Nick said. "Never mind. Hand me my pint back, okay? Let's get one for this guy too; he looks like he could use one. Or a rematch?"

The foreman said flatly, "No, thanks; I think I'm done here." And he walked out.

Nick said to Jonathan, "Is it just me, or was that guy kind of a sore loser?"

Jonathan was still staring. "That was kind of incredible, dude. I've never seen you do that before."

Nick shrugged and took the pint Jonathan passed back to him. He couldn't think of another wisecrack just yet, and right now, it felt like the gaps between jokes were deep and dark, and he needed Jonathan to fill them with something normal, something comfortable and familiar.

Jonathan waited for a long moment, though, and then he turned away, back to their table, leaving Nick standing by the bar with the sweat still running on him and condensation dripping from the pint in his hand.

Nick wiped his face on the hem of his T-shirt and drained the glass and ordered another. He would follow Jonathan back to their seats; he would have a great, normal night out with his best friend. He would. He just needed a bit of help to get his head back in it.

MAY II

● WAXING CRESCENT

Lissa spent an evening at Yelena Ivanova's house, drinking tea poured out of a Brown Betty with a crocheted ruff around the spout.

The ladies of Baba's generation were mostly dead or too frail to go about, but their daughters and granddaughters still convened a couple of times a month. This was the first night Lissa had attended without Baba. Tonight, Olga Rechkina sat in the good armchair, which was still covered in its clear plastic sleeve; her two canes stood propped against one arm, tripping all passersby. Her daughter passed around a plate of rugelach. Yelena Ivanova had filled another plate with store-bought almond shortbreads.

Lissa dressed in what she was beginning to think of as her witch clothes: conservative, dark, too heavy for the weather. She braided her hair and twisted it into a fat knot. The ladies were always winding their hair into high tiers of braid work, stuck full of pins. In the mirror in Yelena Ivanova's hallway, Lissa thought she could see how she'd look in another sixty years.

Everyone addressed her with respect. Some called her *koldun'ia*, as Maksim did. But anything spoken in English was circuitous, avoiding irreligious and difficult words like *witch* and *magic*. Lissa was treated like something between an alternative health practitioner and a Tupperware salesperson. The men she did not see, except for a brief glimpse of Yelena Ivanova's husband passing through the kitchen on his way to the garage.

They sometimes forgot that any of the *kolduny* had ever been male, she thought. Their respect for Baba had always been tinged with suspicion. Lissa would have it worse, being young.

But although the men would not meet her, some of them had given their wives requests, or else the wives were taking liberties, for Lissa departed with a full roster of orders, promising them after the next full moon. Eggs to draw pain, eggs for sleeping or waking, eggs to bring luck, eggs that were the magical equivalent of Viagra. Baba had rarely taken so many orders in a single evening. Lissa thought she was being tested.

Tonight, the sky was thick with red-lit cloud, as it usually was over a city of three million people in smoggy late spring. She descended into the subway tunnels, where the cooler air smelled of mold.

A hundred other people waited on the platform. An elderly West Indian gentleman with a portfolio; two redheaded girls playing a clapping game; a tall woman and a taller man in shiny black PVC skirts and studded collars; a Portuguese couple arguing; a lovely young man with a rainbow of rubber bracelets, and another with a Union Jack on his denim vest. Young dark-haired men her own age, Italian or Greek: a dozen, at least, and most of them wore the kind of clothes Maksim had described, cargo shorts and plain T-shirts and Converse. Even with the cut on his forehead, the guy they were looking for would have a thousand ringers in this city.

Lissa sighed and shifted her weight in her uncomfortable shoes. She wanted to be alone in the quiet of her house—too many strangers, too many church ladies, too many eyes upon her, waiting for her to do something wrong.

When she arrived home, though, and let herself in, the house was muggy and stale. Stella must be at work. The light over the stove had drawn a single fat moth, whose wings beat back and forth over the bulb. In the sink, a centipede ran in circles until she washed it down the drain.

She went upstairs, stripped off her heavy clothes in favor of a cotton tank top and a wraparound skirt, and let her crimped hair down.

Then she went out again. The Duke of Lancashire was an easy ten-minute walk, and it had air-conditioning and the Smiths on the jukebox.

It also had Stella in a ridiculously short kilt, flirting with a table of grad students.

Lissa sat at the bar and waited to be noticed.

The bartender got to her first and tossed a coaster down. "What'll it be?"

"You're British," Lissa said. "That makes sense."

"British blokes do tend to be found in British pubs," he said. "We also serve British beers." He was pulling a pint for someone; she watched the muscles of his forearm shift under the skin as his fingers closed over the tap. He looked strong but comfortable, like he would give good bear hugs.

"You hired my British stepsister," Lissa said.

"Oh, you're family, then!" he said. "Rafe Green." He stuck out his hand.

"Lissa Nevsky."

"But Stella's a Moore, isn't she?"

And before Lissa could get started on the awkward explanation of how she'd taken Mama's surname instead of keeping her father's after he'd left, Rafe went on, "Oh, right, you said stepsister. Steel trap." He tapped his head: topped with a brown toque, maybe shaved underneath. "Half a sec."

He slid the pint down the bar to another customer and came back to pour a pint for Lissa. He smiled as he passed it to her: one crooked tooth made his smile look roguish and sweet. "Organic lager. Everyone loves it. On me," he said. "Ever been in before?"

Lissa shook her head.

"Didn't think so. I'd remember," Rafe said, smiling a little and looking down at the bar. Then he took a deep breath and howled, "*Stella!* God, that's never going to get old."

Stella tossed her ponytail, waved good-bye to the table of grad students, and sauntered to the bar.

"I was wondering if you'd get thirsty eventually," she said to Lissa with a tentative smile quite unlike the bold cheer she'd worn for the customers.

"I had to make sure they were treating you right," Lissa said.

"Everyone's lovely," Stella assured her, and this time, her eyes smiled too, so it seemed to be true. "Rafe's great. The food's even okay." She dodged the damp towel Rafe threw at her head.

Lissa leaned down to retrieve it. So did Stella.

"And he's hot," Stella mouthed beneath the bar before standing up and shaking out her hair. "Are you sticking around for dinner?"

Lissa ducked her chin, feeling heat across her cheeks. "I can't."

"Come on—the special's good tonight. And I can chat when we're not busy."

"Should have plenty of time for that," Rafe agreed. "It's looking like a quiet one." He took the towel back and wandered away for a fresh one.

"Come on," Stella murmured. "You have to admit."

"I don't . . ." Lissa said. She followed Stella's look: Rafe's broad shoulders under a gray T-shirt, a barbed-wire tattoo around his biceps. "I just—I have some reading to do."

"I didn't know you were studying anything," Stella said.

"I'm—"

"Oh my God, you're going to go secretly read *Harry Potter* under your blankets or something. Aren't you? I knew you had to have some kind of vice."

"I shouldn't have come," Lissa said, digging in her bag, face downturned. She found her wallet, fumbled out a ten, and laid it on the bar. "See you later."

She slid off the stool and hurried toward the door. Behind her, Rafe's voice with that beguiling accent: "Where's she off to? I said it was on the house."

Lissa didn't hear what Stella replied. She walked back home too quickly in the humid night, feeling limp with sweat, the very air a weight on her eyes.

MAY II

◗ WAXING CRESCENT

DeShaun was schooling two young women in the ring when Maksim arrived at the gym. Maksim sat on the edge of his old steel desk and watched, twisting paper clips between his fingers. He had put himself on an enforced leave since the night of the full moon, but today, suffused with the calming haze of a couple of eggs, he had missed his regular life too much to hold himself back from visiting. The gym had been his for nearly a decade now, a decade of daily workouts, familiar smells, and people among whom he could feel nearly at home. He was not enough of a businessman to make it thrive, but he was more than enough of a fighter to keep attracting a rotation of students: contenders, sometimes, but people had many reasons to learn to fight, and winning was often the least of them.

The younger of the girls—Concepción, he thought—was developing a powerful straight; she loved to hammer it into the heavy bag, and she would cheerfully spend round after round doing nothing else if Maksim or DeShaun left her alone. Now she was trying to land it on the older girl, without much luck.

The older girl was new, and Maksim didn't even know her name. Whippet thin, with collarbones and sharp sinews standing out beneath Somali-brown skin. She dodged instead of blocking. Concepción lumbered after her, throwing her hard right again and again into empty air.

Both girls were grinning; DeShaun, instead of advising, stood with folded arms and let them have at it. The key sometimes was to give them their mistakes. Maksim had told him so often enough. When the bell sounded, DeShaun said, "Neither of you is hitting the other. Why is that?"

"I'm slow," Concepción said.

"I'm afraid," said the other girl. "If I want to hit her, I have to let her get close, and I'm worried I won't be able to block her 'cause she's too strong."

"Let's start there," said DeShaun, and he strapped on a pair of practice pads and began walking them through exercises.

He didn't acknowledge Maksim, so the girls didn't, either; it wasn't until one of their mothers arrived to pick them up that Concepción waved to him shyly and then saluted him with her fist.

"Shit," said DeShaun when the girls had gone. "No wonder you haven't been around."

"I did not wish to frighten off the students," Maksim said.

"One look at your face and half of them would swear off the

ring for good," DeShaun agreed. "So why'd you come in today? Things are going fine, you know."

"I missed you." It was simple truth; Maksim did not have many friends.

Or many sparring partners.

He'd always have to hold back with DeShaun; it wouldn't be the kind of joyous brawl he could have with Augusta. But he could make it last longer, and neither he nor DeShaun would come away with broken bones.

DeShaun started by holding back too. Maksim laughed at him when he realized this. DeShaun shrugged and stepped it up.

A full twelve rounds. Halfway through, DeShaun stripped off his soaked shirt and slapped it over the ropes. He'd been building muscle lately, Maksim saw; he'd been in the gym every day of the last couple of weeks, with Maksim unavailable.

He'd be more than capable to take over permanently.

Maksim did not want to leave this life. He shook sweat from his eyes and stepped in with a combination of hard, mean uppercuts. DeShaun blocked most of it, tucking to take the impacts on his arms.

Maksim got through, though, and flung DeShaun back against the ropes.

DeShaun wheezed. "Christ!"

Maksim pulled a punch he hadn't meant to throw. He tapped DeShaun on the ear, almost gently, and said, "You do very well."

Then he turned away and pulled his shirt over his head to hide the face he thought he might be making.

Behind him, DeShaun groaned and stretched out his weight on the ropes. "I *thought* I was."

"I might be away for a while longer," Maksim said. "The classes are yours. I will give you a raise."

"Thanks! You think I'm ready to take on the contenders' training?"

Maksim said something; he did not know what. Yes, DeShaun was ready; he would be fine—it would all be fine.

Maksim would not be fine, not until he got out of doors again and ran for a while; not until he could hammer his fists into something unyielding, something he could wreck, something he did not love.

MAY 12

◑ WAXING CRESCENT

Lissa was nearly home from work when the rain began. She held both hands over her head as great fat drops soaked her hair and coursed down her face and neck. The gutters turned into streams and the roofs into sheets of sliding water. Lissa ran up the sidewalk, her sandals slapping flatly.

Lightning rent the sky in the south, over the lake, and in the flash, she saw Maksim's face carved white, eyes closed, nostrils wide, his hat a sharp shadow over the bridge of his nose. He was standing beside her lilac tree again, hands shoved in the pockets of his jeans, ignoring the downpour.

"Good Lord, are you out of eggs again already?" Lissa said.

"Nearly so. And I have something else to ask."

"Want to come in?"

He shook his head. "Thank you, no. Fetch the eggs and walk with me."

Lissa ducked inside, found the carton; she did not bother with her umbrella since she was already drenched, and the rain was as warm as the air.

She came back outside to find Maksim awaiting her stoically. Under the beating water, the tension in him was banked but visible; Lissa found herself unwilling to turn her back to him—not out of fear, exactly, but out of concern that he might do something sudden.

They walked together northward along a street of narrow-roofed Toronto Victorians. Lissa's braided hair clung to her back in heavy ropes.

"So if you didn't only come for eggs . . ." she said.

"I wished to ask you about the spell Iadviga made for me," Maksim said.

"I haven't found it in her grimoires. I was thinking maybe her journals."

"She left you everything?"

"Everything she could. But she didn't have time . . ." Lissa bit down on a sudden hot rush of sorrow.

"Be easy, *koldun'ia*. I am sure she would be very pleased with what you are doing. One cannot go from apprentice to master overnight."

If he only knew. "It's just—I miss her, that's all."

Maksim paced, silent, while Lissa wiped rain and tears from her eyes.

"I'm sorry. I'm just tired, I think." And, she thought, in need of someone to talk to about Baba: someone who was more than an acquaintance, someone who was apparently family of a sort, although she still did not understand exactly how. "Do you think you can make it like this until the full moon? That's the soonest I'd be able to fix anything for you, even if I can figure it all out earlier—it's kind of an important rule for us."

Maksim knit his eyebrows. "I did not know. Of course I will make do with the eggs as long as I must."

It wasn't exactly what she'd asked, but it sounded good

enough to go on with. Soaking wet, hair plastered to his neck below his cap, tank top skinned to his body, Maksim did not look very dangerous; he looked like a roofer or a landscaper caught in the bad weather, the menace in him drowned to ordinary sullenness.

When she looked closer, though, she could see a muscle twitching below his eye.

"Do you need one now?" she asked.

He shook his head. "Not so long as you walk with me. My home is not far." He hastened his steps, though, as they went north.

Maksim turned out to live on Dundas, in one of the old Victorians near Bellwoods, above a Portuguese hairdresser. He fumbled for the key, kicked the door open, and tore at his bootlaces.

Lissa put away the fresh batch of eggs in his refrigerator, which contained a case of Czech beer, an orderly assortment of mustards, and several butcher-paper packages. When she returned to the main room, she could see through the bedroom door Maksim stripping off his wet shirt, and she turned away hastily.

She looked at the walls, hung with a sword of some kind and a couple of antique guns. A map, with characters in Cyrillic. A signed photograph of George Chuvalo. The sofa and coffee table were elderly and graceful. A bookshelf held military histories in English, Russian, and French.

"Koldun'ia," Maksim said, his voice gone hoarse again. "Where?" He had his hand at his bare throat, fingers dug into the muscle above his collarbone.

"I put them in the refrigerator."

"I must go out," he choked, pushing past Lissa toward the door.

"Wait! I thought you wanted me to walk you here so that you wouldn't do anything stupid."

"You are right," he said, turning again and wrapping his

arms about his chest; he was bruised there, a mottling of red and purple over one side of his rib cage, and, beneath the bruising, older scars. "Bring me an egg, *koldun'ia,* and speak to me while you do."

"I'm bringing you an egg. Um. Two eggs? I'm at the fridge already, and I'm—what are you doing?"

Maksim had one fist pressed to his forehead and the other hand blindly extended; she set an egg in it. Maksim punched the shell with his thumb and sucked it noisily, spitting out a fragment of shell into his palm. He held out his hand again, imperious, and Lissa gave him another.

On finishing it, Maksim cast the broken shells carelessly on the floor, tipped his head back, and let out a long sigh.

"You may go now," he said.

"You won't go on some kind of a rampage, without your shirt?"

Maksim glanced down at himself, mouth twisting. He did not answer, only shuffled away toward the bedroom.

Lissa waited. Finally, she went to the bedroom door and cautiously peered in—saw Maksim sprawled, naked, facedown and snoring into his pillow.

She turned out the light and left him.

MAY 13

◑ WAXING CRESCENT

Lissa took Baba's notebooks with her to the Duke of Lancashire, telling herself she needed a change of pace—and anyway, Stella kept saying that shyness could only be conquered with practice. Lissa did not think of herself as shy, exactly, but when she followed Stella into the air-conditioned dimness, she did find herself dropping back, touching her face, hugging the stack of notebooks, not quite looking behind the bar at Rafe.

He smiled sunnily and brought her the organic lager before she could ask and said only, "Hitting the books, I see. I'll keep out of your way." And he bustled back down the bar. He was not wearing his toque today, and she had been right earlier: His head was shaved—lightly stubbled so that the tiny dark hairs lowlighted the contours of his skull. A pale, jagged scar stood out, as if he'd been hit over the head with a bottle; he looked like the kind of man who might have a few fights in his past—but only a few and only for boisterous fun, not like the scars she'd seen on Maksim.

That thought chilled her a bit: scars were a language, and she'd been reading without understanding the meaning. Now it began to come clear. A man like Rafe, a normal guy, might wear the signature of a couple of brawls or a car accident or some extreme sports. Maksim had a whole book traced on his skin, and Lissa had not really been conscious of seeing it the other day, but now her mind served up the picture of him shirtless, wealed with white or red keloid, several long, cruel lines, and one knot that surely must be a bullet scar.

Soldier: he had to have been. It went with the military books and the maps and the collection of weapons. And with the kind of muscle he had, hard and lean and functional.

It also spoke to her of what Maksim might be like when he did not have a witch to calm him down.

She found she was gazing at Rafe again as he leaned on the cash register twirling a pencil behind his ear. Just then, he turned her way, caught her gaze, held it a moment, and then smiled— not the goofy crooked smile he gave everyone but a smaller, sweeter one.

Lissa ducked her head, sipped from her pint, and flipped open the first of the notebooks.

Taken together, they formed a journal of sorts, recording

trials of the spells Baba had later perfected and noted in her own grimoire. Sometimes the recipient of the spell was mentioned, sometimes the ailment to heal, sometimes even the due date for a much-desired child. Lissa found a spell against colic, created for use on herself in infancy. She wondered what her father had said about that: old-country superstition, dangerous nonsense. She knew Baba's influence had been one of the points of strain in her parents' marriage, but by the time Lissa had been old enough to pick up any of the finer points, the marriage was long over, Dad had relocated to London, and Mama was dying.

She turned another page. Baba had always preferred to write in pencil, heavily, every line and both sides of the page, embossing the cheap paper of her notebooks. The words formed an incomprehensible Braille to Lissa's fingertip.

They were nearly as incomprehensible to her eye; Baba switched between Arabic and Cyrillic alphabets and dotted the pages with drawings and symbols, some arcane but recognizable, others possibly nothing more than doodles.

This page, for instance, bore four circles—white, black, and halved each way: clearly the phases of the moon, drawn as on a calendar. Beside the moons, Baba had made a series of tally lines: one for the full moon, three for the first quarter, five for the new moon, and two for the last quarter. Tracking the frequency of something: requests for spells? The church ladies mostly knew that the full moon was the time for that, and so it was possible they would make their requests in advance. What else could Baba have been tracking?

Lissa flipped open her phone and called Maksim. Ten rings, no answer, and nothing to leave a message on. Annoying; maybe she'd bully him into getting a proper phone and voice mail if this situation was going to continue.

Just as she was about to pull the phone away from her ear, he picked up.

"Hey. Maksim. Question about the . . . your thing. Any relation to the phases of the moon?"

He made a sound like a stifled yawn. *"Koldun'ia?"*

"Yeah, it's me. Did I wake you up?"

"One moment." The phone clattered onto a hard surface. In the background, a momentary sound of water. "Repeat your question."

"Phases of the moon. Any relation to your madness?"

"A witch should not need to ask."

Lissa snorted. "You asked me for help, you get to deal with a few questions. I have a page here with some notes about moon phases, and I was wondering if it could be—"

"No. Witches are the only ones who traffic in such things." His voice was rough again.

"I did wake you up. Jesus, Maksim, it's six in the evening."

"I was not sleeping. Only thinking," he said. "You should make more eggs."

"I can't do that until the moon is full again."

"You told me; I remember now. I will try to make the others last, then."

Lissa flipped the phone closed, frowning. She'd figured on a maximum dosage of four eggs a day at most; for a regular person, two ought to be sufficient. Though that was based on eggs that actually worked the way they should, and these were clearly subpar strength. God only knew how often he was taking them. She thought about calling him back and asking how many were left.

"Let me guess," said Rafe, wiping a spill from the varnished wood, setting a fresh coaster before her and upon it, a pint of water with a slice of lemon. "Study buddy is one of those people who expects you to do all the work?"

"Sort of," Lissa said, flashing back again to Maksim's extended hand, imperious and yet desperate.

"What's your major, anyway? Stella didn't tell me."

"It's not a formal program," Lissa said.

"Oh. I'm being nosy again. Professional hazard," Rafe said, touching her elbow in apology and grinning.

Lissa would have answered that smile. She really would. She could not think of anything to say, though.

After a moment, Rafe's face went a bit rueful, and he raised his eyebrows and backed away with his hands held up, empty.

Stella danced over to pick up a tray of pints. "It works better when you smile back," she whispered.

"What works better?"

"Flirting, silly," Stella said and slid away again, leaving Lissa pinned against the wall, fighting the urge to hide her hot face in her hands.

MAY 14

◑ WAXING CRESCENT

Maksim's door stood an inch open. Lissa knocked, and it swung wider, showing her that the elegant coffee table was strewn with dirty mugs. Beside the telephone, a pressback chair lay on its side, one of its legs broken.

"Maksim?"

"Out here."

She followed his voice through the bedroom—unmade bed, a pair of dirty jeans on the floor. A sliding glass door led out to the balcony.

Maksim sat with his back against the brick wall, one leg out-stretched and the other pulled up. As Lissa approached, he raised his head from his knee and held out his hand in a silent demand.

"You're like a toddler," she started to say, and then she saw his face. Older bruises had bloomed to livid color, and newer ones overlaid them, redder and bloodier.

"Oh my God. Maksim, what happened?"

"Eggs," he said.

She set down her bag and pulled out the cartons: all that remained of the sleep spell, plus the leftovers of two kinds of painkillers, made the full moon before Baba died.

She thanked whatever instinct had told her to bring the pain-killers. She gave him one of those first, hoping it was still good. The spells lasted only as long as the eggs did, and the expiration date on these was drawing near.

He slurped it from the shell. One corner of his upper lip was split and puffy, and so was his eyebrow on the same side. He tossed the shell shards to the corner of the balcony, and Lissa, fol-lowing the motion, saw a pile of other discarded shells there.

She waited for a moment until Maksim gestured again, and she gave him one of the sleep spells.

"Another," he said once he'd taken it, wiping a string of albu-men from his lip.

"No. You have to make them last."

"I did not husband them earlier. I am sorry."

"I can see that. Are you going to tell me what happened?"

He tilted his head back against the brick and shut his eyes. Lissa opened her mouth to chide him, but she saw his jaw work-ing and set herself to wait.

"I do not visit with my own kind often," he said. "I have been living apart, because of the spell."

"Right, the thing Baba did for you."

"The *kin* do not love witches. Many of them think it perverse to tamper with our nature."

"No one loves witches."

"I do," Maksim said, smiling faintly. He showed her his left hand: knuckles bloodied and mottled with bruising, two fingers swollen stiff that could not join the rest in a fist. "See? I thought I had broken the bones there, but now it does not hurt at all." He rolled his head on his neck and stretched his arms gingerly. "I would not tell many of the *kin* of you; we all have our ways and secrets. This one is . . . a friend. I asked her for help in finding the boy."

"I take it she said no."

"Oh, no. She agreed. We fought only because it is in our nature to fight."

"I guess you lost."

"I was not myself." Maksim gave her a haughty flick of a glance. "And it made Augusta happy to best me for once. She is capable: she knows the area where it happened. She will ask questions of people who may have seen him."

"I wish you'd told me about this earlier."

"I wish your grandmother had made better provision for me, *koldun'ia*. I wish your eggs would let me sleep straight through until the full moon. I wish I was careless and could let this boy go his way and never think of him again." Maksim rose stiffly and limped to the edge of the balcony, where he knotted his good hand on the railing.

"Why can't you forget about him? What will he do?"

"Die, most likely," Maksim said, leaning out and sniffing at the air. "He will do something rash, and someone will kill him, because he is too young to know his own strength. And if it should come to that, it is still better than watching himself go mad and hurt the people he used to love."

Lissa rose herself and set the egg cartons aside, watching Maksim shift his weight from foot to foot, testing. "How bad is it going to be, having this . . . Augusta on the warpath?"

"She will not hurt you. I have asked her to respect you, and she will not disobey me."

"That's not what I meant, and you know it. What if she hurts someone else?"

Maksim lunged away from the railing, with a section of it still clutched in his hand. He shoved past Lissa and into the apartment.

She heard a crash and ran after him. Maksim hefted the length of railing like a club and swung it down onto the wreckage of the broken chair until both splintered. He set the chair seat on his knee and hammered his fist through it so that the splinters raked his arm. He snapped the railing between his hands and cracked the longer half in two again.

Lissa watched, flinching, from the dubious safety of the bedroom, with her arms hugging the cartoned eggs.

At last Maksim spun about, short, jagged kindling in each hand. The abrupt motion sent a spatter of blood from his arm arcing across the floor.

Lissa jerked back.

Maksim stood rooted, panting, staring at the mess. "Do not touch. You must take care with my blood," he said. "That is how the infection passes. . . ."

He sat down slowly, and his knee buckled halfway so that he sprawled to one side. "I believe that should have hurt," he muttered, easing his leg out straight. "No more easing of pain. I must have something to warn me to stop."

"It's getting worse," Lissa said. "Your madness. Isn't it?"

Maksim's lips skinned back from his teeth, and he would not look at her.

"Jesus. I don't know what to do with you." She put the eggs in the refrigerator, except for one more of the painkilling ones, and sat on the other side of the room from Maksim while he washed up his arm.

He shuffled about slowly, sweeping the broken chair pieces into a corner and wiping the droplets of blood from the floor. Finally, he let himself down onto the sofa and covered his face. He said something in Russian into his hands.

"Maybe I could go out for you, pick up some groceries and first-aid stuff," Lissa said.

"I am not hungry—and for medicine, there is no need to worry; we are all quick healers. All too soon, I will be running again." He smiled, but there was no mirth in it; or maybe it was just the crooked cast of his bruised mouth.

MAY 15

WAXING CRESCENT

Lissa woke up in Baba's bed, and for no reason at all, she knew that today was the day to make it her own bed.

Baba's bedroom was the biggest room in the house. The window looked out into willow branches. Although the floor slanted, it was beautiful age-darkened hardwood. Over the last few years, as Baba's knees increasingly pained her, even with the eggs she made for herself, it had become Lissa's job to do the floors. She'd spent many hours first washing them with Murphy Oil Soap and then rubbing in cinnamon-scented beeswax. The scent mellowed into the rest of the old house, mingling with dust and books and wool, sun on aged paint, mothballs, and cedar.

Lissa tied her hair up and dressed in old denim shorts. She

was halfway through her coffee and Special K when Stella found her at the table.

"You look . . . casual?" Stella said. "What's the plan?"

So Lissa filled her in. "I'm not, you know, handy. I don't want to renovate or something. Yet. I just want to clean out some things. Get some fresh air in."

Stella nodded. "A good spring cleaning," she said. "Mummy does one every year. I mean, the cleaning service takes care of all the mopping and stuff, but Mummy and I sort the things and put everything in its place."

"I don't have a cleaning service," Lissa said, hearing the bite to her tone a moment too late. "I mean, it's just me."

"It's not just you," Stella said. "I can help. I'd like to help."

Lissa started to shake her head and stopped herself. What would it hurt? So Stella's mother had a cleaning service—Stella had been the one with the bucket, cleaning the spot in the kitchen when Lissa couldn't even look at it.

Lissa bit down on her reflexes and told herself to say yes. And when they were finished with their coffee and Special K, she and Stella marched back upstairs to tackle the room.

Lissa had already moved Baba's grimoires to the shelf that held her own in the kitchen sideboard. It was the personal things that remained: Baba's dresser was scattered with powder compacts and a thousand hairpins and the photo of herself with Lissa in its tarnished silver frame. The drawers were full of brassieres and nylon undergarments. The wardrobe held Baba's dresses, gray and navy and hunter green, and her faded eggplant coat. Far at the back, about where you'd expect to enter Narnia, was a shelf of sweaters wrapped in plastic against moths and a jumble of handbags and hatboxes.

Stella took down the curtains to give them a wash. Lissa began with the dresser drawers, sorting out the useful stuff from the things that even thrifty Baba would have thrown away if she'd thought about them anytime in the last five years. The bad went straight into a garbage bag. The good, Lissa folded into a very elderly blue suitcase to take to Goodwill.

"What about the things for you?" Stella said over her shoulder.

Lissa spread her hands flat on the bare wood at the bottom of the last drawer. "Oh."

"You don't have to. I just wondered."

"No, you're right. I wasn't thinking." She stood up then and looked at the things on top of the dresser in front of Baba's mirror. The jewelry case folded open to display a tangle of necklaces. Lissa lifted out a rhinestone collar and found the settings and clasp gummed over with human dirt. One ring box, on inspection, proved empty; that was probably the one Baba had worn most often, which was still in the manila envelope from the hospital. Another box held a ring of clustered garnets set in what might have been white gold. Lissa slipped it onto her finger; it was too big and wanted to twist askew.

All at once, it struck her that Baba had not even been gone a month, and here was Lissa chucking out her things without even asking.

It would be another week and a half before she could speak with Baba again, and she'd have only three questions to spend. She did not want any of those questions to be about the disposal of Baba's belongings.

"She never said, did she?" Stella said, looking over her shoulder. "That probably means she didn't mind, you know. She trusted that whatever you did would be right."

Sighing, Lissa left the jewelry case where it was and went instead to the closet.

Stella talked her into keeping the two silk scarves and a whimsical feathered hat; the rest they hauled downstairs and set by the front door. Remaining in the bedroom were a hatbox of old photos, the framed one, the jewelry, and a little chest that seemed to contain Baba's personal papers. And the urn containing Baba's ashes. Lissa took it in her hands a moment, met Stella's helpless gaze; but Stella couldn't offer much help on that. Lissa tucked the urn behind the bedroom door, which got her a raised eyebrow, but no commentary.

Stella helped move Lissa's clothes into the dresser and the closet and her shoes into the shoe bag on the inside of the closet door. They dried the curtains and hung them again. They set Lissa's comb and bracelets and necklaces and face cream before the mirror.

After Stella left for work, Lissa took the little chest down to the kitchen, where she could go through it in the bright light of her study lamp.

She'd been hoping for private diaries, something that would illuminate the question of what Baba had done for Maksim—or something personal and strange that might illuminate Baba herself, something to tide Lissa over these in-between days until she could speak with her grandmother again.

What she found was her grandfather Pavel Nevsky's passport. He'd been born in Canada, unlike Baba, whose passport must have been stashed somewhere else, if she even still had one. Pavel Nevsky had been a member of the church from birth; Father Manoilov remembered him a little and had said to Lissa once that he was a great bear of a man and had been a builder.

Below the passport, a photo of Pavel himself, a smaller and sharper image of the one Lissa knew from Baba's album.

Below that, a small chaos that included a vaccination document for Lissa herself; an old address book in flaking leather, in which most of the names were inked out and in which Maksim's did not appear; the birth certificate of Lissa's mother; a brass button; the business cards of two carpenters, a plumber and a mason; a handful of old rubles and kopecks.

Lissa tugged at her hair in frustration.

Whatever Baba had done for Maksim was either something so obvious that it had not needed to be written down or something so secret that—

Not secret; not quite. Lissa looked again at the tarnish-dark faces of the coins at the bottom of the box.

Whatever Baba had done, it had been done at the new moon.

Four

◐ WAXING CRESCENT

"Jonathan," Nick whispered. "There's a guy at the end of the alley."

"The wanker, the tweaker, or one of the crackheads?"

"No, another guy. I've seen him before, in Kensington Market." Bent low, Nick crab-walked away from the edge of the balcony and into Jonathan's apartment, taking cover behind the couch.

"Everyone goes to the Market. People from Scarborough go to the Market," Jonathan said.

"I think he's following me."

Jonathan held up the bong. "See this? It has some well-known effects, compadre, and one of them starts with the letter *P*."

"Just because you're paranoid doesn't mean they're not after you," Nick said, accepting the bong and taking a hit.

"Right. Make yourself more paranoid. See if that helps."

"Sarcasm doesn't suit you," Nick said, crawling under the kitchenette table to pass the bong back to Jonathan.

Jonathan, unmoved, sat at the table and contemplated the spread of cards. They were playing Dominion: Jonathan had about five different versions of it that Nick could never keep straight, but the upshot was you had to use a zillion different card combinations to buy as much land as possible before the end of the game. It reminded Nick of Monopoly, only fractally complicated. "I'm going to play this market for an extra card," Jonathan said. "Oh, look—gold. That means I can buy a province."

"Shit. Was that your first province?"

"Nope," Jonathan said, popping the *P*.

Forgetting his fear of the man outside, Nick bolted up and sat at the table again. "How'd you get all those cards, anyway?"

"I bought that Noble Brigand, like, five turns ago."

"Oh yeah. Rub it in, douche bag."

Jonathan let Nick ponder the table for a minute while he got up and mixed them each a rye and Coke.

"I'm going to be blunt. You're kind of fucked," he said, coming back to the table.

"That's a bit premature. I'm going to buy a duchy right this minute—"

"Actually," said Jonathan, "I didn't mean the game. Nick, honestly. You're kind of . . . I don't know."

"I don't know, either. What are you trying to say?"

"I was wondering if you might be manic-depressive."

"It's called bipolar now. And I'm not."

"Come on, Nick—take a drink, chill out, and listen to me. You've been all go-go-go lately. And now with this thing of thinking people are watching you. And all the arm wrestling . . ."

"I *win* all the arm wrestling."

"That actually makes it even weirder, honestly. I mean, you used to be pretty laid back, right? And now you're bouncing off the walls every time we go out, and you want to go out *all the time*. I can't keep up." Jonathan's hands lay flat on the table on each side of his sweating plastic tumbler. He looked at them instead of at

Nick as he kept talking. "I looked up the signs. Increased sociability. Feeling invincible. Sleeping less, drinking more. Paranoid thoughts."

Nick took a too-large gulp of his drink and choked a little. When he recovered his voice, he said, "Wow. I thought I came over to play Dominion, not have a fucking intervention."

"It's not an intervention, for Christ's sake. I just want you to think about—"

"Come here." Nick got down on the floor again and beckoned to Jonathan to follow him.

Sighing, Jonathan did.

They crawled out to the balcony and peered through one of the cutouts in the concrete barrier.

"See him?" Nick whispered.

"The guy in the rugby shirt?"

"Exactly. Rugby shirt. And he's wearing this really strong cologne. Can't you smell it?"

"Nick. He's, like, half a block away."

"Well, he's wearing a lot of it."

"If you're trying to convince me of your sanity here, it's not quite working."

"You were the one who smoked me up, and now you're telling me I'm not sober enough to pass your little test. Fuck off." Nick flicked Jonathan in the forehead with his fingers and stormed back inside.

"Ouch. Fine. We'll talk about it later."

"Jesus, everyone's so *serious* these days."

"Yeah," Jonathan said. "Well. Got to get serious sometime, right? We're grad students now. I have underlings and everything. I was actually thinking about asking Hannah to move in here."

Nick pressed his hands over his ears. "I can't hear you. La, la, la, la, rainbows and puppies and lucky charms. Dude—you know what will happen, right?"

"I'm pretty sure I do. I'll have to keep the place cleaner, maybe buy some matching plates, and be nice to her mom, and in exchange—"

"Jonathan. You'll never be able to smoke pot in your apartment again. *Never.* You'll have to come to my place."

"I hope to God you'll clean up those moldy apple cores from your windowsill before I do. What a buzzkill."

"Already gone, man. I couldn't stand the smell of them anymore."

"Anyway, I'm not smoking that much these days," Jonathan said.

"What? I'm the drinker, you're the smoker. It's the natural order of things."

"Hate to break it to you, buddy, but I haven't even bought weed in a month. I've just been smoking yours." Jonathan started laughing, so that Nick couldn't tell if he was telling the truth or just yanking Nick's chain.

It didn't change his answer, anyway. "My weed is here for you, brother," Nick said. "I am with you in your time of need."

Jonathan stopped laughing then and said, "Look, I'm with you too. Other stuff might change, but not that."

A key in the door: Nick heard it first, snapping his head around, grabbing at the game box to hide the bag of pot sitting out on the table.

Jonathan didn't flinch, though, just lazily kicked his chair back.

Hannah dropped the key on a side table and her purse on the floor and sniffed the air theatrically. "Did I interrupt a moment?" she said.

"Just taking advantage of an afternoon off," Jonathan said, rising to give her a kiss.

"Ugh, you taste all smoky," Hannah said, giggling. "I bet you've already got pizzas on the way or something, right? Don't let me harsh your buzz; I'm just picking up that laundry I left here yesterday."

"Oh my God, and you wonder why I keep calling you Mom," Nick said.

"Ignore him," Jonathan said. "Stick around. Have some, if you want. I haven't ordered pizza yet, but I will."

"Count me out. I've got to go," Nick said, finding himself on his feet already, halfway to the door. "Remembered some stuff I have to do."

"You sure?" Jonathan said.

"Sure," Nick said, making a jerk-off gesture and sticking his tongue out.

"Fine, fine, get out of here, asshole," Jonathan said, flinging the baggie of weed at him. "See you tomorrow."

"See you tomorrow, Nick," Hannah echoed, looking up from the pizza menu on her phone.

Right—he'd almost forgotten the three of them had plans to get together for dinner. Nick let the apartment door swing shut behind him and jogged down the stairs, all at once eager to put some distance between himself and the next day. When he saw them again, he'd open some half-decent wine and maybe wear the shirt Hannah had given him from her trip to Switzerland.

Nick didn't remember having to work this hard before, having to make a plan for how to be nice to people.

He wondered if Hannah had to work this hard to be nice to him or if it was just in her nature—and if the distinction mattered.

Because Jonathan had said the arm wrestling was weird, Nick didn't head toward the Palmerston tonight, but he still felt an itch under his skin, blunted a little by the pot smoking and the couple of drinks he'd had, but not gone—just made whimsical. He thought about dancing, maybe, but it was a Monday, the worst night for dancing.

Then it came to him, and he changed direction: he had a renovation project in the works, and tonight would be a perfect time.

MAY 17

◗ WAXING CRESCENT

Maksim, as the nominal host, suggested a restaurant on Roncesvalles. He chose it because he planned to run in High Park for a few hours first, tiring himself enough to converse without either eggs or a quantity of liquor; he did not like the way Gus looked at him under either influence, assessing and overfamiliar and sad.

Accordingly, he wore jogging shoes and shorts and a Nike T-shirt. He did not mind running in whatever he happened to have on when the mood struck him, but he did mind the looks, and nowhere in Toronto could he find a place free of other runners. He hammered over the trails, breathing deep of the tree scents and the fox musk. His knee pained him, but not enough to make him stop, and after a while, the feeling left it.

Sometimes when he ran his mind would fray away into his surroundings, leaving nothing but smell and sight and rhythm, and he would reach a place hours later and have no words for how he got there.

So it was today: when he finally slowed, at the edge of the park in a place he'd already passed at least once, he discovered he had only five minutes to reach the restaurant, and so he had to run again.

Gus waited for him on a bench outside. She wore a lumberjack shirt with the sleeves torn off, jeans spattered with bleach spots, heavy boots. Her grizzled fair hair had not been brushed.

"I hope you brought plenty of money," she said, grinning. "I have a hunger."

She ordered eggs scrambled with sausage and onions, and a plate of pierogi, which arrived piled high with crumbled bacon and more onions fried crisp. Maksim, despite his run, did not have a hunger. He spooned idly at a beet soup dotted with tiny mushroom dumplings.

Gus, elbows on the table, stuffed her mouth full of egg and said through it, "You're freaking me out."

Maksim shrugged.

"Jesus knows I didn't have a whole lot of use for you the way you've been these last few years, but this is truly unnatural. Eat your fucking lunch."

Maksim's nature had begun to rise up hard as the spell of the eggs wore off, and the struggle left him without an appetite, but he filled his mouth with soup and gestured for Gus to move on.

She rolled her eyes but said, "I haven't picked up anything. A few brawls, but the ones I saw personally were not your guy, and the other ones didn't sound like him, either."

"He was in a place on the eastern edge of your neighborhood."

"It's a big neighborhood. And people come to it from all over."

"What for?" Maksim muttered.

"Vintage clothes, crack, Trinidadian food, you name it," said Gus, and she laughed. "Don't be discouraged. I remember what it was like to be newly made *kin*. He hasn't gone off the rails yet, Maks. When he does—"

"I would very much like to find him before that."

"Yeah, well. Society takes care of stuff like that now. When he causes a big enough problem, someone will step in."

"They will not know what to do with him."

"Of course not. But if he makes waves, it'll be easier for us to find him, if he's still worth finding. And if not, if he goes too far, at least he'll be locked up where he won't hurt anyone for a while."

Maksim pushed his fists together under the table and breathed through his nose. All his fault. He felt as an addict feels, tumbling off the wagon after years of sobriety to discover the high is as wonderful as it ever was and that he's only been half-alive without it; and, at the same time, he's now going to have to tear down again the new life he's built and devote himself only to the old, single, terrible thing.

He felt, in short, very much in need of a friend; but the friend he had was going to be no help at all.

"Welcome back," Gus said.

He looked across the table at her. Bright eyes in a face just beginning to weather, a smile showing faintly yellowed teeth, and a scar at the corner of her lip. She was not as old as Maksim was himself, but still the years had left marks. And the time did not give much in return: neither riches nor wisdom, if he and Gus were anything to go by.

Still, she was smiling, and he almost hated her for it, even as he knew exactly what she meant.

He sighed. "Would you like to drink some whiskey?"

"After you eat your soup, damn it."

"I have never known you to be a mother hen before, Augusta."

"Don't call me that. And I'm only compensating for kicking your ass the other day."

"I hope you enjoyed it, for it is unlikely to reoccur." Maksim raised a brow and curled the corner of his lip at her.

Gus made a rude noise. "You wish. Have you seen yourself lately?"

Maksim let the sneer fall away and trailed his spoon through his soup.

"Whatever it was," Gus said. "Whatever's eating you. It was years ago. Decades, Maks. Things change—even you and me."

"For the worse," Maksim said.

Gus leaned close to look at his face. "Always?"

"Yes," Maksim said, a bare whisper from the depth of his chest.

"But—"

He shook his head and pushed the soup bowl away. A flaw in the glaze scraped the surface of the table, and the sound made Gus twitch and shiver, pale hairs rising on her forearms.

She met Maksim's eyes again. When he would have looked away, she caught his chin roughly.

She said finally, "Okay. I told you I'd help, and I will."

WESTERN RUSSIA: 1952

The borders of nations were drawn and redrawn. Maksim returned to his homeland now and again, but the familiar landmarks aged and the people wandered, and though he stood on the soil of his birth, he no longer recognized it.

Home became a collection of remembered scents and weather and accents and angles of light, which found him unexpectedly in places very far from the banks of the Don.

It was the smell of thunder that drew him this time. He knew what it meant. He'd come across it first in the hut of the *koldun* near his home; the storm smell mixed there with dried blood and old leather and dusty herbs and the thousand other things the *koldun* hung from his ceiling.

He had come across other *kolduny* now and again. One healed his *ataman* of an infected wound; one lived in Rostov and sent evil wishes upon people for the price of a cockerel. He had come to understand that their scent was the scent of their power.

When he smelled it in the rail yard, then, he found it curious.

The rail yard was somewhere in western Russia, and he was crossing it after midnight on his way to someplace warm. As he passed between the shadows of cattle cars, he smelled people: a number of them, some of them ill, all of them afraid and unwashed, and one of them a *koldun*.

The Second World War was over. It had been over for several years. Maksim had spent the last two of them working in various ports on the Black Sea, and he had not been keeping up with politics. His nature craved simple, head-on violence, one person to another. These last few wars, he had been struggling to keep pace with things he did not understand. Camps designed to contain and eliminate civilians. Weapons effective over great distances. Wars fought for abstract political reasons between nations many thousands of miles removed from each other.

War was not what it had been. But apparently peace wasn't, either.

He stalked around the cattle car that held the *koldun* and saw the slats had been stuffed with cardboard and newsprint and rags. He found a gap and whispered into it, "What is happening here?"

Someone sobbed within. Someone made a shushing hiss.

"No one is about," he said. "Only me. I am a stranger here, and I wish to know why you are prisoners."

"Only God knows that," a woman whispered back.

"I stole the silver from a church," said another one.

"Are you all thieves, then?"

Dry laughter. "We are all children of God, and that is all we share."

"Except for this one," said another voice. "Who is a child of Satan."

A blow or a push, then, and a hushed cry.

Maksim slipped around to the door of the cattle car and broke the lock between his fingers.

"Show me this child of Satan," he said, and he slid the doors wide.

Moonlight glinted from eyes and teeth and buttons: fifty women or more, huddled in sparse straw.

They did not move at first. The woman closest to the door flinched away from him—or from the frosty air.

"Show me this witch," Maksim prodded.

Someone hauled the witch to her feet and shoved her toward Maksim. "Take her and be damned."

"Someone has ill-used her," Maksim observed. The witch's coat hung open, most of the buttons torn from it, and her hair straggled down on one side.

Silence, and a few averted eyes.

"*Koldun'ia*," Maksim said. "Point out anyone here who has served you an insult."

The witch raised her eyebrows. "Do you think I care about the scratches of cats when I am in the jaws of the wolf?"

Maksim laughed at that. "This wolf has a healthy respect for witches," he said.

"I did not mean you," said the witch. "We are in the grip of the Gulag. There are guards in the station office; they will take us north in the morning. They will put us to work in one of their camps, along with all the others impolitic enough to question them."

"Not you, *koldun'ia*," Maksim said. "Unless you wish it, of course."

She tipped her head to one side. "I do not," she said. "Though I wish to know the price of my freedom."

Maksim did not tell her right away, because he heard voices at the door of the station office and saw a lantern bobbing in the hand of a man.

He killed the lantern bearer, the other two guards outside the door of the station office, and the three remaining within. For good measure, he killed the engine driver, the mechanic, and another man who had been playing cards with them.

He returned to the cattle car to find that most of the women had departed, leaving only the prints of rag-wrapped feet in the frost.

The witch waited for him with her arms wrapped tight around her body.

"The price," Maksim said. "You have been watching me, yes? You have seen what I can do. Someday . . . someday I might not want to do such things anymore. And I will need someone to make me stop."

The witch sighed. "Not yet, I hope. It is many miles to the border, and this country is full of madmen."

"Not yet," Maksim agreed, smiling and wiping his hands with dirty straw.

"How do I know you will not turn on me? Your *kin* are not known for constancy when your temper takes you."

"We are not," Maksim allowed. "And I cannot promise. Yet I do not think it likely that my temper will run unsated in these parts."

"I suppose that is something."

"You remind me of home," he said. "I think it will be enough."

And it was: enough to get them out from under the Gulag and all the way across Europe.

When had it stopped being enough? When had the memory of home lost its power to calm him?

Perhaps it had never been enough; perhaps it was only that he'd met Iadviga at the end of almost thirty years of warfare and that for much of his time with her, struggle was in constant supply.

Perhaps the world had let him fool himself, year after year after year. Perhaps it was only a miracle that he had not gone fully mad much earlier.

MAY 17

 WAXING CRESCENT

Nick could see right away that this wasn't going to go well.

He had a bottle of pinot grigio on the table; he didn't own an ice bucket, but he'd improvised with a plastic camping cooler. The place was cleaner than it had been in his whole tenancy, probably; he'd always been lazy about food in the past, leaving banana peels on the counter until he had ants, but now the smell of rotting fruit bothered him so much he'd given up on having any produce in the place at all.

He'd washed all the counters, walls, and floors, first with cleanser powerful enough to make his nose smart and then with a ton of plain water to get rid of the cleanser scent. And he'd eliminated a bunch of musty-smelling things, like the curtains and his old armchair and his futon. He had no problem sleeping on a Therm-a-Rest until he could find a mattress that didn't reek of chemical treatments.

But it wasn't the new spartanness of the place that had drawn his friends' attention. It was the heavy bag he'd mounted from the ceiling.

"That's . . . different," Jonathan said.

"Can I try it out?" Hannah socked her fist into the leather. "Ouch."

"You let your wrist buckle," said Nick. "You have to get your forearm straight, like this, and line up your knuckles." He demonstrated, causing the bag to jerk on its chains.

"How does your landlord feel about the ceiling?" Jonathan asked.

"He's not allowed to come in here without giving me twenty-four hours' notice," Nick called over the thunderous pummeling of a series of one-two punches. "I figure I can cover it up with something."

"What if you get a noise complaint?"

"What? Sorry, I couldn't hear you." Nick finished off the bag with a right hook and stepped back. "I bought some of that iced tea you like," he said to Hannah. "In the cooler over there beside the wine. I figure it will get me brownie points with the judge."

"Don't be that way, Nick. We're your friends."

"Sure about that? Because that message sounded more like a summons." But he opened the iced tea for Hannah, seated himself on a pressback chair facing the sofa, and spread his hands. "Go for it. I'm ready."

"This isn't a test, Nick," Hannah said. "Really. I can see it feels that way to you, but think about it. You've known Jonathan for ten years. You've been in all kinds of trouble together, and he's been right there with you. That's why he's concerned now."

"Then why isn't he speaking for himself?"

"Because I'm no good at that shit," Jonathan said. "You got mad at me yesterday when I tried."

"Damn right, I got mad. You pulled all this hypocritical crap while we were supposed to be having a good time."

"That's just it. The good times are going weird lately, Nick. And it's not me that's changing."

"The fuck it's not. You told me you wanted Hannah to *move in with you*. That is some serious change, my friend." Nick pointed a stabbing finger at Jonathan while he spoke and half rose from the chair.

"What?" said Hannah. "You told Nick you want me to move in?"

"It's called growing up," Jonathan said. "What Nick's doing is *fucking* up."

"He didn't tell me," Hannah said blankly to Nick.

"Maybe he's not sure," Nick snapped.

"I just hadn't got around to it! And don't change the subject. I'm not the one with the problems here."

"Oh, seriously? You think you can just sail on and pretend to be a grown-up and play house with your girlfriend and forget everything you used to be? You think you can start, I don't know, buying espresso makers and shit? What are you going to name your fucking kids? Yeah, I didn't think you'd thought about that yet. Ask *her*. I bet she's got a boy and a girl name already picked out for you." Nick paced around the chair while Jonathan and Hannah sat frozen on the sofa. "You aren't that guy, Jonathan."

"Hey," Jonathan said. "This is going off the rails. This might be news to you, but most people grow up to buy houses and have kids. Just because I haven't got names picked already doesn't mean I won't be happy when the time comes."

"Happy," said Nick. He wound up and punched the bag. "How can you be happy like that?"

Jonathan covered his eyes with one hand. "I love Hannah. I like Toronto. We'll buy a condo here when we have enough money. This is how life goes, Nick. When you're normal."

"Maybe I'm not fucking normal!"

"That's kind of what we've been trying to say," Hannah said softly. "Listen, just listen. I know you don't like me. But I want you to know it's not mutual. I like you, and you're important to

Jonathan, and I want you to be happy. So it's kind of hard to watch whatever is going on with you."

"Of course I like you," Nick said after a slack-jawed moment. "Where do you even get that?"

Hannah rolled her eyes. "Your face is not subtle, Nick. But I'm glad you try to be nice, anyway. For Jonathan's sake, especially. You've been friends for so long—I'd hate to be the thing that drives you apart."

Nick bit his tongue on a rush of pure hot fury. *Drive me and Jonathan apart? I'd like to see you try.* Only that was what was happening, wasn't it? Nick growled in frustration. "I think you should leave."

"He's right," Hannah said to Jonathan. "All of us getting upset isn't going to help anything. Nick, maybe we can get together again in a couple of days, once we've all had time to take a deep breath."

She led Jonathan out into the hall. Nick shut the door very firmly behind them, not quite a slam.

"You see what I mean," Jonathan said heavily, out in the hall. His voice came to Nick as clearly as if he'd been miked.

"I wonder if he's jealous of you," Hannah said, a bit more muffled, as if Jonathan was embracing her.

"I wonder if he's trying to distract us so that we won't ask him the right questions."

"Which are . . . ?"

"Hard drugs? I don't know." A sound of fabric sliding roughly against paint, as if one of them had leaned back against the wall. A sigh.

"I'll be happy to move in with you," Hannah said after a while.

"That wasn't how I meant to ask you."

"That's okay. I was going to ask you, if you hadn't said anything by the time I needed to house hunt."

"Do you have names?" Jonathan asked.

"Sorry?"

"Our kids."

Nick stood stock-still, breath held, waiting for the answer to come amid the sounds of traffic and pigeons and distant street-cars.

"Abby and Noah," Hannah said finally. "Abby for my sister; it's her middle name. And Noah—"

"My grandfather," Jonathan said. "Yeah. That's nice."

Then the soft sound of a kiss. Nick wondered who'd made the first move, and then a moment later, he was disgusted with himself. Or with Hannah and Jonathan. Or with the whole fucking mess.

He turned on the stereo and pressed play on his iPod, which was halfway through a workout playlist. He raised the volume until he couldn't hear Hannah and Jonathan walking away. Then he uncapped the pinot grigio, took a long chilly swallow straight from the bottle, set the cooler near the heavy bag, and went to work.

MAY 18

◑ FIRST QUARTER

Maksim slowed to a stop on a stretch of dusty sidewalk in front of a nail salon, a municipal campaign headquarters, a pawnshop. He smelled toasting spices: delicious for a moment and then almost nauseating. He was soaked with sweat, his shirt wet all the way through, the waistband of his shorts chafing at his skin.

A woman was coming toward him, a youngish Indian woman in pink and yellow. The glass bead of her bindi sparkled in the morning sun.

Morning. Not too early, either: the sun was above the nearby apartment buildings, the street was lined with cars, and the sidewalk scattered with shoppers and baby carriages.

Maksim had no idea where he was.

The woman with the bindi was staring at him.

He turned his face away casually, instinctively. Wiped sweat from his forehead beneath the rim of his cap. Saw her hesitate and then continue on.

He saw a street sign on the corner and headed for it. Something was wrong with the letters: the shapes looked familiar, most of them, but they didn't sort themselves into anything that made sense.

He would ask someone for directions. He saw an elderly man crossing the street, bracing himself with two canes. Opened his mouth to call out. Found his voice knotted in his throat like a choke pear.

He turned away and walked quickly down a side street, head hunched, hand pressed over his throat. He knew this feeling. His body took longer, sometimes, to come back to him than his thoughts did.

What had he been doing?

He had been running. Obviously. Running was fine.

He sat down on the guardrail of a parking lot to look at himself. His shirt was one of the ones from his own gym, and apart from being sweat-drenched, beginning to stain with salt as it dried, it was unremarkable. No bloodstains, no tears.

His shoes were on his feet. They were gray brown with dust, with all the running he had been doing lately. His calves were dusty, and the dust showed sweat trails through it. Sweat, nothing more.

His knuckles were scabbed still from fighting with Gus. The

bruises had darkened to green and gray purple. He flexed each hand in turn and felt no new stiffness.

But there was yellow on his left palm: bright yellow like pollen, smeared across the central lines and the web of his thumb and up to the pads of his index and middle fingers. He sniffed at it. Not pollen: something synthetic but not strong-smelling, some kind of paint, maybe. He spat into his palm and rubbed it on his thigh. Nothing came off.

In the sunlight, the color looked too vivid. So many of the colors did now. A house painted coral pink across the way. The subtly iridescent red of a stop sign. A car painted the same pearly green as the beetles Maksim used to see among the ash trees in eastern Russia, an age ago.

He blinked his eyes. The sun jumped.

His shirt was nearly dry now. When he ran his fingertips over his skin, he felt the fine grit of salt.

He got to his feet and felt the ache of the long run halt his steps a little. There was a young man standing on the corner now, handing out leaflets. Maksim cleared his throat and approached.

"Can you tell me which way is downtown?" he asked, pleased that his voice came out this time, hoarse but his own.

The boy looked white-eyed at him and handed him a leaflet.

Maksim began to repeat himself and then realized he was speaking Russian.

He shied away from the boy when he realized, dropping the leaflet.

"Are you okay, man?" the boy said in English.

Maksim understood him; at least there was that.

"You have a little . . ." the boy said, gesturing at his own upper lip.

Maksim nodded. Got himself away.

Safely around the corner again, he ran his fingertips down his face and felt the crust of dried blood below one nostril without much surprise. He rubbed at it until it seemed to be mostly flaked away.

This was not good. The last thing he could really remember was before sundown yesterday. Maybe. He hoped it was yesterday. He'd awakened from a restless nap to a breath of fragrant air and headed out toward the park . . . maybe.

Nothing in his pockets: nothing at all, in fact, no wallet, no cash. He still had the key to his flat, which he'd taken to clipping to a carabiner on his belt loop.

Nothing at all to show him what he might have been doing except for the trace of blood crusting his nostril and the streak of yellow on his palm.

And the sweat, and the thirst on him, and the dragging ache in his legs.

Nothing to hint why he'd lost his voice, why he'd lost an entire language for a little while.

He would have to go home. See if he'd merely left his things behind or lost them too, somewhere in his irretrievable night.

He picked a direction and began walking.

MAY 18

◐ FIRST QUARTER

Lissa came home from work with her nose tingling from the smell of ink and heated paper and her own sharp sweat; the air-conditioning in the shop couldn't quite keep up with all the printers going at once. She washed her hands with Ivory soap and let the fresh cold water run over her inner wrists for a minute or two.

Stella wasn't home. At breakfast, she'd said something about art galleries. Lissa stood still in the relative cool of the house, breathing the flat air.

She had not heard from Maksim for several days; good news or bad, she was not sure. She should call him, she thought.

Later.

Now she just wanted a tall glass of sparkling water over ice and an hour to herself. She sat by the window in the front room, in the late afternoon sun, listening to bees in the lilacs outside.

Her eyes passed over the pages of one of Stella's *Vogue* magazines without taking anything in. She'd been fretting over Stella's constant presence, and yet now that she had a bit of time alone, the silence in the house oppressed her. Everything still smelled like Baba. She wondered how long it would last. Already the upstairs smelled like Stella too, a breezy, rich scent composed of expensive facial moisturizers and hair silkeners.

Lissa could not call this *grief*. Half-grief, maybe. As if Baba had moved to a far foreign country with poor telephones.

Before Lissa could grow too pensive, Stella swung in with an armful of grocery bags. "I found the most darling market. It had Pim's biscuits, of all things! Have you ever had them? No—stay there. I know you've just got home from work. I'll get you something cool."

Lissa sat by the open window for a few minutes, listening to Stella putting the groceries away, opening and closing cabinets, stirring ice in glass. She could not pretend, even for a moment, that the physical presence in the house belonged to Baba. Baba's step had been slow and heavy, even in Lissa's childhood. Her wiry soot-gray hair had been tamed by a musky-smelling pomade. Her voice, even when she sang, was pitched low and dark.

Stella came in with a cocktail. It was a gin and tonic, with a slice of lime perched on the rim.

"I never drink gin and tonic," Lissa said. "I mean . . . I never think of it, that is. Thanks."

Stella set the glass on the windowsill, hesitated for a moment, and walked away.

Lissa thought about following. Instead, she remembered how many times she herself had walked from this room, leaving Baba behind at the window, still and ageless and full of silence.

Maybe Baba had felt this way about Lissa's presence in her house, after Mama died. Maybe solitude was the way of witches.

Stella came back a few minutes later with a drink of her own and a plate of rice crackers topped with cucumber and curls of salmon. "You're off tomorrow. Yes?"

"Yes . . ."

"Eat up, then. I made us an appointment for half six."

Lissa blinked. "Appointment?"

"Pedicures!" Stella said, extending one foot and wiggling the toes, which were painted brilliant coral. "Look at the chips—I haven't been for one since leaving home."

"You said 'us.'"

"Sure. You haven't been, either, what with all the stuff that's been going on. Right? Time for a bit of pampering, isn't it?"

"My grandmother wasn't much into that kind of thing."

"Haven't you ever? It's not scary—it's nice. They massage your feet with sea salt and things. Then you get to pick a color. And you chat with the people while they do it, and they give you a little glass of tea or something. Never?"

Lissa shrugged.

"I've put my foot in it again, haven't I? I thought you could use something relaxing, is all. I'm sorry."

"No. No, it's nice of you . . . it's just . . ."

"You're not coming, are you?"

Lissa shook her head.

Stella filled her mouth with a rice cracker and crunched determinedly.

"It *is* nice. Really. I just need, I don't know . . ."

"I don't know, either," Stella said, dropping her feet to the floor and dusting crumbs from her shirt. "I'm trying, but I can't figure it out. I want to *help* you. Only every time I think I have a great idea, you look at me like I'm from bloody Mars instead of London. So I've had it, and I'm going to get my bloody feet done. See you 'round."

Once she was gone, the house still smelled of her hair product. Lissa stayed exactly where she was, listening to the tick of melting ice cubes in Stella's emptied glass.

Five

◖ WAXING GIBBOUS

Nick went back to the sports bar in Parkdale. It stank.

He didn't see anyone he recognized. He asked for Johnnie Walker and drank it down quickly; it felt as necessary as water, a thought he kept having lately and kept dismissing. He asked for another.

The people in the sports bar—midafternoon on a workday— were a sad assortment of older men and two women, all with the leathery skin of serious drinkers. They stank too. Nick buried his nose in his scotch instead, inhaling the tear-jerking fumes of it.

Drinking alone sucked. He didn't like being one of the people alone in this bar. When he'd been here with Jonathan, he had felt protected, exceptional; they were travelers from someplace better, observing the locals like they were a different species. Now Nick felt a bit too much like he belonged here.

He kept catching people looking at him, though. Maybe they didn't agree that he belonged. Maybe they all knew one another, and the silence in the place was just because they didn't have anything to say to one another. Maybe Nick was the only stranger.

Having a best friend meant you weren't a stranger anywhere you went—you were one of the citizens of a two-man country. Only Nick's country was undergoing some kind of annexation right now, and how was he supposed to deal with that? Half of him knew that marriage—if that was really where Jonathan and Hannah were heading—was a two-person country too, only maybe even richer and better than friendship, and of course it was normal and sweet to want that and to take it when the world graced you with it. And the other half of Nick wanted to nuke that country right off the map and keep Jonathan for himself.

Nick didn't think he could be a country all by himself.

The logical thing to do would be to find a girlfriend of his own: as Jonathan kept pointing out, that was a normal thing for people their age to do. And it wasn't like Nick wasn't hot, he thought, preening a little. He had great abs and a tan and cool-looking eyes. Girls gave him the once-over all the time.

He hadn't dated anyone since Sue Park, though, and if he was honest with himself, it had only been a few dates before she'd stopped returning his calls.

Maybe it would be different now. Nick was different now. Maybe he would call Sue Park later and see if she picked up.

He'd come here to Parkdale for a reason, though: a vague reason, sure, but since he was here, he might as well explore. He paid up and went outside, around back.

The place looked seedier in daylight. Nick observed the Dumpster and the security light and the gravel and the sparkle of broken glass.

He didn't see anyone in the alley. Hadn't expected to, really. Now that he was here, he didn't know why he'd thought seeing the place again would mean anything. It was only that things had changed for him that night, in a way he hadn't yet comprehended. He felt a bit like someone visiting the grave of an old friend.

He followed the alley west, aimlessly kicking at beer cans and chunks of broken paving. Weeds grew lush here, massive dandelions and other bitter things, leaves weighed down with a patina of dust and soot. Nick found an old mattress, springs rusting through; an assortment of gas cans; a discarded sweatshirt that his nose, even from ten feet away, told him was stained with come. He didn't think he'd always been able to identify stains by smell, and he was not sure he enjoyed having this particular ability.

Nick found a homeless man sleeping on an opened-out cardboard box. He found a trio of black kittens playing beneath a flat-tired Topaz; the car's windows were all open, and in the backseat, the kittens had made a nest of rags. He found a small baggie of pot, also by smell, which was cool.

He found a fight.

Two guys were beating up another guy. The victim was on the ground, wheezing through bloody lips. The two attackers circled him, kicking and cursing.

When they saw Nick coming, they stood still and turned their heads to him like jackals. "Stay cool," one of them said. "You're cool, right?"

Nick ran at him, swinging. Everything he didn't know about fighting felt flooded out by the sheer strength in his body. He broke the first guy's nose on the third try. The second guy jumped him from behind and tried to trap his arms. Nick threw him off, twisted around, and kicked him in the stomach.

The one with the broken nose grabbed a bottle and swung at Nick with it. Nick slid away, faked right, and punched left and hit the guy in the broken nose all over again. When the guy fell down, Nick stamped on the hand that held the bottle. More breakage. The sound of it was like meat between his teeth. He stamped on the guy's other hand, for good measure.

The one he'd kicked in the stomach was still on the ground, moaning.

"You suck at this," Nick said. "You shouldn't be in this business." He knelt down and took the man's earlobe between his fingertips. He put his lips to the ear and shouted, "Got me? You can't go around beating people up!"

He stood up, light-headed with adrenaline, and looked around. The third guy, the victim, was limping up the alley as fast as he could, looking over his shoulder; he rounded the corner and was gone.

"You're boring," Nick said to the two on the ground. "Next time, fight back a bit."

He walked on, shaking. Tasting the air through his nose and his open mouth, the smells on it of blood and food and drink and heat.

He'd had a plan, earlier, hadn't he? Yes: to call Sue Park and make her his girlfriend or something. Something stupid. He didn't care about that anymore, not with his blood up like this. He didn't think quiet, musical Sue Park could even handle who Nick was becoming.

Nick might be living in a country of one, but right now he felt like the king.

AFGHANISTAN: 1981

It was the second time Maksim had joined the Red Army. He saw right away that he was not going to have as much fun this time around.

For one thing, the Red Army was bigger than ever, and its web of allegiances ever more tangled. Its opponents, the *mujahideen*, were made up of several factions nominally united by their faith, but as far as Maksim could tell, it was the same faith practiced by most of the Afghans who were Soviet allies. Maksim saw that he would not be able to take much satisfaction in the idea of fighting for his homeland, which was not under threat from the *mujahideen* at all. He would have to fight for his comrades, which meant he would have to get to know them. And in turn, they would get to know him, something he did not always wish to chance.

For another thing, he was not issued his own *Afghanka*. Supply of the heavy winter uniforms was limited to two per squad, said his commanding officer, *Starshina* Petrov. They would go to whoever pulled night duty or was posted in the windiest spot.

In Maksim's long experience of soldiering, complaining was one of the things every soldier enjoyed and a quick way for him to form bonds with the rest of the squad, among whom Maksim was the newcomer. So he complained about the *Afghanka* shortage to one of the other men in his squad over mess one night.

The man gave him a long look. "We are fortunate to have *Afghankas* to share," he said. "*Zampolit* Ogorodnik would not order us to share if it were not for the best." He moved away from Maksim and sat by himself near the tent flap.

Later in the evening, Maksim heard someone else toasting *Zampolit* Ogorodnik, wishing the political commissar long life and excellent health, wishing him the pick of the loveliest brides, wishing him fortune in battle and untroubled sleep.

Sarcasm. It had to be. No one loved an officer that much. The rank of *Zampolit* was a new one since Maksim's last campaign, and he began to see it meant something unfamiliar to him.

Maksim did not find out much more until he met Ogorodnik himself, coming from the hastily dug latrines a few days after their deployment into the Panjshir. Ogorodnik said to him, "You seem like a sensible fellow. Quiet."

"Sir."

"People like to talk to those who'll listen," Ogorodnik said.

"Not to me. Sir."

"No? I find that . . . surprising."

Maksim inclined his head.

"If you ever feel a need to talk to someone . . . share confidences . . . you may talk to me—Volkov, is it?"

"Yes, sir."

Maksim thought for a moment that he had been propositioned.

Then he understood that he had been asked to report on his comrades.

Maksim could not go running—not here, in a hostile valley, with orders not to stray beyond the pickets—but he stormed back to his squad's tent and sat stabbing his bayonet into the dirt until *Starshina* Petrov ordered him to stop.

He made more of an effort not to be separate after that.

His squad numbered eight, including himself; they and two other squads made up the platoon, led by *Starshina* Petrov and Junior Lieutenant Ushakov. His squad slept together and messed together; in addition to sharing a duty roster, they shared a single light machine gun.

"Lady Wasp," they called it; no one told Maksim who had stenciled the name on the gun's dark, lean cheek, but there it was, in slightly crooked Cyrillic. They took turns carrying Lady Wasp. Maksim's turn came more often than not, because whoever had the gun could not have one of the *Afghankas*, and Maksim was one of the ones who minded the cold less.

They all—even Maksim—had thought Afghanistan would be warm.

They met the *mujahideen* two weeks after deployment—or rather, the *mujahideen* met them.

Maksim's platoon was in convoy, his squad walking beside one of the tanks. Maksim was paired with the radio operator, Netevich, who was sweating under the weight of his extra gear. The road ran down the dry cleft of the valley, where a river must have run once. Maksim was not the only man scanning the ascents; scrubby trees and stone outcroppings offered too much cover for anyone's comfort.

When the first of the *mujahideen* sniper bullets winged in, he felt it as a comfort: action at last. Maksim relaxed into the *Starshina*'s orders. His binoculars spotted a muzzle flash, and if he didn't manage to mark the sniper right off, he at least sent the man scuttling to different cover, and Lady Wasp took him down on the way there.

The gunners were few, though, and the skirmish over far too soon. Maksim had to walk on in the convoy, chest tight with unsatisfied blood rage. He thought he would choke.

He had an hour, no more, to simmer and clench and chew upon his lip. Then the *mujahideen* came back in greater force.

The Soviet tank gunner, Trinkovich, tossed a couple of shells out, but the *mujahideen* were thin spread, fast, and not in any kind of order Maksim could see. They spilled down the hillside like pebbles, right into the convoy, yelling in breathless voices. Maksim did not need to know their tongue to understand what kind of thing they said.

He met them laughing.

He did not recall the fight once it was over. It seemed to happen more than ever, recently, that he lost the consciousness of what he did in battle. But he came to himself by degrees, crouched beside the tank, with the blood song subsiding into a delicious comfort that could come from nothing else in the world but this.

He smiled at the nearest man: Aleksei Andreev, he thought.

Aleksei Andreev shouldered Lady Wasp and made a surreptitious face-wiping motion.

Maksim raised his eyebrows. After a moment, he understood what he was being told, and he swiped his sleeve across his mouth, bloodying the khaki.

"That's right. Even wolves lick their jaws clean," Andreev scolded.

They called him the Wolf after that; it was not the first time he had been nicknamed so, given his patronym. His squad, having given him a pet name, owned him now. They learned, as his Cossack brethren had in times past, that Maksim was good enough in a scrape to make up for his strangeness at other times.

The man who bunked next to him, Sergei Stepanovich, who had no sense of self-preservation, even grew teasing with him, cuffing him in the back of the head sometimes and laughing when Maksim turned on him. The laughter disarmed Maksim somehow; at least he never really hurt Stepanovich, always recovered himself quickly enough. It helped that he had real enemies.

He began to have a friend, too, in Stepanovich. Just as the other men were wary of Maksim's temper, they were often annoyed with Stepanovich's nonstop talk, but Maksim found he could relax into it, as Stepanovich did not truly expect him to respond. Stepanovich talked about anything: birds he had seen, books he had read as a boy, the shapes of clouds, his great-aunt. On the occasions when he talked about something he should not, Maksim would clap a hand over his mouth until he shut it, and Stepanovich would dissolve into snorting giggles once Maksim let him go.

Stepanovich knew how to sew and darn; once Maksim realized this, he began to switch his socks with Stepanovich's every time they grew worn, and it took Stepanovich at least four socks to figure it out. When he did, he kept right on mending in exchange for Maksim washing his mess kit after meals.

Nine months they had together, his squad; nine months in which Maksim could live almost as he was meant to live. He came to like, or at least tolerate, the taste of the bulgur porridge that augmented their rations. When Stepanovich received the news of his great-aunt's passing, Maksim got him drunk. When Maksim got his arm broken, Stepanovich strapped it up for him secretly so that no one would think of invaliding him out, and Stepanovich had the sense to keep quiet a week later when the strapping was back off again.

Maksim nearly had a skirmish with *Zampolit* Ogorodnik once, but they were both drunk when they should not have been, and so nothing was said afterward.

They got to know the Panjshir end to end, or so it felt, although the *mujahideen* kept enough secret places to continue surprising them. The squad finally received enough *Afghankas* to go around.

"Means we'll be staying awhile longer," Stepanovich said to Maksim as they both sank their faces into the new-smelling quilted collars.

Maksim said, "Good."

"What, Volkov? Afraid if you go home, your wife will cut off your balls? I knew you were hiding from someone!" Stepanovich did not wait for an answer but laughed uproariously and ran away around the camp perimeter, Maksim in pursuit.

Winter returned. With it, illness. Trinkovich and Tretiak, on the tank squad, took sick first, limp and yellow and vomiting, and by the end of the week, a third of the platoon had it.

Something to do with their livers, said the medics, and so everyone was ordered not to drink. Something to do with contaminated rations, said rumor, and so rations were stopped and started and stopped again. Men grew thin. Tempers grew unpleasant. At half-strength, the squads had to pull double duty. Even Maksim grew fatigued.

Still, it was war, and he much preferred it to peace.

Or so he told himself, even as he watched himself fret at his leash, growl at his comrades, say the wrong things to the *Zampolit*. He told himself he was too tired to run off his anger. Told himself it did not matter that there was no liquor ration now, because he didn't love it the way Augusta did.

Told himself it was not taking him any longer than usual to come back from his battle rages; told himself he had never been able to remember much from them, anyway.

Told himself he could handle everything. Told himself this was better than desertion.

Until he proved himself wrong.

MAY 21

◗ WAXING GIBBOUS

"I'm so tired of Russian food," Lissa said into the refrigerator, where a gallon jug of borscht was getting down to the dregs, separating unattractively, pulp floating atop a livid purple brine.

Stella made a face. "I didn't want to say anything, but thank God. Want a falafel?"

"I don't know how to make a falafel."

"Well, you walk into a Middle Eastern fast-food place, and you hand them a couple of quid, and you tell them whether you like hot sauce—"

"Seriously?" Lissa said, laughing.

"What? I don't like cooking."

"Me neither."

"And yet when I first got here you were messing around with

all kinds of things—which I don't think I even got to taste, now that I think about it—"

"I'm not any good. It was just to keep me busy." More true than she'd meant.

"Fair enough, but it doesn't really help right now, does it?"

Lissa shut the fridge and leaned on the counter. "I just want french fries."

"Come with me to the Duke, then. We can grab a bite before my shift. Rafe would love to see you."

"No. No, no, no. You can't—"

"Can't be a matchmaker? Come on, it's a grand old British tradition, meddling in people's love lives."

"I don't have a love life," Lissa blurted.

Stella looked at her, really looked, drawing her sculpted brows down. "You're not joking, are you?"

Lissa felt her face going hot, blotchy, shamed pink. She shook her head.

"Do you mean right now? Or never?"

Lissa shrugged one shoulder.

"Never? Seriously?" Stella said. "Like . . . wow. Okay. No wonder you don't . . . no wonder we aren't always on the same page, you know?"

"I don't think it's that weird," Lissa said.

"Of course not. You wouldn't, I mean. And it's not. It's only, my friends and I, we were kind of . . . precocious, you know?"

"This is really awkward."

"Yep. Kind of," Stella said, and she burst out laughing. She swung her hair back and whistled up at the ceiling. "Hey, at least there's something I can really do for you, you know?"

"No. You can't."

"Oh, yes, I can. You're going to be kissed, sister. I can make it happen."

"Shit," Lissa said, trying to back away.

"So what is it? You don't seem that shy. And you do like boys, right? Maybe your baba scared all of them away with a broom or something—"

"Stop pitying me," Lissa said, and it should have come out firm and cool, but somehow there was a laugh in it.

"Ha," Stella said. "You're into it. I can tell. Put on a nice top, then—that candy-striped kind of one. You're coming with me. There's chips in it for you, anyway."

"That'll make me feel much better when I'm dying of embarrassment," Lissa said, but she went upstairs and found the candy-striped cotton blouse, twisted her hair up into a loose knot, and stuck a chopstick through it.

"Lovely," Stella said. She'd changed into her little kilt, black sneakers, and a black tank top, an inch of skin showing at her narrow waist. As if anyone would look at Lissa when Stella and about ten other nineteen-year-old stunners were dancing around like that, Lissa thought.

At the Duke, they sat at the end of the bar closest to the kitchen. Rafe grinned hugely, showing his off-kilter canine, and said to Stella, "Good girl—that's worth a nice bonus right there. Now there's a raise in it for you if you can get her to actually talk to me."

"Get Seamus to make her some dinner first," Stella chided. "Can't you see she's about to keel over? She wants chips."

"Let her speak for herself, you overbearing brat. What'll you have, Lissa?"

"Yes. Chips, please," Lissa managed. "And a pint?"

Rafe brought her the organic lager without being reminded and said, "Your money's no good here, you know. Just get comfortable and let me know if you need anything at all. I'll be right here when you're ready."

"See?" Stella said as soon as his back was turned.

"He's just nice," Lissa said. "Or you're putting him up to it somehow."

"Just let him talk to you. You don't even have to talk back."

"Well, *that's* a relief."

"Come on—you know how to talk to other people. I've seen you. It's the same with guys you think are fit, only you might also eventually get to have sex."

"That's what I'm . . ."

Stella's face shifted, her brows going wider and her chin tilting, signaling readiness to listen.

"—not going to talk about," Lissa said. "Look. I think I'm doing pretty well. I'm still here, right?"

"And now you have chips," Stella said as Rafe went to the kitchen pass-through and brought over a plate for Lissa and a burger for Stella.

Lissa doused her fries with vinegar, earning an approving grin from Stella. They were crisp, with the skin on, deep brown, just the way she loved them. She added extra salt.

Just as she'd filled her mouth, Rafe asked, "Did you bring your books tonight?"

Lissa shook her head.

"Did you come to check up on your sister? We haven't broken her yet—I think she's going to be okay."

Lissa shook her head again.

"So you came just to see me," Rafe said, hand to his toque.

"Fries," Lissa said through the last of her mouthful.

Rafe sighed. "I'm being such a git. I shouldn't be talking at you, should I? How about I'll be over here at the bar, and you come and say something when you feel like it?"

Lissa blinked after him.

"See?" Stella whispered. "Smarter than he looks." And she tucked away the rest of her burger, wiped her mouth, and went to start her shift.

Lissa finished her fries. She twisted up her napkin into a greasy corkscrew. She finished her pint.

She ran lip balm over suddenly dry lips and wrapped her hand around her empty glass.

"Hey," she said. "Rafe? I'd like another, please. And . . ." What could she talk to him about? She couldn't tell anyone about magic, of course. He wasn't going to be interested in the gossip of the church she wasn't allowed to attend. Her job at the print shop was utterly uninteresting. They had Stella in common, but another person wasn't the right thing to talk about with someone you wanted to date.

She took a deep breath. "You were asking the other day about what I'm studying. It's Russian folklore. My grandmother left me some books—she was kind of a specialist. . . ."

AFGHANISTAN: 1982

Maksim came to himself like a sleepwalker awakened by a shout: he stood dizzy and shocked for a moment, quite blank, before a flare of pain caught up with him. He saw that his hand held a Zippo lighter, and the flame bit hard against the web of his thumb.

He snapped it shut, cursing. His voice came out in an overused rasp. He swayed a little.

He'd been fighting, then: the fatigue told him so, and the way his voice did not answer. And he could smell blood.

He was standing in some of it. He felt the warmth and wetness on the bare soles of his feet. And he was standing on something soft.

He looked down and saw that it was an ear.

He looked around him then. He was in the rough, single-roomed house that his squad had been using as a barracks. But instead of orderly sleeping bags and a card table, the room held a haphazard haystack of splintered planks, bundles of straw, kerosene-soaked rags. And bodies.

Maksim wondered in that first bare moment, coming to himself among the wreckage, if the *mujahideen* had come into the town, had penetrated the house. If he had somehow driven them off. If he had somehow survived such an incursion alone.

All the bodies in the pyre wore the same, familiar Russian uniform. There were no strangers. No *mujahideen*.

His hands trembled with fatigue, the muscles of his arms swelled with oxygenated blood. His chest heaved with breath. Splinters pricked here and there in his palms.

His right hand, when he looked down at it, was still clenched over the blistering-hot Zippo lighter. His forearm was red with gore up to the elbow.

He had done this himself. He, Maksim Volkov. This was his work.

Maksim looked at the pyre. Most of the bodies were tumbled, chaotic, facedown or thrown like dolls into the man-high heap of scrap: it looked as if Maksim had built it out of every piece of wood in the building, every door and window frame and cot and chair. But at the peak of it, laid out cleanly with arms crossed, lay Stepanovich.

As Maksim jolted forward in shock, he knocked against the pyre, and the balance of the loosely piled kindling shifted, sending Stepanovich's body rolling down. Maksim caught him reflexively, smelling the reek of his long illness, seeing the gauntness of his stubbled cheeks.

He had not killed Stepanovich. He remembered that much:

Stepanovich had been taken by the same illness that had taken so many others. Maksim had been holding one of Stepanovich's dry, bony hands in his own while Stepanovich made wordless gasping moans and turned his yellowed eyes upward.

It was the last thing Maksim remembered with any clarity, although he thought maybe someone had offered to pray.

He did not think he had taken the idea with good grace.

He would have taken it now if he could. But his voice had not returned to him yet. And he had to make himself face the fullness of what he had done.

Maksim hefted Stepanovich's body in his arms, carried him a few feet from the pyre, and laid him down. His weight was too slight, eaten away by weeks of sickness; his mouth caved in around jutting teeth. He looked nothing like the Stepanovich who was always talking, always joking, keeping Maksim's temper from rising too high.

Without him, Maksim had barely lasted ten minutes.

Maksim returned to the pyre, digging at the rubbish, flinging planks aside. He found *Starshina* Petrov's body next: face mostly unmarked, eyes unclosed. Gutted. It looked as if Maksim had reached his knife all the way into Petrov's abdominal cavity.

Why Petrov? He had always been kind to Stepanovich, hadn't he? And tactful toward Maksim himself; surely he wouldn't have said or done something to set Maksim off.

Trinkovich was next. Trinkovich had been shot: once in the shoulder and once in the face. Maksim wondered dully why he had used a gun instead of his hands.

He went on unbuilding the pyre, plank by plank. Comrade by comrade. Looked each of them in the face.

Andreev, who had first given Maksim his nickname.

Junior Lieutenant Ushakov, who always carried with him a picture of the two hounds he had left at home in Moscow.

Tretiak, who had a pair of sunglasses he'd said had come from America.

Netevich, who could not grow a beard.

And *Zampolit* Ogorodnik. It was his ear Maksim had been standing on.

When he saw the place he had cut it from, Maksim fell down in the bloody wreckage and lay there for a while. Of course it would have been Ogorodnik he'd killed first. His body was there at the bottom of the heap, and he was the one Maksim had always disliked.

He had probably said something stupid or cruel. Probably while Maksim's hands were still feeling the warmth ebb from Stepanovich's skin.

Probably Maksim had killed him without thinking at all, and the others would have reacted, of course. They tolerated Maksim's nature when he was using it on the *mujahideen,* but they would be duty bound to stop him when he used it on one of their own.

And Maksim must already have been too far gone to do anything but kill again.

He thought this was how it must have been, but he could not know. Maksim was the only one left alive, and he did not remember anything much, and so there was no one to bear witness to his squad's passing. He lay boneless in the dust. Kerosene fumes and the stench of opened bodies surrounded him. He did not move until he felt a warm, slow crawl upon his shoulder. He slapped at the place, thinking it was a fly, and the flare of pain told him instead it was a bullet hole he had not noticed before.

It broke his paralysis. He had a duty to these, his comrades. He should see it through.

He rebuilt the pyre then. Neater this time. He tried at first to close everyone's eyes and lay their hands in place, but he had waited too long and could not. He could not pray, either, his voice still gone from him: when he tried to force it out, he ended up vomiting at the base of the pyre.

He doused everything with more kerosene, which stank. All the doorways were open, since he had torn the doors from them; there was plenty of oxygen to fuel the blaze. He lit the Zippo lighter and tossed it onto the pyre.

The ball of flame was so sudden and hot that he reeled right out one of the open doors into the yard. He tripped backward over nothing and lay where he fell.

The rescue squad found him there, some time later: both eyebrows burned off, bullet holes in his biceps and trapezius. No one imagined it was anything other than an insurgent attack.

Maksim let the medics stitch him up. He thought, while they did so, about Stepanovich, who had died of illness as mortal people often did. He wanted to blame Stepanovich for leaving him or for being his friend in the first place. He was coming out of his madness enough to know those thoughts were mad thoughts.

He thought about how Stepanovich would not have died of illness if Maksim had made him *kin*.

Maksim could have made any of his comrades *kin*. All of them, even. He thought about what he'd done instead.

He did not mind having killed *Zampolit* Ogorodnik, but the others had been good enough comrades. Kind, even. Now that he was less mad, he did not see how it made sense to turn them all into some kind of tribute to Stepanovich instead of letting them go about their lives. Stepanovich would not have appreciated it.

Stepanovich would not have appreciated being made *kin*, either, he saw. Not when being *kin* led to things such as this.

While Maksim was thinking, the medics, careful and clinical in their latex gloves, washed the worst of the blood from him. He had bled enough from his unnoticed injuries that they did not seem to realize not all the blood was his own.

He had bled enough that he was slow and shocky with it, which kept him from doing anything rash right away. He saw the *Starshina* of the rescue squad enter the infirmary tent and come to stand before him, and he heard the man's questions about the *mujahideen,* about their numbers, about the direction from which they had attacked.

He saw that there was no point in answering these questions, even if he had been able to speak. Eventually, the *Starshina* shook his head sadly and departed again, and finally Maksim was alone.

Maksim still had his pistol. He spent a calm half hour sitting on his cot in the infirmary tent with his mouth around the muzzle. As long as the pistol was there, he could think about his options. He did not need to move quickly.

He thought of only one thing that made sense: Iadviga Rozhnata and the promise she'd made him years ago.

Two things that made sense. Iadviga Rozhnata and the pistol.

The pistol tasted salty. After a while, Maksim found that it was because his tears had run into his open mouth. He put the pistol in his pocket, slipped out of the infirmary, and began running north.

MAY 21

◐ WAXING GIBBOUS

Maksim met Gus at the roti shop this time.

"He was here," she said without preamble. She had a beautiful black eye.

"Did I do that to your face?" Maksim asked.

"Forget about it. The guy you're looking for, that's who I'm talking about. Here. In my part of town. Did some damage to some people who probably deserved it. A man I know said it was a young white guy, a stranger, came up the alley and just laid a beating on these other guys. Knew I was looking for a white kid mixing it up with people. Came and told me. I found the place; I'll show you the way."

"Now."

"No, Maks. When I'm done eating. And don't give me that look. You know I can take you, especially these days."

He did know. He was still limping from whatever she'd done to his knee.

He sat in tense silence, rubbing his thigh, while Gus ate her roti and drank unsubtly from a bottle of something in a paper bag.

"You should have something," she said. "It's killing me to watch you."

Maksim accepted a slug from the bottle, which turned out to be Canadian Club.

"I guess you'd prefer vodka," Gus said at his wince of distaste.

"It is only that nothing tastes right."

"Because of what your witch is giving you. Well, it's unnatural. What do you expect? You'd be better off living like me."

"I would not be happy." An understatement. He'd rather die than live like Gus. She did not manage to hang on to anything precious, neither people nor belongings. She said she liked Parkdale, but that couldn't be more than a half truth. He'd always believed she came to this city because in a pinch she could ask Maksim for help, money, a sofa to sleep on.

Gus drained the bottle and led Maksim outside. The alley was not far from where he had met the boy in the first place. "Did he return here because of what happened? Or because he comes here often?" Maksim wondered.

"What happened," Gus said. "It's got to be. He didn't just come and wander around; he came and kicked some ass. He's starting to figure it out. That means he'll probably be back again, even if we can't find him today."

"If he is beginning to understand his nature, we *must* find him today."

But the trail of scent stopped at the Lansdowne subway station.

Maksim, enraged, overturned a newspaper box and kicked the glass in. Gus had to punch him in the ear to get his attention. A bystander shouted that he was calling the police, and the two of them ran away together, Gus laughing breathlessly and Maksim almost sobbing.

"Five more days until I may stop rationing eggs," he said to himself aloud when they slowed in a laneway a kilometer or two on.

"You sure you can make it that long?" Gus asked.

"No."

He sat down against the door of a garage, covering his face. Gus slid down beside him and gently touched his hair. He let her leave her hand there, but the pressure made his scalp crawl as if with lice until his whole body wanted to twitch miserably away; and still he sat unmoving, clenching his teeth.

"Let me take this for you," Gus said.

"If I do not have something to do . . ." Maksim said.

"What are you afraid of? You'll trash some of your stuff?"

Maksim shook off her hand then, shuddering. "Look to yourself, Augusta. Have a care."

She leaned in and scrubbed a rough hand over Maksim's scalp. "You raised me right," she said. "I'm not an idiot."

Maksim slapped her hand away and replaced it with his own, tugging on the short hair at his nape. "God help me, I will agree," he said. "Take it for me. See me home and go hunting without me. I cannot."

"It's okay. It will be okay. Truly, Maks."

He could only shake his head. "God help me."

MAY 24

◑ WAXING GIBBOUS

Hannah was visiting her parents. Jonathan arrived at Nick's place with a guilt gift: two-thirds of a bottle of wine and a tiny foil-wrapped lump of hash.

"That smells amazing," Nick said, turning from the sink.

"You're doing dishes," Jonathan said. "Why are you doing dishes?"

"They were dirty."

"That's new. Not that I'm complaining. I was just wondering if your head injury had more of an effect than we first realized."

"Ass-kisser." Nick angled his face toward the lamp over the stove. "All good. Look. Hardly any scar, even. Pour me something, will you? I'm almost done." He fastidiously rinsed the sink of soapsuds and dried his hands on his cargo shorts. "Tell me you want to go to Parkdale tonight."

"I'm not in the mood for a dive bar, honestly. Maybe one of the new hipster places there."

"I fucking hate hipsters."

"The Cammie, then. Whatever."

"We can start there," Nick said, smiling with teeth.

"Oh, no. It's not going to be one of those nights. I'm too bagged," Jonathan said, thinking of the next morning's classes.

"Sure, the Cammie, then. We'll just have a pint or two on the patio and head back here for a bit. But first . . . you brought me a present."

"I was feeling bad about letting you smoke me up all the time, and then I happened to run into that guy who used to live next to me in the Annex, and look what he was carrying." Jonathan was already crumbling the hash into pellets the size and consistency of mouse droppings. He mingled them with some shreds of tobacco and filled the bowl of Nick's bong.

"Fantastic," Nick said through a held breath, tendrils of smoke escaping from his lips and nose.

"It's kind of strong. Go easy on it."

"I," said Nick, "am not in the mood for going easy."

Jonathan, in the bathroom twenty minutes later, splashed cool water on his face and sipped some from his cupped palms. He was higher than he'd meant to be, high enough that he didn't want to deal with Nick's weirdness, and thought he'd suggest that they stay here and play video games.

He came out to find Nick waiting for him on the other side of the door with a shot glass.

"Take your medicine," Nick said.

Jonathan sipped. "Wild Turkey?"

"Bulleit, idiot. Clearly, it's wasted on you." Nick reached for the glass, so Jonathan dodged him and swallowed the contents.

The taste of it, the burn of it, tripped an old reflex. He had a half-conscious sensation of dropping the reins. "Wouldn't that be nicer with a beer chaser?" he said.

"The Cammie has beer. Get your shit together. I want some air now."

Nick nearly dragged him out of the apartment, while Jonathan dithered and stumbled. "I'm high," he muttered. "Go easy on me."

"I'm not," Nick said. "Not high enough, anyway. Come on."

At the Cameron, the patio was crowded. Nick and Jonathan found a seat by the railing, sandwiched between a table of guys in polo shirts and a table of young women in tube tops.

"I had a great fight," Nick said.

Jonathan hid his face in his nice chilly pint and didn't meet Nick's eyes.

"Some guys were beating on another guy. I stopped them. I felt like a superhero."

"Why were they beating on him?"

Nick shrugged. "Didn't stop to ask."

"Why's it your business, then?"

Nick slammed his palms on the table, causing his pint to rock and splash. "What is it with you? Nothing I do is right for you anymore." His words sounded too loud in the sudden silence that followed the impact of his hands. The girls in tube tops looked over anxiously.

"Dude . . ." said Jonathan.

Nick smacked him playfully on the side of the head. "Give it a rest. For tonight, at least."

"Ow."

"I mean it. We'll talk about something else. Something you can't judge. So. You and Hannah. When are you moving in together?"

"End of summer," Jonathan said after a heroic gulp of pale ale. He signaled the waitress for another round. "She thought it was romantic, actually. How I hadn't asked her, and then it came out in that—never mind. Anyway, we were thinking about how to break it to Hannah's parents, because you know they're kind of a bit conservative."

"Holy Christ. Oh my *God*, dude. You're going to propose *now*?"

"Not yet. I think we need to live together first. I was going to take her mom and dad out for dinner, though. You know. Show them I'm the kind of guy that won't do anything awful to their daughter."

"Except, like, have premarital sex with her."

"Right."

The waitress came with pints and bourbons.

"I thought you wanted a quiet night," Nick said after she'd

gone. He leaned over the table and let his eyes fall half-closed, inhaling the aroma of the bourbon.

"I do want a quiet night," Jonathan said. "And I'm clearly only going to get one if I make you drink yourself stupid. So those are both for you."

Jonathan ended up having one himself, though, of course, and then another. He came back from the bathroom to find Nick had introduced himself to the tube-top girls and bought them a round of some kind of nasty-looking layered shots.

"When was the last time we even had shots? This is stupid," Jonathan said, but he took it, anyway, and shared in the high fives of the girls, who were celebrating a bachelorette.

Then at some point, the girls were gone, and he leaned on the wrought iron patio railing and tried to light the wrong end of his cigarette, which he should not have been smoking in the first place. The guy who'd given it to him seemed to be talking about psychotherapy or something. Jonathan turned his cigarette around and got it to burn properly.

"There you are," Nick said from the other side of the railing. "God! Put that out." He snatched the cigarette from Jonathan's lips. "What a stink."

"You used to like them."

"Only when I was drunk."

"I'm drunk. Right now," Jonathan said, raising his hand. Nick came around the railing and led him away. "Where are we going?"

"Someplace more interesting."

"Don't we have to pay and stuff?"

"I took care of it."

"Are you, like, mad about something?"

"You sound like a girl," Nick said, slowing. He turned to face Jonathan. Under the streetlights, his face looked open and wild.

"I just can't . . . I can't figure you out right now," Jonathan said.

"Nothing to figure. I'm just me. And I'm really, really, *really* tired of getting shit from you."

"Not giving you shit," Jonathan said, spreading his hands. "Really. Can we talk about it tomorrow?"

Nick wrapped his fist in the collar of Jonathan's T-shirt. "No."

Jonathan flailed at Nick's hand. "Let go. What the fuck are you—"

"Trying to get you to shut up," Nick said. His eyes were narrow and dark and too close for Jonathan to focus.

And then they were far away, and the ground was much closer.

Six

◐ WAXING GIBBOUS

Lissa didn't tell Stella about the date until Stella caught her prepping for it, winding her hair up into a crown of braids and dabbing gloss on her lips.

"That's . . . new," Stella said, leaning around Lissa's shoulder to pout in the mirror.

Lissa didn't say anything. In the mirror, she watched the color rise in her face, hot pink and patchy.

"And it's Rafe's night off," Stella said. "Hmm."

"Don't say anything else. Or I'm going to cancel it."

"And punish an innocent man for my nosiness?" Stella said, grinning. She tapped her comb on the careful coil of Lissa's hair. "D'you think that's a bit tightly wound? You don't want to make him think you're tightly wound."

"But I am."

"Okay, I guess you are, a bit. But—"

"Seriously!" Lissa said. "Just be quiet. Quiet!"

Stella doubled over laughing and flung her hair back and

skipped out, calling over her shoulder, "Don't do anything I wouldn't do!"

Lissa had no idea what Stella would or wouldn't do on a date. What was normal on dates, anyway? What was normal in love? How did anyone figure this stuff out?

The last time Lissa remembered having a clue was back in high school, and so many of the things she'd believed then had turned out to be incomplete or untrue or just hopelessly naïve. She believed Crystal Brink had given blow jobs to the entire football team in a single night; she believed true love meant roses and diamonds and waiting until marriage. She believed her mother was a bad wife who hadn't been able to make Dad stay.

None of it gave her any idea of how to get what she wanted from another person or how to figure out what he wanted in return.

She opened by saying as much to Rafe while she twisted her unbound hair around her hand as they sat on the patio at an Italian place on College.

He laughed and shrugged one shoulder. Everything about him was asymmetrical: his body language, one eyebrow higher than the other, that one crooked tooth. "I think it's like that for everyone," he said. "No, really. If we're being honest."

"I just wanted to warn you."

"Warn me," Rafe said. "Huh. Fair enough. I guess I'd better bring my A game."

"'A game'? What does that even mean?"

Rafe spread his hands. "Sorry. Sorry. It's just . . . I guess you don't know this, but honestly, everyone pretty much has to start at square one every time. That's part of the fun. Finding out what the other person likes and whether you'll, you know, fit together."

"And if you don't?"

"Well, then you go your separate ways. No hard feelings."

"That sounds really . . . not as bad as I was expecting."

"Oh, there's hard stuff, sometimes," Rafe said, a bit of the cheer dimming in his face. "Let's not do it that way, though. Okay? Deal?"

"Deal, I guess." They toasted: Lissa had a very pale pinot grigio, and Rafe had something called barbera, meaty red, tinting the glass.

"So what goes on in the world of printing?" Rafe said. "Stella tells me that's what you do."

"It's a job," Lissa said. "It's a paying-the-bills kind of job. It's not what I do."

"Bartending's what I do," Rafe said. "I guess I'd better get that right out there. I like it, and it likes me. I'm not saving to go back to school or anything. I'm a lifer at this."

Lissa thought of how he looked behind the bar—that cheery quirk to his face, the easy movement from tap to cash to refrigerator—and felt an answering cheer come to her own expression. "I could tell," she said. "You're a natural, right?"

"If only you could tell that to my da," Rafe said. "Wanted a surgeon. Would've settled for something else as long as it came with a Bentley and a really nice flat."

So this was what people did on dates, Lissa thought—talked about their families and the things they were and weren't and the things they knew and didn't know. She didn't think she'd ever had a conversation quite like this. With Stella, a bit, but she'd thought Stella was one of those people who would talk about everything. Before that, Lissa's normal was a lifetime of Baba and her meditative silences and the long evenings she spent reading her grimoires while Lissa did homework or wrote letters to Dad, which would rarely be answered.

Talk. She soaked it up. Rafe's voice, a bit hoarse; his accent, which she was beginning to realize was upper class, veering into broader dialect for effect. Once in a while, he started to wind down and she had to ask him a question, and then he'd wind up again, his hands rising, touching his glass or his toque. Or her hand.

She agreed to a second glass of wine and then a cup of tea, and the tea was what she tasted on his mouth, under the black walnut tree at her front walk, where they said good night.

MAY 25

○ FULL MOON

Nick got all the way up the steps of the Greyhound before realizing what a terrible idea he'd had.

The smells of people and air freshener throttled him, the smells of McDonald's fries and Cheetos and the prickly upholstery on all the seats. Blindly, he turned and shouldered his way back down past the other people trying to board the bus. He stumbled through the line and out onto Elizabeth Street, where he found a piss-stained wall to lean against while he squeezed his eyes shut and put his hands over them for a minute.

Three million people in this sprawling city, and just now they felt like three million bricks in a very high wall. He could not travel in this state or ride a bus or a train. And he couldn't fly.

He could drive, maybe, but he did not have enough cash at hand to rent a car, especially now that he'd bought the bus ticket. If he used his line of credit or his Visa, they'd be able to find him.

The police. The police would be able to find him. No point in refusing to think of the word, like a child afraid of monsters. Police.

Jerkily, Nick shouldered his pack and began walking south.

The morning grew brighter and hotter. A cop car passed him on Yonge, and he ducked his head a little so that his cap would shade his face. The cap was of the John Deere trucker variety, with the synthetic mesh and the plastic snap band at the back.

He'd found it in an alley last night while he was running. It was not very clean, but at least it had been rained upon.

He could not walk through Nathan Phillips Square. Instead, he went into the alleys again, this time on the south side of Queen. He knew where he was going now: the place in Parkdale. He had beaten two men there, and no one had noticed or cared.

Parkdale had had a bad name for a long time, though lately it had begun to gentrify. Jonathan used to like to flirt with the badness, back when he still had his edge, the way some of Nick's high school buddies had been into butterfly knives. Until lately, Nick hadn't quite believed there was anything to it. Until a month ago, when the place had somehow possessed him. Did places have spirits? Evil, violent, craving spirits? How did other people live there? Nick had seen mothers there, nice people, pushing babies in strollers, buying coconut juice, checking out romances from the library.

Maybe they were not nice. Maybe they didn't return the romances by the due date. Maybe they shook their babies.

Maybe it was just Nick.

Just Nick, alone now, on the crazy train.

He bit down on his knuckles until his teeth parted the flesh; he told himself to stop, but his hand kept rising back to his mouth, and his tongue kept worrying at the gash there and liking the taste of the blood.

Something was different, new and nightmarish, rising up through the broken rind of Nick's old self. Like those ants on the nature show with David Attenborough, the husks of them standing still, hollowed out, transfixed by massive fungal eruptions from the centers of their skulls. If ants had skulls.

If Parkdale was infected, where was the chancre? Where was the cholera-tainted well? Was it the sports bar? The alley behind it?

Was it the man in the low-brimmed cap, all solicitous until he pressed his tongue into Nick's open cut?

Was it Nick himself, or even Jonathan, coming back around, buying shots, looking for a fight?

When had the world gone so weird? Why hadn't he noticed before now?

MAY 25

○ FULL MOON

Someone was holding Jonathan's hand. Hannah. Hannah was holding his hand.

"Do you want to get married?" he asked her. His voice came out a bit funny.

Hannah made a sobbing sound. "It's good to see you too."

"I think I have a hangover," he said.

"You have a concussion," Hannah said. "You're in the hospital. Do you remember what happened?"

Jonathan propped himself up on his elbows and looked around. The hospital: he was surprised he hadn't noticed before, but here it was, all white and baby blue, with curtains around his bed and the smell of latex and the noise of monitors and other people beyond.

"What happened?" he asked.

"I was hoping you'd be able to tell me that."

"Nope."

"You were out with Nick. Do you remember that?"

"Oh. Yeah. I went to his place. I think we were going to play video games."

"You were found alone, lying by the wall of a garage on Brunswick Avenue."

Jonathan thought about this hard enough to make his head hurt. "Is Nick okay?"

Hannah bit her lip. "He wasn't with you."

"Nick wouldn't ditch me."

"If he was confused, maybe. If he was drunk or something."

"If I was being a dick to him, maybe. Give me my phone?"

"I've already called him a few times. He's not picking up."

"Well, call the police, then!" Jonathan said, pushing himself up. "What if the muggers got him?"

Hannah put both hands on his shoulders and leaned in close, pushing him back down. "You weren't mugged," she said very quietly. "You still have all your stuff. Even the cash in your wallet."

Jonathan blinked. "I'm too stupid right now. I know you're trying to tell me something, and I can't figure it out."

Hannah whispered, "I think he might have hurt you. And I know I'm not a nice person for thinking that. Only he hasn't been himself lately, and . . . and if it was him, I don't want to be the one who calls it in."

Jonathan pressed his palm to his aching head. "I don't fucking know."

"Can we just wait?"

"I think I'm going to be sick," Jonathan said.

Hannah handed him a kidney-shaped dish.

"Give me a moment?" he said, and she pressed her lips together but withdrew beyond the curtain.

MAY 25

◯ FULL MOON

Stella solved the full-moon problem herself, inadvertently, by calling up a friend she'd met while backpacking in Australia. The friend lived in Barrie, conveniently a half hour away by train, and she invited Stella overnight. It only remained for Lissa to steer her stepsister toward the correct day.

The house felt huge and echoing the moment she left, but Lissa spent no more than a moment standing before the screen door; after that, she began pulling out her spell equipment from the places she'd stashed it, checking all the while for the moment the sun would set.

She had just begun taking eggs from the refrigerator when the doorbell rang. She could see Maksim's head through the glass, face shadowed by his cap, looking away.

He stood awkwardly, weight canted to one side, and when she opened the door, he seized its edge.

"I can go away if I am not wanted," he said. "I hoped since the moon is full . . ."

"Stella's out tonight. You can come in."

"Thank you, *koldun'ia*."

He followed her into the kitchen and settled carefully on the same stool as before. He bowed his head and folded his hands together. The two fingers still looked bruised, and Lissa could see fresh marks across some of the knuckles.

"I'm making extra tonight," Lissa assured him. "The last week hasn't been easy on you, has it?"

He shook his head.

"Did your friend find anything?"

"The boy was sighted in Parkdale, near where I first found him. We tracked him as far as the subway, but that was all." Maksim hunched one shoulder and winced, but Lissa couldn't tell if it was at a memory or at a physical pain. "Did you?" he asked.

"You mean, did I find anything? About Baba's spell?" Lissa turned away to shut off the electricity and light the candles. She'd thought about it a number of times in the past week and had changed her conclusion each time. "Some," was what she said now. "Maksim . . . I think it was against the law. Our witches' *Law*, I mean."

He looked up sharply from beneath his cap.

"It's not any of the regular spells. I've figured out that much for sure," Lissa went on. "For one thing, all the regular ones are impermanent—you have to take frequent doses. They're almost all in fresh eggs, like the ones I give you. For more permanent spells, you have to do other things. Bindings with blood or hair. Sometimes there are eggs in those too. Ever hear the story of Koshchei the Deathless, who hid his life in an egg?"

"Koshchei the Deathless," Maksim said, pronouncing it in a way that let Lissa know she hadn't quite got it right. "I remember."

"Well, he was evil," Lissa said. "And eventually, some prince broke the egg, and then he wasn't deathless anymore. The point is, there's a price for the kind of magic that pushes natural laws too far. Until now, I believed my grandmother always followed the rules. I know she wouldn't have broken them unless it meant a lot to her."

"She owed me a great debt," Maksim said, raising his brows. "Perhaps it was great enough to cover such a thing." He slid off the stool and paced unevenly across the kitchen, still favoring one leg. "I did not know what I asked of her, though."

"To tell the truth, I don't know, either. I mean, I know there's a price, whether or not you get caught; but it depends on what you've done, and I still haven't figured out all of it."

"She was good," Maksim said, pacing back. "A good person."

"I know."

"I do not like to drag good people into my dealings."

Lissa sighed. "D'you think she would have done it, whatever it was, if it was really bad?"

Maksim pressed a fist against his forehead over the brim of his cap. He went to the window, where his breath troubled a candle flame. "I wish I could think. I wish I could sleep."

"You will once the eggs are done. Want a drink or anything? I'm ready to get started."

All Lissa could find in the cupboard was gin, but Maksim accepted it gratefully, and he sat on the floor in the corner with his bad leg outstretched while Lissa began her work.

She didn't have milk from a human mother this time; it wasn't the kind of thing you could just pick up. Instead, she substituted fresh, unpasteurized goat's milk from the Tuesday night farmers' market, where she'd managed to converse with the farmer while Stella lingered over a selection of honeycombs. She worked quickly, consulting the grimoire, determined to get it this time. The memory of last month's imperfect working was still fresh. If anything, this time her concentration was aided by the presence of Maksim, who trusted her. He made no sound except for the occasional breath and the tilt of liquid in glass.

Sometime after midnight, he rose quietly and left the room. Lissa barely noticed. She was finger-painting eggs by then, hastily, for the power in the mixture only lasted the length of the night it was brewed, and there were quite a few eggs to get through.

The front door opened and closed.

Two hours later, or thereabouts, it opened and closed again, but Maksim did not return to the kitchen. He went upstairs and turned on the water.

The next time Lissa thought of him, she was closing the last carton. The mixing bowl was empty but for a few lavender smears, and she set it in the sink, too tired to wash up. When she turned on the tap to rinse it, the water pressure was low, and it came to her that she could hear the shower still going upstairs. She thought it had been running for a long time.

She took the final carton in her hands as she hurried upstairs.

The bathroom door stood ajar an inch. She knocked and pushed it farther inward. The air from the room felt strangely chilly.

"Maksim?"

A shuddering, indrawn breath; in the near-darkness, Lissa could see the pale shower curtain shifting in the breeze from the open door.

"Maksim? Are you okay? The eggs are done."

"*Koldun'ia,*" he said. "Thank God." He drew the curtain back. He sat in the bathtub, fully clothed, visible by the white T-shirt pasted to him like papier-mâché. Water broke on his head, his shoulders, sending chilly spray all the way to where Lissa stood.

Maksim leaned out from the water, reaching.

"Turn that off," she said, and he did. "Aren't you freezing?"

He nodded. He beckoned. Lissa gave him the egg carton.

"Shouldn't you get yourself dry?"

Maksim cracked two eggs in quick succession and sucked them from the shells. "Thank you," he said, slouching back against the shower wall.

"You're shivering, Maksim."

"I think you turned off the hot water," he said, closing his eyes. His mouth fell open, and his hand relaxed, letting the eggshells fall.

The eggs had turned out stronger, then. That was a relief, even if it did present her with a new problem.

"Don't go to sleep there. I mean it. Come on, that's it. Eyes open."

Lissa went to fetch him a towel and herself a candle to see by.

She came back to find Maksim out of the shower, hunched on the bath mat, with his T-shirt off and his arms wrapped around his knees. Water puddled from the cuffs of his jeans. Eggshell fragments decorated the top of one foot.

Lissa draped the towel over his shoulders. "I don't have any pants for you."

He made no move to hang on to the towel, which slipped off one shoulder.

"God," Lissa said. "How do you survive in the wild?"

"It is easier when there is a war," he murmured. "No one notices the things I do."

With some assistance from the towel rack, Maksim managed to get to his feet.

"Can you handle the stairs?"

He shook his head and leaned over into the wall.

Lissa gritted her teeth. Why hadn't she thought to warn him to start with a single egg? "This way," she said, and she led him toward her own room.

Maksim limped and shuffled and left a trail of water on the hallway carpet. Lissa helped him to prop himself against the door frame, and she gathered up her pillow and sleepwear and hairbrush.

"The bed's there," she said. "Take off your wet pants before you get in it, or so help me, I'll . . . I don't know, I'll do something witchy to you. I'm too damned tired for this. Next time, you're putting yourself to bed. Somewhere else."

"I am sorry," he whispered. "I am a sorry creature." He pressed his fist to his forehead. His eyelids were swollen.

"Stella's coming back on the two o'clock train. If you're not up by eleven, I'm going to wake you. And you're going to help me tidy the house."

He nodded again and twitched a hand at her.

Lissa left him and went to the bathroom, where the floor was awash in cold water and Maksim's T-shirt lay in a sodden grayish wad in the bottom of the tub.

She did nothing with it. She brushed her teeth and went downstairs to put the fresh cartons of eggs in the refrigerator, and finally, she could retreat to the front room and drop into the armchair by the window.

The doll, in its wrap within her bag, looked like its hair was getting a little matted, but the eyes still worked; they blinked open and shut when she took it out and set it upon the windowsill.

She offered it a crumbled slice of heavy rye bread and a pinch of salt.

By the white rider of dawn, by the red rider of day, by the black rider of night, I call to you: Iadviga Rozhnata, your scion desires your counsel.

"I've had a month to think about it this time," Lissa said. "I won't ask anything stupid."

"*Vnuchka*, you have never been stupid," Baba said from wherever she was: cold and old and far.

"What are the *kin*? It's nothing to do with our family at all, is it?"

"Cursed with a hunger for violence. Blessed with long and hale lives," Baba said.

Lissa waited, but this seemed to be the whole of the answer.

"Are they evil?" she asked next.

"Are you?" Baba said.

"Come on," Lissa said after a moment. "That can't be all you have to say about evil. Evil's a big topic."

"You might answer my question for yourself and see what comes of it," Baba said.

"Fine. Okay. I'm not evil by nature. I guess that means the *kin* aren't, either. But the way Maksim's acting about this guy—the guy he might have, whatever it is, infected? He seems to think it's the end of the guy's life. If being *kin* isn't evil, why is it such a bad thing—never mind. Don't answer that! That's not my question!"

Baba laughed. The laugh was not comfortable. Lissa physically cringed from it, in fact, and shivered in the warm night air.

"What new-moon ritual did you do for him?" she blurted. "I'm sure you did. He needs it again. It went away when you . . . when you . . ."

"When I died," Baba said. "I am sorry I could not make it permanent. I liked to see him happy."

"Then tell me what you did to make him that way."

So Baba told her. Lissa wrote it all down in the faint light from the window: egg, ink, black wax, rusty nail. Spit. Blood. Three nights leading up to the new moon. The words she must speak, and the shapes she must inscribe upon the shell of the egg.

"Place it within a casket, and bury it where it will not be disturbed," Baba finished. "But—"

"But?" Lissa said. "I know this one's against the rules. What's the price?"

The price counted as a separate question, apparently. Baba did not answer, and the place in Lissa's brain was comfortless and empty once more.

Lissa folded up her notebook and placed it and the doll back in her bag. She turned the power back on, listening to the refrigerator hum to life, but she didn't bother to switch on any lights, using the candle to light her way back to the front room. She did not want to lie on the sofa, which was Stella's bed, still. Instead, she sat in her chair again, sliding down a bit against the cushions.

By the time her eyes fell shut, the room was gray with dawn, the birds outside had begun to chat, and the air was already warm. She turned her face against the high chair back and covered her eyes with the tumbled mass of her hair.

MAY 26

◐ WANING GIBBOUS

"There's a gin bottle on the front steps," Stella sang out. "Oh! And you're in the armchair. You haven't been on a *bender*, have you, Lissa?"

Lissa rubbed her eyes. They felt crusted and swollen. "What time is it?"

"Ten," said Stella. "I know—ungodly, right? I've had a ghastly night, and I escaped as soon as I possibly could. And I want to know about *your* night."

Lissa sat up slowly. She could think of nothing at all to say.

"Bit the worse for wear?" Stella said. "I'll make some coffee, and you can tell me all about it. And you *will* tell me."

Lissa stumbled after her into the kitchen. The eggs and the grimoire she had put away, but the lavender-stained mixing bowl rested in the sink, with an inch of scummy water in it, and the shoe box of baby-food jars sat in plain sight beside the refrigerator.

"Cooking up a frenzy, I see," was all Stella said as she bustled about, putting on the kettle and measuring coffee into the grinder. "I've just had the unforgettable experience of seeing an entire high school football team share a bad acid trip," she confided. "One of them was a bit sweet and told me he was gay and he'd never come out to anyone before. The others were animals."

"What brought this on?"

"Anne's sister is a cheerleader," Stella said. "Anne told me their parents were out of town. She didn't happen to mention there was a party on. Good God, your Canadian kids can drink."

"Can they?" Lissa said.

Stella paused at the stove. "Are you all right? You look a bit peaky."

"I didn't sleep well."

"Might have something to do with being in the armchair."

While Stella fussed with the coffee, Lissa had a few minutes to think of what to say to her and how to either explain Maksim away or, preferably, get rid of him completely, eggs and all, before he could invite unwelcome questions.

But the scent of brewing dark roast undid all that. Before Lissa had anything like a reasonable idea, she heard the floorboards creak upstairs, and Maksim shambled into the kitchen, shirtless and scarred and clothed in still-damp jeans.

He stopped when he caught sight of Stella. "I smelled coffee," he said apologetically. "I will go now."

Lissa sighed. "Now that you're up, you might as well stay for breakfast. Stella, this is Maksim Volkov. Maksim, my stepsister, Stella. Be very polite to her, or I'll make your life hell somehow."

"My life is already hell somehow," Maksim said, unsmiling.

"It's a pleasure to finally meet one of Lissa's friends," Stella said, extending her hand. "How do you know each other?"

"Church—" Lissa began.

"I knew *koldun'ia* Iadviga," Maksim said and shook his head. "And somehow, I think I have not said until just now how sorry I am for your loss."

Lissa dissolved into unexpected tears, groped wildly for a napkin, and spilled her coffee all over the table.

By the time Lissa had located the napkin, smoothed her damp hair back from her face, and wiped up the coffee, Maksim was gone, and with him, two cartons of eggs from the refrigerator, although the wet T-shirt still lay in the bathtub.

Stella had made herself scarce when the crying started. Lissa found her in the front room, hunched over her phone.

"Your friend owns a boxing gym?" she said. "Now I know why he looks like *that*. Wow."

"Were you just . . ."

"Googling him? Yep. Haven't you? Or . . . maybe you're just not curious." Stella rolled her eyes. "I know, I know. He's too old for me, right?"

Lissa choked on a hysterical laugh. "Definitely."

"What about you? Is he your lifelong crush or something? Is that why you've been taking it so slow with Rafe? No, you didn't look at him like that—and he said that thing about your grandmother . . . okay, no, wait . . . I know! Russian Mafia! What's it called again? That's why you didn't want me to meet him—and come on, boxing and organized crime always go together."

"Russian Mafia?" Lissa said. "Seriously?"

"Okay, you don't have to make me feel mental just because I don't know about organized crime. Just tell me."

"He's . . ." Lissa said.

She swallowed. Whatever she said now, Stella would remember it. There was no getting rid of Stella; it was too late for that. Maybe out of the house, maybe even out of Canada for the moment, but not forever. Lissa was going to be on the hook for this lie for the rest of her life.

She had already waited too long.

"So it's not organized crime," Stella said. "But it's something old country, definitely. Wait—let me think. Dad used to rant a bit about your grandmother and her superstitions and how it wasn't right to bring up a child that way. Is it something to do with that?"

Lissa nodded.

"So I'm warm. When did your grandmother come over to Canada?"

"She escaped from the Gulag," Lissa said. "I can't remember what year exactly."

"So he can't have known her then. There's no way he's more

than forty, right? Whatever . . . that's all beside the point, isn't it? What I really want to know is why is he here *now*."

"He's dangerous," Lissa said. "I mean it. I don't want you Googling him, I don't want you thinking about him, I don't even want you to answer the door if he shows up when I'm not here."

"And yet you let him stay overnight," Stella said, brows high. "Forgive me, dear sister, but you are completely full of shit."

"I'm serious."

"I can see from your face that you are," Stella said. "That doesn't mean I'm wrong."

"You don't understand."

"Of course I don't, since you won't tell me. I'm going to let him in," she said. "I'm going to *invite* him in, and I'm going to give him the third degree until I figure out what's going on here."

"Two weeks' notice," Lissa blurted.

"No fair. That's the nuclear option."

Lissa deflated.

"Coward," Stella said, perfectly calm. "You know where to find me when you're ready to chat. Until then, I'm going for a pedicure."

"Again?"

"They don't last forever. I'm on my feet all day, you know."

And she left the house in a haughty swirl of scent, and Lissa moved slowly to clean up the kitchen, as tired as she could remember being in her life.

MAY 26

◖ WANING GIBBOUS

Maksim limped homeward, two egg cartons under his arm. The sun felt uncomfortably hot on his shoulders; after a long, blinking moment of thought, he understood that it was because he had no shirt.

He didn't remember where he had left his shirt. At the witch's house, no doubt. He did not want to go back there. That house was so oppressively still. Though he thought he remembered it being even more so when *koldun'ia* Iadviga had been alive.

The first time he'd visited it had been in the early eighties. He'd come straight from Afghanistan. Traces of blood still under his fingernails. Three days awake, trying not to dream about the thing he'd done. Three days of travel among crowds of civilians. He wore a sore into his inner cheek with his teeth.

He hadn't seen Canada before; didn't see it now. He took a taxi from the airport, because he didn't know the way and it would be faster; he made the driver roll down all the windows, and he sat quite still with the harsh air beating on him, and he pressed his fingers to his eyes until the driver stopped the car.

Maksim did not see the house right away. What he saw was Iadviga Rozhnata on the front steps. Iadviga Rozhnata, no longer young.

She smelled familiar: a smell like thunderstorms, which he knew was the smell of witchcraft. But the bright hair was all gone gray, and the limber carriage slumped and rigid under the burden of nearly thirty years. She folded her arms and did not smile.

Maksim stood at a safe distance on the walk, twisting his fists into the canvas of his kit bag. "You made me a promise."

"There is no place for you here," she said.

"You made me a promise," he repeated.

"I did not think you would come."

Maksim felt the winter cold then as he had not in years. He missed his gun very much; he had thrown it away before leaving Afghanistan, and in the rush to get here, he had not yet tried to find another.

"*Koldun'ia . . .*" he said and paused. Even if he had his gun, he could not shoot himself right here, in front of a person who'd been kind to him once. And there was the matter of how to keep people away from his blood.

He would have to go somewhere else and get money and buy a new gun and then find an empty field.

The thought was so exhausting that he dropped his kit bag and wept. He stood on Iadviga's front walk with tears dripping from his nose and chin.

The taxi driver shouted in English, and Maksim had forgotten the words to respond. He only stood and watched, and finally Iadviga paid the man and took Maksim by the arm into the house.

"My daughter and her husband live here too. I will send them away," she said. "It will be three days. You are right: I made you a promise."

She sent him to rest in the garden shed while she made her arrangements. He did sleep a little, but his nightmares woke him; mostly he sat in the dim, cold mustiness and ran the point of a rusted screw around his cuticles to scrape away the blood traces. When the daughter and son-in-law were no longer present, he was allowed to come inside and shower and finally, properly, wash his hands.

Two days later, he received the enchantment. Iadviga, fatigued, hair slipping in strings from her crown of braids, said words over a black-shelled egg. She set the egg in a stone bowl and had Maksim spit upon it and smear it with a drop of his blood.

Maksim didn't know what it meant, but it worked. He felt the restless fury of the *kin* spirit subdued, as smoothly as a gas flame shrinks when the stove is turned down. It was still there, burning, but low and blue and not the searing thing it had been. It would not goad him into doing things like he'd done in Afghanistan.

It would let him walk among people again, people who were not soldiers. It would let him swallow down the desire to hurt, to hunt, to rend.

Without that desire, he was not a person, yet, exactly; he did not know what he liked or what he could do, apart from violence. He would have some time to find out, though.

Now, nearly thirty years later, Maksim paused on a street corner, remembering the recently departed weight of Iadviga's spell. Not as heavy or slow or horrible as these eggs. Under it, he had been able to read books and enjoy food and spar with DeShaun. Yet he had often thought of himself as a golem of clay. Cold and inhuman and slower than he should have been.

And this was what he would be asking *koldun'ia* Lissa to do to him once again.

He would miss the molten heat of his nature.

He sighed, tucked the egg cartons closer to his chest, and began limping across the street.

From his left, a sense of bright motion, a flash of sun on glass.

He half turned. Something lifted him up and threw him down again, far and hard.

He couldn't catch his breath. Shells and yolks everywhere. And blood. He trailed a hand through the mess, tried to sit up, and went to sleep.

Seven

◐ WANING GIBBOUS

Nick smelled the woman coming: she wore the essence of Parkdale distilled. Meat and sweat and blood and bourbon, old cloth
and curry, and a whiff of gasoline.

"I haven't got any change," he said, not looking up.

"Welcome to the life," she said: crisp and wry, a bit foreign-
sounding. "You don't look as if you're enjoying it so far."

Now he did look. The woman was older than Nick but not
quite middle-aged. Kind of butch-looking, with a fading black eye.
She was clearly the kind of person who had lived in the area awhile.

"I can help you," she said, and then she laughed. "That's an
outright lie. I can't even help myself, mostly. But I can take you to
someone who can."

"I'm not . . ." *A homeless person,* he was going to say. But he
was a homeless person, unless he wanted to go back to his apartment to wait for the cops.

"Don't you want to know what you are?" the woman asked.

"Crazy. I think I'm crazy. To be honest."

She squatted down beside him and nudged him companionably with her shoulder. "You're not normal anymore. That's right. But your life isn't over. Not for a long time yet."

When Nick said nothing, the woman stood up again. "The way forward is with me. And I don't much care if you don't want to come. You'll come regardless."

Nick raised his eyebrows.

The woman picked him up by his hair and shoved his face into the wall. "I'm bigger than you, and I'm a bit of a bully."

Nick started to struggle away, and the woman shoved his face into the wall again, harder this time. It sent a starburst through Nick's head, so that he slumped from her grip like a kitten in its mother's mouth.

"What have you figured out so far?" the woman asked.

"Ow," Nick said. "I don't know what you want me to say. Fuck."

"About yourself," she said. "What have you observed?"

"You sound like a drill sergeant," Nick said.

"You've clearly never joined an army," said the woman, and she mashed him into the wall again.

"Okay, okay, okay. I'm . . . this is going to sound really stupid."

"I've heard it all," the woman said, and the utter flatness of her voice made Nick believe her.

"I have superstrength," Nick said and waited for another blow. Nothing happened.

"I . . ." Nick said. "I told you I think I'm going crazy, right?"

The woman nodded.

"That's pretty much it," Nick admitted. "Oh, and I can smell better."

"What can you smell right now?"

"Booze," Nick said.

The woman laughed a little. "How's your head feeling? Ready to walk?"

"You haven't told me anything."

"Fair enough," the woman said. "You're right about all that, and also, you're going to have a very long life. Me? Couple of hundred years and counting. And since you're not going to die of age, you're going to die by violence."

"But . . . not right away, right?" Nick said, flinching.

"Depends on how smart you are."

"Not as smart as I should be," Nick said. "Can you, like, let me up now?"

The woman stood him on his feet again and brushed grit off his cheek. "Don't worry. You'll be much tougher in a few more weeks, once it's had a chance to sink in. I think I took a full year to hit my stride."

"So you're crazy too?" Nick said.

"I'm Gus," said the woman. "I'm one of the nicest people you're going to know from now on."

"I'm not nice," Nick blurted. "I think I'm a bad kind of crazy. I hurt someone. I don't know if he's going to make it."

Gus sighed. "You loved him, didn't you? That never goes well."

"No! I mean . . . he's my friend. My best friend."

"We don't get to have friends," Gus said, unsmiling. "We don't get to have family. We get to have each other, once in a while, although it's hard to spend much time together. I hope you're the kind of kid who doesn't like your mother much."

"I don't know. She's okay. Oh my God, what am I going to say to her?"

"Nothing," Gus said. "Not now. In a few more weeks, you'll start to figure out what comes next."

"Jail," Nick said. "If they find me."

"I don't recommend it," Gus said.

She led him up out of Parkdale and over toward Bellwoods.

"I like walking and everything," Nick said, "but how far are we going?"

"That doesn't matter," Gus said. "What matters is whether you can conduct yourself properly on a streetcar."

Nick shook his head. "I tried the bus. It wasn't good."

"Would you believe I still have problems with transit?"

"No one likes transit," Nick said. "That's not that crazy."

Gus rolled her eyes. Nick couldn't even see her face, following slightly behind her, but he could see the eye roll in the set of her shoulders and head.

He followed, anyway, up through the park and onto Dundas and into the entryway of a converted Victorian, while Gus told him some unbelievable shit about Maksim Volkov and herself and what they'd done, what they were.

"You wait here," Gus said, stiff-arming Nick into the wall. "We don't enter each other's places without a very sincere invitation."

He dumped his pack on the floor and sat upon it. Gus climbed the stairs. She moved like a young woman, he thought, energetic and sturdy—and caught himself, because by her own account, Augusta Hillyard was two centuries old.

Crazy. No two ways about it.

He knew it, and at the same time, he could do nothing but play along with her, with himself, with the day as it unfolded. This level of craziness was so complete and well knit that he didn't have any idea how to begin unraveling it, short of checking himself into the hospital, which never seemed to go well for anyone.

For the tenth time that day, Nick thumbed his phone open without turning it on and then snapped it shut again and stuffed it back in his pocket.

He could smell himself: sweat and booze, the dirt of two

nights outdoors without a change of clothes. He could smell Gus and the reek of Parkdale. He could smell someone else, the person who lived upstairs: familiar and somehow *good*. He'd put things together enough to figure out that it was probably the guy who had put his mouth on him the night he was mugged.

He couldn't hear much, though; no more than before. Apparently, it was only smell that got superpowered. And strength. And temper.

Nick shot to his feet, turned about, paced the cramped hallway. Being told to stay like a dog. Why did she think that was okay?

She wasn't in any hurry to come back, either. He couldn't hear anything at all from upstairs—no footsteps, no voices.

He sat down and kicked the opposite wall a few times, getting comfortable only to thrust himself up again.

At last he swore under his breath and jogged up the stairs and through the open door of the apartment.

It was a nice apartment. Not what he'd have expected, except for the weapons on the walls.

Then he saw the bedroom.

"Did someone break in?" he called to Gus, who knelt beside the bed.

"Nah. He did this himself," she said.

"Oh. All his books." Nick came in and stood in the litter of torn paper and broken spines.

"He's going to be really sorry about that when he gets back," Gus said. She turned away from Nick and rubbed her face. "And he's going to be even sorrier that he gave me a key, if I don't get the hell out of here. Come on."

She wrapped a fist around Nick's wrist and pulled him from the apartment and back downstairs. "Leave your shit there. No one will bother it. Got any money?"

"Thirty bucks?" Nick guessed.

"That's a start. We've got some drinking to do."

She didn't lead him to a bar. Instead, she headed for the liquor store farther down Dundas, where she loaded a basket with as much cheap whiskey as Nick's money would cover.

"I think he thought we were street people," Nick muttered as he followed her out of the store.

"I kind of am," Gus said. "So are you, now, right? You get used to it. I have an apartment, but I like being outdoors better."

"We could go there."

"No, we couldn't. I'd kill you in a couple of hours if I have to share my four walls with you."

"Have you ever killed someone?" Nick said, swallowing.

Gus glanced over her shoulder at him, expressionless. "Yes."

She took him to Trinity Bellwoods. They sat on a bench under a great spreading tree. Gus uncapped the first of the bottles, and Nick could see her throat working as she drank very deeply.

He edged away a little.

Gus passed him the bottle, wiping the mouth of it on her sleeve, which did not make Nick feel any better about its sanitary qualities.

He drank anyway, though, shuddering. "Does this really help? Or are you an alcoholic?"

"Both," she said with a wide, mirthless smile. "It keeps me calm. Calmer. As long as I don't let myself get too sober."

"Will I have to be an alcoholic too?"

"Aren't you already?"

Nick shrugged. "I figured I'd slow down when I got older."

"We don't," Gus said. "Slow down, I mean. It's as bad as ever. We just learn tricks to keep ourselves amused."

"Eternal life as a rubbie," Nick said. "Doesn't sound like a great deal. This other guy, though—Maksim Volkov—he seems like he has his shit together. His place seemed nice, except for what he did to the books. How'd he manage that if he's like you—us?"

"A witch," Gus said. "It's unnatural."

"Coming from the two-hundred-year-old person, that's kind of funny."

"You won't think it's so funny when you meet Maksim. You'll see why I've not made his bargain."

"Why did he, then, if it's not a good bargain?"

She would not answer that. When Nick pressed her, she turned to him with her gray eyes intent in her weathered face, and said, very low, "I'm not drunk yet, and you're not *kin* enough to fight me. So be quiet. Please."

Nick opened his mouth.

Gus shoved the bottle in it and poured whiskey into Nick while he spluttered. She held him down as if she were bathing a cat.

When she let him up, Nick coughed and gagged and somehow managed to keep from spewing whiskey all over his shirt.

"I wonder why he did not just kill you," Gus said quite seriously.

Nick shrank against the bench seat, wiped his streaming eyes, and thought about bolting.

But Gus smiled and slapped him on the arm and said, "You're Greek, right?"

He nodded.

"I was in Greece during the first Balkan War," she said and laughed. "I was on the Turkish side, though."

"I didn't know women fought in that war."

"Women fight in every war," Gus said. "Men don't always notice."

She was quiet for a while. Nick held still.

"It's something we can do," Gus said. "Remember that if you need it. Join the Légion Étrangère or the nearest available substitute. *Vive la mort, vive la guerre.*"

"This is crazy," Nick said for the fiftieth time, and, helplessly, he began to cry.

"Hey," said Gus. "Hey. Here, wipe your face. You don't want to look all messed up in front of the witch."

"We're going to see her?"

"We're going to see her. As soon as I think I can do it without hitting her."

MAY 26

◖ WANING GIBBOUS

Saint Joseph's Hospital. Lissa stood just within the doors, struck hard by the memory of Baba on the gurney with her face slack and the blood already pooling in her veins.

If she had been home a few hours earlier, that day a month ago, she might have come in through those doors with a baba who was still living. Might have been able to say a real good-bye. Might even have seized a few more months for Baba. A few more years.

A family came in behind her, and she stumbled out of the way, shaking her head. She dug into her bag, closed her hand around the doll within its wrapping of scarf, and went to the admission desk.

They made her wait for thirty minutes, but finally a nurse took her through into the emergency ward, past rows of curtained cubicles and a few beds parked in the hall. A boy in a wheelchair spun himself in bored circles. A woman wept quietly.

"Mr. Volkov's almost ready to go," the nurse said. "You've brought him a change of clothes?"

She drew back a curtain. Lissa stopped short.

"They told me you'd been in an accident," she said.

Maksim smiled sleepily with the side of his face that was not scuffed raw. "I walked in front of a truck," he said.

"On purpose?" Lissa said.

Maksim laughed as if Lissa had been joking. He pushed back the coverlet. "My clothes?"

Lissa was going to ask what had happened to his others, but she could see the answer: deep scrapes marked the entire right side of his body that she could see around the hospital gown, all the way down below his knee. His right wrist was in plaster, and his hand bandaged.

He slid stiffly from the bed and took the bundle she passed him: the T-shirt he'd left at her house, laundered, and a pair of cargo shorts she'd picked up at Old Navy on the way over.

Lissa waited outside the curtain with the nurse while Maksim dressed himself.

"Someone close to him should keep an eye on him," the nurse said softly, watching Lissa.

"Of course," Lissa said blankly. She was wondering if her eggs would show up on a tox screen. Probably not. Even if they were superstrong compared to the last batch—strong enough to make Maksim unaware of his surroundings.

"The witness apparently said he just wasn't looking when he stepped into the road. But still, someone should watch him. Okay?"

"Okay," Lissa said. For a moment she wasn't sure how those things went together, and then she understood: the nurse was hinting that maybe Maksim hadn't stepped into the road by accident.

Nothing she could say seemed adequately reassuring. "Okay," she repeated.

From the other side of the curtain, an intake of breath, which could have been laughter or a sound of pain, made Lissa fairly certain that Maksim had heard everything; but when he nudged the curtain back with his cast, he nodded politely at the nurse and thanked her for her care.

In the waiting room, Maksim went outside while Lissa called a taxi. He paced carefully. When Lissa joined him, he said, "My eggs were broken."

"There's more at home; I made lots this time."

"*Koldun'ia . . .*"

"Yes?"

"I did not see it," he said. "The truck."

"I didn't think you were trying to kill yourself."

"The nurse thought I was. I told her I was sick. Hepatitis, so they would be careful of my blood."

"But you weren't."

"No. I was only stupid."

"Because of my eggs," Lissa said. Her fault. When she'd been so pleased with getting the recipe right this time.

"Because of my nature," he said. "Because I must do something to make myself safe, and whatever I do, there is always a price, only this one is higher than before, and I am afraid."

He said it simply, without shame, and he did not look at her.

Lissa saw the cab approaching. She held the door while he gingerly climbed in, and then she followed him in and gave the cabbie her own address.

"I'll take you home in a bit," she said, "but I didn't think to bring any eggs with me."

He laughed a little and winced. "They broke all over me when I fell. I still cannot think."

"I can make you some food too. You've been at Saint Joe's for hours. You must be ready to chew your own arm off."

Maksim shuddered. "No . . . no, thank you, *koldun'ia*."

Lissa watched bars of sun and shadow slide over the scraped side of his face and the eye that slowly closed.

She resolved to do it.

A moment later, she'd changed her mind.

Break *Law*? When she didn't know the penalty? On behalf of a man she'd known only a month? She owed him something on behalf of Baba, and maybe something more because she hadn't been more careful to warn him about the eggs, but how much?

He might be pitiful now, but he had not always been. He had done terrible things. He hadn't told her any of them.

He was sleeping now, with his head tilted back against the cab seat, his breath whistling quietly between his teeth. The near side of his lip was swollen. Lissa didn't think she'd ever seen him without an injury of some kind.

She paid the cabbie and tried to help Maksim out; he waved off her hand and heaved himself unsteadily up and onto the walk.

He followed her in, a little too close, dumb and blinking. She led him into the kitchen and microwaved some frozen chicken noodle soup for him.

She watched him drag his spoon through the bowl without taking a bite.

"Aren't you normally kind of a big eater?"

He nodded, shrugged.

"Look, if it's not good, I can get you something else. I didn't even make this; it was one of the church ladies."

"It is only that I have no hunger," he said and then ate a big bite as if to oblige her.

Lissa went about packing up two dozen eggs, wrapping them

in two layers of paper bags and then a plastic one. She'd made a lot this month, but she hadn't counted on so many of them being hit by a truck.

A truck, for Christ's sake, and here she was wondering why Maksim had lost his appetite.

She came back into the kitchen to see Maksim curled against the wall, with his plastered hand sheltered against his chest. He might have been sleeping.

"I'm thinking you ought to have someone give you a hand for a day or two. Your friend's name is Augusta, right? How do I get hold of her?"

Maksim, without opening his eyes, said, "She does not have a telephone. But she will come to me in any case."

"How will she know to do that?" Lissa asked.

"She will find the boy, or she will not. Either way, she will want to tell me."

"But how do you know?"

Maksim jolted up, spilling his soup, and began to laugh, a sweet and slightly mad sound. "She is nearly here," he said. "You may ask her yourself. And I would tell you to put away your breakables, only I do not think there is time."

MAY 26

◖ WANING GIBBOUS

"He's here," Gus said, seizing Nick by the wrist.

Nick already knew. The good smell. It was stronger, and there was blood in it. He edged up the walk behind Gus, nostrils and eyes wide, cataloging. Lilacs; a tree with nuts growing on it, like the one near the patio at the Cammy; someone cooking Indian food a few doors down. And something else.

He elbowed Gus in the hip.

"I know," she muttered. "I know that stink." The other smell, the storm smell, she meant. She didn't tell him how she knew it.

It did not belong to Maksim Volkov, of that much Nick was certain. And it did not exactly smell like a storm, but that was the closest thing Nick could find to it in his nascent library of scents. It was the kind of smell that made his hairs rise, made him want to check the horizon.

It came, he discovered, from a girl.

She was his own age or thereabouts. Long fair hair in braids; round-cheeked, pink, plump. She looked like a Swiss girl in a butter ad, except that she was not smiling or wearing a frilly blouse, and she was blocking the doorway.

"Maksim's been expecting you," she said coolly.

Gus, despite all the whiskey, stood squarely in her heavy boots and crossed her arms. "You must be the witch."

"You may call me *koldun'ia,*" the witch said.

"Where is he? What did you do to him?" Gus said. Her hands fisted in the fabric of her sleeves. Nick felt his own knotting in response.

"Nothing," the witch said. "He'll be okay. He walked in front of a truck." Her eyes stayed level on Gus. Her breathing was even, though Nick could see the pulse beating in her neck.

For a second, Gus only stared back.

Then she bulled forward, tossing the witch away from the door like she weighed no more than a child, and disappeared into the house.

Nick followed. The witch had landed sprawling in her hall-way, back against the stairs. She was coughing.

"Are you okay?" Nick said, lifting her easily to her feet. He could tell she wasn't really that light, but it didn't make a differ-ence to him, the way he was now, any more than it had to Gus.

He steadied the witch and tugged her tank top back into place over her bra straps and got another lungful of that crazy smell.

She rubbed a hand over the reddening bruise on her arm and nodded.

"Sorry about that. Gus is afraid of you," Nick said.

"She should be," the witch said, shaking off Nick's hands and heading away down the hall.

In the kitchen doorway, the witch stopped, hands on the frame, blocking Nick's path. But he could see over her head: Gus had Maksim in a headlock, her chin pressed into his hair. Her back was to them. Nick could hear the low thread of her voice growling incoherent words.

"I'm Nick Kaisaris," he said to the witch, tapping her on the shoulder.

"Lissa Nevsky," the witch said, without turning.

"Can you fix him?"

She shook her head and shrugged. "I'm doing what I can."

Maksim and Gus both lifted their heads at that, turning. Gus's eyes looked feral, bloodshot, pupils nearly eclipsing the blue; Maksim's only looked human and very tired.

"Please," Maksim said, in his low rasp, and Gus went slack, dropped her arms from about his head, and slouched against the witch's kitchen table.

"I don't like it," she said, almost plaintive.

"I know," said Maksim. "Please."

"You aren't yourself."

"I cannot go on this way," Maksim said, spreading his hands, showing the raw flesh where he'd met the road.

Gus made a low, unhappy noise, butted her head against his, and began to lick the dried blood from his face.

In front of Nick, the witch put her hand over her mouth.

"I kind of want to do that too," Nick said. "Weird."

"Is that . . . sanitary?" the witch asked.

"I guess they can't catch anything they haven't already got," Nick said, watching Maksim shut his eyes and lean into Gus. "Wow. It's like they can't even hear us."

Nick ducked under the witch's arm. The blood scent was stronger with every step. After a moment, he realized he'd come closer and closer and was kneeling there with them and was putting out his hand to touch Maksim's injuries and was bringing his fingertips to his tongue.

He tasted family. He knew now what it was that made a dog want to roll in its master's soiled clothes. He put his head down to press into Maksim's hand, and although the hand was swollen and stiff, the fingers coiled into Nick's hair and held tight.

And Nick thanked God that Gus had made him drink the whiskey, because he thought that was what made it possible to watch himself do these things without going completely batshit insane and even to wonder, with some excitement, what might come next.

Halfway through that thought, Nick smelled lilacs and heard footsteps in the hall and looked up to see the most adorable girl standing in the doorway. She was wearing tiny shorts and flip-flops and a Kawasaki-green halter top, and a fine gold chain slid over the arc of her breastbone, and Nick imagined how good she'd taste if he could put his mouth right there . . .

. . . and that made him remember that his mouth was currently pressed to the forearm of the man who'd seriously fucked up Nick's life and that maybe Nick wasn't going to make a great first impression.

Nick stood up and wiped his mouth on the back of his hand and said, "Sorry." He couldn't think of what else to add—*Sorry I'm doing unspeakable things with another dude in your kitchen?*—and he just laughed a little, nervously.

The new girl turned to the witch and said, "Well. Now I can see why you haven't wanted to introduce me to your friends."

English. She was English. Too awesome.

"That's Nick, and that's Gus," Lissa said, pointing. *"Don't* offer to shake, Nick. That's disgusting. This is my sister, Stella, who you are not going to mess with."

"Wow," said Nick to Lissa. "It's like you can read my mind." And then he remembered that she was supposed to be a witch, and maybe she really could read his mind, and the humor fell right out of him.

Lissa's eyes held his as she said, "Nick and Gus just came to take Maksim back to his place, because he's had a bit of an accident. They were just leaving."

And damn it, she was a real witch, because in about five seconds flat, Nick found himself on the porch of her house, with Maksim propped up between himself and Gus, and the door shutting firmly behind them.

MAY 26

◑ WANING GIBBOUS

Stella waited, arms crossed, while Lissa shut the door and washed her hands and poured a glass of water.

"I had an idea," Stella said, just when Lissa thought she might not speak. "A bit of a crazy idea, but you know, I'm open-minded. I could sort of maybe believe there are things in the world that are stranger than philosophy—or whatever it was from Shakespeare; I think I mangled it. And you know what? My crazy idea? It wasn't even half as weird as seeing these people drinking each other's blood in your kitchen."

"I didn't know they did that," Lissa managed.

"What, you never read *Dracula*? Oh, wait, I guess they're not vampires because of the part where they didn't burst into flames when they walked out the door—but seriously, you can't pass off the Russian Mafia thing on me anymore, because I know for a fact that being in the Russian Mafia does not make people drink blood."

"I really didn't know," Lissa said. "Honest to God. Baba told me Maksim was *kin,* and at first, I thought she meant he was related to us somehow."

"Wait a second. I have a vampire stepfamily?"

"That's not what I said—"

"To go with my witch stepsister. I guess it all makes sense now."

"Wait. How did you know?"

"Do you think I'm completely daft?" Stella cried. "You have an entire bloody library of magic books. Just because I can't read Russian—there are, like, pentacles and things all over them, for Christ's sake. I mean, I didn't think it actually *worked*. I thought maybe you were one of those people who believe in crystals and all that too, but clearly, if there are vampires—"

"They're not vampires." Lissa set her glass down roughly enough to spill cool water over her hand. "I don't think. They're people. Really old, violent, scary people."

"Nick doesn't look very old."

"He's not. He's brand new. Maksim just infected him, or whatever you call it."

"Whoa," Stella said. "That must be a mindfuck."

"Yeah. Wait. Stop. You do *not* go there. He is not your new fantasy boyfriend."

"What? Come on, Lissa, I just met him! I only meant he doesn't look as scary as all that, not like the other two."

"Well, he is."

"I didn't see you hiding under the table while these scary people were making out in your kitchen."

"They were not making out."

"Whatever. You've been having them over for breakfast. All the time when I'm not around. Don't you think I notice how many eggs this house goes through? Who knew vampires liked omelets?"

"They're not vampires," Lissa said again, weakly.

"If they're so bloody dangerous, *explain* to me," Stella said. "Tell me what you're doing with them. Tell me the whole goddamned story. Give me my two weeks' notice if you have to, just *talk* to me."

Lissa gulped in a breath that hurt her chest. "Okay. Okay. Hang on. I will . . . I'll tell you. I just need . . ."

"A stiff drink," Stella decided. "A nice, strong G&T, and then we'll settle in to share the weirdest family secrets *ever.*"

Eight

◐ WANING GIBBOUS

"Wow," said Stella. She squinted into the bottom of her glass. "I don't think there's enough gin in the world."

"You asked." Lissa shivered a little at a breath of cool from the window; night had fallen while they talked.

"I'll get my head around it," Stella said. "I mean, it's like everything else, right? You think the world is one way, and then you find out it's another way, and you have a few days where you have to keep reminding yourself *that guy I thought I loved is actually a creepy stalker,* and then it kind of integrates itself into your reality, and even if it sucks, you start moving forward."

"Does it?" Lissa said. "Suck, I mean?"

"The vampire stepfamily?" Stella looked startled. "I know, I know, not really family, not really vampires. But come on—of course it doesn't suck. It's like finding out there's really a Saint Nicholas."

"But there was really a Saint Nicholas. In history. Wasn't there?"

"Whatever. The point is, magic's real, and people can have superpowers."

"Superpowers they want to get rid of," Lissa reminded her.

"I meant you, idiot."

"Oh."

"And you're going to show me, right? How you do the magic?"

Lissa shut her eyes. She had already had her three questions of Baba for the month, and none of them had touched upon this.

Though she couldn't quite see how showing Stella the magic could make anything worse. That part was safe enough—came with rules and guidebooks. No. The things she really wanted to keep from Stella were already out there, and she had a dismal feeling that Stella wasn't taking them seriously.

"That shirt," she said, her mouth dry. "You'll have to change it for something that doesn't have ties or hooks. And your hair, leave it down. And turn off the lights upstairs on your way back. We'll work in the kitchen."

"Right now?" Stella asked, eyes huge.

"It's the second night after the full moon," Lissa said. "We have three days for our workings. That's the first rule."

"Oh my God. I'm going to learn the rules of magic. Look out, Hogwarts, here I come."

"What?"

"Don't you have *Harry Potter* in Canada? Never mind—it's a book. I'll lend you mine if I can get Mummy to mail it to me."

"Slow down," Lissa said, fighting laughter. "I promise you won't think it's very cool once you see it. It's like cooking, only even more boring."

Stella embraced her, squeezing tight. "It's going to be perfect." She ran for the stairs, almost skipping.

Lissa put their glasses in the sink, biting her lip on the fear that Baba was going to be furious.

But Baba was not here, and she had left this to Lissa, and Lissa would have to leave it to someone too, wouldn't she? And Stella *liked* it, liked her. Wasn't slamming the door like Dad had done.

"I'm ready," Stella said, sliding into the kitchen, barefoot and braless in a loose T-shirt. "What are we going to do?"

Lissa stood on the step stool to fetch down the grimoire she wanted. "A remedy," she said. "Most of it is stuff like this. This one's for Izabela Dmitreeva, who's one of our best customers."

"What kind of a remedy? Is she sick?"

"It's for fertility," Lissa said.

"Does it actually work?" Stella said.

If I get it right this time, Lissa didn't say. "It would probably work better if she and her husband didn't live with her husband's mother."

Once she and Stella had the giggles forced back down, they faced each other over the kitchen countertop and the array of grimoires and ingredients and a stack of egg cartons.

"So like I said, it's basically cooking," she said. "Only a bit weirder. Think of it like cooking Communion wafers or something."

"I'm Anglican," Stella said.

"I don't know how they're made, actually. I was trying to prepare you for the part where I have to . . . sort of pray over them."

"Seriously?"

Lissa covered her eyes. "It's kind of embarrassing."

"No. No. You know what's embarrassing? I didn't know you had your own money in Canada. I thought I could use regular money from home. *That's* embarrassing. Saying magic words? That's just quaint and unusual."

Stella gamely held each egg and dabbed it with paste and then passed it to Lissa, who muttered over it in as unintelligible a manner as she could manage.

"Dad must know you're into this, right? I mean, didn't he used to live here too? Only I don't remember him ever saying anything about witchcraft, and that's not the kind of thing you forget," Stella said as she piled Lissa's grimoires in an untidy stack at the end of the counter and swept around them with a damp cloth.

Lissa bit the inside of her lip. "He's not totally cool with it," she said.

"But it's obviously good witchcraft," Stella said.

"There's a word for it," Lissa said. "For a witch who works with eggs, I mean. We're called *kolduny*. It just means 'sorcerer,' basically. If you meet some of the people from church, you might hear them call me *koldun'ia*."

"Yeah. Maksim said that too. I remember."

"Anyway, Dad . . . it wasn't his heritage, you know? Good, bad—didn't matter. He didn't want Baba teaching me. He won't like it if he knows that you're involved."

"Then we just won't tell him, will we?" Stella said brightly.

Lissa shelved the stacked grimoires in a high cupboard and turned back to Stella, who was setting the last batch of eggs carefully in their carton. "Thanks," she said. "For your help. Do you want to come with me later this week when I drop them off?"

"Gah!" said Stella, fumbling an egg.

"Okay, I guess that can wait. The church ladies will be scandalized anyway. They'll think it's all wrong that you're not my full sister."

"Look what I did," Stella said mournfully, pointing at the mess on the floor.

"Don't get that on your hand," Lissa said.

Stella jerked her hand back. "I could be fertile just by touching it? Well, I guess it makes sense, if you have to have them all the time. There's only so many fried eggs a person can eat, anyway."

"Raw," Lissa said.

Stella shuddered, gingerly wiping up broken yolk with a paper towel. "Now I get why you were laughing."

"Welcome to the glamorous world of real magic."

"Shut up, or I'll give you fertility," Stella said, brandishing the paper towel. "Oh my God. I just figured out why you're so weird about dating Rafe. How do you come out as a witch?"

"I told him my hobby was Russian folklore," Lissa admitted. "You know, in case he's ever curious about my books."

"That's . . . not bad. He might buy it. As long as you can persuade your freak friends not to drink blood in front of him."

"Shut up."

"Aww. You told me to shut up," Stella said, grinning. "It's like we're real sisters now."

"I don't even know what that means," Lissa said, more honestly than she'd meant.

"It means I pester you to include me in everything, and you try to get rid of me, and you can't; if anyone hurts me, you threaten them with something awful; we cry at each other's weddings; we steal each other's clothes—"

"Wait. Have you seen my blue camisole top?"

"We watch *Pride and Prejudice* together; we eat ice cream together when one of us has boy troubles—"

"That's like the Hallmark version of sisterhood," Lissa protested.

"Well, I've never had one, either."

"Make it up as we go along?"

"Make it up as we go along."

MAY 27

◐ WANING GIBBOUS

Nick woke.

Blood-warm night air, rich with blossom scent, wafted in from the balcony. Indoors, everything smelled of Maksim. Nick wanted to run outside; he wanted to jerk himself off all over Maksim's furniture; he wanted the others to wake up and drink with him; he wanted Jonathan, all at once, very badly, and then he wanted to punch a hole in the wall.

He did that. His hand smarted, and he sucked on the knuckles. Around the fresh scrapes were the scabs of other scrapes, and he thought he remembered licking those clean as well.

No one woke; no one scolded him.

No one was in the apartment with him. He rolled to his feet and stood still. Maksim's bed was empty but for a twisted sheet; the sofa where Gus had been was in darkness, but Nick could tell from the lack of scent that she was not there.

Nick padded out to the balcony. Green pallor in the east told him dawn was an hour off; far down Dundas, a streetcar swam heavily away, trailing sparks.

He shut his eyes. The scent of Maksim's blood was out here too, some old and some new. And liquor sweat, though some of that was Nick's own.

And voices: hoarse and hushed. One of them might have been saying Nick's name.

He rested his elbows on flaking iron and leaned over.

They weren't talking about him at all.

"Outside of Durban," Gus was saying. "Haven't been there in a dog's age."

"It might be best," said Maksim.

"Not until you're ready, though. Right now, you need a minder."

"I need to mind myself."

"And I'm here to make sure you do," Gus said.

"I wish you would leave."

Gus did not answer, or if she did, Nick, above, could not hear.

"Sometimes," said Maksim, "I catch myself wishing for war."

Gus made a sound, a laugh or something else. Then a door,

opening; a confusion of footsteps. Nick hurried to lie back down.

In the morning, when he woke again, Gus was out. Nick did not ask Maksim, and Maksim said nothing.

Maksim ate raw eggs cracked from the shell and went back to sleep.

Nick took a twenty from the bedside table and wandered out to Dundas Street to find a Starbucks.

He sat over his coffee like a regular person, browsing the headlines in the paper. *Wishing for war*. He wouldn't have to look far, if war was what he wanted: Sudan, Afghanistan, Chechnya. He wondered why Maksim was here instead of out there.

Gus was into war too; Nick remembered her saying as much.

Yet here they were, both she and Maksim, fucking about in Toronto the Good, where a black eye earned stares on the street.

Crazy. Clearly someone was—and maybe, in fact, it wasn't Nick.

After his coffee, he went for a walk, which just happened to take him past the witch's house. Nick stood on the sidewalk, not quite bold enough to go closer. Were the witch and her sister at home? He thought he could smell them, a softer, sweeter scent than before, like fresh sheets or baking bread. A homelike scent. Maybe they were cooking. Maybe they were sleeping late.

He kept walking.

MAY 28

◖ WANING GIBBOUS

Maksim kept returning to the pyre. The splintered planks and the reek of kerosene. The ear.

He had managed not to think about it for thirty years. Thirty years: a long time in a human life. Not long enough in Maksim's life.

The ear. The feel of it under the toe of his boot.

He did not want to be there again.

His reverie was broken by a chilly touch upon his lips. He reared away.

A spoon clattered on the floor. "Damn it, Maks," Gus said wearily.

Maksim opened his eyes. "I thought it was something dead."

"It is," she said. "Dead cow, with vegetables. I took it out of the can all by myself." She retrieved the spoon, wiped it off, and stuck it back in the bowl. "Remember what to do with this?"

Maksim took the bowl and propped it on his knee and, with his good hand, stirred the gelatinous brown mess and then lifted it to his nose. The stuff smelled chemical.

Gus read it on his face. "I can shove it down your throat," she said.

Maksim shrugged his good shoulder. "I would like an egg."

"They're not good for you." She gestured at his cast, at the cracking scabs down the right side of his body.

Maksim's last egg had been long enough ago now that the haze of it had mostly lifted, leaving physical pain and bleak confusion. He wanted to ask Gus if the witch had said anything more about the spell he needed; he could not remember for himself, although it was so important. The last few days were a series of blurry tableaus, silent film stills, nothing at all in the soundtrack.

"Stay awake for a while," Gus said. "Talk to me."

She nudged him with her hip, and he curled his body to make space; he was on the sofa, though he thought he recalled putting himself to bed.

"I wish you would leave," he said.

Maybe he had said it before, for Gus sighed. "Nope."

"Then give me an egg. Do not anger me. I am afraid I will hurt you."

She snorted. "With one hand? Not bloody likely. Besides, you're not in top form just now."

"I was not then, either," Maksim said.

"When?"

He shook his head.

"When, Maks?"

"I hurt someone I did not wish to hurt."

"As is our nature to do, Maksim."

"This was worse."

Gus turned an inquiring gaze to him.

She'd done things, her look said—knowing and cool and sad. She was his. She could not be shocked.

She was his, and she should not be here, and the surest way to drive her off would be to tell her the story. And still, he could not bear for her to know it.

He buried his face in the crook of his arm. Tried to think of something else. Failed.

MAY 28

◖ WANING GIBBOUS

The apartment was nearly dark, just after sunset. Nick let himself in. He stepped on something just inside the door, which crunched wetly.

"Gross," he said.

Flame kindled in the center of the room and touched the wick of a candle.

"You came back," Maksim said.

"Um. Yeah. No place else to go right now."

"But you went."

"Just . . . out. Read the paper, hung out in the Market, went to a pub, that kind of thing," Nick said, wiping egg from his sandal. "Should I have left a note or something?"

"You've been fighting," Maksim said. "Show me."

Nick came and knelt by the candle, tilting his face to show the split over his cheekbone. He was reminded strongly of the night all this had begun. He trembled very slightly under the touch of Maksim's fingertip and less slightly under the rasp of Maksim's tongue.

"You must be very careful with your blood," Maksim said. "You can infect others if you are not."

"It didn't bleed much at all."

Maksim waited, sitting back on the sofa with one hand open and relaxed upon his knee and the other, the bandaged one, curled over his stomach.

"Some people in an alley," Nick said. "They were giving a hundred bucks to anyone who would challenge this one guy. He'd already taken down two other guys. He was a huge mother-fucker, so I thought he'd be interesting. You know?"

"I know."

"So I took the hundred. I think it's a frequent gig, this thing. They had tape for my hands and everything. Maybe fifty people watching. Long odds on me," Nick said, and he felt mad laughter bubbling up. He'd been small as a kid. Avoided the neighborhood bully—played soccer rather than hockey. Couldn't remember if he'd ever hit anyone in real rage in all his life before now.

Oh. Wait.

The knuckle he'd split on Jonathan's face hadn't even finished healing, and what the fuck kind of best friend could do that and then forget about it? Even for a second?

"You like it," Maksim was saying.

"No. What kind of freak likes getting off on hurting other people? I mean, I do, but I don't want to . . ."

"You like the life."

"My other life was full of shit, to be honest. I couldn't seem to get through it without a whole lot of booze."

"I still can't," Gus mumbled, rolling out of Maksim's bed and padding into the room. Her plain white tank top was twisted around her body. She sat on the floor beside Nick and drank water from a cracked cup.

"That's what I mean," Nick said. "I like being tougher and everything, but I still have to figure out what to do with myself, right?"

"If you could see yourself now," Maksim said, reaching out and touching Nick's cheek again and a lock of his hair. "You are like an angel."

Nick lurched back. "I don't want that."

"It is not that," Maksim said. "It is as if I gave you wings of wax. The fault is mine, but you will find your way to your own ruin."

Nick had no idea what to say to that.

"Come here," Maksim said. "Sit. Lay your head down. Be still if you can."

Nick obeyed. He was still for a while, and Maksim stroked his hair, and the candle flame flickered.

Outside, someone argued in Portuguese, and someone drove by with the Gorillaz on the car stereo. Nick felt the restlessness rise in his limbs, slowly but inexorably.

"Before the new moon," Maksim said, "the witch will have to make a choice."

But he did not say what the choice was. Maksim sat, dreaming, and his hand moved more slowly until Nick could not bear it anymore and bolted up.

Gus gave him a significant look, but whatever she meant was lost on him.

In a moment, Nick got his reactions under his control again, and though he was breathing heavily, he managed to shake his hair back from his face and go to the refrigerator for a cold glass of water.

"Go," said Gus. "Here, take some money. Go pick up some more beer or something."

"Okay, I can do that," Nick said. "I'll be back. In a bit."

Nick opened the last two bottles of pilsner for them before leaving and descended the stairs while Gus sang a song about Spanish ladies.

He would come back. He wanted to come back, even. Not right away, though, and not forever.

MAY 30

◖ WANING GIBBOUS

Stella danced through the pub with even more than her usual brio. Rafe watched her for a second, eyebrow up, and said to Lissa, "Like a five-year-old who's got into the jelly beans. What did you do to our kid?"

"Our kid?"

"Well, sure. You're the big sister, I'm the boss; she's our kid."

"We're getting along," Lissa said, even though she knew he hadn't been looking for a serious answer.

"You're not shipping her back to Daddy?"

"She told you that?"

Rafe grinned. "Let's just say you're the quiet one in the family."

"It was never up to me," Lissa said. "She's the one who decided to stay here."

"In your house."

"Well, yeah, I guess that part was up to me."

Rafe reached out and took the tip of Lissa's braid in his fingertips. "You're doing good by her. In case you wanted my opinion. Which you probably don't."

Lissa made herself look at him. "She's your kid too, right? Someone's got to make sure I don't mess her up."

Rafe seemed to think she was joking. He laughed and tugged her hair and leaned across the bar to kiss her cheek. "Want to get brunch tomorrow? It'll be breakfast for me, but you're probably a disgusting early-morning person, right? We could meet up at that place on College at noon."

"Sure," Lissa said, dazed. Another date. Where were all these people coming from? People in her life, making plans with her, making jokes—had they all been waiting somewhere until Baba was gone?

She had one more drop-off for the church ladies tonight, and she wouldn't mind sleeping late herself. She pictured warm morning air, the light sheet covering her, sun slanting at the window—the anticipation of brunch at the patio on College—and what if it was more than a brunch date later? Would she someday ask Rafe to sleep over? Would they wake side by side in the big bed, tangled in sheets, hands touching?

Lissa felt heat wash over her face, and she gripped her hands together under the bar, arms tight to her sides. Rafe wasn't looking at her; he'd gone to take someone's order at the other end of the bar. She was not allowed to have these thoughts. She was not permitted. What would Baba think?

She slipped off the stool and slung her bag over her shoulder.

One pint and look where her mind had gone. There was work to do, and she had to call and check up on Maksim.

She didn't cancel the date, though. She only mouthed, "See you tomorrow," to Rafe and waved to Stella, and then she was outside in summer heat, and it seemed as if, all the way home, everyone she saw was holding hands.

Nine

Nick knocked too hard on the witch's door and split his knuckle again.

"Crap," he said, and he sucked the blood away. It tasted faintly like Maksim's blood. He wondered when he had stopped finding this creepy.

A wad of Band-Aids bulged in his pocket. Maksim and Gus between them had told him twenty times already that he needed to be careful not to contaminate anyone else. He peeled one and covered the cut and, for good measure, smeared the door clean with his fingertip and licked that too.

Then he knocked again, more decorously.

The sister opened the door. Nick was the luckiest son of a bitch ever. Stella was just as tall and peach-skinned as he remembered from the other day, and she smiled at Nick in a hesitant way that made him wonder how old she was.

"Hi," he said. "Remember me? Nick Kaisaris." He held out his unbloodied hand. He knew he was rumpled from living out of his backpack; he had not shaved today and maybe not the day before, and he smiled at her with all his usual ease. Somehow in the last few weeks, he'd lost the need to excuse himself for anything.

"I remember. We weren't properly introduced, though. Stella Moore." God, that classy English voice, and her hand felt clean and warm.

"I had a question for your sister, but I'm glad to find you instead."

"She's not in," said Stella, angling her torso to block the doorway. She didn't look like her sister at all, except for the body language. That much was the same.

"I'll wait," said Nick, showing her his open hands. He wasn't the kind of person who'd knock a girl aside to get into her house, not like Gus.

"I can't let you in," said Stella. "But I'll wait outside with you, if you want. She shouldn't be long. I suppose I shouldn't offer you a beer."

Nick didn't ask why he didn't rate a beer. He sat down cross-legged on the porch boards and leaned back on the cool yellow brick. After a minute, Stella came outside, handed him a glass of lemonade, and arranged herself just beyond his reach.

"What were you going to ask my sister?" she said.

"Witch things," Nick said and laughed. He wondered if he laughed too much these days, with nothing exactly funny but everything so marvelously strange.

"Eggs? I can do that. Which ones did you get the other day? The sleep ones?"

"Not for me," Nick said. "I tried one. I don't need it; I can handle myself." The egg had felt like quicksand, he thought; he'd been hoping for a pleasant, lazy high, like a Vicodin or something. But it wasn't at all similar. He didn't know how Maksim could stand it.

"For Maksim?" Stella asked. "Is he okay?" She leaned forward so that Nick caught the scent of her hair.

He swayed closer himself, entranced. "He's not so good. He doesn't eat. He doesn't even drink water unless you remind him."

"Since his accident?" Stella said.

"That's right; he's not healing up very well, either. Gus is worried. I'm supposed to . . ." He could smell the sweat that gathered in the hollow of her throat and the blood that ran beneath her skin. "What was I saying?"

Stella pursed her lips. "Drink your lemonade."

Nick did. It was delicious. He probably hadn't been drinking enough water himself, what with all the bourbon he'd been putting away, taking turns with Gus watching Maksim sleep. He probably reeked of it. He was not a credible person anymore, and he could not bring himself to do anything about it.

"Anyway," he said to Stella, "I wasn't bound for greatness. I would have got a job in a call center. Or a chain bookstore. And they would have had to fire me sooner or later."

"You were telling me about Maksim," she reminded him. "You need to focus. Tell me if he needs medical care."

"No," said Nick. "It wouldn't do any good."

"And you?"

"Me?"

Stella rolled her eyes. "Are you always this spacey, or is there something wrong with you? Look, never mind. You're above my pay grade, anyway. I'll let it pass until Lissa gets here. You just drink your lemonade. It's good for you. It's got vitamins and electrolytes."

"You remind me of Hannah," said Nick. "Wife material."

"Not for a couple of years yet," Stella said, laughing. "Who's Hannah? Your sister?"

"My best friend's girl," Nick said. "I've lost both of them." His eyes spilled over, and he wiped them on his wrist. "I don't know what's wrong with me. I can't have a reasonable conversation anymore. No one told me about that part."

"Hey. Hey." She touched his shoulder. "We'll do what we can."

Nick tilted his head back against the bricks and pressed until his scalp felt like it would split. That was better. He would not cry now. He would be nice and sane and charming for the witch's sister.

He raised his head and looked at Stella's peach-pale face and scented her perfume again and the fresh sweat of her body. In it all, the very faintest trace of thundercloud.

"Are you a witch too?" he asked.

Stella's face lit. "I'm learning."

"I think I like witches. I don't think I'm supposed to. Gus doesn't."

"Her loss," Stella said. "More lemonade?"

While she opened the door, Nick shut his eyes tight and smelled the breath of the house: dry wood, oil-based paint, lemon polish, and a much heavier blast of the witch scent. It chilled him.

By contrast, Stella smelled like a spring storm, the kind that sweeps in gladly with a fresh, hard wind to crush the petals.

She stepped out of the house again with a pitcher in her hand and leaned down to refill Nick's glass.

He caught her arm and pulled her down beside him, where he could press his face to her jawline. She was trembling, or maybe it was the strong thrum of blood through her body.

"Look, I'm pretty sure you're harmless," Stella said, "but what you're doing is really inappropriate."

Nick tasted, just barely, the lobe of her ear.

"Fair warning," said Stella. She fumbled for a moment at the neck of Nick's shirt.

Something cracked. Chill slimed the small of his back.

Nick jolted back against the wall.

Stella slid back out of reach.

Nick went to follow. He tripped on the toe of his sandal and hammered his knee into the porch flooring.

"You egged me," he said wonderingly. "It's a strong one."

"It had better be," Stella said. "My sister made it. Just sit there. I have more where that came from."

Nick shook his head. Sleep fumes curtained his eyes: the heavy, inexorable sleep that comes with sickness. "Damn it," he said. "You didn't have to do that."

"You wouldn't listen," she said. She examined one of her fingernails and buffed it lightly against the floorboards.

Nick lolled back, blinking. He thought he might feel better if he got the mess of egg out of his shirt and waistband, but he could not quite be bothered. He rubbed at his eyes and face; his skin was half-numb and prickling.

"I've just crossed the ocean to get away from a presumptuous tosser," Stella told him. "I'm not in the mood to put up with more of the same from you."

"I didn't mean to be a tosser. Sometimes I can't stop myself."

"Erick always said that kind of thing too. Show me you're different."

"So sure of yourself," Nick said, and he shut his eyes; beyond his lids, the summer sun loomed bright and vague.

"I know what I know."

She couldn't know. She was young, younger than he was. She'd find out; he wasn't some annoying little shithead like her ex. He was powerful. He could make things great for her, or he could make them awful. Nick wanted to tell her, to warn her; to take away the calm confidence from her face; to put fear into her, proper fear. No, that was not right; why should he be the one to take away the fresh strength of her? Why should he want to be cruel all of a sudden? Had he always wanted to be cruel?

He said none of this. He forced his eyes open again and plucked a lilac bloom from the tree and tore at the petals with fingers gone clumsy and cold.

JUNE I

◑ LAST QUARTER

Lissa took the sunny side of the table and watched the fine blond hairs on her arm stir in the warm breeze. She ordered iced coffee.

Rafe arrived before she had time to get too insecure. She saw him strolling up, recognized his walk, a bit shambling, in his skateboard sneakers and cargo pants, the chain of his wallet swinging. He wore dark Oakleys, and she couldn't see through the lenses at all, but the lines of his face turned happy when he saw her.

So she stood up and kissed him. Was that okay? Did people do that?

Rafe answered her by sliding a big hand over her hair and kissing her back, grinning broadly as he took the chair opposite, nudging her foot with his.

"Now I'm glad I set the alarm," he said. "'Fraid I went for a nightcap with the boys after closing. Going to need some eggs to put me right."

Lissa bit the inside of her cheek to keep from laughing. She ordered banana pancakes, and Rafe sang part of a song about them in a husky but tuneful voice; the lyrics matched so well with what Lissa had been thinking last night that she couldn't help but smile.

"I was in a band," Rafe explained, breaking off. "A third-rate cover band playing Tuesday nights in a sports bar in Bloor West Village."

"You were the lead singer," Lissa guessed.

"I did a truly awesome Billy Bragg when they'd let me."

Lissa didn't know who Billy Bragg was. It must have been obvious from her expression.

"Someone too British for the Canadian sports bar crowd," Rafe said, shrugging. "Remind me next time you drop by the pub; I'll put him on the jukebox."

There it was again, that easy assumption that this would continue. Rafe didn't even notice he'd done it and just went on naming bands, singing bits of songs. Some she knew, and some she didn't, and one she could even sing along with him. As if she were a person who sang or ate breakfasts with men or lazed in the sunshine on a morning off.

Her pancakes came with a scoop of custard on top, and she couldn't finish them, but Rafe polished off the part she didn't want, finally sitting back and patting his belly. It was a solid belly that went with the muscular arms and the breadth of his shoulders.

And she was sitting there looking at him and not talking, and maybe she should be doing a better job of this date thing.

She looked quickly to his face and saw that he was smiling below the dark glasses.

"I don't have to be at the Duke until six," he said. "Want to take a wander with me?"

So she got to see College Street in a way she'd never done before, at strolling pace, looking in the windows of boutiques. Helping to flip through bins of used vinyl outside the music shop, because Rafe said he had a vice. Buying herself a tortoiseshell hair clip and wearing it right away, liking the weight of her hair lifted off her neck and the brush of Rafe's fingers over the warm skin exposed.

It wasn't until they stopped for espresso, midafternoon, that she thought of anything else. Rafe was at the counter, paying, and Lissa thumbed her phone open to see a voice mail and three more missed calls from Stella.

When she called back, no answer.

JUNE 1

◑ LAST QUARTER

Nick opened his eyes to Stella's face, blurry and way too close, and her hands tugging on his arm.

"Here's the deal," she said. "I have more of the eggs in my bag. I don't know where I'm going, though. You'll have to take me there."

"Can't walk," Nick said, yawning.

The hands left his arm and tugged at his shirt.

"Stoppit," Nick mumbled. The shirt peeled stickily away from his skin, and he fought to free his head from the fabric.

"Wow," Stella said. "You'd be kind of pretty if you weren't covered in egg."

A chilly, rough cloth swiped over his back, and he made an unhappy noise.

"Stop whining. You'll feel better in a moment. Just don't do anything stupid, or I'll put the whammy on you again."

She sat with Nick while he scrubbed his fists into his eyes and worked spit around his mouth and finally sat fully upright.

"Good to go?"

"Um," he managed. "Sort of."

She hauled him up by the biceps. "Put this on."

It was a T-shirt from the Duke of Lancashire, brand new, size M. It was tight over Nick's shoulders and smelled unappealingly of cheap dye.

He stretched hugely, cracked his neck, shivered at the touch of his still-slimy waistband against his skin.

"What are we doing again?"

"Taking eggs to Maksim. It's what you came for, right?"

There'd been something else, and probably Gus was going to kick his ass if he came back with the wrong sister and the wrong magic, but Nick just couldn't wrap his head around it at the moment. "Whatever," he said and stumbled after Stella down the walk.

Thank all the gods she hailed a cab, because Nick thought it was at least a few miles, and fuck if he was going to walk all that way with traces of egg still sending pulses of nauseating sleep through him. He sat there dumbly in the backseat with the cab unmoving and Stella staring at him. She finally snapped, "Tell the man where we're going."

"Dundas. And, uh . . . Dundas and Bellwoods."

Stella wouldn't let him lean over against her. He opened his window all the way and leaned his head there instead, breathing cab fumes. How did Maksim deal with this all day? No wonder he didn't want to eat.

When the cab pulled to the curb, Nick fell out and leaned on a newspaper box while Stella paid. "You owe me fifteen bucks," she said, but he was too busy swallowing down sick saliva to even answer.

It was better out of the car, though. He could smell trees. And home. Home was right there.

He had a fuzzy moment where he couldn't quite remember

why Stella was with him. She smelled mostly nice, but there was something.

"Right," he said. "This sucks. Come on, he lives up here."

He stumbled up the stairs. He got halfway, and then Gus popped out from somewhere and tackled him into the wall.

"Eggs!" Stella yelped, holding the bag above her head.

Gus sniffed along Nick's neck and wrinkled her nose at the new shirt. She let Nick drop and gave Stella a flame-edge blue glare.

"Jesus, Gus, stand down already," Nick said and yawned. "Her sister was out, so I brought her. Would you chill?"

"You were gone a long time," Gus said.

"Nothing happened. She egged me. No, fuck, it's fine; I was being a dick."

"Thank you for that," Stella muttered.

"You egged him," Gus said. Her voice was flat.

Nick edged protectively in front of Stella.

Stella pushed at the flat of his shoulder with her hand. "Don't be an idiot, Nick. Get out of my way, or I'll do it again."

Gus laughed: a real, normal, amused chuckle. Nick opened his eyes wide.

"A witch I could like," Gus said. "Who knew? Hey, I've forgotten your title, but I'd use it if I had half a brain for Russian."

She was drunk, Nick thought: not very, but he could smell it, along with the smell that meant *family* to him now.

Stella, behind him, was laughing too. "I can't say it, either," she admitted. "We'll get Maksim to walk us through it, shall we? How's he doing? I've got more of the sleep eggs, but I'm afraid if there was anything else you needed, Nick didn't manage to tell me."

"Sure. Blame it all on me," Nick grumbled, trailing after the two women, "when you egged me before I had a chance."

Stella didn't seem to hear him, and he was still too damned

sleepy to bother to raise his voice; he only plodded upstairs and picked at the crusty egg drying on the back of his shorts.

JUNE I

◑ LAST QUARTER

Lissa was getting better at lying spontaneously, at least to people who didn't know her well yet.

Rafe seemed to believe she was really getting a migraine. He offered to take her home, and when she demurred, he hailed her a cab, kissed her gently, and told her to come by the pub tonight if she felt better.

When she reached her house, though, she wished it hadn't been so easy. She was already getting used to the warm and solid presence at her shoulder. She stood on the porch and looked at the bits of eggshell scattered there. What the hell had happened?

The front door was locked, the kitchen tidy, all the lights turned out. She found Stella's note, thank God, in an obvious spot on the counter, weighted with the sugar bowl. *Gone to drop off eggs to M.*, it read.

Gone, without Lissa, to the home of the very person she'd been told to keep away from. And why was Maksim out of eggs again?

She didn't waste any time getting back out the door and into another cab—the amount of money she was spending on cabs these days, for Christ's sake; what about the house bills?—and when she was speeding up Ossington, she took out her phone again and tried Stella once more.

"Hey," said Stella, picking up.

"You're okay?" Lissa asked, feeling it come out breathless. "You're at Maksim's?"

"Yes." Stella sounded puzzled. "Didn't you get my note?"

"I was worried. I called you back, and you didn't answer."

"Oh, sorry. Must've missed it. Yes, I'm here. Brought some eggs, though it turns out he still had some."

"No one's hurt you?"

"No. Really, I'm fine. Maksim, though . . ."

"I'll see for myself in a second," Lissa said. "I'm just pulling up." She flicked her phone shut and paid the cabbie. Her head ached for real now, in the backwash of fear. Stella said she was fine—but so much could have gone wrong, and all of it would have been Lissa's fault.

Stella met her at the downstairs door.

"I'm glad you came," she whispered. "I don't know what to do."

Lissa seized her hand to stop her going back up. "Is anyone giving you a hard time?"

"Nothing like that. Nick got a bit handsy, but—hey, don't go all big sister. I'm trying to tell you something here. You know how Gus really doesn't like you?"

"I got that, yeah."

"Well, she sent Nick to ask you for help. And I'm starting to get why." In the shadow of the foyer, Stella's eyes were liquid and dark, beseeching.

"You think I should fix him," Lissa said.

"Can you? For good? Is that how it works?"

She didn't answer, patted Stella on the arm, and went up.

Gus was sitting on Maksim's sofa with a bottle of rye between her knees.

"He's over by the refrigerator," she said unnecessarily, for Lissa could see Maksim's legs sprawling in the kitchen doorway.

She knelt beside him without touching; she remembered what he was like when surprised awake.

He lay curled on his good side on the linoleum; someone had put one of the sofa pillows under his head. He wore the same jogging shorts she'd given him at the hospital and nothing else; the waistband was grimed with old blood. He'd taken the plaster off his arm; the injury still looked swollen and unhealed.

"*Koldun'ia*," he murmured.

"I thought you were asleep."

"Am I?"

"That doesn't make sense," she said, but he only made a dismissive gesture and winced and curled up tighter.

Lissa went back to Gus and Stella on the sofa. "He wasn't that thin before."

Gus's lip lifted. "I feed him."

"I didn't send him home with you so that he could lie on the floor," Lissa started.

"Of course you feed him," Stella interrupted, soothingly, hand hovering an inch above Gus's knee. "You're doing just about everything for him, right? Nick's useless, I can see that."

Gus's mouth worked. Her hands were wrapped tight about the rye bottle, bloodless, showing the ugly, dark scars on most of her knuckles.

Lissa bit her tongue and let Stella keep talking.

"But you want him to go back to doing things for himself. I know. It's frightened you, hasn't it, seeing him like this?"

"God help me, yes," Gus said, taking a drink, her mouth twisting at the taste. "All he does is sleep. And the dreams he's having . . ."

"You can see inside his head?" Stella said, wide-eyed.

Gus shook her head. "Wouldn't want to. What's on the outside is bad enough."

"And you left him on the floor because . . ." Lissa prodded, ignoring Stella's glare.

"Every time I turn my back, he fucking lies down there!" Gus spat.

Maksim roused a little, opening one eye. "She made me take a pillow."

Gus scrubbed a fist over her mouth. "He doesn't want to be comfortable." She watched Maksim until his eye shut again, and she leaned forward, beckoning Lissa and Stella close. "He did something. I don't know what it was. After it, he went to your grandmother," she whispered, breathing rye fumes. "He won't tell me. But he's afraid he'll do it again."

"And he thinks I can stop him," Lissa said.

Both Stella and Gus looked at her, waiting.

"There's something I can do."

Gus shuddered, a full-body reaction. "I won't like it, will I?"

"I doubt it."

Gus took a deep breath and shut her eyes for a second. "I'll go to my place until it's over. You can send Nick to get me."

"Wait. Just wait. I can't do it right this minute. There are rules." The most important rule she was going to break, but maybe Gus didn't need to know that. "It has to be done on the new moon. That's a full week out."

Gus winced.

"You can manage to look after him until then," Lissa said. "What with none of you having a job or anything. Where the hell is Nick, anyway? He's not missing again, is he?"

Gus pointed at the open door of the bedroom. Lissa could just see an unmoving lump lying diagonally across the bed.

"Your sister egged him," Gus said, her drawn face lighting. She clapped Stella on the shoulder. "I'm going to be laughing about that for ages."

"Hey," said Lissa, returning to kneel beside Maksim. "I'll see you in a week, okay?"

She watched his eyes drag open, dazed and wet.

"A week. *Koldun'ia*, are you certain?"

She nodded.

He wrapped both hands around her arm and pressed his forehead against them, breathing in short little gasps. Not quite sobbing.

Lissa pulled her hand away as gently as she could. "Hey," she said again. "My grandmother wanted it. Okay? Just hang in there until it's time. And stop sleeping on the floor."

Maksim fisted his hands to his mouth and nodded.

"Jesus," said Stella once she and Lissa were outside, walking south through Bellwoods Park. The air felt wide and fresh after Maksim's apartment.

"Yeah," Lissa said.

"He needs psychological help," Stella said.

"Well, he's got us."

"And Nick. And Gus," Stella said. "Poor bastard."

Ten

◖ WANING CRESCENT

"I was hoping you'd be in yesterday," Rafe said. "Headache stayed bad, did it?"

"It's fine today," Lissa said, sliding onto what was becoming her favorite barstool, at the end away from the door. She hung her bag from one of the convenient hooks underneath the bar and looked up again at Rafe's smile: the private one she was coming to know, not the one he used for customers, even regulars. "I went to work and everything."

"They make you dress up at the print shop?"

Lissa felt herself blush. The black dress. She'd actually forgotten she was wearing it, in her haste to shake off the foreboding quiet of Izabela Dmitreeva's mother-in-law's house. The fertility eggs had not worked yet—no surprise, if her first batch of sleep eggs had been anything to go by—and while Izabela coolly kept right on knitting baby blankets, her mother-in-law had given Lissa a truly grim look.

"I had to visit a friend of my grandmother's," Lissa said now, thinking it felt like another lie even though it was not.

Rafe's face warmed. "And you didn't show up with blue hair and multiple piercings? You're a better person than I am."

"Blue? Really?"

"Why d'you think I shaved it off?"

Lissa laughed aloud at that. Rafe bowed with a flourish of his hands. "Stella tells me that's hard to do."

"What is?"

"Making you laugh."

"It's not fair, you getting dirt on me from my sister. Who am I supposed to ask if I want to know things about you?"

"Me," Rafe said. "I'll just tell you. No secrets at all. I'm silly that way."

"Really? What's your worst fear?"

"I love that your mind went straight there," he said, rolling his eyes a bit. "Blood. Can't stand it. I pass out."

"Where did you get your toque?"

"Board shop on Queen Street. Best twenty bucks I've spent all year. Why would I keep that a secret, though?"

"It was the next thing that came into my head," Lissa protested. "Ever broken the law?"

"Smoked quite a bit of pot in uni," he said right away. "Stole twenty bucks off my da to buy it once too. Let's see . . . climbed over a few fences in my time, climbed up the downspout of a cathedral onto the roof—and then fell off, no bones broken thanks to all the lager I'd had—oh, and I stole a stuffed stag's head from a pub once too. No idea why."

"But those are all funny. Just pranks," Lissa said. "And most of them involve climbing."

"I was skinnier then," Rafe said, shrugging. "I don't know. What were you looking for? Really serious lawbreaking? I've got nothing. Never locked myself to any construction equipment or threw any Molotov cocktails. Wasn't thinking ahead to when I'd have to impress you, obviously."

She let it go and took the pint of organic he slid across the bar to her. And when she was ready to leave, Rafe went on break and met her in the alley out back and gave her a much more serious kiss than he'd given her before. The most serious kiss she'd ever had, really. Black dress and all.

She gave it back to him, and that was breaking a rule too, and so it seemed he had very useful advice on the topic, after all.

JUNE 5

◑ WANING CRESCENT

Nick ran around the track at the high school near his old apartment. He had forgotten his running shoes, but it turned out not to matter.

He ran for three hours, maybe four. At sunset, he slowed to a walk and left the track. Sweat dried in his hair. He strolled north from the school grounds, hands in the pockets of his cargo shorts.

Jonathan's street. He passed the corner and turned down the alley. The same graffiti marked the garage doors. The same Labrador puppy came to a rear fence to watch him pass.

He leaned on a cinder block wall beside a froth of blossoming vines, and he looked up.

At first, the fading sunset glared off Jonathan's window too brightly to let him see anything; not that he expected to see anything.

He wondered if he was holding a wake and wished he'd brought something to drink, after all.

Dark came on slowly, with the scent of frying onions. Above him, windows brightened, here and there and there.

And there.

He saw a hand—whose hand?—turn on the old wicker lamp at Jonathan's window and then pull the cord of the blind.

Nick left the alley, circled around to the fire door, and tugged. Locked.

He bit his lip and went to the front entrance. Suicidally dumb, he told himself.

He didn't listen.

A woman approached with an armload of groceries. Nick said, "Be right up," toward the intercom speaker as the woman opened the outer door.

She paid him no attention, flashed her keycard to the inner door, and smiled distractedly at Nick as he held the door for her and followed her in.

Too easy. He rode the elevator to a random floor and took the stairs to Jonathan's so he could approach from the far end of the hall.

Even from there, once the stairway fire door was open, he could tease out the unique smells of Jonathan's apartment: sandalwood soap from Chinatown; microwaved popcorn; stale beer; Aussie shampoo; a fading underlay of pot smoke.

Nick crept almost up to the door, listening. If only his hearing would do what his sense of smell had done.

It wouldn't, but the apartment building was not new and the soundproofing was imperfect.

From within the apartment he could hear a woman's voice— Hannah?—very faintly, and then, from right by the door, "Got it. You sure?"

Jonathan.

Footsteps receded. More speech from farther in, too quiet for him to make out.

Nick leaned right against the door, straining. Jonathan was in there. Alive, together with Hannah, doing normal things. Making dinner.

He thought he heard them laughing. Scraping chairs, sitting down to eat.

He could have been there with them. Had been a few weeks ago. They'd teased him about getting a better haircut, finishing his degree on time, getting a girlfriend, a whole bunch of the normal things he hadn't managed to figure out yet.

Would never manage now.

It was a long time before he could tear himself away.

JUNE 6

◗ WANING CRESCENT

The pub was full, and someone was sitting in Lissa's usual spot, and though Rafe was glad to see her, he didn't have time to chat, moving briskly up and down the bar, pulling pints and slapping down coasters and hip-checking the cash drawer shut.

Lissa was only having the one pint, anyway, to kill the rest of the time until dark. She fed coins into the jukebox and put on, for kicks, all the songs she could find with "moon" in the title. She had already eaten at the roti shop after work, and she had all the information she needed on the ritual, and she'd been to check on Maksim.

He'd been mostly asleep, again, but on the sofa this time. And he'd showered, although he was wearing a wrinkled U of T Athletics T-shirt that probably belonged to Nick. And Gus had gone back to protective glowering, which Lissa thought indicated that she was sober, or at least less drunk, which she'd count as a win.

For this step, she didn't need them. She explained as much

and watched Gus shudder whenever Lissa got too close, watched Nick pace in and out of the room, watched Maksim lace his fingers together over his knees, the injured ones still swollen and dark. He didn't seem to feel them, and that was creepy. No one looked sorry when she said good-bye.

Through the window at the Duke of Lancashire, she saw the sky dim down: orange to bruise purple to the dull dark red that passed for night in a city of this size. She tried to get a good-night kiss from Rafe, but someone was pounding a glass on the bar, and someone else was brandishing a twenty, and she gave up and only waved.

The walk home, through heavy, bloom-scented air, did nothing to ease her nerves. Inside her bag, her fingers twined themselves into the hair of the doll.

At home, she'd left the windows open all day. The house felt humid. She moved around the kitchen in darkness, unbinding.

The first part of the ritual called for wax. Black wax and a rusty nail. Lissa had found the nail in the gardening shed, lying beside a tomato sauce can full of more of the same. Now she sat close to the candle, tucked her loose hair back behind her ears, dipped the nail in the pool of wax around the wick, and began scribing: rough lines, awkward and uneven, the wax clotting heavily at the beginning of a stroke and then too quickly scraping away to nothing.

It was the first time she'd had to do this: instead of just painting the egg with a paste, making an actual design upon it. The design wasn't too complicated, fortunately: a black circle that might represent the new moon and a few Cyrillic letters arranged around it. Baba had not told Lissa what they stood for, but at least it was the kind of design she'd been able to describe verbally, while Lissa took notes, back during their last full-moon conversation.

Before Lissa had finished the first section, the point of the nail broke through. Yolk slimed her fingers. She tossed the ruined egg in the compost, washed her hands, and tried again.

The second egg she crushed in her own hand, startling when the house settled and a stair creaked.

Quiet, she told herself, wiping her hands again. *You're not used to the quiet anymore.*

She could not put on the stereo with the house powered down, but she hummed to herself a little while she set up again. *Whistling in the dark,* the spooked part of her brain said, and so she shut up.

Third egg was the charm, of course. She scraped the point of the nail over the shell, thankful there weren't too many curved lines. Thankful she didn't know enough Russian to guess what the Cyrillic letters might stand for.

Ridiculous. Spooked again. A full-grown, practicing witch ought to do better. She elbowed her hair back and let her shoulders fall square again, deliberately exposing her back to the kitchen doorway.

When she had finished the design, she propped the egg on a mini-tripod to let the wax harden, poured herself a glass of tap water, and stepped out to the porch.

Light, high clouds covered the sky, red with the reflected lights of Toronto. If they had not been there, she would have been looking at an empty sky or maybe at the dark, covered face of the moon. She was not usually awake on such a night.

The heat wave had broken sometime while she was indoors. Air flowed up from the lakefront, almost chilly. Lissa let her hair fall forward about her neck and crossed her arms.

When she went back indoors, she lifted the drying egg into one of the high cupboards, where she had a faint chance Stella might not look at it.

Lissa had already, in a scant few weeks, introduced Stella to

Maksim Volkov, who had to try very hard not to be a monster, and to Gus Hillyard and Nick Kaisaris, who did not seem as if they were trying as hard, and she still did not know what that meant. She did not want to be the one to introduce her stepsister to forbidden new-moon rituals. She was only just getting to know them herself.

Not that she knew Stella so well yet, either; but she did know Stella well enough to wait up.

Stella bounced in after three, just as Lissa had begun to nod off on the sofa. "I'm brilliant!" she said. "Look at all the tips I made. It just keeps getting easier."

She cast herself down beside Lissa, stretching out her long legs. "It's true Canadians are polite, you know. Even the rowdy lads."

"They know you'll have Rafe chuck them out if they cross the line."

"The power! The power!" Stella cackled. "I've never had any before. I think it's rather nice." She rubbed her eyes with both hands and yawned indelicately. "Beddy-bye," she said. "You too. You look fagged."

Lissa shuffled upstairs, shivering a little in the late cool. She actually unfolded a blanket from the chest at the end of Baba's bed and wrapped it close about her neck and shoulders.

She thought she would lie awake, but sleep came down over her as thoroughly as if she'd had one of her own eggs.

JUNE 7

◐ WANING CRESCENT

The ritual's second night demanded more.

Lissa drank a cup of coffee as soon as Stella had left for work. She washed her hair and let the damp mass of it hang down her back; the heat had come again, steamy and stifling, and the house smelled damp.

She drank a glass of water and used the toilet as if in preparation for a long car ride.

Lissa stood on the porch to watch the sun setting peachy orange at the end of her street, between a factory converted to lofts and a row of Victorian houses, and breathed in the scent of trees.

In the twilit kitchen, she took the egg down from its hiding place. The design of the spell, drawn upon it in black wax, looked ill done and crooked. She ran her fingertips over the letters.

She took the egg up to her bedroom, where she'd set up the necessary things on top of her dresser, in case Stella came home before she was done. Last night's candle had only half burned; she lit it again and set another one, unlit, beside it.

She uncapped a bottle of black ink bought in Chinatown: cheap, slightly gritty, and as dark as anything she'd ever seen. She poured it into a stone bowl she had found in the back of one of the lower cupboards. It looked heavier than water, and it reflected the candle flame like an open eye.

Tonight's charm must be spoken. Baba had given it to Lissa in English, because Lissa's Russian pronunciation had never been very good, and apparently the rune required a great deal of repetition:

As a horse is curbed to the bit, as a river is bound under ice, so, I ask you, bind this one to stillness. Riders of dawn and day and dusk, I ask you. I, Vasilissa, granddaughter of Iadviga, ask you to bind this one by blood.

Then she said it again, three hundred times.

She lost count, of course; but she figured one repetition per minute, for five hours or thereabouts. Baba had told her to repeat it until the hour of the hag, which she figured out was a particularly unpleasant way of designating three in the morning.

With the clocks unplugged, she could not be too sure of the time, but she felt it, nonetheless. Her voice had almost given out, her throat dry like an old bellows, squeezing air between cracked leather.

The air in the house cooled. The candle began to gutter.

Lissa licked dry lips with a dry tongue and stopped speaking. She had to work her mouth for a moment, but she managed just enough saliva; she leaned over the bowl of ink and spat.

Beside the bowl was a box cutter, with a fresh blade, which she'd dipped in rubbing alcohol at the beginning of the night. She pricked her thumb with it, and squeezed. A single, fat droplet of blood fell into the ink and sank.

Carefully, using both hands, Lissa took the wax-written egg and bathed it in the ink, turning it over and over until the faint greasy marks of her fingerprints had vanished.

She took it out and set it back upon the tripod. The ink dried quickly, first marbling in the currents of air and then turning matte.

Lissa watched it, heavy-lidded. After a while, she blew out the candle and went to fetch a glass of water.

Downstairs, the door creaked open. Stella fumbled about, set down her bag, bumped into something, whispered a curse.

The power in the house was still off. Lissa had not thought.

She stood, breathing silently, at the top of the stairs, while Stella tiptoed into the living room; she heard the flick of a flint, saw a faint bloom of light. She waited until the candle was extinguished again and then counted off ten long minutes before she crept downstairs and reset the breakers.

The hallway light flashed on for a second and then died in a fizzle of overstressed filaments. The refrigerator hummed to life.

Stella murmured in her sleep. She sounded distressed. Lissa

stood outside the living-room door, but she was quiet after that, and finally Lissa went up to her own room and tried to sleep.

JUNE 8

● NEW MOON

On Tuesday, Maksim arrived on foot, limping, leaning on Gus.

"You made him walk?" Lissa said.

"He wouldn't get in the cab," Gus said. Under the streetlight, her eyes showed white, too wide. "Your sister's not here, is she?"

Lissa shook her head. "At work."

"What's up with your voice? And that smell?" Gus said. She shivered and tossed her hair. "Ah, Christ, I've been over and over it, and there's fuck all I can do on my own. Take him."

She shoved Maksim at Lissa. He stumbled and caught at Lissa's shoulder but kept his feet. It helped that he had lost weight.

"I'll be back for him tomorrow," Gus said, and she shoved her hands in her pockets and walked away, too quickly, boot heels loud on the sidewalk.

From the corner, she shouted, "Don't fuck this up!" And then she ran.

Lissa left Maksim sitting on the porch steps while she prepared the house. She brought the black egg down to the kitchen, turned off the power again, took down her hair.

Outside, Maksim seemed to have crawled up and slumped against the door, his weight holding it shut. Lissa kicked it before she realized, and she heard the hollow rap of Maksim's head against the wood.

A shuffling confusion of noise, and the door was jerked from her hands. Maksim bulled inside, all awake now, all menace. He crowded Lissa into the kitchen, saying nothing, pressing his fist against his forehead.

He took the glass of water she offered him, but he only set it aside. His face looked clay-colored and heavily lined.

"Do you need a sleep egg before I start? I can't have any interruptions."

"Your voice, *koldun'ia*," Maksim said. "Are you ill?"

"Stayed up all night chanting," Lissa said. "So? Do you?"

Maksim shrugged. "I had two before I left so that we might walk here. Gus did not like it."

"She's not the only one."

Maksim angled his head oddly. In the candlelight, his pupils were dilated all the way so that his eyes looked black. "I smell witchcraft," he said.

Lissa brought down the stone bowl, impatient to get this done now that she was committed.

"And something else," Maksim said.

Lissa opened her notebook to the page where she'd written Baba's instructions.

"I should not ask this thing," Maksim said. "I should go."

"What? Don't be an idiot. It's almost done, anyway."

"I should go," he said again, folding his arms around his body, shaking his head. His eyes looked spooky, blown open wide like that; maybe because his face was thinner than Lissa was used to seeing it.

"You've already made the choice," she said. "Sit." She pointed to the stool by the counter.

He sat. The tendons in his arms and neck stood out harshly beneath his skin.

Lissa placed the black egg in the bowl and poured more ink around and over it. She began to say the charm again.

After the first hour, her voice went, scraped down to a husk of sound, but that did not matter. Her mouth, a witch's mouth, formed the words. Her mind, a witch's mind, held the intention.

Maksim moved only once, to release his grip on his own forearms and pick up the glass of water. Lissa could see the marks on his flesh where his fingers had pressed. He held the glass too tightly also and lifted it to his lips with a grim care that made Lissa wince; and then she turned her eyes away so that she would not lose the thread of the words.

Finally came the hour of the hag.

Chill swept the house. The candle went out.

In darkness, Lissa took Maksim's wrist and led him to the stone bowl. She made him spit in the ink. The egg was bound to her from last night's working; now it must be bound to him, as well.

She held his hand over the bowl, felt for the pad of his thumb, and handed him the blade.

Maksim inhaled sharply.

"Cut," Lissa rasped. "You don't need much."

He said nothing, only sighed out. Lissa heard the blood splash into the ink. She let Maksim go, and she snapped on a pair of latex gloves. Then she reached into the bowl with both hands, turning the egg, coating it.

When she drew it from the ink, her gloves were black up to the knuckles. She found the tripod—her eyes had begun to adjust to the lack of light—and set the egg to dry.

"Now we wait," she whispered.

On her words, the candle flared back to life.

It showed her Maksim, cradling his cut hand against his chest; he'd cut deeper than she meant him to, for blood had run into his palm and down his wrist.

It showed her the familiar kitchen made stark and strange by looming shadows. It showed her the hairs pricked upright on her own arms.

For a moment, unheralded dread stopped her mouth.

She swallowed, swallowed again, gestured to Maksim to pass her the water glass.

He did not seem to see her, sunk deep within himself. Lissa got up eventually and went to the tap. She peeled her gloves off, binned them, washed her hands twice over, and drank straight from the running stream, letting it splash her chin and hair.

When she lifted her head again, Maksim had wrapped his hand into the hem of his shirt. He met her eyes.

"I felt it," he said. "I felt it take." His voice sounded rusty too. He waited until Lissa had finished at the sink, and he held his thumb under the cold tap and then slipped off his shirt to rinse it.

"Thank God," Lissa said, almost light-headed with the lifting of a worry she hadn't even known was so heavy.

"Rest your voice," Maksim said.

Lissa took his place on the stool and drank another glass of water, while Maksim went carefully about her kitchen, pouring out the mess of ink and fluids from the bowl, washing it with plenty of soap. He hung his wet shirt over the back of a chair and went without, though he shivered occasionally. Lissa could see on his skin what the last few weeks had cost him: new livid scars, scour marks, starkly knotted muscles.

"Your sister," Maksim said. "Is she well?"

"She's working late," Lissa said. "It's convocation week for the universities." Elsewhere in the city, people were laughing. Celebrating their achievements. Getting ready for their new lives.

Maksim sat down beside her. "And you?"

"I have to do the last thing," Lissa said. She slid off the stool.

She'd hidden it in her bedroom, in the closet that still smelled of mothballs and Baba's clothing. She brought it out slowly, almost ceremoniously: a steel urn, designed for the ashes of a beloved cat or dog. She'd already stuffed it with a nest of green plastic Easter grass.

In the kitchen, Maksim sat with his face in his hands. He lifted his head when Lissa returned. He did not bother to wipe his swollen eyes; he turned away a little only when Lissa looked at him.

"Why did the candle light again?" he asked as Lissa slid it closer to her.

She shook her head and shrugged. The egg had dried. She wrapped it in a rag and held it gingerly, close to the flame. Nearest the heat, the waxen Cyrillic characters warmed and slid. Lissa wiped away the melted wax with her rag, exposing the bare shell the wax had kept free of ink.

Bit by bit, she revealed the design. Maksim watched. The letters looked uneven, childish; but when the shell was quite smooth and free of wax, Maksim shivered again and looked to Lissa.

She placed it gently within the urn and packed more Easter grass around it.

"Would you like to seal it?"

Maksim shook his head, twisting his hands together on the countertop. Lissa sealed the urn herself, first screwing the lid into place and then dripping hot wax all around the seam. She burned her fingers a little, but she could be sure the urn would not take in any groundwater.

"I'll bury this in the yard," she told Maksim.

"Now," he said.

He followed a few paces behind, out to the garden shed. He dug the hole, two feet deep, between the roots of her grandmother's favorite tree. He would not touch the urn. He stood back while Lissa leaned down to set it in the ground.

He shoveled earth over it as quickly as he could, breathing hard. He filled the hole and stamped it down with his boots.

Only then did he rest, leaning on the shovel and smearing sweat over his forehead with the back of his hand.

"My God," he said. "I am hungry."

Lissa restored power to the house. They took turns in the shower. Maksim fried a pound of bacon while Lissa toasted rye bread and chopped mangoes, bananas, and strawberries.

Just before dawn, Stella came in. She stood in the kitchen doorway and frowned. "Lord, you're weird," she said.

"I am better," Maksim said. "I am sorry I behaved badly before."

"Actually, I meant you were weird for having breakfast in the middle of the night," Stella said and helped herself to bacon.

JUNE 9

◐ WAXING CRESCENT

The food tasted right, as food had not done for so long. Blueberry jam, crusty toast, ripe buttery mango. He ate almost all the bacon himself, some of it right from the pan, hot enough to burn his fingers and his tongue.

Stella made a pot of tea, but she and Lissa were both drooping over the table by the time it had finished steeping.

"Go and rest," Maksim said. "I will tidy up. Thank you for breakfast."

Lissa whispered, "You're welcome." Her hair lay in a wet tangle over her shoulders where she had not bothered to comb it all out. That, and the fragile little voice, would make her seem childlike if Maksim was not what he was and could not smell the heavy thunder on the air.

It made the hair rise on him, even now, with the thing safely sealed up and buried.

He watched Lissa stifle a yawn and pad toward the stairs and turn to wave good night, and he flashed back to the memory of her soft hands gloved and black with ink, a few hours ago, maybe, the memory cloudy and dreadful. The night had gone blurred, everything before the moment when the spell had taken and he'd come to himself, with his own blood pooling in the palm of his hand from a gash in his thumb he did not recall receiving.

He had a pink Band-Aid over it now, and it still hurt: a proper, sharp hurt. A lot of things hurt. Bruised ribs and scabbed-over skin and the knitting bone in his wrist, which had begun to ache when he was digging under the tree.

He relished it. Too many days of smeared-out numbness, burying himself down deep so that he could not do harm, could not do anything at all.

"So," said Stella.

Maksim spun. He'd forgotten her; the new, darker thunder scent covered everything else. And he was tired.

"She didn't want me to see it," Stella said. "It was a bit of a pain, really, not being able to come home. I had to go to an after-hours club with a couple of the girls from the pub and dance to house music. Which I hate."

Maksim raised his eyebrows.

"Well?" said Stella. "Aren't you going to fill me in?"

"If she did not want you to see it . . ."

"Someone's got to look out for her while she looks out for you," Stella said. "Or are you just fine with letting everyone else take the heat for your mistakes? Because I know you've made some, and so far, it looks to me like Lissa's the one who's been cleaning up after you."

"Her grandmother made a promise," Maksim felt compelled to point out.

"Her grandmother was a horrible old hag who kept her away from the rest of the family," Stella said.

Maksim remembered Iadviga, young: all pride and temper, almost like one of the *kin*. He had shepherded her across half of Europe, because *kolduny* were rare and his home was long gone. He'd been glad when he realized she was with child, thinking there was a husband somewhere to whom he could restore her; but she only said fiercely that there was not and kept her head up, glaring.

Sometimes it was hard to remember it had been more than fifty years since he'd found Iadviga in the grip of the Gulag and thirty since he'd asked her to repay that debt. And perhaps the things he admired in Iadviga, the fury that had kept her alive in war and the honor that had urged her to help Maksim, had not made for an easy legacy.

"Her grandmother gave her the spell," Maksim said now, "to give to me. I do not know more than that."

"You know it worked? For sure?"

"Yes," he said, feeling the truth of it: his nature leashed, with a choke leash, barbed enough to hurt if he strained against it.

"Her voice was all shot."

"She prayed for a long time," Maksim said; he was not sure how long, but he had a recollection of the husking whisper continuing in a long broken stream while he sat, struggling slowly and dumbly with himself, at the bottom of a sticky well.

Stella frowned. "I just don't know enough about this yet. But it seemed like the other ones only took a moment."

"The other eggs were only to give sleep for a few hours. This one was to bind a piece of my soul."

He'd meant it figuratively, but it sounded right, now that he said it. The dark piece of his soul matched with the black-stained egg.

"That sounds a bit sinister," Stella said, shivering a little. "Lord, why's it cold in here? It's going to be ninety degrees again by noon."

"You are tired," Maksim said. "You waited up all night. Go, rest. It is enough for now."

He spoke to her as he would to a fellow soldier, and she must have taken the tone correctly, for she straightened and nodded and rose easily.

She stopped and leaned toward the window, though.

"Gus," she said, and both of them stepped quietly to the front door.

Gus stood on the front walk. She had taken a bit of care with herself, Maksim saw: clean, damp hair curling in the warming dawn, two layers of white tank top, bare shoulders dotted with freckles and old scars. He could see her nostrils pinching. If she'd been an animal, her ears would have been laid flat. He realized she did not want to approach any closer to the house.

"Come out to me," she said, voice pitched low.

Maksim did. The sun warmed his bare skin; dew lay heavy on the grass. Gus stood very still until he was within reach, and then she embraced him tight, strong arms about his shoulders, cheek against his.

He felt her look up over his shoulder after a minute and draw breath to speak, but she said nothing.

She let him go then. "Are you ready to come home?"

"I promised to tidy the kitchen. Come inside."

She glanced at Stella on the porch.

"Come," said Stella. "I think there's still tea."

Gus came, though Maksim could see how much it bothered her. She took her tea black and stood in a corner while Maksim balled up his soaked and stained T-shirt and put it in the trash and wiped the bacon pan.

Stella tidied away the fruit peels and toast crumbs and stacked the dishes beside the sink. She kept looking at Gus, quick flashes of her long-lashed eyes. Finally, she said, "You're his sister. Right?"

Gus barked out a laugh. "Close enough." She grinned at Maksim, daring him to offer a different word.

He did not. He was the elder by a century, give or take, but not by enough to gainsay her, not any longer.

JUNE 9

◑ WAXING CRESCENT

The night after the new moon, Lissa went to bed very early.

She'd fallen asleep in front of the television with a glass of water in her hand and only realized when it slipped to the floor and spilled. She left it there.

With Stella out at work, she hadn't bothered to make dinner. Her stomach felt tight and hollow; she only gulped more water and crawled between her sheets.

She dreamed of a mass grave in Greenland. She'd seen it in *National Geographic*, maybe, when she was a child.

The grave contained bodies preserved by the ice: several adults and a baby. The baby had been wrapped in a shield of hides, securing it to a carrying frame, as its mother or father would have used to tote it around in life. The baby's skin and hair, the wool of its swaddling, had all been tanned by the earth to the same palette of browns as the wrapping of hides.

The mouth, gaping open, showed a single brown tooth. The eyes had withered away, leaving empty sockets.

Lissa knew exactly how the baby felt.

She woke with her mouth open on a soundless howl. Her voice had worsened. She could not make a sound at all.

The thin cotton of her sheet rasped her skin as she turned over. The air in her room had gone cold and flat while she slept. She groped for the water glass on her bedside table.

Empty, and her throat ached.

She sat up, knuckling at her eyes. Without her sheet, the cold bit deep. She reached for the switch of her lamp.

No power. The room stayed dark.

It was still on her, the feeling of the dream. Dread and despair. She snatched her hand back from the lightless lamp and huddled as close to the center of her bed as she could get.

In the dimness, the shape of her doll, lying on the bedside chair, reminded her of the mummified baby. And of the chill in Baba's voice, when she spoke, from wherever she was now.

Wherever she was, Lissa would be there too, eventually. Maybe it was the price. She'd made a binding at the dark of the moon. How had she thought this could ever be forgiven?

Then the clock ticked over.

Outside, a bird called.

Lissa raised her head. Warmer air breathed in through the window.

Beside her, the bedside lamp bloomed to light.

"Holy shit," Lissa croaked.

Her face was smeared with tears and snot, her hair pasted to it. She put on a light nightgown and went to the bathroom to wash. In the mirror, under the fluorescent light, she looked puffy and too pink; she could not meet her own eyes.

The wrongness had left her, whatever it was; but she felt the bruise of it still. She wished Stella was home and was then violently thankful she was not. Lissa was afraid to go back into her bedroom.

She ended up drawing a bath and fell asleep in the warm water, with her head propped up by an inflatable neck pillow.

She woke up chilly again, but only because the water had cooled around her; and downstairs, she heard Stella's key in the lock.

"This house smells funny at night," Stella said when Lissa came down, hair wrapped in a towel.

"Does it?"

"Like a cave," Stella said. "You know. Stone and cold water."

Lissa's skin prickled.

"What are you doing up, anyway? You look like the dog's breakfast, quite frankly," Stella continued. "Why don't I make you some tea?"

Eleven

◑ WAXING CRESCENT

On the first day, they built bookshelves. Gus proved to be handy.

Nick was not, but he liked carrying lumber; he ferried over several loads of it from the nearby shop, delighting in the chance to use his strength. He sawed where Gus measured; he did the coarse sanding.

Maksim cleaned up the wreckage of the previous shelves and the books they'd held. He smoothed bent covers, taped torn pages, arranged titles spined alphabetically across the bedroom floor.

Around nightfall, Gus brushed sawdust from her jeans and stood back. "Not half bad," she said.

She helped Maksim carry the books in. Shelved, they covered up the scars in the plaster where Maksim had hammered the wall with broken chair legs—or Nick with his fists.

On the second day, they cleaned.

Nick swept up the sawdust and then vacuumed. He swept the balcony and washed off the albumen stains of two broken eggs.

Then he took everything out of the refrigerator and washed the inside of it.

He threw away the rest of the eggs, but he figured the mustard and beets were okay, and he knew he and Gus would drink the beer, even if Maksim didn't.

He cleaned the kitchen cupboards. He mopped the floor and then dried it.

When he looked up from buffing, he saw Maksim and Gus sitting on the balcony outside. Not helping. Bristling, he approached.

"—until you figure out what to do with him," Gus was saying.

"It is not up to me," Maksim said. "I wish it was."

"And? I don't remember you giving me much of a choice about leaving Cadiz."

"It was not the same. Those days were not the same."

"Because I was a girl, you mean."

"Yes: a girl in a country of men, in an age of men."

Gus scrubbed her fists through her hair. "I don't know why I'm fucking arguing with you. I have to go."

"Augusta . . ."

"You don't need me right now." She pushed past Nick, boots heavy on the hardwood.

"Hey," Nick said.

"Christ, will you shut up?" Gus said, pausing at the door, her hand clenched on the upright of one of the new shelves.

"I was just wondering if—"

"No," she said, and she cast down the shelf.

Nick flinched back. Books cascaded. Nails shrieked in the wood.

Gus's boot heels drummed down the outer stairs. The door banged open and shut.

Maksim sighed. "Will you help me clean up?"

"I have been. All day, in case you didn't notice," Nick said. "And it's not really what I pictured doing with my superpowers, so far."

He kicked a tumble of books out of his way and stormed out. He thought about following Gus, but her scent led toward the park, and Nick was tired of sitting around drinking out of paper bags like a street person, and so he went the other way.

He heard Maksim calling him from the balcony. He kept running.

JUNE 10

🌘 WAXING CRESCENT

On the following night, Stella did not have to work. She went out for a while and came back with a grocery bag bristling with frisée and baby lettuce.

"I've got the makings of a great big salad," she said. "And a bottle of pinot grigio. I thought we could have a nice night in."

"Sure," Lissa said.

"I thought we could watch a chick flick."

"Okay."

"Throat still sore? I can do a soup, if you'd rather."

"Salad sounds good," said Lissa.

"For real? Because you don't sound very excited," Stella said, taking her head out of the refrigerator.

"I didn't sleep well," Lissa admitted.

Stella hugged her. "I know. That's what gave me the idea. We'll have a sleepover in the living room, you and me. Braid each other's hair, watch our film, have our wine. Just the thing."

The movie was about an editorial assistant at a fashion magazine in New York, and Stella seemed to find it hilarious. Lissa sprawled on the sofa and drank the pinot grigio and fell asleep while Stella was still sectioning her hair into tiny braids.

It did not help, though.

At the appointed hour, the cold came over her, and she woke gasping.

She reached out to rouse Stella, in a panic, but her hand stopped just short.

Lissa had broken *Law;* she had fraternized with evil. Maksim had blood on his hands. She had not even taken the time to find out what he'd done. Maybe she should have let him kill himself.

She had not seen, until now, that he'd meant exactly that when he said he should go before the ritual, but it was so clear now—he'd meant to go to the subway and throw himself on the track, and instead of letting him make his amends, she'd done a very wrong thing.

And after, she'd shared food with him. She'd let Stella share food with him. Stella would never shake it now, the wrong like a cancer infecting her house and her family and following her even back over the sea. And Lissa . . . she'd been wrong since childhood, wrong since Mama was ill, and she had been too small to help. People who needed Lissa would always be disappointed.

She might as well take her punishment.

She snatched her hand back and bit down on it and lay in silent terror until the hour passed.

JUNE 11

◗ WAXING CRESCENT

Almost three weeks since he'd taken off. The air smelled flat and dusty when he got the door open. A piece of paper lay half-crumpled on the mat: a testy note from his landlord, inquiring about the June rent. Nick tore it in half and dropped it back on the floor.

He'd been three years in this apartment, and now he followed his old habits: dropping his keys on the table, toeing off his sandals, giving his heavy bag a quick pummeling, going to the refrigerator to uncap a beer, and then leaving a trail of sweaty clothes on the floor on his way to the shower.

The products in his shower smelled too strong to him now, but the water pressure had always been excellent. He stood under it and had a good wank, which had been a bit hard to accomplish lately, considering he was pretty sure Maksim and Gus would know if he did, and the idea of them knowing anything about his sex life was just fucking weird, like incest, and that was not a thought he wanted to be having while trying to get off, which meant he had to start over, thinking about Stella instead.

When he'd finished and thoroughly rinsed off the scented soap, Nick dried himself off with the cleanest-smelling towel he could find. He stared into the open dresser drawer: two stacks of folded T-shirts in dark, dull colors and a strip of expired condoms.

He opened the next one. Five pairs of cargo shorts and two pairs of pants. The informal uniform of every guy his age in Canada; in any country in the world, probably. He'd blend in the way he always had. He grabbed whatever was on top and got dressed.

He strode quickly to the kitchen and opened another beer. He could use his credit cards again, his bank card. No one would be monitoring them. Even if Jonathan had reported him, no one would pay so much attention to the perpetrator of a simple assault; and since Jonathan was fine, he probably wouldn't have said anything to anyone at all.

Nick would be able to go wherever he wanted, so long as he

could stand to get on the plane. Maybe he could ask a travel agent, find out flights with the fewest seats sold.

If he knew where he was going.

Someplace wild, he thought; someplace with fewer people and more space. Up north, maybe.

He rolled up his shorts and pants and some of the T-shirts and packed them into a duffel bag, along with extra socks and underwear and toothpaste. He did not pack any of the scented soaps or shampoos. He found a stack of maps left over from various summer holiday backpacking trips and added those and his passport.

He did not pack any of his books or his camera or his iPod or his PSP. He had not even thought about those things in the last three weeks.

He set the duffel bag by the door and looked around. On the table was a wide brown ceramic bowl given him by Hannah last Christmas; she'd filled it with clementines and pomegranates and told him someone needed to make sure he was getting his vitamins. After the fruit was gone, he'd mostly filled the bowl with overdue bills and unanswered family letters.

Now he ruffled his fingers through the paper, smelling the adhesive of stamps. He picked up the bowl and dumped out the mail on the tabletop. The ceramic felt chrome-smooth and faintly cool.

Nick raised it and brought it down hard on the table's edge. The bowl split into five asymmetrical wedges, sharded with fractured glaze.

As a gesture, he thought it was perfect.

He wasn't done smashing things, though, so he retrieved all the condiment jars from the refrigerator and broke them like eggs into the mess. He opened all the windows and tore out the screens to let the flies in. Then he shouldered his duffel and left.

JUNE II

WAXING CRESCENT

"Does midsummer mean anything to us?" Stella asked.

"Us?" Lissa echoed.

"Witches." Stella pointed to a page in the book she was reading. Lissa looked more closely. *Witchcraft and Sorcery*, it was called, and it looked to have come from the library.

"I don't think so," she said. "Not our kind, anyway."

"It might help with my research if you told me what kind we were," Stella said.

"What kind I am," Lissa said. "Not you."

She stood there looking at Stella's face and hearing the echo of her own words in the heavy air.

"What I mean is—" she said.

"You're right," Stella said, snapping the book shut. "Thanks for reminding me you don't actually want me around."

She set the book very gently on the coffee table, picked up her bag, and walked out the front door.

Lissa waited. After a long time, she went out to the front porch, but Stella was not there. She could not remember whether Stella was working tonight, and she thought in any case it would be a bad idea to barge in on her at the Duke if she was upset.

And why should Stella be upset? She *was* pushing in. She and Lissa weren't real sisters.

And who was a real sister if not a person who'd stay up with you, braiding your hair, while you tried to avoid nightmares?

They'd even started to fight like sisters, Lissa thought—at least she had—fixing on the thing she suspected would hurt Stella most.

She settled for leaving a message on Stella's cell phone. "I'm sorry," she said. "I'm being a jerk. It has nothing to do with you, and I'm sorry. I'll try to do better." She hesitated. "Love you." And hung up.

Lissa cleaned the bathroom in penance, very thoroughly, taking a brush to the grout in the shower.

When the doorbell rang, she struggled up, dried her hands hurriedly, and ran downstairs to answer.

Maksim stood there under the porch light: clean-shaven, dressed in khakis and a T-shirt with the logo of his gym on it.

He looked rather shy as he held out a bundle of carmine-red alstroemeria. *"Koldun'ia,"* he said. "I did not thank you properly the other day."

"That's very sweet," Lissa said.

He followed her inside, politely accepting her offer of a glass of wine.

"I suppose I am still not thanking you properly," Maksim said, looking into his glass, "because I have come with a question. Can it be worked upon someone unwilling?"

Lissa blinked. "I don't get it," she said. "I thought you didn't like it, what it does to you."

"No," he said simply. He shook his head and took a deep swallow of his wine, looking for a moment almost the way Lissa remembered from before.

Maksim set down the glass and looked at his hands. "It is not pleasant. It is a shackle, or a weight, and beneath it, I struggle sometimes."

He looked up again, eyes catching the light. "You do not know what it is to fear your own self," he said. "To know that if you fail in your vigilance, you will destroy whatever it is you care about."

"Sure I do," Lissa said. "Everyone does. People hurt their loved ones all the time." She thought of Stella's eyes and the careful way she'd set the book down.

Maksim gazed at her, steady and cold. "Most of your mistakes do not end in murder."

Lissa did not have an answer for that.

"My mistakes," Maksim said, "are visited upon my progeny. If I wish to protect them from harm, I must protect them from doing harm."

"You want me to do the ritual for Gus and Nick too? I thought they both hated the idea."

"They do."

In the house next door, someone played piano: long arpeggios, an exercise, marred here and there with hesitations. Lissa felt the weight of her sleepless nights.

"I can't," she said.

"Because they have not agreed?" Maksim said, a rough edge in his voice.

"I just can't." Lissa's turn to hide her face with a too-large sip of wine. "You were a mess for a while there. Do you remember me telling you about the ritual? About how it was against the rules?"

Maksim shook his head.

"Yeah. We're not supposed to do anything at the new moon. And when I asked Baba about it, what she'd done for you, I didn't ask all the right questions."

Maksim frowned, the lines in his face deepening. "That smell," he said. "I thought the magic smelled wrong."

"Yeah. I don't really want to discuss it in detail, but it's not something I can do again. Not now. Maybe not ever."

"Your sister?"

"Hell no," Lissa said. "You're not listening. There was a price, and I'm paying it. And it kind of sucks, and there's no way I'm going to let Stella do that for Gus or Nick or anyone else."

"Break the egg, then," he said, laying his hands flat on the table. "Dig it up and break it."

"No. No, Maksim. I know what you were thinking of doing when you offered to leave before the ritual."

She could see from the look on his face that she'd been right. He didn't have to speak.

"Were you suicidal before, when you first came to my grandmother?"

He made a motion with his head that might have been a nod.

"That's why she did it for you, then."

"She owed me a very great debt, *koldun'ia*."

"She never told me about it." And Maksim did not look likely to tell her either, Lissa saw.

He pressed his hands to his eyes. "All I knew was what she owed me; I did not know what I asked of her or of you."

"My grandmother was willing to pay the price. She asked me to do this. She must've known it wouldn't be easy, but she thought you were worth it."

"I will try to find a way to thank you, *koldun'ia*," Maksim said, unsmiling. "And I will not ask again."

He left then, leaving his wine half-finished.

Lissa flipped through a grimoire and set it aside. She'd been through it all earlier, looking for the ritual in the first place; she wouldn't find answers here or in any of Baba's full-moon books. She'd have to wait and ask Baba herself.

How to stop the nightmares or live through them, of course. And what Maksim had done for her, whenever he had done it.

Lissa did not think she would ask anyone what Maksim had done later to make him fear himself so much. It had been bad enough that he'd rather die than do it again, and that was all she wanted to know.

JUNE II

🌒 WAXING CRESCENT

Nick's sense of smell worked even better now. He was learning. And he had, also, the memory of Maksim's address book, which had listed an apartment on Dunn Avenue.

Who even used an address book anymore? People who were hundreds of years old and hadn't really got used to computers, apparently; but he guessed there was the factor that *other* people who were hundreds of years old had shitty subsistence-level lives and weren't on Facebook, and so you had to remember it somehow. At least Maksim hadn't written it in Russian or something.

He'd forgotten the street number, but it didn't matter. All of Dunn Avenue smelled faintly of Gus, as if she'd been walking up and down it for decades. Maybe she had.

Nick stood in the middle of the street. A taxi honked at him. He gave the driver the finger and turned in a slow circle.

South, toward the lake, stronger scent beckoned. Not far.

He followed the thread down an alley between two old Victorians. They'd been beautiful once. Dead vines dangled from the walls; gingerbread trim rotted below leaking rain gutters.

Of course Gus would live here. Nick climbed the fire escape on the outside of her building and knocked upon the boarded window of her door.

She threw a bottle, by the sound of it. It didn't make it through the plywood barrier, but Nick heard it burst and shower shards onto a tiled floor.

"Are you done?" he called.

"Fuck off!" Gus shouted from within. "I told you. We don't enter each other's houses."

"We both spent the last week in Maksim's," Nick said with syrupy reason, hoping it would piss her off even more.

She banged the door open. "I'm going to Durban," she said.

"Why? Oh, wait, I know. To visit your old girlfriend or something. Right?"

"She wasn't my girlfriend," Gus said, hanging on to the door frame.

"How drunk are you?" asked Nick.

Gus laughed and backed down; Nick cautiously stepped into the apartment.

"What a shit hole," he said, without thinking. The window over the fire escape wasn't the only broken one. The fire door led into a cramped main room furnished with a sofa and one wooden chair. The door into the kitchen had been torn from its hinges and left propped against the nearby wall.

The kitchen barely rated the name: it held a laundry sink with the tap wound about in duct tape, a bar refrigerator, and a hot plate mounded with a mess of melted plastic and scorched food.

Gus saw where he was looking. "I forgot I was cooking," she said. "It could happen to anyone."

"Anyone drunk," Nick said.

Gus sprawled on the sofa. "Did you come to fight?"

Nick shrugged.

"You know you're not up to my weight yet," Gus scolded him.

"Maybe not. But no one else is up to mine, really, so I don't have much choice. I'd rather get my ass handed to me than completely mangle some random shithead who happens to be in the wrong alley."

"That's a lie," Gus said. "You'd love to mangle a random shithead." She tongued over the words mockingly, nearly missing a few of the consonants.

Nick shrugged again and helped himself to the open bottle of rye, making a face at the taste.

"If you don't like it, you could have brought me something else."

"I did," Nick said, remembering. He dug through his duffel bag and brought out an unopened bottle of Jameson's, half a mickey of rum, and two airline-sized bottles of vermouth. "The leftovers from my place," he explained.

"Raising anchor?" Gus said and began singing "Spanish Ladies."

"What is it with you and that song? Don't you know anything from this century?"

"It reminds me of the first girl I kissed. In Cadiz. A long time ago."

"I think I'm going to have girls all over the world too," Nick said. He felt a smile spreading over his face as the rye sank in. "I'm going to start with Stella Moore."

Gus went quiet and looked at him.

"She likes me," Nick said. "I know she does."

"She hit you with an egg."

"That's because she has a lot of self-respect."

Gus covered her eyes with her forearm and reached out her other hand for the bottle, which was nowhere nearby; Nick uncapped the rum and guided her fingers around it.

"I think I'll take her with me on a trip," he went on. "Her sister would never let me hang around their place; and anyway, Stella's not the kind of girl who will stay in one town for long. Maybe we'll go to Greece."

"Nick," said Gus.

Nick blinked.

"You came to my home," Gus said. "Against my wishes. You have about five more minutes before I finish drinking your rum and start doing violence. I suggest you say what you came to say."

Nick bit his lip and inhaled. "You aren't really going to Durban, are you?"

Gus laughed. "How would you know?"

He was right; he could tell by the flat look on her face, but she seemed to want him to show his work.

"You're here drinking," he said, "instead of at the airport or on a train. You don't have any things to pack. You know Maksim is okay now. You could be out of town in about ten seconds if you meant to go."

She nodded.

"Why?" Nick said.

"Why do you think?"

"You know she wouldn't take you back," he guessed. "She's your ex for a good reason. Right? You've been here in Toronto for a long time, years, and you wouldn't have been if you could have gone back to this girl anytime."

"She isn't a girl anymore," Gus said, but she didn't disagree with any of what Nick had said. "I haven't seen her in a decade, at least."

"What did you do? Cheat on her? Act crazy? She didn't like your drinking?"

Gus shrugged. "All of the above. Also, I hit her."

Nick whistled.

Gus narrowed yellow-gray eyes at him and lifted off the sofa. "So would you have."

"I'd never . . ." Nick paused.

"Hit a woman? Tell that to the bruise on my ribs," Gus said. "A person weaker than you? Didn't you skip out of your flat because you think you killed your best friend?"

"He's okay," Nick said, hands out, warding her off.

She kept advancing. "Maybe you got off easy this time," she said, "but you won't always."

"I can control myself."

"You have to want to. That's the thing that keeps fucking us up," Gus said. She turned away, wiping at her face.

"Why do you even give a shit?"

"Because you're my kid brother," she said, and she whipped around, catching him in a headlock, and she scrubbed his hair with her fist.

Nick twisted his shoulder into her gut and tried to throw her.

Gus's apartment didn't contain many breakable things, but they managed to crack an arm of the sofa and decorate the kitchen floor with vermouth and broken glass before the pounding of the neighbors below began to register.

Nick spat a strand of Gus's hair out of his mouth and sat up. "Fuck," he said, falling back again, picking a glass shard from the ball of his thumb.

"You did better this time," Gus mumbled through swollen lips.

Nick grinned. "I feel better."

"Don't get comfortable."

"Not much danger of that." His knuckles ached, and his cheekbone began to swell; his scalp stung where Gus had thrown him into the corner of the refrigerator; the little toe on his left foot felt broken, and maybe the one beside it too. But all of that paled beside the weirdness that had been creeping up on him unnoticed during the fight. "Is it magic? Something's really seriously making me want to get out of here."

"Animal instinct," Gus said, shrugging. "This is my territory. Not yours." She bared her teeth.

"I'm going. I'm going," Nick said. "See you around."

He shouldered his duffel again and left by the fire escape, kicking broken glass from the stair treads.

Gus thought Nick would have to be like her, drinking alone in a shit hole apartment, reminiscing about people whose lives he'd ruined. Not bloody likely. What a waste of a very long life.

And Maksim wasn't much better. Castrating himself with the witch's magic. He smelled different, even: duller and less compelling. A boring relation of the graceful, menacing creature Nick had first seen in the alley six weeks ago.

Nick did not have to be like either of them. He was going to enjoy his new life—his long, powerful life—to the fullest.

The only bad thing Nick had done was hit Jonathan. And Jonathan was fine.

JUNE 11

◗ WAXING CRESCENT

Lissa went to the Duke anyway, since Stella hadn't phoned back. Probably hadn't even got the message yet, and Lissa hated the idea of her going through a whole shift with her usual cheer pasted on over a sore heart.

Rafe was in the middle of serving someone. She took her usual seat at the end of the bar and waited for him to notice her.

When he did, the look that crossed his face wasn't anything she'd seen before.

"Oh, love," he said, and he came to take her hands.

She opened her mouth to say something—what did he mean? what was he looking at?—and Rafe's expression changed to something else, and he ducked around the edge of the bar and pulled her close, face against his brown T-shirt. And when had she started crying?

Rafe cupped the back of her head in one big hand, murmuring,

"Hey, hey, hey." She could feel his voice through his chest. His other hand rubbed between her shoulder blades.

She ducked away and wiped hard at her eyes.

"Okay," he said, "no hugging, then, but what about tea? It's a cliché, but help me out here—I have to do something."

Lissa nodded and took the Kleenex he handed her and bit down hard on the inside of her cheek. By the time he came back with a mug of tea and a slice of lemon on a saucer, she was breathing without that shuddering hitch, and she'd managed to dry her face.

"Sorry," she said. "Sorry."

"Don't apologize. Unless you're upset because you're here to break up with me, in which case, I'll have my tea back," he said, smiling in a way that wasn't quite as cocky as he might have meant it to be.

"No. No. It's just everything."

"Bad few days? I wondered when you hadn't been around much, and then I thought, well, she's a nice girl, probably going to work and evening Mass or something."

"I'm not," Lissa said. "I can't even go to church—and Stella—"

"Hey, it's okay. You don't have to. Look, whatever you want to tell me. Or not." He smoothed his hand down her arm. "Let me get you another tissue."

He was gone a few minutes, pulling a series of pints and setting them on a tray for one of the waitresses, a gangly brown-skinned girl who looked barely of age in her kilt. Lissa blew her nose and drank some tea.

Rafe was right; it did seem to be working.

When he came back, he looked rueful. "I'm terrible at this. You'd think a bartender would be better at the tea and sympathy, wouldn't you? I don't have anyone to fill in right now."

"No, no, it's fine. I'm fine."

"You don't look it," he said frankly. "I mean, you're still adorable and all that. But look, whatever it is . . . is it more migraines? You've been poorly?"

"It's . . ." How to even begin to translate? She hadn't thought about it at all, had stupidly not even expected to see Rafe here. "I said something awful to Stella," she admitted.

"That'd be why she called in," Rafe said. "Well, she's a talented barmaid, but I know which sister I'd rather have around." He tugged Lissa's hair affectionately. "She thinks the world of you, you know. You'll get things patched up in no time."

"Wait, she's . . . not here?"

"Hey, don't look like that. She's a big girl. Probably went to let her hair down somewhere."

"You're right." He was right. Stella wasn't an idiot, and eventually she would check her phone, and things would be fine tomorrow.

Lissa was only tired and strung out and not used to dealing with people. All she had to do was get through the night.

Twelve

 WAXING CRESCENT

"This was a great idea. I needed to get out," Stella said, stretching her long legs under the patio table, one calf just brushing Nick's.

She glinted in the lantern light: straight teeth and mink-brown eyes and diamond stud earrings. She tilted her head back to get the last drops of her wine, and the skin of her throat looked as delicate as a magnolia petal.

They were the only customers on the patio. The fence between them and the neighboring yard was overgrown with Japanese honeysuckle, just beginning to bloom. Between that and the scent of Stella and a tart Rueda, Nick felt absolutely dizzy with pleasure.

"That's usually when you should stop," Stella told him, sliding his glass along the table, away from his hand.

"I can drink much more than other people. In fact, it's good for me. Gus says so."

"Gus sounds like a bit of a bad influence, if she really said that."

"You have no idea." Nick chuckled.

"I should probably slow down too," Stella said.

"It's okay. I'll look after you."

"I prefer to look after myself," she said, meeting Nick's gaze with a wry smile.

Good God, he was glad he'd had a chance to jerk off in the shower earlier. He retrieved his glass and drained it.

"Really," said Stella. "It's nice to get out from under everyone's thumb a bit. But this bad-boy thing you have going on is sort of . . ."

Nick smiled slowly.

"Transparent," Stella said.

Nick blinked.

"I mean, I know your life has changed a lot lately," Stella said. "Mine has too. You think you know exactly what's going to happen next, and then you find out you were wrong, and you have to figure it out all over again. And you find yourself on the other side of the ocean, or whatever, with people who don't really like you that much. But all this, like, Ernest Hemingway stuff—I mean, the black eye and the drinking and the dark hints . . ."

"What are we talking about?" Nick said.

"I'm giving you unwanted advice," Stella said, laughing bitterly into her empty glass.

"Damn. I thought you were flirting with me," Nick said.

"I'm taking a break from men," Stella said.

"Some of us never go back," Gus said from the other side of the honeysuckle hedge.

"Jesus!" said Nick. "Where'd you come from?"

"Behind this plant," said Gus, strolling around it. "Smells great, doesn't it? You'll learn to use that kind of thing."

Now Nick could smell her, *kin* to him, but he wasn't sure if he would have noticed it on his own, not with the heady flower scent drowning everything.

"Pretty good," he said. "You're like a ninja. A fun-killing ninja."

Stella, without asking, filled her glass with the rest of the wine and handed it to Gus. "Give it a rest, Nick. I was never going to sleep with you," she said.

Gus laughed hard at that, pounding her fist on the table.

"I'm going home," Nick said, wondering if he sounded as sulky as he felt.

"I thought you were going to Greece. With Stella."

"He said that? That's kind of creepy." Stella gave him a raised eyebrow.

"It's no creepier than Gus going to Durban to stalk her ex," Nick said.

"Who's got a packed bag under the table?" Gus said, kicking it with her boot.

"Seriously?" said Stella, turning to Nick.

He shrugged one shoulder. "I just went by my old place to get some stuff."

"When were you going to invite me on this supposed trip?" Stella demanded. "Christ, you've known me how long? And I've already had to egg you once."

Fuck. He had nothing. It did sound stupid when she put it that way. He didn't think he'd always been this stupid with women. When had he turned stupid?

When Maksim Volkov licked him was when.

He needed advice from someone smart, someone who wasn't neck-deep in supernatural bullshit. If he wasn't going to get laid, he needed something to go right, just one thing.

He made himself turn to Stella and apologize. Maybe she wasn't as into him as he'd thought, but he'd learned at least one thing from the whole Sue Park debacle.

Gus, though, she could fuck herself. Nick grabbed his duffel from under her boot and walked away without saying good-bye.

JUNE 12

◐ WAXING CRESCENT

Lissa sat in her kitchen until two o'clock in the morning. She read grimoires, paged through one of Stella's celebrity magazines.

More than a week before the full moon, when she could ask Baba for help. She wondered how long she could stay awake.

She hadn't tried getting out of the house yet, she thought. Maybe it would help if she wasn't asleep when the hour struck: if she were someplace beautiful, someplace else.

Outside, the air held no trace of the weird nightmare chill. Not yet, anyway. She looped her bag over her shoulder and strolled north. The maples were in full leaf now, haloed brilliant lime in the streetlights. They hardly rustled, the air hung so still.

She walked aimlessly, too tired to hurry, even if hurrying could have taken her further from the nightmare hour. North and a little way east, through two parks, passing a man sleeping beneath a bench, another man on a pair of flattened cardboard cartons.

A few houses showed lights at upper windows or the flicker of a television. A raccoon trundled across the street ahead of her; two cats stood, backs up, eyeing each other in a tableau of hostility.

She was only a couple of blocks from the church. She saw the onion spire above a cloud of maple leaves.

Even at night, empty, the church felt hung about with a special quiet. Lissa found the door locked, of course. She ascended the fire escape, which led up to a side door into the choir loft. Also locked—but she could curl up in the deep embrasure of a window and rest her head against cardinal-red and finch-yellow panes.

Father Manoilov would be furious if he knew, but it wasn't as if he could do much to her, not now. She was already barred from the sanctuary. And she wasn't breaking his edict; she was on the church, not in it.

She even prayed, one of the prayers she used to say with Baba. It didn't help.

An hour later, queasy with weeping, she uncurled her body and crept down the fire escape again.

The walk home took longer than ever, and she had to stop once and lean on a trash can while she decided whether or not she was going to be sick.

She wasn't. She kept walking.

She was. She vomited bile into someone's flower bed, while a cat watched from a nearby stair.

Shaking, she wiped her mouth on the back of her wrist and trudged on.

JUNE 12

WAXING CRESCENT

Maksim dreamed of Afghanistan again.

It was not the full-color horror of the dreams he'd had over the last few weeks. The sleep brought on by the eggs had seemed to make those brighter, more vivid, than anything he truly recalled. He knew he did not have complete memories of much of what he did in his battle fury, but his dreaming mind was all too willing to fill in the missing bits with stench and hot blood and bone-cracking sounds.

Instead, this dream was unpeopled, spare, and fragmentary.

In it, he wore his *Afghanka*, and he walked the perimeter of a camp alone. Sunrise glinted from the windshields of the infantry trucks. Behind him, the main battle tank loomed, still in the shadow of the hills.

Dust coated the grass at his feet. His boots were worn; steel showed through the leather at the toes.

He smelled the distant river, fast and fresh, and the grease of his gun. He heard wind and his own footsteps.

He felt quite peaceful, even though he knew in the dream that he would be fighting again before noon.

As he began to wake, he remembered what he would do a few months later. He wondered if peace was ever real, ever a thing unto itself, or whether it was only the temporary absence of violence.

The dream fell away then, and Maksim rolled out of his bed, finding that the sunrise, in reality, was still an hour away.

He drank yesterday's cold tea, black. He tore a chunk from a loaf of bread and ate it on the balcony, watching a rat creep down the gutter on the opposite side of the street.

He thought he would buy meat at the market today; he would visit the gym, see how DeShaun was doing with the competitors; he would buy wine and bitter greens, and he would cook. Nick would like his steak rare, and if he ate well, he might feel his other appetites less.

Only then did Maksim wonder when he'd last seen Nick.

JUNE 12

◑ WAXING CRESCENT

Stella was sitting on the porch, just outside the shadow of the lilacs.

"Did you forget your key?" Lissa asked, hurrying up the walk.

"Nah," Stella said, waving her hand languidly. "Gus doesn't like it inside, is all."

Then Lissa saw that what she'd taken for a dismissive gesture was Stella patting Gus on the shoulder. Gus Hillyard, who was a pale smudge lying sprawled in the dark of the lilac leaves.

"What is it? Is it Maksim?"

Stella giggled. "Nothing's wrong. Sit." She slapped the porch beside Lissa's feet, overloud. "Have a drink. Unless I drank it."

"No, I did," Gus said drowsily.

"Seriously?" Lissa said. "This is what you decided to do with your night?"

"You were mad at me; Rafe was working. I don't know anyone else," Stella said. "Are you still mad?"

"No. I called you to apologize."

"Oh. I don't know where I put my phone," Stella said, and she began digging through her bag.

"Forget it," said Lissa. "You can listen to it later. I just wanted you to know."

"That's lovely," Stella said, and she hugged her around the legs.

"You're not going to be sick or something, are you?" Lissa asked, looking down, twining her hand in the loose strands of Stella's hair.

"I wouldn't let that happen," Gus said and chuckled, low and hoarse. "She's only a little foxed. I, on the other hand . . ."

"You still walked me home. Mostly," said Stella, and she yawned. "I have to go to bed."

"Me, too," said Gus and she did not move.

Lissa gave Stella a hand up. "Are we okay? Really?"

Stella hugged her again and kissed her on the cheek. "One of these days, you're going to tell me all about whatever is going on in your head," she said. "And I'm going to steal your blue camisole top and make you watch romance films again."

"Deal," Lissa said. "Gus? Want a cab?"

"What? Christ, no," Gus said, struggling up. "I prefer to go on foot."

"The sidewalk is that way."

"Ignore my patronizing sister," Stella said. "Thanks for looking out for me."

"You're welcome," said Gus, and she took Stella's hand and kissed the back of it before stepping heavily off the porch and down the walk.

"And she didn't like me giving Maksim eggs," Lissa said.

"Maybe it is the same," Stella said, watching Gus weave around the corner. "They only want to be able to get by, right? But it seems like life should be more than just getting by. Especially when your life is that long."

Lissa wasn't really listening. "Bed," she said, tugging Stella's hand. Her mouth watered at the thought of toothpaste, clean sheets, cotton nightshirt. The night was nearly over and the worst hour past. She would sleep in, long after the sun was up. She would drink tea and listen to the news on the radio, and maybe, later, she would see Rafe.

JUNE 12

◖ WAXING CRESCENT

Maksim saw Gus coming up through Bellwoods Park; she was off the path, kicking heavy boot prints into the soft grass. He changed direction to meet her.

"Why did it get worse for you?" she said without preamble. "Why did you go off the rails?"

"*Koldun'ia* Iadviga died," he said.

"No. Before that. The thing you never talk about."

He took a breath into tight lungs. "I still do not truly know why."

"That's not good enough," said Gus, gripping him by the shoulders. "I need to know."

"I need to look for Nick."

She shoved at him and nearly fell. "I need to know! Why didn't you see it coming?"

"Augusta . . ."

"If I'd been there, I could have stopped you."

"If you had been there, one of us would be—"

She cut him off with a wild haymaker. He didn't let the blow land; he just caught her arm and squeezed until he felt her skin start to pulp against the bones.

She didn't make a sound. She looked at him with her eyes wide and wet and still young-looking, somehow.

"I must look for Nick," he told her again, letting his fingers ease open. "He has not been back to my apartment."

"I saw him," Gus said, holding her arm against her chest, stroking the skin where it would bruise. "He was at a wine bar."

"Then where is he now?"

"I don't know," Gus snapped. "Not with Stella. That's what matters."

"Oh," Maksim said.

Gus hit him again, faster and with better aim this time.

Only once, though, and then she backed down and let her shoulders slouch. "I'll show you where the wine bar is," she said while Maksim ran his fingertip over the tooth-cut on the inside of his lip. "After that, I'm going to crash at your flat, because I'm too damned drunk to be up past dawn."

Maksim held his tongue on the things he could have said. He had said them before, anyway, in other languages and in other countries, and he did not think they would sound different enough in this.

JUNE 12

◑ WAXING CRESCENT

Scientists would want to examine him if they could see him now. The military would run tests on him. Vials of his blood would be marked with biohazard symbols. They'd keep him in a cell underground in the Arctic. For centuries.

Nick nearly laughed aloud. Jonathan would get such a kick out of this. Jonathan would have all kinds of great ideas of how Nick could use his powers.

Jonathan, he realized, would be asleep right now. Jonathan was just a person and would not get up until long after dawn.

Rather than ring his bell, Nick dumped his bag in the alley and decided to climb the wall.

He and Jonathan had done some wall climbing together the year before at a gym on the lakeshore. Without ropes, this was a bit more frightening, but Nick's hands were so much stronger now. Even without chalk, he could use his fingertips to grip the edges of the cheap yellow bricks of Jonathan's building. He could kick off his shoes and wedge his toes in the tiny holds. One toe hurt—he thought he'd broken it fighting with Gus earlier—but he knew by now that it would heal up quickly and well.

He took a break on the balcony below Jonathan's, stretching his arms and legs. Only a minute and he was fresh again, ready to keep climbing.

He wrapped his fingers about Jonathan's railing and swung himself neatly up, a campus he never would have been able to manage before, even at his training peak. This was more like it; forget cleaning floors and building shelves. He could become a hit man or a spy.

Jonathan's balcony door was not locked. Why would it be?

Nick slid it softly open and stepped inside.

The apartment smelled of last night's dinner—oil and vinegar, peppery sauce—and of people who'd sweated together in love and gone to sleep without washing up.

Nick stood in the doorway of their bedroom and watched.

Hannah lay with her back to Jonathan, face nested in her own tangled hair. One hand rested at her mouth, as if she'd almost forgotten not to suck her thumb.

Jonathan's hand curled over Hannah's stomach. They were going to have children, Nick remembered. Surely not yet?

As sweet as it all was, he was bored and a bit hungry. He cleared his throat.

Jonathan sat up fast. Hannah tried to, but Jonathan pressed her behind him.

"It's just me," Nick said. "Didn't mean to scare you."

"Shit, man," Jonathan said, rusty-voiced, after a moment. "Just about gave me a heart attack."

Hannah was squirming beneath Jonathan's arm, dragging the sheet up.

"Oh," said Nick. "You aren't dressed. Well, I'll wait in the living room."

He heard them whispering together as he turned his back: urgent, sharp, argumentative. Maybe there was something wrong between them. Maybe they'd break up.

Jonathan came out alone, in boxers and a U of T shirt. "My head's okay now," he said. "Thanks for asking."

"Oh," said Nick. "Shit."

"Yeah. It was you, then."

"Yes."

Jonathan sat down on the sofa, staring at Nick with an expression that reminded him of being reprimanded by his father. Nick dug his bare toes into the pile of the carpet.

"Hannah has to get up early," Jonathan said. "Maybe you should keep this short, whatever it is."

"I just wanted to see you," Nick blurted.

"In the middle of the night? After disappearing for a few weeks? We were worried, you know. Hannah wanted to report you missing."

"But you didn't?"

"I haven't forgotten that time you randomly took off for Edmonton. I thought maybe you'd suddenly decided to go tree planting or teach ESL in Japan or something."

"I had," Nick admitted. "Forgotten the road trip, I mean. That was a good time, camping and everything. That music festival. Wow, the hash brownies. What was that girl's name? With the VW van?"

"No fucking idea," Jonathan snapped.

Nick shook off the memory. "I actually came to tell you something."

"If it isn't an apology—"

"No shouting," said Nick, stepping closer and laying his hand over Jonathan's mouth. "You said Hannah needed her sleep."

Jonathan's eyes widened. His breath, through his nose, whistled faster. His smell changed.

"You're afraid," Nick said, wondering. "Of me. Is it because I hit you?"

Jonathan nodded.

"That was a shitty thing to do," Nick said. "I'll try not to do it again."

Nick removed his hand and laid one finger to Jonathan's lips to remind him to be quiet. Then he crossed to the bedroom door and shoved a chair under the doorknob.

"There. Now it's just us," he whispered, returning and standing over Jonathan. "I came to tell . . . I don't even know. Maybe you won't like it."

"Look," Jonathan said, even more softly now. "Give it a shot. Tell me. It can't be any worse than the stuff I've imagined, can it?" He didn't sound sure.

"I've changed," Nick said. "I'm different. I'm not like you anymore." He couldn't quite bring himself to say *not human.* "When I met Maksim . . ."

Jonathan actually laughed. "Are you trying to tell me you're gay?"

Nick slapped him across the mouth. "Stop interrupting!"

"Fuck!" Jonathan said, feeling his lip where the blow had landed, checking his fingertips for blood.

"Would you just let me speak?" Nick said.

"There's nothing wrong with being gay."

"Of course there isn't," Nick said. "But that isn't what I am."

"Have you been in the psych ward?" Jonathan said. "Is that where you met this guy?"

"Stop it," Nick said, reaching out. "Stop fucking *assuming* things. You don't know. You don't know everything."

Jonathan's breath wheezed through his nose again. Nick found he had clamped his hand rather tightly, and he loosened it a little, but not enough to let Jonathan talk.

"When did you start thinking you were better than me?" Nick said. "I thought it was her, for a while, but she's too nice for that, isn't she? You came up with it all on your own."

From the bedroom, Nick heard footsteps and a thump.

The doorknob twisted on its short arc. Hannah: "Jonathan? What's going on out there? Jonathan?"

"He's fine," Nick said over his shoulder. "Be quiet."

"You're scaring me," Hannah said.

"You're scaring yourself," he said. "I just came to talk."

"Nick," she said, "I know you don't want to hurt anyone. I'm not sure you're feeling like yourself right now."

"Of course I don't want to hurt anyone," Nick said. "Unless someone wants to hurt me."

Jonathan twisted under him, jerked at his arm.

"Don't do that. You aren't strong enough anymore," Nick said. "That's part of what I'm trying to tell you."

"Nick, you need to let Jonathan talk to me," Hannah said. "If he needs help, I'm going to have to call someone."

"Threats?" Nick said. "You don't have to do that."

He let go of Jonathan and shouldered open the bedroom door.

It came off the hinges and knocked Hannah off her feet. "Oops," Nick said. "Didn't mean to break it. Give me that." He snatched the phone from her hand, turned it off, and threw it at the window; plastic pieces scattered, though the window glass remained whole.

Hannah backed away, hands out.

"Just stay in here. Shit, you're not going to do that, are you? Come with me." Nick took her wrist, dragged her into the living room, threw her down on the sofa beside Jonathan. "I'm trying to be nice here."

They didn't speak. Nick looked at their faces, identically wide-eyed and blank.

He clutched his own hair in frustration, squeezed his eyes shut. "Fuck!" he said. "You're making this so much harder."

When he opened his eyes, Jonathan had his hand on another goddamn phone.

Nick lunged, seized his arm, twisted.

Jonathan came off the sofa, yelling, and dropped the phone. When Nick released him, he knelt on the floor, cradling his arm against his chest.

"You should have listened!" Nick said. "I just wanted to talk."

Jonathan looked funny: sallow-faced, eyes too dark. Nick wondered if he was going to vomit.

Hannah looked nearly as bad. But her eyes weren't focused on Nick.

Nick glanced over his shoulder.

JUNE 12

◐ WAXING CRESCENT

The sandals at the base of the wall were familiar. Maksim laid his face against the brick for a moment, and the scent there was clear.

He untied his running shoes and removed his socks. This close and he wanted to slow down, wanted to turn back, almost. Wanted to walk back to his apartment and make coffee for Gus and tell her that Nick was gone. If Nick had any intelligence, he would be, after tonight.

Maksim did not smell any blood, though. Not yet. He might still have a chance to keep Nick from shedding it.

He cracked his knuckles and set his palms to the wall.

Climbing proved awkward, with several of his fingers still stiff and the healing scabs down his side still cracking. He had never liked heights, either.

He could hear nothing from within the building. Nick's scent stopped abruptly. A thread of fabric caught in a cracked brick smelled of him, and then nothing.

Maksim craned his head around. Above and to the left, the base of a balcony: Nick must have taken that route. Maksim hugged his weight close to the wall, pressed up on his toes, and swung up and out.

The iron rail creaked when it took his weight. Even underweight, he was bigger than Nick. He clambered up hastily, tearing his shirt.

Through the open door, a young woman watched him, open-mouthed—and before her Nick, poised and thrumming with violence.

Maksim bulled in and took him.

Nick had time to turn and inhale. Maksim caught him by the throat and squeezed.

Nick kicked and swore and hammered at Maksim's forearm. Maksim held on.

"You're hurting him," the woman said. Maksim looked to her. She was backed into the corner of the sofa, hands raised protectively before her.

"Look to your own," Maksim said. The other man was hunched on the floor, and he wasn't breathing quite right.

The woman darted forward, falling to her knees beside the other man.

She stammered something. Maksim did not listen.

He waited until Nick was purple-faced and gagging for breath and then let him fall.

"I will take him with me," he said to the man and the woman. "You will not see him again."

"But . . ." the woman said.

"What the fuck," the man said.

"I am sorry," Maksim said. "I should not have let him escape me. I hope you are not badly hurt."

He bundled Nick up, arms behind his back. Nick wheezed and drooled.

Maksim asked, "Where is the door?"

The woman pointed. "When you take him back, are visitors allowed?"

Maksim blinked. "I would not recommend it."

A few minutes later, hauling Nick down the fire stairs, he asked, "What did she mean, your friend? Where does she think I am taking you?"

He'd thought Nick capable of answering by now, but Nick only gasped and choked and leaned on his arm.

By the time they reached the ground floor, though, Nick had recovered enough to point to the place he'd left his bag. Maksim hefted it easily in his free hand.

"Will you follow, or must I force you?"

"I'll follow," Nick rasped.

He was lying, of course. Maksim had to force him.

ANOTHER COUNTRY: A CENTURY AGO

Maksim had nearly ended Gus, once. He no longer remembered what city, what country, but he had found her in a barn. There had been a cock crowing, and Gus had been wearing a blue smock like a butcher would wear, and it had been bloodied like a butcher's too.

Maksim remembered waiting for her to wake up—from one of her rages? From a blow to the head? From a few days' worth of drink?—while he sat upon a milking stool, empty hands upturned on his knees. She looked childlike, still, in sleep, with the stained fabric bunched around her, hiding the wiriness of her limbs.

As he watched, the lines of her face tightened, and her eyes squinted. He met her gaze and smiled a little. "Augusta," he said. "You have been busy."

She did not smile back. "People busy themselves with me. You cannot blame me for answering."

"Oh, but I can," he said. "I ordered you to lie quiet."

"That was days ago, Maks," she said, stretching, her hands

finding the rents in her smock and covering them over. She wrapped the garment closer around her, shivering a little under Maksim's gaze.

"You did not come away clean this time," he said, shaking his head at the mess of scratches on her bared legs, the torn soles of her feet.

"I had to run away," Gus admitted. "But some of them could not run after."

"Is this what you wished for yourself?" Maksim said. "When you fretted inside the walls of your father's house?"

Gus shrugged one shoulder. It looked as if it hurt her.

"It need not be forever," Maksim said. He turned fully toward her and withdrew the silver-chased dueling pistol from the pocket of his coat. "You need only ask," he said.

Gus sat up straight, wincing. "Of course not."

"Are you quite sure? This is no life for a girl."

"I am no girl," she said, baring her teeth to him. "And I like this life very well."

He laughed and put the pistol away, and no more was said about it.

He wondered now if he would have done differently in a different age; if the very reason he'd let her live was that he did see her as a girl, still, despite all the harm she could do. And by the time he learned to see her as she really was, he also learned to love her and forgive her all her tempers and lawlessness.

She, in her turn, learned the virtues of discretion and learned to point her temper where it might do good as well as harm and was better at all of it than Maksim was, although time would no doubt wear her down.

Nick, now: part of the problem was that he did not want to learn. And the other part was that neither Maksim nor Gus had learned to love him yet.

JUNE 12

◖ WAXING CRESCENT

Maksim kept Nick in a hammerlock all the way back to his apartment. Nick bore it, seething silently, though Maksim could feel the deep tremor in the joint of his shoulder. He hauled Nick right up the stairs and through the door and into the shower, where he let go and cranked on the cold tap.

Nick hissed through his teeth and shied away from the chill.

"It will keep the bruising down," Maksim told him. "And perhaps your temper, for now."

"I had it under control."

"No. I had you under control," Maksim said. "Hush, now, and clean up."

Nick scowled, but under the icy water his mutiny was leaving him. He nodded and shivered; he stripped off his sodden T-shirt, wrapped his arms about his lean chest, and tilted his throat to the spray.

Maksim left the shower curtain half-drawn and stood in the bathroom doorway.

Gus, on the sofa, rolled over and set her bare feet to the floor. She padded close and leaned on the door frame opposite Maksim and whispered, "I will kill him for you, if it must be done."

Maksim looked at her: bloodshot eyes, hair flat on one side, a tiny scar at the corner of her lip that he thought he might have given her once upon a time.

"You don't need another reason to hate yourself," she said.

"No," Maksim said. "Neither do you."

The shower turned off; from within the bathroom, Nick coughed painfully.

Gus shrugged and stretched and knuckled at her temple. "Offer stands if you change your mind," she said, and she got up to make coffee.

Maksim watched her—the still-youthful grace under the clumsiness of her hangover as she ran water and measured grounds and rinsed out a couple of used mugs. She didn't look at him. She was giving him time to see she meant it.

Like a cat offering her master the corpse of a songbird, he thought; but that was not right, because animals were innocent, and the *kin* were not.

The coffee finished brewing. It did not smell as rich as it would have before the spell tamed his nature again, but still it was good. And still he did not know what he should do.

Nick, subdued and pale-faced, dried off and put on clean clothes. He ate a piece of bread and a plum, in small bites, swallowing carefully.

"Are you ready to listen now?" Maksim asked him.

Nick nodded.

"I am going to send you away," Maksim said. "With Gus, if she will take you."

Gus, sitting on the kitchen counter, dangling her boots, shrugged and nodded. Looked keenly at Maksim.

He met her eyes and blinked.

"I think," Nick said, and he paused to clear his throat. "I think I know where I should go."

"Oh?"

"Jonathan said it. I knew he'd know . . . only I fucked it up . . . Whatever. Look. There's a job—you might've heard about it—where you plant trees. Up north. You live in a camp in the woods. It's hard, and the pay's not great, but you work outdoors."

With the words, his voice came a bit easier. Gus lost a bit of her wary poise and leaned forward, interested.

The job would only last the summer, Maksim understood. Nick would be back in town and restless by fall.

But maybe it was enough time for him to come to terms with his nature. And if not . . .

Maksim nodded and gestured for Nick to continue.

JUNE 23

◯ FULL MOON

The full moon fell the day after midsummer.

"I thought it was significant somehow," Stella said, tapping the calendar with a manicured nail. "It always seems to be a big thing in stories."

"It's different every year," Lissa said.

"Oh, right; I keep forgetting how the moon shifts about. Doesn't that drive you a bit mad?"

"When I was a kid, maybe. Now I just make sure to look at the calendar."

"Oh, snap! Some of us haven't had a lifetime of witching," Stella said. "I've got the patio tonight. Come and tell me how it goes, if you don't mind."

Lissa kissed her on the cheek and waved her off.

Restless, she prowled the house for almost an hour, running her fingertips over shelves that hadn't been dusted since Baba's death, reminding herself that she still had not canceled Baba's credit card and that she owed Anna Malinina a batch of painkilling eggs.

She'd take care of those later. First, her questions.

When the moon showed a broad yellow face over the east end of the city, Lissa was watching from the porch with the doll cradled in the crook of her arm, a torn hunk of French bread ready, and the saltshaker.

By the white rider of dawn, by the red rider of day, by the black rider of night, I call to you: Iadviga Rozhnata, your scion desires your counsel.

"On what matter may I counsel you tonight?" Baba asked, her voice harsh and still her own and very far away.

Lissa felt her eyes flood over. "I performed the new-moon ritual," she said. "The thing that's happened, ever since . . . I hate it. I haven't had a full night's sleep in two weeks. Stella worries. I worry. I worry you're angry at me, and I worry I haven't done the right thing."

Baba remained silent.

Lissa supposed none of what she'd said was a question, after all. "How do I make it stop?" she asked.

"Oh, *vnuchka*," Baba said. "You do not. You bear it, because it is the price of breaking *Law*."

"How long?" Lissa asked. Her voice gave out again. She wondered if it would ever come back all the way.

"Until the price is paid," Baba said. "Not forever. Long enough."

Lissa drew in a shuddering breath. She had two more questions to ask, and only one could be answered.

She bit her tongue on it, holding on to the sense of Baba in her mind. Until she had her last answer, she would not be alone.

She kept sitting, cradling the doll, watching the moon brighten to white and rise up into a halo of thready cloud.

Baba waited with her, endlessly patient.

Finally, "Maksim says hello," Lissa said. "He thanks you. He says he did not know what he asked of you."

Something in the quality of Baba's silence gave Lissa her decision.

"And Stella," she said. "Stella never got a chance to know you, and she wishes she had." Lissa could not say Baba and Stella would have loved each other, although she wished it were true. She forged on, "She knows what I do now. She's curious and smart, and I think she's capable. Should I teach her?"

"You have already begun," Baba said.

And that was all she said. She didn't go, right away, though. Lissa felt her there, lingering in the chilly open space that was not a space.

She kept talking, telling Baba about the changes she was going to make to the house, about Stella's job, and even a bit about Rafe.

Sometime around her description of how they'd set up Lissa's old bedroom for Stella, Lissa noticed that Baba was gone, leaving a warmth behind, or maybe it was only the contrast to the sense of chill she brought.

Lissa wrapped up the doll and put it away.

She tied up her hair in a loose knot, glossed her lips, and went to the pub.

Thirteen

JUNE 23

◯ FULL MOON

The work was hard. He'd known that going in. He'd wanted it. But it was hard.

Nick's shovel stripped the skin from his right palm. His left hand, the one he shoved into the dirt a thousand times a day, had grains of dirt jammed up behind the fingernails. The sun raised crackling, bleeding burns on the tips of his ears and the nape of his neck. His boots blistered his feet raw. His planting bags, hanging from padded shoulder straps, rubbed welts into his thighs where they swung with his steps.

The roof of his mouth ached with dehydration until he learned to drink well before he felt thirsty. His right Achilles tendon seized up most mornings so that he fell on his first steps out of his tent as often as not.

"Aren't we supposed to have some kind of awesome healing powers?" Nick asked Gus, retaping his ankle with duct tape over his wool sock as they sat at the cache at the end of a day, waiting to be picked up by one of the crew ATVs.

"We do," she said. "Imagine how the regular people are feeling."

"I don't have to," Nick said. "I can hear them bitching every night when I'm trying to sleep."

"Work harder," Gus said, completely unsympathetic. "Tire yourself out enough and you won't notice what anyone else is doing."

She stretched out her booted feet and cracked her back with a sigh of satisfaction. She wasn't in any better shape than Nick was—worse, probably, because as far as Nick could tell, she'd spent the last few years just hanging around getting drunk, not keeping up any kind of a regular fitness program. But she seemed fine with it, somehow. She meticulously bandaged any injuries that broke the skin and then covered them up with extra duct tape, but she didn't seem to care about anything else; she limped around like a drunken sailor for days after twisting her knee sliding down a trench, and she refused the foreman's offers to take her to town for an examination.

She was supposed to be some kind of role model for Nick, and sometimes he just wanted to smack her.

He leaned over and did just that, right upside the head, and then he laughed at the look she gave him.

"See?" Gus said. "If you were working harder, you'd be too tired to start shit with me."

"Does that mean you're too tired to take it?" Nick said.

Gus pretended to think about it for a second, but Nick could see the grin starting on her face. She didn't even get all the way to her feet, just launched in and bowled Nick off his log seat. He got one arm mostly around her head and then half flipped her, only she grappled him along somehow so that they both rolled headlong into the rutted ATV track.

Nick spat out a mouthful of bark chips and roared out a laugh.

He slammed Gus in the ribs with his knee, and she let go for a second, long enough for Nick to kip up and get into something more like a fighting stance. Then Gus was on him again, taking him right back down into the dirt.

"Our ride," Nick panted, grabbing Gus by the hair. "Quit it. I hear the ATV."

It was too late to pretend they hadn't been doing anything: the clear-cut offered long sight lines. Their foreman looked thunderous as he brought the ATV up to the cache. "We have a policy for this shit," he said, glaring at Nick.

Nick glared right back. "Fuck policy," he said.

"Sorry. We were just sparring," Gus said, her expression mildly apologetic but her hand pinching hard at Nick's backside. "We go to the same boxing gym at home."

"I don't care what kind of jujitsu you know. You don't speak to me that way," the foreman said to Nick, pointing. "Policies are there for a reason, and it's my job to keep you guys safe."

"Sorry," Nick bit out as Gus kept up the pressure. "Potty mouth, that's me."

"Oh?" the foreman said. "Well, try keeping a lid on it, or you'll be shipping out on the next town day. I don't want to pay workers' comp for some kind of bullshit sporting injury, and I don't want to deal with any attitude, either."

He dismounted from the ATV then to stow their shovels on the side rack, and while his back was turned, Gus wrapped her fingers around Nick's wrist and squeezed until Nick gasped. She didn't need to say anything. By the time the foreman looked back at them, Nick had his daypack on and his face as neutral as it was going to get.

Nick and Gus sat up on the back of the ATV, shoulder to shoulder, while the foreman stood up and steered over logs and slash and rutted mud. Gus looked over at Nick and mouthed, "Better?"

Nick nodded—of course he was going to say yes to that; he wasn't stupid—but he still felt angry energy prickling over him, joining the chafe of dried sweat and the itch of mosquito bites. He looked back over his shoulder at today's work site.

They had not been able to fill in all the available trenches today, so they'd be coming back tomorrow, to the same depressing clear-cut bounded by depressing stands of scrubby, dense forest. Nick hadn't bothered to find out what kind of trees they even were, but there were another twenty-odd boxes of them waiting under a silver tarp for him and Gus to put in the ground.

He did feel a little better, he guessed, like he might be able to get to sleep after dinner. It was the later part of the nights that got bad, more often. He complained about the other workers, but it was even worse when they were all sleeping, when the wind dropped and the silence was the deepest and widest Nick had ever heard, hundreds of miles from the next closest human settlement, and the dark so heavy he couldn't tell whether his eyes were open or shut.

In those moments, he almost wanted to crawl out of his tent—fuck, out of his *skin*. Out of this wilderness and on to someplace different, someplace he'd never been.

JULY 14

◑ WAXING CRESCENT

Smoke rode the prevailing wind to their camp, staining the sun dull red. By noon, all the tents were struck, the shitters were filled in, and the radio pole lay lengthwise along the tree line. The cooks were disassembling the stoves on the patch of bare earth that had been the cook shack. Nick sat on his backpack, rolling a joint.

"Put that fucking thing away," Gus said without lifting her

arm from over her eyes. She lay on the ground with her feet propped on her kit bag. "How d'you think these fires get started in the first place?"

"Everyone knows bears smoke in bed," Nick said, and he ran his tongue down the seam of the fragile paper. He tore a rectangle from the cover of the packet of Zig-Zags and rolled it into a cylinder to serve as a filter. Overhead, another water bomber roared by, slow and full, on its way to drop its quenching payload on the fire. Flights had been passing all day: they looked like they held as much water as a swimming pool, Nick thought, but what was a swimming pool against the might of a fire that spanned a hundred hectares?

"—out of Pikangikum," Gus was saying as the noise of the plane retreated. "I'd like to see that."

"Maybe we will."

"Nah," said one of the other crew members nearby. "They'll put us in a no-tell motel on the highway somewhere, and we'll spend all our fucking money at the peeler bar while we wait around."

"Or they'll draft us and give us piss packs," said Gus.

"I vote for the motel," said the other guy.

"I dunno. Fighting fires sounds like fun," Nick said.

"Yeah, but you're hard-core," the other guy said with an eye roll. "Some of us actually like to relax."

"Hey, I like to relax," Nick said, holding up his joint.

"Whatever, dude."

"What do you mean, 'whatever'?" Nick demanded.

Gus reached over with the arm that wasn't covering her eyes and felt around until she got hold of his knee. "You are not fucking relaxed is what he meant," she said. "Sit tight. Once we get to the motel, you can smoke that thing and chill out."

Nick held the joint to his nose and inhaled the resinous scent of it. Fucking fire ban. Who cared if the forest burned? People like him would just plant more of it.

He had that slip-sliding feeling that he wouldn't have felt that way before, but he had that feeling about a whole lot of things now, and why the hell was Gus in his face all the time, anyway?

She was right up against him, blinking her bloodshot eyes a few inches from his own.

"Calm. Down." She breathed it against his ear and then backed off. "Nick, I feel like a peach. Do you feel like a peach?" She pulled her bowie knife from her boot and a peach from her daypack and started slicing, efficient sweeps of the blade through the thin skin.

Nick watched. She was right. He knew she was right. He just couldn't always keep the knowledge right up front where he needed it. He hypnotized himself on the motion of her hand. When she held out a slice on the blade of her knife, he took it in a grasp a bit too tight, and juice welled over his fingers where they bruised the flesh.

After another hour of waiting, the word came from the foremen: evacuation. Motel in town. They boarded the crew buses and rolled out, and Nick sat by a window with Gus between him and everyone else, and he turned his joint over and over in his fingers, waiting for the moment when he could set it alight.

It didn't come for hours. Hours of jouncing over pitted gravel roads, hours of vibrating out of his skin; but finally they were spilling off the bus, and Gus was inside getting them a room, and Nick could pace the perimeter of the parking lot until she told him where to go.

The motel room smelled of bleach and mildew. Nick stripped his filthy clothes, dumped them on the bathroom floor, and stood in the shower with his joint between his lips and a beer on the ledge of the tiny window.

"I'm going on a liquor run," Gus said from the other side of the shower curtain. "I'll pick you up some of that bourbon you like."

"Hurry it up," Nick said on an exhale of pot smoke. Fucking finally.

"Don't do anything stupid," Gus said.

"Depends—do you think jerking off is stupid?" Nick said back, and he heard her snort of laughter before the bathroom door clicked shut.

He did that. He wasn't lying. He rubbed one out and then did it again, which was one of the more awesome things he'd discovered about his new nature. Got clean: scrubbed off the ground-in dirt of a long contract, four weeks marooned in the bush with only the rest of the crew for company. Ash caked over sweat and bug dope, salt crusted in his hair: all of it swirled down the drain, leaving a grubby ring in the tub. He finished his beer and padded dripping over the stained motel carpet to fetch another.

The shower went cold. Gus didn't come back.

Nick drank the third and final beer while pacing naked from one window to the other. It didn't take him very long. Gus had said to wait, but he got dressed instead in the cleanest things he still had—cargo pants and a wrinkled T-shirt from the bottom of his pack—and strode out to the motel balcony.

The air reeked of smoke, just as much as it had in their camp. He couldn't really see it, except in the red haze over the sun, but somehow, since his new nature had taken hold, scent had become important enough to him that it overrode his other senses. He could look at the late carmine sunset and see that it was pretty, but he could not ignore the smell of imminent harm. It fretted at the edges of his temper like blackfly bites.

He knocked on a few doors, looking for his crew. Someone shouted, "Fuck off!" Someone else was having sex. One door opened, and a girl he didn't like gave him a dizzy grin and asked if he wanted some mushroom tea.

He shook his head. "Seen Gus?"

"Your better half? Or are you the better half? Isn't she at the bar?" the girl said with that twist to her mouth that people always seemed to have when they were talking about Gus.

"Don't you fucking judge her," Nick said, fist clenching empty at his side as if he wasn't always judging Gus.

The girl laughed, not noticing his anger. Nick left her standing in the doorway and pounded down the iron stairs and across the parking lot to where a yellow-and-red plastic marquee advertised the One Spot, Liquor and Beer.

As he neared the door, he caught the scents of stale drink, trucker sweat, chips, and cigarettes, stronger and fouler for the weeks just spent in the bush, ash and all. He glanced back over his shoulder at the motel, and beyond it, the deep blue sky and the dark fringe of trees. That forest went on for more miles than Nick could imagine, broken only by logging roads, reservations, and bush camps, the ribbon of the Trans-Canada Highway and its string of lonely towns.

And the fire. The forest was broken by the fire. How many square miles now?

His feet, blistered and callused by weeks of work, still felt like running. He hesitated, on the brink of letting them.

Instead, he made them march up to the tavern door, and he made his hand reach out and open it, and inside the rank dimness he saw Gus, at the bar, palming matted hair out of her face and wrapping dirty fingers around a glass.

"I told you to wait," Gus said, her gaze flicking from Nick's wet hair to his clean shirt to his feet, which he'd left bare.

"I didn't feel like waiting," Nick said, hoping it didn't come out as hostile as he felt.

"Pull up a stool, then," Gus said. "I've got your bourbon in my pack, but they didn't have any of the stuff I like, so I stopped in for a refresher."

Knowing Gus, she probably meant two or three. Not that Nick could really blame her right now. She looked sad and old and kind of pissed off, and if she felt half of what Nick did lately, she was a damn saint for giving him the first shower and picking up bourbon, and he shouldn't complain about her taking a bit longer than he'd expected.

He still wanted to punch her in the face.

He slid up next to her, brandishing a fifty, all crumpled and warm from the pocket of his cargo pants, and even as his mouth watered for drink, he wondered once again how long he'd be able to keep on not leaving.

JULY 15

◐ WAXING CRESCENT

Gus woke up with a sudden urgent kick, jerking her flannel shirt from around her head. It reeked of her own work sweat.

Her mouth tasted like bourbon. She smacked her lips together and threw off the motel coverlet. She could smell the water inside the pipes, chlorinated and stale. She turned it on cold and put her mouth to the tap.

Water roiled down into her belly and chilled her from the inside.

The whole room was colder than it should be. She could still smell Nick—a funk similar to her own—sweat, swamp muck, booze and pot, waxy soap that didn't quite scour down all the layers of dirt.

But the scent wasn't fresh.

She was supposed to be keeping an eye on him. This wasn't the bush, where he had a choice of trackless woods or a single logging road. The Trans-Canada Highway was right outside their motel. It had Greyhounds and trucks, family sedans, and the Broncos and 4Runners favored by blueberry pickers. Nick could have charmed his way into any of them; hell, he could have bullied his way into any of them too. He could be well on his way to the American border already.

Gus was still wearing her sport top and road-filthy jeans. The motel key and roll of bills were still in her pockets. She kicked through the tangle of clothes on the floor until she found her boots. Half of the stuff there was Nick's dirty laundry, but his day pack was gone.

And his tent. That meant at least a chance he'd picked the woods.

She stepped quietly down the iron stairs from the motel balcony. Whiskey still slopped around in her head. It made her feel loose and warm despite the night chill on her bare arms. But she'd only had a few shots' head start before Nick came into the bar, and she hadn't been alive this long without learning to handle her drink.

If he'd meant to put her under the table, he hadn't done a very effective job of it. No, she thought, he'd just been seized with the desire that overtook them all sometimes, and a few drinks behind, he hadn't been able to sleep it off.

She shoved her hands in her pockets and strolled around the perimeter of the motel parking lot, breathing deeply. No need for haste, was there? She didn't want to risk missing the scent.

On the second round, she caught it, elusive but unmistakable. The woods.

Under the trees, pupils jacked open uselessly, she saw texture in the blackness where there was none and nothing at all where there were branches to scratch at her hair and face. She slowed down and shut her eyes and groped forward along the thread of scent. Behind her, the sound of the highway faded and faded and was gone.

The scent was obscured now and then in the heavy overlay of ash, but she was going upwind, and she was very good at this, and she always found it again. And after a long, slow time of it, the sun began to rise, red and evil, and she saw she was going east.

It took her hours, but finally she ran Nick to ground at the edge of the burn. Less cover here: black, ragged spikes of tree trunks with all their branches and bark fired off, and the ground smoothed with drifts of ash.

She could see Nick now, plodding forward, misshapen by the pack on his back, his legs gray to the knee.

The fire itself was close enough that she could see towers of fresh smoke above the trees, northeast. She could hear it too, a dull crackling rush; or maybe that was only the hangover piling up at the base of her skull.

No ground crews, though; maybe the burn they had reached was a firebreak, and the crews fought on another front.

She did not want to shout, her throat and chest tight and aching. She quickened her pace and closed the gap between them, ash puffing around her boots.

He turned when he heard her coming. She saw the resignation on his face.

"Should've known I couldn't get out from under Big Sister's eye," he said, his voice raw with smoke and fatigue. "Come to take me back? Did you bring any water?"

"Nope," Gus said. She slowed, bent to set her hands to her knees, and coughed.

"Jeez," Nick said. "Next time I run away, I'll make sure to take along a care package for whichever warden comes to put me back."

Gus fell in beside him and nudged his shoulder to direct him a bit farther north.

"Where are we going?" Nick said through a yawn. "Not straight back?"

"To the fire," Gus said.

"Knew you wanted to see a water bomber in action," Nick said, smiling, teeth white in ash-smudged, dark-tanned skin.

"Let's not talk," Gus said.

Her eyes stung. Her mouth tasted like bourbon and smoke.

Closer to the fire line, step by aching step. And then she heard it coming, a ripping bellow of engine noise. She held Nick still with a hand on his wrist. They looked up.

There came the water bomber, belly full, streaking directly over them toward the thickest smoke. Gus's eyes teared up. The plane vanished over the trees before she could see it drop the payload.

She looked down just in time to catch Nick's fist swinging around into her ribs. She tucked her arm in and tightened her core, took the blow harmlessly on her bicep, pivoted for a punishing counterpunch.

"Gotcha!" Nick crowed.

Gus pulled the counterpunch, instead smacking him lightly in his solar plexus. Nick coughed out a laugh and dropped his pack. "Never too tired to spar, huh? I'll let you try my Wu-Tang style!"

He made some kind of bullshit hand-chopping motions. Against her will, Gus felt herself grinning. She did some theatrical shadowboxing and charged in.

Damn, it felt good to fight, even so tired. Fists, flesh, the thump of bone. Weight against weight. Breaking apart and closing again, each laughing when the other scored.

Maybe she could keep this. She caught Nick in a headlock. He nearly threw her over. She kicked his feet out and got her grip again.

"Surrender!" she said. "It's a long way back to town, and I want breakfast."

Nick snorted air through his nose. "Guess it would be a waste of time to offer you whatever's left of my cash advance to just let me skip out."

He made it sound like surrender, but it wasn't. Nick was always joking and never joking.

Gus felt the fun evaporate right out of her and blow away with the smoke.

She braced her feet, felt Nick react to the minute shift of weight with a shift of his own.

She wanted to say something, but she was too tired to start it all up again.

She set her free hand to the side of Nick's face, let the gesture be comforting for a fraction of a second, and then gripped tight.

From there, it was the work of a moment to snap his neck.

JULY 16

◑ FIRST QUARTER

"Skol'ko volka ne kormi, on vsyo v les smotrit," Lissa whispered to Stella. "My grandmother used to say it. It means, 'No matter how well you feed the wolf, he still looks to the woods.'"

Stella giggled. "You'd think he'd be more at home here, after all the time he's spent on your sofa."

Maksim prowled between the windows, looking both menacing and uncomfortable. He had worried the knot in his tie low enough to expose the unbuttoned collar. The last month had been easier on him, the new-moon spell allowing him to live as normally as he ever had, but Lissa was still conscious of his other nature, chained.

He was supposed to be pouring tea, but Lissa had given up reminding him of that. He did remember to serve out vodka for the men.

A few of them had spoken to him in Russian, quietly, when they thought no one was near. Lissa watched them do it but couldn't get close enough to hear.

The ladies crowded her, patted her hair, pinched her cheek. Yelena Ivanova's rugelach were eaten up in no time, and Stella re-filled the plate with shortbreads. She had asked Lissa to braid her hair for the occasion, and she'd dressed soberly in a silver blouse and gray skirt, but she still looked ridiculously young and English. She sat like a secretary, notebook balanced upon her knee, and wrote down the orders.

Izabela Dmitreeva took over the tea service. She whispered to Lissa, "Mr. Volkov used to come sometimes, when your grand-mother was still with us. We wondered if he was all right."

"He is very well," Lissa said.

It had been his idea to come, in fact; he had even, amazingly, helped her vacuum the house.

He had done the most important thing of all: when the ladies were filing in, he'd stood with the sisters, shaking hands, as Lissa introduced Stella.

"Stella Moore," some of them had repeated. "From England, are you, dear?"

And Maksim had glowered, without saying a word, until the ladies more properly said, "*Koldun'ia*, it is a pleasure to meet your sister."

The men who'd come—few, as always, and only the elderly ones—nodded to him, their eyes dark and grave, and bowed their heads over Lissa's hand and then over Stella's.

By the end of the afternoon, they'd taken a page and a half of orders; they'd gone through six pots of tea and three dozen cookies; and Maksim had broken the brown teapot with the sudden pressure of his fingers.

"I am very sorry, *koldun'ia*," he muttered. "Very sorry. It is only that I sometimes forget myself."

He did not seem in a mood to break anything else, so Lissa merely handed him a rag and a dustpan and asked him to clean up the mess.

She and Stella saw everyone out into the halcyon summer evening. The house smelled pleasantly of tea and furniture polish.

Stella went up to change out of her nice clothes, and Lissa sat with Maksim in the front room.

"Thank you," she said. "We will have a much easier time of it now, even if you don't wish to come again."

"You would have made an easy time of it for yourself without my help, *koldun'ia*," Maksim said. "You do very well."

"I try," Lissa said, abashed.

"I have not forgotten," Maksim said. "The nightmares, do they still trouble you?"

She shrugged. They did, but she had no intention of rubbing Maksim's face in it.

He understood, anyway, by the tension in his posture; he looked away from her, out the window again, and shifted restlessly.

"You want to go out running or something, don't you? It's such a gorgeous evening," she said. "I'm glad you're well enough again."

He was more than well enough, really. He'd regained much of his lost weight, eating well and training, and his skin shone brown with sun, except for streaks of pale scarring on the right side. He no longer limped at all.

"Go," Lissa said. "We'll finish the cleaning ourselves. Thanks again."

He brought his attention back to her with an effort and smiled. "Next month, *koldun'ia*. Or anytime I can be of service."

Once out the door, she saw him walk away swiftly, yanking at his tie, shoving his sleeves up his forearms.

Stella came down in a halter top, hair still damp and kinked from the braids. "We should bring him to the pub with us," she said.

Lissa bit her lip.

Stella swatted her. "Joking. I'm not an idiot," she said. "Though it *would* be funny, watching Rafe wonder . . . still joking, still joking! Want to get a falafel?"

JULY 16

◑ FIRST QUARTER

Maksim reached the park, almost running now. He dropped his tie in a waste bin and then tore at the buttons on his shirt and let it flap open.

He stopped under an old oak and spread his arms wide, opening his chest, flaring his nostrils.

"Hey," Gus said, edging up behind him.

Maksim turned and embraced her.

Gus stood stoically; just as Maksim began to release her, she hugged back, hard, and butted her head against Maksim's for a second.

She was thinner and darker-skinned, hair bleached sun-gold. She looked boyish and wiry, the way she had when they'd traveled by sea, only even dirtier: army pants mottled gray, shirt nearly worn through, showing a salt-bleached sport top underneath. Fingernails worn to the quick, with dirt rammed up beneath them. A dozen bracelets of woven embroidery floss about her wrist. She reeked of smoke.

She was also alone.

"Shh," she said, though Maksim had not spoken. "I said I'd take it on, and I did."

Maksim wrapped his arms around her and pressed his face against her unwashed hair.

"I'm going to skip out for a while," she said. "Someone's going to notice he's gone."

"Maybe I should come with you," Maksim said. "His friends might be able to tie him to me."

Gus was shaking her head, hard. "Fuck that," she said. "You're staying. This is what you wanted. This is what you built."

Maksim waited and held on until the fierce tremor in Gus's body stilled and she stood away, holding her breath.

"I will stay," he said. "I will be here when you are ready."

Gus exhaled.

"And I think you might make the time for dinner before you leave," Maksim said.

Gus looked down at her hands, all the knuckles dark with scars.

"How about a drink?" she said.

Maksim felt his throat tighten with something, pity or pride or guilt or all of those.

He would have taken her to a pub, at least, but she led him southwest through Parkdale to the LCBO. She let him pick out a bottle of bourbon that wasn't the cheapest on offer while she fidgeted with the bracelets at her wrist.

Back outdoors, she was easier. They walked south past Gus's old flat and sat on a bench overlooking the highway and the lake. The evening began to cool, fresh air drifting in off the water. Gus drank quickly until Maksim could see the tension loosened in her shoulders. She talked about the job a little and the places she had seen, forests on forests.

"I think that's the kind of place I'll go next," she said, fingers tearing idly at the edge of the paper bag holding her bottle. "Someplace with gorgeous things."

"Not South Africa," Maksim said. "Choose a place where you will be a stranger."

"If you'll lend me a bit of blunt for a ticket," Gus said, with her blinding grin, sunset haloing her tangled hair. "Right now, I have enough to make it as far as, oh, New York, and that's if I don't expect to be hungry when I get there."

"Where are you staying? I will come by with money."

"Nowhere," Gus said. "Not now. I'll be on a flight tonight, if you can get me drunk enough."

And so midnight found Maksim bundling Gus into a security line at Pearson, with her kit bag and her bowie knife safely checked, her clothes still filthy, and her face, puffy and flushed, looking every bit as old as the faked passport said.

She didn't look at him once she passed the scanners. Just kicked her feet back into her boots and walked on.

JULY 16

◐ WAXING GIBBOUS

Sooner or later, the nightly terrors would fade; but in the meantime, thought Lissa, she could not be expected to keep her life on hold.

She arrived at Rafe's apartment—he called it a flat—carrying a little box of Portuguese custard tarts and a bottle of the barbera she remembered him drinking the first time they'd gone out.

"Wow," he said when he opened the door.

"Too much?" Lissa asked. She'd worn her hair down, rippling over her shoulders, over the thin straps of the top Stella kept trying to steal. It was a flattering top.

"Custard tarts," Rafe said, skimming his palm over her collarbone. "Can't resist 'em."

"You're not supposed to resist them."

"Come," he said. "There's pesto salad and salmon steaks. If you can keep from distracting me while I finish cooking."

"I'll do my best."

"You'll have to do better than that."

"Rafe. There's some stuff I don't know—"

"I know. Remember? Everyone starts at square one, every time."

"Yeah, well, I've never even played the game."

"It's not a game," he said, taking her hand. "Hasn't been a game for a while now."

He kissed her mouth and the hollow of her throat and led her inside to the table he had prepared.

Later, when she woke at the accustomed time, shivering, with the dream of the mummified baby terrible and familiar in her mind's sight, she did not reach out for his hand. But she listened to his breath and knew he would still be there when the hour had ended.